DERAILED
The Dominion Falls Series 2

Sarah Cass

Historical Western Romance
Erotic Romance

Sarah Cass
www.authorsarahcass.com

Divine Roses Ink Publishing
www.divinerosesink.com

A Divine Roses Ink Book
http://divinerosesink.com

Historical Western Erotic Romance
First E-book Publication: July 2013 with Secret Cravings Publishing
Second E-book Publication: September 2015
Third E-book Publication: April 2018

Other Books in
The Dominion Falls Series

Independent Brake
Derailed
Dark Territory
Green Eye
Runaway Train
Home Signal
Red Zone

Upcoming Books in
The Dominion Falls Series

Dust Raiser
Blizzard Lights
Dead Man's Swish
Birdcage
A Highball Arrangement
Ball of Fire

Books by Sarah Cass

The Tribe Series
The Tribe
The Wolf
The Chief
The Raven
The Lake Point Series
Santa, Maybe
Deep-Fried Sweethearts
Stalled Independence
Witch Way
A Thorough Thanksgiving
Eve's New Year
Heartstrings & Hockey Pucks
Luck of the Cowgirl
Stars, Stripes & Motorbikes
Free Falling
Love for Hire
Haunted Hearts
Stand Alone Novels
Masked Hearts
Leap

Dedication

As with all my books, this book is always thanks to the support of my amazing hubby.
Erik, you have supported me through it all, even when I maybe didn't always deserve it. None of my books would ever have come to be without you.
Thank you for your unconditional support.

To my kids,
You will always be too young to read this in my eyes…so don't you dare.
But I love you anyway. The way you proudly tell anyone that "Mommy is an author" makes me so happy. You're all my little inspirations with your indomitable spirits to overcome everything life has thrown in your path.
Never give up.

Table of Contents

There is peace and rest and comfort in sorrow.
-Soren Kierkegaard

Jane's whole body hurt. She wanted nothing more than to be back at Cole's side. Still, the importance of her examination by Daisy had defeated most of her protests. Cole's near-constant state of sleep eased the last of her worries at leaving his side.

In order to agree though, she'd insisted Cole never be alone. If anyone was inclined to tell him about the secrets that had emerged when the stranger had kidnapped her, she wanted to make sure she told him the truth first.

The unvarnished truth, told without the cruel twist of people like Graham. Graham, who'd poked his head in to taunt and threaten her any time Cole was unconscious. So Daisy had sat with Cole while Michael carried her to the next room, and then they'd switched places.

With the exam concluded, only one question still burned in her soul. The aches and pains she could live with. The broken ankle, the twisted wrist, even the gunshot wound—those wounds were physical and would heal in time. However, she did not quite know how she would survive the knowledge of the child being gone. Though a surprise, and knowing that Cole might not be so inclined to be happy about the news like herself, she knew already she'd become attached.

Daisy said nothing. She set about washing her hands, her gaze focused unnecessarily strong on the task. Once Daisy had washed and dried her hands, she reached out to help Jane sit.

Jane couldn't wait for Daisy to initiate, the burning question burst from her throat. "Am I still with child?"

"Yes." Daisy's cheeks took on a delicate pink hue, though her features were stoic. As always when in doctor mode, Daisy was all business. "You are."

Jane breathed a huge sigh of relief, which made Daisy lift her head.

Daisy's eyes widened slightly and her jaw dropped. A few seconds later she recovered enough to close her mouth. "You're happy?"

"No one is more surprised than I am about that." Jane's hand shook when she lifted it to brush a curl from her forehead.

"How long have you known?"

"Not long." Jane ducked her head. "Right before Cole was hurt, actually. That very morning I had realized the truth. One stray thought brought it all together. I hadn't truly had time to realize what it meant before everything went mad."

"With everything you've gone through you're quite lucky, if you wish to see it that way, that you are still pregnant."

"I do choose to see it that way." In all the hell she'd been going through, this baby gave her hope. The idea of hope was so rare in the darkness. "I hold no illusions over Cole's reaction."

"So it is Coles?" Daisy's voice squeaked and she flinched. "Sorry."

Jane sighed and glanced toward the window. The response wasn't surprising. She'd certainly made a good show of being rather free with her person, but it had all been an illusion. "What if it is? I can't I imagine he'll have much joy at the prospect, of course. But what if it is?"

"He isn't…he doesn't…I, oh, I don't know what to tell you, Jane." Daisy might not know Cole as well as Jane, but she had been under contract to him as a whore for three years. She did know how good Cole was at keeping anyone and everyone at a distance. Cole had always been proud of how far he could push his own emotions away.

Jane laughed weakly. "You don't need to try. I know Cole well enough, I suppose, that advice is unnecessary." She didn't know the story behind his former wife and daughter, but she did know he'd run far away and not let anyone in since.

No one until her. Jane closed her eyes again, fighting against the tears that threatened to form again. One step at a time. Cole was still far too injured to be dealing with this. Plus, she had other details to discuss with him; like Clara's past, the missing boys, and the telegram she'd just received. Cole's unconscious state had left him rather uninformed and she had to fill him in before it was too late.

Once the dust settled, if he wanted anything else to do with her, she'd tell him about the baby. No matter what the cost. All she'd need to do was screw up the courage to admit it on top of everything else.

"Jane." Daisy set her hand on Jane's, the warmth a shock to her cold extremities. "I must ask that you take it easy. Your body has already been through such trauma. If you are happy about this, then promise me you'll be careful."

If only fate would be so kind as to let her do as asked. "In case you hadn't noticed, Daisy, the state of my existence does not allow for much relaxing. I know you've heard the rumors already. Everyone in this town but Cole has."

"I have, but rumors are cruel whispers. I know from experience."

Jane smiled, for the first time thinking perhaps she and Daisy could overcome whatever battle used to rage between them. One day she might even call the doctoring whore before her a friend. "It is good to know that one or two folks are, if not on my side, at least understanding. I suppose I should see if I could get that number up to three. Will you go send Michael in to fetch me? I'd like to get back to Cole's side."

"Of course." Daisy patted her hand. "I'll want to see you again in a few days. Like I said, the trauma you've been through could have some lasting effects if we aren't careful."

"Thank you." Jane took a shaky breath when she left. As Michael entered a few minutes later, she considered letting him in on her little secret, but then thought better of it. Clara's brother had been hurt deeply, and still mourned over the new revelations. In time she would tell him, as she imagined she would one day need help to raise the child.

"What did she say?" Michael took her hands in his. "Are you going to live?"

"If I keep going the way I am, most likely not. I believe Cole was right."

"That is something I don't hear often. Please, expand on this idea."

"He once told me I have a knack for getting myself injured."

A smile broke through the serious, morose lines on Michael's features. "I do rather despise that he's right in this. You must stop worrying me so. I'll soon look older than you."

"You already do." She allowed his tight hug. "Thank you, Michael."

"Hush. Don't do that." He released her. "Let me take you back to the impatient man in the next room."

"He's awake?"

"And grumping that you weren't there when he woke."

She hummed her understanding, but said little else. Cole wasn't the only one upset she'd missed his waking. With him out of it so much since she'd been back, she wanted to enjoy as much time in his presence as she could.

Without further ado, Michael lifted her. Though his broken ribs had to still be healing, he hardly made a grunt of pain. When they got into the next room, Daisy was fighting with Cole over the bandage on his head.

Jane sighed. "Cole, why are you hassling her?"

"Who says I'm hassling? She's the one won't leave me alone." Cole brushed away Daisy's hand again. "Now get over here."

"Not until you let Daisy finish her exam." She smiled at Michael when he set her in the chair instead of on the bed.

Cole glared at Jane, but stopped fighting Daisy. "Daisy says you're good?"

"Good as I can be after being tossed about like a rag doll on that train." When he reached toward her, she allowed their hands to touch. She smiled. "And much happier to see you being so ornery. I know you're feeling better now."

"Other ways to be feelin' better. Ya done yet?" Cole narrowed his eyes at Daisy.

"Thankfully, yes. I'm done with you for today." Daisy snapped her bag shut and swung around the bed. She offered Jane a smile. "Good luck."

"Thank you." Jane smiled in return. After accepting Michael's kiss to her cheek, she watched the pair leave. She didn't miss how Michael's hand dropped to Daisy's waist as he held open the door and led her out.

"Good luck for what?"

"Dealing with you." Jane softened the smart edge of her words by gingerly getting herself transferred onto the bed. Once she'd managed to get her broken ankle to a comfortable position she snuggled against Cole.

"I ain't about to fall asleep, ya know."

"I can tell. You're more alert than you have been."

"So are ya gonna tell me now why you're so worried? What happened?"

She swallowed against the sudden lump in her throat.

"Don't gotta worry about me. Known plenty of bad deeds. Don't make no difference."

"How can you be so sure?"

"Already told ya. You ain't Clara."

She smiled at his simple cutthroat take on the situation. "What I say may change what you think about that."

"Words always complicate. Keep it simple. You're Jane, and Jane ain't Clara."

"Just remember that as I tell you, okay?"

"Ain't gonna forget it."

"Promise?"

"Promise."

We view ourselves on the eve of battle.
We are nerved for the contest, and must
conquer or perish. It is vain to look for present
aid: none is at hand.
We must act now or abandon all hope!
—Sam Houston

"Get out of here, ya lyin' jezebel!"

Jane's throat tightened automatically to Cole's ferocious snarling yell. Moments before the door behind her had opened, so his yell had likely been heard through the whole saloon. Cole's curses pierced her heart worse than any rumor or whisper since the revelation of her likely criminal past.

She'd known what Cole would say, she'd expected every heart wrenching word, but the impact was far stronger than she'd expected. It had happened too quickly, too soon for her liking. Before she could disclose her feelings, or the truth of the child she carried.

A familiar, low, chortling laugh sounded behind her. Her fists clenched to restrain her visceral response to Graham's amusement. Now was not the time for biting commentary or physical reaction. Her body was far from healed. What she needed most was to get out of the saloon and go home. She needed privacy right then, time to herself to cope with all that had befallen her in recent weeks.

"Told you he'd see what you were." Graham's dark voice lumbered in her ear. His large, threatening form hovered inches away, his hand dangerously close to grabbing her arm. If he did, she couldn't account for the consequences. "Now get outta here."

She didn't dare lift her gaze to look at Cole. If she did, she'd break. With her crutch she nudged Graham back so she could turn away. She hobbled the few inches to the door, stopping at the threshold. Fear and pain kept her gripping the crutch like a lifeline. "Goodbye, Cole."

"Goodbye."

Graham stopped her exit. The flood of tears she held back couldn't block the triumphant gleam in his eye. He leaned closer. "Look forward to Davie hauling you to jail. Now get outta my saloon and don't ever come back."

Jane yelped when he shoved her out the door so hard she stumbled. The door slammed behind her before she caught herself on a chair. Her crutch clattered to the floor. That was when she noticed the saloon's booming silence.

She closed her eyes against the well of tears. She wouldn't cry, not yet, not here. When she opened her eyes to face the silent saloon, she found dozens of eyes on her. Those that had greeted her with friendliness now stared in hostility and suspicion.

Rather than confront them as she might have otherwise, she bent to grab her crutch. Their suspicion hurt. She'd done nothing to anyone there, but she had locked herself in a room with Cole for three days and not dealt with the talk. They knew nothing, and they would know nothing. Not today.

Let her pain shine through; let them see the hints of her deeply aching soul she couldn't find the strength to hide. She hurried through the saloon, past the peering eyes fast as she could on her broken ankle.

Michael's arm circled her waist the moment she stepped outside. His smile of greeting faded. "Jane? What is it?"

"Word travels fast. I have been dismissed from the saloon, from Cole's presence."

"No. Cole couldn't believe you did this."

"Well, why not? Everyone else does."

"Not everyone." He led her across the street toward the wagon. "Cora doesn't think you did this intentionally. You know that."

"Michael, please. Just take me home." She couldn't keep a conversation going. Her emotions wouldn't remain under wraps that long.

"Cora wanted to see you."

"Take me home. I don't wish to be out right now. Word traveled fast and I don't want to be here. Please, just take me home."

"All right." He paused next to the wagon and set a hand on her shoulder. "You do know you're stronger than this, don't you, Jane?"

"I know nothing of the sort."

"Jane."

"Michael."

He sighed, lifting her up into the front of the wagon before climbing into the seat. He took up the reins, but didn't urge the horses on. "Why don't you stay at Cora's tonight? Once I drop you off, I need to report to the jail. David is going out with another search party this afternoon so I need to keep an eye on things here. I'll be there all night. I hate the idea of you being home alone."

"I need to be alone." She folded her hands in her lap and kept her eyes lowered. The jolt of the wagon beginning to move was the distraction she needed to avoid his gaze. "I need to figure this out. I am alone again."

"You're not."

"For all intents and purposes—I am. My actions have caused a great deal of pain for people here, Michael. People are dead and injured because of what Clara became after she left David. No one trusts that I truly have amnesia, and even if they do believe it, they still don't trust me, or they blame me."

"David will come around."

"Should he?" The wagon jolted over a bump. The action stirred her back to life and she lifted her head to stare at the road ahead. "I don't think he should. It's best that he doesn't, because I assume he will be coming to arrest me soon as we have an idea of where this murder was committed."

Michael shook his head. "You didn't kill anyone. I won't believe it. Ever."

"That's why you should leave. Get out while you can."

"No."

When he stopped in front of the house, she kept her hands folded in her lap. Her jaw clenched and she scooted away from him to the edge of the seat. "Then you're as big a fool as Clara ever was. You didn't know her, Michael. No one did."

He reached for her hand, but she was already halfway out of the wagon. Broken ankle or not, she wasn't going to be an invalid, nor would she extend this conversation any further. He frowned. "Let me help you."

"I can do it." She landed with a wince. "I want to be alone. Do not send anyone to check on me. Let me be in peace."

"Did Cole really kick you out?"

"Called me a lying jezebel, among other things, and then said goodbye." She adjusted her crutch for a more secure stance, and then lifted her tear-filled eyes. "Now go away."

"I'll be back to check on you first thing in the morning."

She hobbled to the door and let herself in. The moment the door closed, she leaned against it. She listened intently until the wagon had rattled away before she let out the tears she'd been holding back.

In the three days since she'd returned to Dominion Falls, her whole world had been in chaos. She'd spent the first night wrapped in his arms, enjoying his proximity in the moments he was awake. Both shunned the world and the revelations of her past for those few hours.

They survived that way for a full day before her appointment. They'd been granted one more day together, before the world had fought its way in.

After days of searching for the boy and for Arthur, David had returned. He'd dragged her from the sanctuary of Cole's room and demanded answers. She'd sat in Cora's restaurant for hours explaining what little she knew in vivid detail.

Cora, Michael, and David had needed to hear it, and she was as honest as she could be given want little she knew. David continued to question her for hours, and she didn't blame him. Clara had hurt him, lied to him, and taken away his son. He had every right to be angry and not believe a word she'd said.

Michael and Cora had both balked at David's accusation that she'd kidnapped Arthur and arranged for the boy to be taken as well. They'd been surprisingly firm in their defense of her, and she wasn't sure why.

The knowledge of all the pain the sins of her past had caused formed her own internal prison. She had to make it right somehow. The truth was the only thing she needed. She wanted to know the truth of the seven missing years. How could she ever learn?

There was only one thing she could do, and she knew what it was.

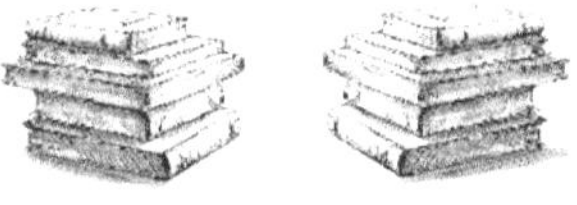

It is easier to find a score of men wise enough to discover the truth than to find one intrepid enough, in the face of opposition, to stand up for it.
—A.A. Hodge

He wasn't supposed to be out of bed.

But when had Cole Mitchell ever done what he was supposed to?

Never.

Cole twisted against the stitches in his back to test his range of motion before he pushed himself to his feet. That morning Daisy had told him not to push it, but he couldn't sit around. He had to know what was going on.

The door opened to reveal Graham's smug face. Cole wanted to punch the man, and shake his hand for his behavior the day before.

Cole picked his shirt up off the chair. He did his best not to wince as he slid it on. "What's the word, Graham?"

"Davie and the search party got back a few minutes ago. No surprise, but no sign of the boy or Arthur. They went up to Denver this time."

Cole fought to keep still, a nugget of fear almost forced away his calm control. "Why in hell did they go there? The bastard was headin' south."

"There wasn't no sign of them all the way down to Santa Fe. Guess they figured they'd see if they went the other way. Why?"

Cole forced his calm back in place. He buttoned his shirt slow and steady as he composed his thoughts. Graham said they saw no sign, and hadn't said much else, so perhaps his panic was misplaced. "But they found nothing. Like anyone really pays attention in the big cities. Don't he know better?"

"Guess not." Graham chuckled heartily. "Gotta say. It's been mighty peaceful around here. You went and kicked out the liar finally, and this morning you sent Daisy packing again."

"Daisy's only been here for doctoring. It ain't sending her packing, idiot. And we're still three girls shy and you ain't done nothing about it." Cole glared at Graham before passing him to head into the bar. Between selling Daisy's contract and all the other chaos they were down three whores. "You're too busy passing judgment to do any actual business."

"In case you forgot, this isn't my only business! I've been packing people in pine boxes the past few days while keeping this damn place afloat." Graham smacked his hand on the bar. "So don't go snapping at me. You'll get a new girl and then you'll find another one after her. All of them'll be a damn sight less manipulative than that Janey."

"Ya know what?" Cole grabbed a bottle from the shelf. He fought a wince when the stitches in his shoulder pulled. Last thing he could do was show any weakness to Graham. He poured two full glasses and drank them both before continuing. "Why don't ya go back to the dead bodies? Stay there—they're the only ones you're smarter than."

"Don't take it out on me. I tried to tell you that you were getting played."

Cole grabbed the man's collar and yanked him half over the bar. "I don't get played. Ever. I do the playing."

Snorting, Graham pried his collar free. "Sure, Cole. Still gotta say, it was worth it all to see the look on her face yesterday. She really thought she could still fool you."

Cole could only focus on the whiskey bottle in his hand. His jaw clenched tight. He poured two more glasses, remembering all too clearly the look on Jane's face the day before. His words had hit her hard, and she'd toppled like a house of cards. "Yeah. Guess she did."

"Cole!"

They both turned to the door at Mike's shout. Graham chortled. "Oh look. It's the only one left defending the strumpet. You aren't welcome here."

Mike strode up to the bar and glared at Cole. "What the *hell* did you say to her?"

"Exactly what she deserved." Graham grinned and leaned on the bar next to him. His lip curled as he sneered. "Or did you forget what she did? I knew she was a liar. I told everyone. And I was proven right!"

In a flash, Mike's arm shot up. His elbow rammed right into Graham's nose. Before the larger man could react, Mike spun and landed a solid hook to his eye.

Half the saloon was on their feet, staring at the scene with a mix of amusement and surprise. No one had ever seen anyone knock down Graham so well or so fast, certainly not a man half Graham's size. Before their eyes, Mike landed one more blow from the left and Graham dropped like a cadaver.

Mike righted himself with two solid tugs to his vest.

Cole chuckled, lifting his glass in a toast. "Impressive."

Mike ignored him in favor of giving the saloon's patrons, whose attention he now had full command of, a dark glare. "All of you knew her! She bought books for the school and more food than any of you for the families that were attacked by renegades. She was nicer to all of you than you have been to her since she got back. You turned your back on her—she didn't lie to you."

"He's right." Cole took his chance to give each of his patrons the once-over. Most of them shrank from his scowl. "The lot of ya liked her well enough when she was flirting and being friendly. All the talk that's been going around is just that—talk. Jane ain't a liar. She says she don't remember, she don't."

Mike spun around so fast, Cole had to jerk to catch a glass before it shattered on the ground. Mike's eyes narrowed. "What the hell?"

"Let me guess." Cole smiled as he lifted his glass. He knew what had the shrimp all hotheaded. "She ain't home."

His hands gripping the edge of the bar so hard his knuckles were white, Mike leaned closer. "What the *hell*?"

"Come on. We gotta talk." Cole wasn't about to reveal the whole story in front of this lot of nosy bastards. He grabbed the bottle of whiskey. He nodded to one of the girls. "Get that bastard up and outta the saloon, Iris. I don't wanna see him when I get out. Prim, get Cuddy to man the bar."

Mike remained silent, fists clenched at his side. "You called her a lying jezebel in front of everyone. You told her to get out. *Now* you come to her defense?"

"Yup." Cole smirked and held open the door the room he'd been spending his recovery in. When Michael wouldn't move, he offered a glare of his own. "Ya won't hear nothing without getting in here."

Though he hesitated like he might protest, Mike stormed into the room. He refused the chair Cole pointed to, instead pacing the length of the room.

Cole groaned as he sank into a chair. All he'd done was gone for a couple drinks and he hurt from head to toe. Damned if he'd tell Daisy she was right, though. He tilted his head side to side, then turned to Mike. "Ya got it right. That's just what I did."

"I don't have time for your games. What the hell happened?"

"Jane was in here for near two days before David came and dragged her off. What did ya think we were doing?"

"I've got a feeling you could be on your deathbed and still be looking for nothing but a good time, Cole." Mike paused his pacing to glare at Cole. His nostrils flared. "And Jane would do anything for you—especially that."

In any other situation, with any other woman, Cole might have found the statement amusing. Not this time, the insult to Jane was too great. "You really don't got a high opinion of your sister, do ya?"

"Excuse me?"

"I ain't saying we didn't..." Cole smirked. So Mike wasn't entirely wrong, but he was far from right, too. "Have a reunion. But she was injured. I was injured. And that ain't all we did. We talked."

"You're not a talker."

"No. But she is."

Mike sank into a chair, remaining silent while Cole managed to drink two glasses of whiskey. "So she told you everything."

"Before she told you."

"Then you know where she is? Why she left so much blood—"

"Blood?" Cole shot to his feet, panic taking hold. Had the stranger tricked her? Got to her before she could make the drop? "No. I don't know a damn thing about blood. What the hell happened?"

"You tell me."

"What blood?"

"I got home this morning and there was blood all over the place. Looked like she was slicing a cucumber when it happened, but the blood was all over the floor, her room. The gun was gone and so was her horse."

"That crazy bitch." Cole went to the window. He stared out into the street, the people passing by without a clue. "What was she thinkin'?"

"Cole!" Mike shot to his feet and glared at him. "You tell me! You're the one that isn't the least bit surprised she's gone."

Cole returned to his chair. "Yeah. She's probably halfway to Frisco by now, if she did what she was supposed to."

"Frisco?"

"Yeah."

Cole stared at the folded square of paper she waved before him. All he knew was when Daisy had brought their food; she'd dropped the paper with Jane, a whispered exchange between them. "What is it?"

Jane rested her hand on his chest. Her brows rose, amusement tickling her lips into a teasing grin. "It's called a letter. People get them all the time."

"Jane." He didn't have time for games. They didn't have time for games.

"All it says is 'Frisco depot. September the fourth. Bring everything'." Her hand shook when she deposited the paper into her pocket. "I must go, Cole. I have no choice. He has Arthur; perhaps he has my son back by now. I have to make this right. It's all my fault."

He took her hand in his, incapable of true comfort. Still, he was urged to try. "It ain't your fault. It's Clara's."

"I was Clara once. Amnesia is not a defense. Whatever Clara did is her fault, and by default, mine as well. Guilt by more than association." Her eyes closed when he cupped her

cheek. A soft sigh brushed his wrist as she leaned into his hand. "I cannot let Arthur suffer at the hands of that man. I cannot let him be off with my son again should he have him as well."

"Ya don't even know how much money he wants. It's a fool idea." She'd already told him everything the insane bastard had said, and what he'd been after. It didn't take much of a leap to figure out what he meant by 'bring everything'.

"I have to try."

"They're never gonna let you leave. Ya try to put one foot on a train and they'll have you dragged to jail." He wrapped his hand around the nape of her neck and pulled her down. Once she nestled against his shoulder, he laced his fingers with hers. "If you have to do this…"

"I must."

"You're gonna have to get out of town a different way."

"How? I'll have to leave soon. The fourth is only a few days away. I have money. After the fallout with Jackson, I started to keep the bulk of my funds at the house."

"I got a couple thousand upstairs."

"What? No!" She sat up in an instant, so fast she winced in pain. Moisture welled at the edges of the depths of blue as she shook her head. "There is no way I am taking your money for this. You might never see it again."

"I might never see you again either." He frowned when the dam broke and her tears flowed free down her cheeks. He pushed himself to sit and reached out to gently tuck his finger under her chin. Once he'd lifted her eyes to meet his, he nodded. "I ain't saying that you're gonna take off with my money. I trust ya."

"So in this crazy situation my past has gotten me into, somehow saying a man is probably going to kill me is reassuring."

"As opposed to me saying I think you're lying. Yeah. I think so."

A weak laugh broke through her tears. "The scary thing is—you're right."

"You're gonna take the money. If it gets Arthur back...but Jane."

"What?"

"No trading. You ain't worth no less than Arthur. You ain't a criminal. He's lying somehow. I know he is."

Her smile faltered and she nodded. "I'm sure you think so."

"Promise."

"I will not trade my life for his. I promise."

"Good. Now come back here. I was doing better planning when I was layin' down."

"Liar."

"Fine. Ya just feel right. If you're gonna be leaving, you're staying here until I say otherwise."

"Yes, sir."

"That's why she made me take her upstairs the other day. It wasn't for books." Mike's face was buried in his hands, an edge to his words.

"It was, and it wasn't." Cole glanced at the book on the table beside him. He couldn't read it, but it was Jane's favorite and she'd been happy to read it to him.

"She lied to me."

"We figured the best way to get her out was to give her a chance to escape." Cole rubbed his hand over his face, still upset she had to leave at all. Without him. He was injured, but so was she. Unfortunately, she'd been right again to point out his absence would be noticed sooner than hers would be if they did it right. Unfortunately the right way was not pleasant.

Michael kept his face buried in his hands. A frustrated groan filled the room. "What exactly does that mean?"

"I ain't an idiot. Neither is she. We both knew soon as he had a chance, Graham would be tellin' the truth his own way. He didn't like her around. Didn't like her puttin' her nose in around here. He really don't like that I let her keep her independence."

"Let her?" Mike snorted. "Like you had a choice."

"Graham don't know that." Cole shrugged. "So we let him think he won. I said to her all the things he wanted to hear. Didn't take but one minute for him to think he won."

"And you kicked her out. I thought she could lie to me, but yesterday I really believed you'd kicked her out; hurt her deeply. She was so upset."

"Don't imagine she liked hearing it." Cole poured another whiskey and returned to his post by the window. He'd seen the look on her face when he'd said the nasty things to her. She'd protested to help build the game, and he'd had to keep going. Every word had been difficult for both of them.

"I guess not." Mike sounded doubtful.

"I didn't much like saying it." Cole kept his back turned to Jane's brother. He stared out the window and sipped his whiskey, his stomach churning at the memory. It had taken a lot of effort not to pull her close and remind her he didn't mean a word of what he was saying. After she'd left he'd had to put up with Graham's gloating—his own version of hell for sure. "She wasn't lying. She was hurting. Tough knowing there ain't no one that believes ya. 'Specially ones you been so nice to."

"So she refused to stay in town so she could run away."

"If she did it right, she should be in Frisco by tomorrow, a day early. She didn't tell me what she was planning. We talked about some ideas, but then decided we'd best stop wasting time with our talking."

"You gave her money?"

"Whatever I could spare. Got Chauncey in Pueblo now picking up Tempest to bring her home. When David came to get Jane to give her the inquisition, Graham took his chance and put his spin on the story with me. Ass that he is, he made it worse than even Davie's calling it. Speaking of which, nice work out there. Ain't no one that's been able to give Graham what-for in a long time."

"Five brothers and Jane—and I was the runt. I learned a few tricks." Mike managed to grin. "Graham needed to be knocked down. Dumb bastard doesn't have a lick of sense."

"You gonna tell David?"

"I have to. First, I'm going to find out how much money she took, and then I'm going to handle David. He already is threatening to take my badge. This should seal the deal. Can't have a deputy you don't trust."

"Right. I'd go, but I ain't much good to ya."

"And you think she is with a broken ankle?"

Cole shook his head, giving Mike the once over again. He frowned. "I'll say it again. You really don't got a high opinion of your sister, do ya?"

"What's that supposed to mean?"

"Well, I get that ya don't like me. That you think I'm a rake, because I am." Cole smirked. "But first, ya think all she did in here with me for over two days was screw. Now you think she ain't strong enough to fight through that pain for what's right?"

Mike stood silent for a long time. He looked Cole up and down with an appraising stare before levelling his gaze at him. His eyes narrowed at Cole. "You do realize that if you hurt her again, I will do worse to you than I did to Graham? She has enough chaos and hell right now. She doesn't need a bastard playing tug of war with her heart."

"She's a grown woman. She knows what's here."

"I'm not kidding." Mike dared to stride across the room to glare up at him, chest to chest.

"Get outta here. Only one train leaving today. If ya want to catch up, you're gonna need to move fast." Cole held his gaze steady, breaking a brief smile when Mike moved to leave. He had to admit he admired the shrimp wasn't afraid to stand up to him. For the first time, he could see the family resemblance.

The thought made his heart catch. Once again the realization that Jane might not come back shot through him. The last she'd have heard was words he didn't mean. He shook his head and cleared his throat. "Mike."

"What?"

"Bring her back."

Full of wiles, full of gile, at all times,
in all ways, are the children of men.
-Aristophanes

The door slammed shut. The lock clicked in place and the key slid from its slot. They were alone again.

Arthur shifted his weight. A frenzied race of sparks up his arms drew a groan of pain that made little noise through the gag in his mouth.

A movement in the shadows under the windows drew his attention. He sat straighter to get a better look at the boy hiding there. He'd seen the boy in Dominion Falls, where they'd said he was the son of the man holding them prisoner. Of course they'd also said the man was French, but he'd heard him speaking clear English to Jane on the train. Every conversation since had also been in English. Another lie from the man. He had to be lying about Jane, too.

Arthur tried to talk through the dirty barrier. When that failed, he tried to gesture the boy closer with his head.

Painfully slow, the boy crept toward him until he was sitting right next to Arthur. The boy held a finger to his lips. After a glance to the door, he tugged on the gag and pulled it free. The second Arthur's mouth was free, he jumped back a foot.

"Thank you." Arthur fought against the dryness of his mouth to say the few simple words. He scrunched his nose when nothing helped. "Water?"

He drew in a ragged breath when the boy scooted away. For a week, they'd been locked up in some fashion or another. In all that time, he'd come to realize the boy was close to Isaac's age, but he'd not heard a peep from him at all.

The boy seemed obedient, even terrified, of their captor—not that Arthur blamed him. Arthur remembered the declaration on the train that the boy was Jane's son—and David's as well. Tears filled his eyes before he could stop them, thinking of his own family.

His pa had taught him to be strong, and he was smart. Somehow he had to find a way out of this. He'd heard their captor say someone was dead, but he didn't know who. Wondering who could have died tore at him, but he tried to push it aside. He'd never get away if he remained scared.

A cup was held to his lips, and thirsty as he was, he sipped instead of gulping. If he drank too fast he'd get sick to his stomach, his pa had taught him that much. As he finished sipping down all the water he sighed in relief.

He leaned his head back against the wall. He tried to still his racing thoughts. The boy stayed a foot away, glancing back and forth between him and the door. Arthur didn't want the boy any more scared than he was. He smiled and looked over at the boy. "My name's Arthur. Do you have a name?"

With wide eyes, the boy stared at him before looking back at the door.

"He's gone for a bit. I heard him. He said he was scoutin'. We'll hear him before he gets in. Can you talk?"

The boy nodded and looked down.

"He don't know, does he?"

With a fierce shake of his head, the boy gripped Arthur's arm, sending a jolt of pain through it. At Arthur's groan, he scrambled away.

"No! Wait. It's all right. My arms hurt being tied up is all." Somehow he found a smile and nodded to the boy. "It's okay. I ain't gonna tell him you can talk. But it's good to know. Do you have a name?"

"Secret."

The faint whisper barely registered in his ears, but Arthur grinned to hear the boy speak. "Oh, I'm real good at keeping secrets. I got a brother your age—he tells me all kinds of secrets. Do ya remember seeing him? His name is Isaac."

The boy kept his eyes lowered. A small smile formed and he nodded.

"Can you tell me your name?"

Scrambling close, the boy cupped his hand over Arthur's ear. "Jesse."

"Jesse? That's a good name. Where'd you get it?"

His eyes wide again, Jesse shook his head and backed away.

"Too big a secret?"

Jesse gave a fierce nod and looked back at the door.

"Guess if he don't know your name, he didn't give ya one." Arthur shifted, trying to ease the ache in every joint. "Jesse, I don't know how, but we're going to get out of here. Soon. I'll need your help to do it. Will you help me?"

Fear covered every inch of Jesse's face then poured through him into trembles.

"I know it's scary. But he can't keep us. He ain't family. He's a bad man."

"Bad man," Jesse echoed. "Bad. Hurt."

"Yes. I think he's hurt a lot of people." Arthur looked back at the door when Jesse did. In the past week, he'd been unable to do much. The whole time he'd been tied up and gagged, but he'd been able to listen.

For one thing, he was sure the man was unstable. His ramblings weren't always clear, but it was evident he was angry with Jane. By this point, Arthur wondered if he hadn't been the one that killed the man he'd said Jane had killed. The whole puzzle was confusing, but he wanted to figure it out.

He liked Jane. She couldn't be capable of murder. But then he looked at Jesse again, wondering how she'd let the man take him. Closing his eyes, he sighed and thought back to what he could remember from the train.

She'd thought he was a half-breed, but he didn't know why she'd think that. He also knew that Jane didn't remember. His pa had always said he had good instincts, and he trusted them now. Jane didn't remember, and she wasn't bad. He just wondered how a smart lady like her had been fooled.

"Eat."

Arthur's eyes flew open and he grinned at the sight before him. He took a bite of the bread Jesse held out to him; grateful the boy had been kind enough to bring the bread. Within minutes, he'd devoured it and was relieved to see the cup of water refilled. "Thank you, Jesse. I needed that."

Jesse held up the drink for Arthur again. Soon as Arthur finished, Jesse was cleaning up every crumb, removing any trace of the transgression.

"It's smart of you not to tell him that you can talk. You ain't an idiot like he says, Jesse. You're smart. Real smart."

Jesse beamed, carrying the cup back to the table.

Arthur watched Jesse take great pains to set the cup back exactly where he'd found it. His mind was set. They'd have to try to escape the next day. "I'm going to need your help, Jesse. The bad man talks a lot. I think he's got something big happening tomorrow."

Jesse nodded. "Trains."

"Right. He mentioned watching the trains for someone. I think he's gonna be gone a while. Will you help me? I promise if we get outta here, I'll keep you safe. The bad man won't hurt ya again. Will you help?"

"Bad man hurt."

"We'll go back to Dominion Falls. They won't let no one hurt you. I promise."

Jesse sat back next to him, trailing a finger along the designs in the carpet. "Bad man."

"Will ya help me? We have to try."

"I'll try."

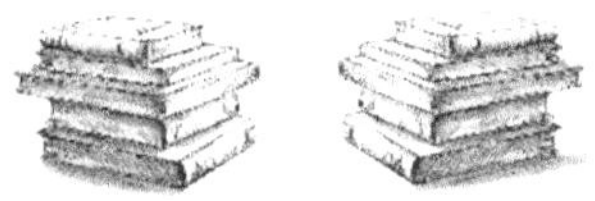

The solution of every problem is another problem.
—Johann Wolfgang von Goethe

Michael stood in the doorway of the saloon until he'd caught Cole's attention. Soon as the man saw him, Mike went out onto the porch and leaned on the hitching post. He lifted his hat to scratch his head and stared into the street.

What he'd found at the homestead hadn't been at all what he'd expected based on what Cole had said. He wondered if Cole would be as confused as he was. When Cole joined him, Mike handed him a piece of paper he'd found in the safe.

Without even looking at it, Cole handed it back.

"Aren't you going to read it?" Mike eyed him, noting the sour look on the man's face. Could it be that Jane had fallen for a man unable to read? One that could not share her love of words? If he weren't so worried, Mike might have been amused. "Ah. I see. Fine, then I should inform you that your funds are securely locked in our safe at the homestead."

"What?" Cole's eyes flashed and he reached to grab Mike by the collar. Before he made contact he paused, then withdrew his hands. They clenched at his sides. "Why?"

"I don't know the whole reason. Jane only took about one thousand, and it was her own money. I don't know what fool idea she's concocted, but she's not going in with anything." Mike turned to grip the hitching post. "She wanted you to know she couldn't use your money. I'm to give it back to you when it's convenient."

"What else did she say?"

Was it just his imagination, or did Cole look hopeful? Did he want a message for him? Despite his concern for Jane, the idea Cole was that hopeful for word was a definite distraction. "Why? What would you like her to say to you?"

"Just curious is all."

"Of course you are." Mike could have pushed the issue, and enjoyed seeing the man squirm. Unfortunately, time wasn't on his side. He instead unfolded the note Jane had left behind, her easy curving script so familiar, yet just different enough, like the writer herself. "There's not much here. She says that in the end, she couldn't take your money. She told me to get to Sacramento, that she will do everything she can to get Arthur there."

Cole's hands fidgeted, a display of nerves Mike wasn't used to seeing. They refused to rest anywhere for more than a few seconds. "She's smart."

"Impulsive."

"She don't remember."

Puzzled, Mike furrowed his brow and glanced at Cole. "I know that."

"But I think part of it is still there."

"Again…I know."

"No. What I mean is—whatever this guy had her doing those seven years, I think something in her remembers. She's got dead-on aim, she's been running investments and raking in dough, speaking French."

"You've got a point there. She couldn't do any of those things. We were taught German, not French. She sure as hell couldn't shoot. Shot Nick when he was teaching her." Michael rubbed his hand over his face, one key problem with the situation reared its head. "How can you outsmart someone that remembers everything when you remember nothing?"

"Don't figure she thought of that."

"Impulsive."

"Proud."

"Crazy."

Cole snorted. "Got no argument here. She's plum crazy. Best go tell her husband where she is and get after her. She's gonna get herself killed the way she's going."

This time Mike was certain he wasn't imagining the strain in Cole's voice. The man was more than worried; he was almost panicked. He frowned. "Jane says you're honest, so tell me the truth. Why do you care?"

"Ain't none of your business, and that's the truth."

If there weren't a pressing matter at hand, Mike would have been happy to prove Cole wrong. Instead, he headed toward the jail. David wouldn't be willing to listen to anything Mike had to say, but Michael would force the matter. A child's life was at stake, and so was Jane's.

Rather than risk being cut off before he had a chance to say anything, Mike threw open the door. "Arthur is in San Francisco."

The group of men huddled around the desk all turned to stare at him. Michael narrowed his eyes and gestured outside. "All of you, out. Now. I need to speak to David."

"I'm not interested in any more of your lies, Mike." David folded his arms across his chest. "You've got no right to give orders in my office."

"If you want to find that child, you damn well better listen. Everyone out." Mike glared at the men until they began to file out. Only Archie lingered behind, and knowing he was mayor and had a clear, level head, Mike didn't balk. He slammed the door. "Jane went after him. She left sometime yesterday."

Archie frowned. "Why would she think he's there?"

"Because that's where he told her to go. He sent her a letter and told her to be there by the fourth." Mike turned to

David. Desperation pulled him closer to the desk. "She's going to do something foolish. She's trying to make this right."

"She can't!" David slammed his hand on the desk. "And you're wasting my time."

"Then you'll let Arthur, and possibly Jane, both die!"

"Wait a minute." Archie raised his hands, stepping between the two men. He looked from one to the other before landing his gaze on Mike. "Why should we believe it? What makes you think she didn't just take off?"

"Because if she was going to, she would have taken the money and ran. She didn't. She's made sure we knew where she was going and where to be." Mike frowned. "And she wants to make this right."

David snorted. "She wants to make it right? Well, it's too late."

"You told her you *believed* her. That you knew she wasn't Clara."

"That was before I learned what good liars you both are, Mike!"

Mike shook his head and looked down at the floor. "We made mistakes. I can't even apologize for not telling you the truth. I thought she'd be back, and then it was so long. Look, I don't care if you believe me now. I'm going after them. Stay here with your useless maps and hopeless search parties."

"David," Archie leaned on the desk, "you know we've got to go if there is any chance Arthur is there."

Mike could see clearly now why Jane believed Archie would be a good mayor. He was managing to remain levelheaded in this chaotic mess. "The train leaves in twenty minutes. I'll be on it. If you expect to get there in time for whatever Clara is planning, you need to be on it as well."

David stared at the maps for a long minute before nodding. "You're right. We've gotta go. I'll gather some men."

"No." Mike frowned when David's head snapped up. "The more we take, the worse it could be. You, me, and one other is best. One can stay in Sacramento and the other two can head on into Frisco."

"Why Sacramento?"

"I'll explain on the way. We've got to move now."

*The wise man avoids evil by
anticipating it.
—Publilius Syrus*

September third dawned early, bright and cool in San Francisco.

One day before she'd been told to be there, Jane took up a spot on a bench inside the depot. The crowd bustled and thinned in shifts around her; life sprang from every corner, from every car that arrived and departed.

She sat stoic, dressed in an elegant black mourning gown with a veil pulled low over her face. Her hair was powdered so what was exposed appeared white, and she'd left her crutch behind in the hotel. Wrapped tight as it was, her ankle still throbbed in protest against the abuse of being used before it was truly ready.

Still she sat, stitching a panel of embroidery. The needle stuck her finger every time it ran through the fabric. She'd rather have been reading, as needlework was not proving to be something she enjoyed. However she'd made a choice to pull on none of her favorite things to pass the time or blend in.

Despite her apparent attention to her work, her gaze frequently found its way around the building. From under the relative safety of the mourning veil, she observed as many people as she could, looking for one man.

After several hours, a sore well-stuck thumb, and a halfway decent orchid on the panel, her patience was finally rewarded. This time, a mere two weeks after she'd seen him last, he was slender. A well-groomed goatee graced his features, his hair cropped quite short. She ripped her gaze away fast, maintaining intense focus on her needlework.

Once she counted to twenty, she lifted her gaze again, studying his features to be sure she had the right man. Her stomach flipped and fell to the floor when she came to the conclusion that it was, indeed, him. The man wandered through the depot, his sharp gaze on his surroundings.

Rather than be caught under his gaze, she gathered her needlework without any rush. Last thing she wished to do was draw attention to herself, so she moved slow even as he passed right before her.

She kept her head lowered. She rose with her bag in hand. With a hard bite to the inside of her cheek in anticipation of the pain, she started to leave, noting he was only feet away, though his gaze was on the far exit.

Every step sent a sharp shock up through her leg, and her ankle made threats to collapse beneath her. She forced herself to walk straight, and prayed her ankle would hold just a while longer. If he noticed her at all, she could not appear injured, as she would have been in the accident. She had no idea if he'd known of her injuries, but she wouldn't risk detection on such a simple matter.

By the time she made it across the street to the small café, tears slipped down her cheeks. She brushed away the evidence of her pain before it could wash away the powders she'd used to cover her lingering bruises.

As she ordered a coffee and a sandwich, she kept her eyes on the depot across the way. She'd suspected he would also be there a day early, acquainting himself with the depot and the available escapes. It was a relief to know her instincts had been right.

The problem now was if her plan would work. It was a long shot, but she could think of no other way. She hadn't been able to take Cole's money, though he'd freely offered. It wasn't right. She'd made this mistake, whether she remembered or not. It wasn't his to pay for.

The coffee arrived and she took a sip, keeping one eye on the depot while her mind wandered back to Cole. The relief she'd felt when he'd believed her had been immense. Even though in her head she knew he believed her, his parting words had carried a sting that still left an ache in her heart.

She refused to focus on that, pushing right on past the bitter memory to when he'd told her he believed her.

Cole's hand ran up her back, squeezing her shoulder. She knew he wanted her to turn around, but she didn't dare. What if he hated her? The past weeks had been so difficult; she didn't think she could bear it again so soon after getting him back. She selfishly wanted to cling to this joy while she could.

"If ya don't look at me, I ain't gonna be able to tell if you're lying."

She took a deep breath and turned as he'd asked her to. Still, she couldn't bring herself to meet his gaze, worried over what she'd find there. He'd always been honest with her, even when it hurt. These days everything hurt. "Everything is pointing to Clara being a horrible person."

He tucked his finger under her chin. One gentle nudged forced her gaze even with his. "First, you aren't Clara. Second, you ain't a killer."

"If what he says is true, then a lot of people believe I am."

"Don't matter what they think."

"Yes, it does."

"He ain't said one honest thing since he showed up."

Her heart thumped hard in her chest. She gripped the muslin in a weak, failing fight against tears. "That's not entirely true. On that train, he did. He admitted the boy is my son. David's son. Cole—"

"Look at me. Look me dead in the eye and tell me ya don't remember."

"I don't remember." Her lip trembled with the tears she'd pushed back, but she held his gaze. "I'm terrified of what will happen because of what I don't remember."

"I believe ya."

"Why?" She was afraid to believe he truly did believe her. Afraid of that faith going away. "You're the only one that will. You know Graham will be all too happy to make this all worse, turn everyone against me. Those that aren't already."

"Graham's an idiot." He grinned when she laughed despite her tears. "Won't ever deny he's an idiot, but he's good to get your back in a fight."

When his hand rested on hers, she let out a gust of relief and clung to it like a lifeline. The horrors of the past week crashed in on her until she lost control of her tears again.

Before she knew it, he had her wrapped up tight against his side.

Curling into the comfort of his arms, she stopped trying to fight off the crushing waves of grief and guilt. She cried until her eyes were dry, lingering in the quiet once the last tear slipped from her cheek to his chest.

As she settled, his thumb ran along her arm, but he remained blissfully silent. Once she felt calm enough to speak, she tilted up to rest her chin on his chest. "You're a damn fool."

"Probably."

A short laugh escaped and she placed a gentle kiss on his chest. She rested her cheek on his chest, soaking up his warmth and comfort. The strong steady thrum of his heart beat against her tension until she sighed. Being right there was bliss, and she hoped it would never end.

He squeezed her shoulder. "You're gonna get your answers. I got no doubt."

For once she was glad he'd misinterpreted her sighs. His words were surprisingly soothing. She nodded. "I hope so. I'd hate to face a trial without any knowledge of the crime itself. However, that might just be what happens."

"If there was a crime."

That might have been soothing if it weren't for the nightmares. She lifted her head again so she could meet his eyes. "I can't believe that after everything that's happened, you would still believe me."

A frown tugged his lips down and he looked away. "Weren't all your fault."

"Damn straight it wasn't." That managed to pull the corners of his mouth back up so she kept going forward with

it. "You're a stubborn mule of a man that refuses to listen to reason when you get fired up. If just once you'd have listened to my cooler head, we might not have wasted any time."

"If you'd ever let me get a word in, I might be more willing."

"You don't like words."

He turned his focus back on her and his eyebrow popped up. "No. Not much."

"Thank you." The words escaped in a rush before she could censor them.

"Don't."

Nodding, she lowered her gaze and cleared her throat. Such deep emotion was risky. His hand on her cheek startled her. Before she could protest, she was pulled into his lips. Relief poured through her and she welcomed the wordless review of his feelings. By the time their lips parted she had to gasp for air. "Actions over words?"

"I wouldn't mind a few more actions."

"Cole. You're still in pain. We both are."

"We both got apologies to make."

"You can't apologize well in pain." Damn him. His grin was far too contagious and she felt a giggle bubbling. It took much effort to force it down and shake her head at him. "You need to heal. We both do."

"You don't play fair."

"You're the one that decided to be a fool and try to save this lying jezebel's life."

He sat so fast she almost fell off the bed. Cupping her face in his large hands, his icy eyes flashed fire as he held her gaze. He shook his head fiercely. "That weren't foolish. And you ain't a liar."

Her heart caught in her throat at the ferocity of his defense. "You really believe that?"

"Yeah."

"Thank you." She closed her eyes in relief and her hands rested on his chest. "I'll never be able to thank you enough."

"Sure ya will. I can think of a few ways."

"Is that so? A few?"

"Yeah. Maybe more."

"Tell me all of them."

A smile managed to find its way to her lips as she remembered all the colorful and enthusiastic ways he'd suggested. Despite her best intentions to let him heal, she'd allowed for several. He'd reminded her over the next day that he believed her, and reminded her often enough she should have no doubts.

She looked down at her untouched sandwich with a frown. Her appetite tainted by her own disgust with herself. The words he'd said were a ruse, they shouldn't let them cut her so deep.

She wasn't sure if it was the compilation of emotions she'd been put through, or the child inside that was making her so susceptible to the despair. But it was always there now, grasping at her like bony fingers pulling her into the grave.

With a shudder, she looked up at the depot again. She kept distracting herself from her task. It wouldn't ever work if she missed Johnny's departure. Everything hinged on it.

She nibbled at her sandwich and sipped her coffee, praying that she hadn't missed him in her diversion. It wasn't until she'd almost finished the sandwich that he emerged.

Dropping some money on the table, she headed outside without bothering to hide her limp. She waved down a carriage and climbed in, sitting up and giving the coachman instructions.

When he gave her a funny look, she placed a handful of cash in his hands and repeated her request. Relief flooded her when he nodded and turned back to his horse. Sighing, she dropped back into the shade of the cab.

She searched the streets and saw the man again, turning a corner several streets down. Reaching up she tapped on the door and with the jolt the carriage moved in the direction she'd indicated.

From there the route wound through the streets, turning and weaving without any particular direction. Then it would backtrack and go back down streets they'd already gone down.

The whole time Jane kept her eyes out the window; once in a while she'd give the driver a new instruction. Every time she saw the man their route changed, winding around and back to where she could find him again.

After what seemed like ages she saw him disappear into a restaurant. Giving another instruction to the driver, the carriage never stopped. Continuing to weave through the streets before she saw him again.

Almost two hours after they'd left the depot she sat forward as the man walked up the steps to a hotel and went inside. Closing her eyes, she sat back and let the coachman continue the crazy route around the city.

Once she was certain they'd passed by the hotel at least twice more, she sat up. She ordered the driver back to her own hotel and got herself to her room. Safe as she could feel inside the room, she sat on the couch and lifted her foot.

She unwrapped it with great care, trying not to wince at the increased bruising and swelling. "I only have to last through tomorrow. Then I will use the crutches again."

Sighing, she ran her fingers through her hair and pulled it from its bindings. She let it fall over the arm of the couch as her eyes closed.

Get out of here ya lyin' jezebel!

Jane's eyes flew open and she stared at the ceiling, the fear cutting through her like the knife had her finger the other day. Lifting her hand she studied the finger, contemplating removing the bandage.

In that moment when the pain of the wound had started to hit her, so had the emotions she'd been holding back since she'd woken up in the hospital. The self-loathing, the fear, the anger and shame rolled into a vicious ball that gnawed and roiled, crawling through her stomach and along her flesh.

Her eyes closed again slowly. "It'll work Cole. Don't worry…it'll work."

Faith means belief in something concerning which doubt is theoretically possible.
-William James

The coin spun through Mike's fingers, up one side, down the other. They were going to get into San Francisco so late he worried they'd be too late.

"Maybe they're already on a train to Sacramento." He couldn't put any conviction into the words. His head spun with the possibilities. "She's smart. Maybe she did it."

"I've got a question for you." Archie remained the picture of calm, sitting with his hands in his lap. He was a large man, years of blacksmithing adding to his bulk, but quiet and subdued.

"What?"

"She lied to you as much as she did David. Why do you trust her?"

"She didn't lie to me." Mike met the man's sharp gray eyes. "She can't. That's why she didn't write to me for seven years."

"A lie of omission is still a lie."

"If that woman I found in Dominion Falls remembered anything, I'd know it." Mike knew in his heart she couldn't lie to him. She hadn't been able to hide a lot from him since his arrival, though she'd tried hard. Even right then, before she'd left, there'd been something.

He couldn't put his finger on what, but something had been bothering her since the incident on the train. Something beyond the nightmare they were currently living. She was wrapped in a level of distraction that made him worry over her focus when she needed it most.

Mike turned to stare out the window at the passing miles of land. "Maybe Clara did do those things, but Jane doesn't remember them. I know it. I didn't hear from her for seven years because she couldn't lie to me. Jane or Clara—she still can't."

"How can you be so sure?"

"I just am. She's my sister and I know she didn't do those things. She may have been confused and allowed herself to get involved in some crazy things. Maybe she even thought she needed to run away, but she wouldn't ever kill someone. She couldn't."

"You've got a lot of faith in her."

"We were always close." With a sad smile, his mind drifted beyond the scene outside the window to the past. "She never could lie to me. She tried, but always failed. No matter what, I always caught her."

"Still. Seven years is a long time. If she's been taught to lie real good, maybe she can lie to you now."

"Maybe she can." Mike sat back in his seat, allowing the coin to drop into his empty hand. "I'd like to think that in the end, she's still Clara. That no matter what circumstances did to her, that even without the briefest memory of me, that she still knows me, she still couldn't lie to me."

"Sometimes faith can be misplaced."

"Do you have any sisters? Brothers?"

Archie stretched. His arm rested across the back of the seat, still studying Mike with the same appraising gaze. He nodded. "One of each."

"If they did something terrible. Would you hate them? If they made a huge mistake that changed their life into something evil and dark, would you give up hope?"

"I suppose not." Archie sighed. "Her past is catchin' up with her. If David can't find reason to lock her up, there's probably someone out there that has real charges against her if what she told David after the train accident is true."

"I know." Mike looked back out the window as the train made its way into the depot. "I know. She knows. It's inevitable if this guy told her the truth."

Archie fell silent as Mike while they waited for the train to make its final stop. Around them folks gathered their things together, but the two men had nothing but their persons and their weapons. Mike had refused to waste time with gathering clothes or any other items in favor of getting to Jane as fast as possible.

The train jolted one final time, signaling time for them to move. Mike flew to his feet and worked his way through the handful of passengers to make it to the door soon as it opened. Archie was more polite about disembarking and didn't join him for several minutes.

The depot overflowed with passengers from three trains within fifteen minutes. Mike glanced back at Archie when he finally caught up. "Keep a look out for Jane. If he's changed his appearance once, he's likely to change it again."

After exchanging a nod, Mike moved through the crowd. When he spotted a nearby bench, he hopped up to get a good vantage point. His heart pounded as he searched the crowd, looking for any sign of her familiar features.

There were so many people. Worse, he had no idea if Jane had already met with the man. Their entire search could all be in vain, but he searched anyway. Desperation fueled him to look at every person he possibly could.

The crowd thinned as most of the travelers made their way out into the city beyond the depot's walls. Every muscle in Mike's body trembled; he had to find her. He just had to. He searched every shadow, every crevice. Near the telegraph office Archie stood on a bench doing the same thing as him.

Then Archie pointed across the depot and shouted. Mike spun, his breath caught in his throat.

There she was.

The dress she wore was the same she'd worn to meet the stagecoach in Dominion Falls. A hat with a veil covered her features and most of her hair. She stood by a pillar, her satchel on the floor next to her. Then for some reason she took a step back. Another. Another.

That's when the movement of the man caught Mike's eye. For every step he took, Jane took another one back. Pain seared through Mike's chest as the man drew closer like a panther on the hunt. Mike's throat closed, his heart raced.

"Clara." The yell burned through his throat and echoed through the depot.

She froze, whipping toward him, then back to the advancing man. A shaky hand flew to her chest and her head whipped back and forth before her gaze settled on the satchel.

The man reached the satchel and Mike could finally see him. Though he had a goatee and appeared slimmer, it was him. The man's gaze went from Jane to Mike and a cruel smile twisted his features.

She jumped and turned, racing from the depot. The man followed right behind.

Mike jumped over the back of the bench in hot pursuit. Before he ever got outside, screams reached his ears. A police whistle sounded through the doors when he and Archie burst through them at the same time.

A crowd gathered near the alley beside the depot. A woman was screaming, "She's dead. He just ran up and killed her."

"No." Mike's whole body went numb and he collapsed to his knees. "Clara."

Water splashed his face. Arthur gasped, jumping awake.

Jesse stood over him, a cup in his trembling little hands. Wide brown-green eyes focused on him, then the door.

"What is it?" Arthur tried to move into a more comfortable position, but he knew one didn't exist. He'd tried for days.

"Bad man. Gone."

Arthur paused and glanced around the room. "Good. Help me."

He tried to move his wrists and work the rope, but only found pain for his efforts. With a grunt, he shifted and scooted along the floor enough to give Jesse access to the wretched knot of ropes. Jesse's hand touched his wrists, and Arthur grew still. "Take your time. He's gonna be gone for a bit."

"He'll find me. Always."

"We won't let him, Jesse. Just help me and I'll get ya somewhere safe. I promise." If he were honest he had no idea where he'd take the boy, but he knew anywhere would be better than here. Somehow he'd find a way to get them home. He had to.

Jesse's whimper pulled his attention back to the room. Arthur glanced over his shoulder and found Jesse's features screwed up tight in concentration and frustration. After a deep breath to calm himself, Arthur spoke as reassuring as he could. "It's all right, Jesse. I know he tied them tight. Just keep trying."

The minutes passed slow as molasses. Arthur did his best to keep still so Jesse could work. If he panicked, Jesse would too and that would make everything worse. His heartbeat raced and he took a ragged breath. Closing his eyes, he tried to focus like his pa had told him to do when he was afraid.

"When we get back home, Ma will make us the best meal you ever ate." Arthur didn't know if he was talking to keep himself or Jesse calm, but he wasn't about to stop for anything. His feet twitched with nerves he couldn't contain. "And I'll show you all around Dominion Falls, all the best places. You'll like Isaac."

Blood rushed to his hands in a firestorm of tingles as the rope finally began to loosen. Arthur tried to move his wrists a little to help Jesse along. "We'll go exploring, and fishing. And maybe you can go to school Miss Becky's real nice."

Suddenly the ropes got real loose and Arthur fought against them until he tugged his arms free. Fire shot through every nerve. He shook his arms out; there was no time to waste on pain. He grinned over at Jesse. "Good job. You did it!"

Arthur rubbed his raw wrists and flexed his fingers. He could only hope they'd work well enough to untie his feet. He tugged at the knot, working it faster than Jesse had worked on his hands. "Just a few more minutes and we'll be free, Jesse."

"Arthur." Jesse's voice scrambled against the wall.

"It's all right. I'm almost done." Arthur grinned over at the boy before turning back to the knot. Just a few more moves and he'd be free. "We'll get out of here, Jesse."

"Arthur!"

Arthur grinned in triumph when the knot came free. He looked over at Jesse and took a shaky breath. "We need to get out of here. Fast. I gotta get some money so we can send a telegram. Maybe get out of this city."

Jesse trembled. "Arthur."

"Maybe something I can use for a weapon. Just in case."

"Arthur," Jesse squeaked again. "Door!"

Arthur froze and looked from Jesse to the door. When he heard what Jesse'd been trying to tell him, his eyes widened. Someone was fighting with the lock. He ran toward Jesse just as the door burst open.

It is vain for the coward to flee;
death follows close behind;
it is only by defying it that the brave escape.
–Voltaire

"It wasn't her."

Archie gripped Mike's arm. "What? Are you sure?"

"It looked like her. Her hair was the right color, and that was Clara's dress. But it wasn't her." Mike sat down hard on the bench; his body sagged under him. He planted his elbows on his knees and buried his face in his hands.

He'd thought for sure it was Clara. The way the man reacted to his shouts left no doubt he'd been Johnny, or whatever his name truly was. That woman, whomever she was, was dead. It could easily have been Clara. The coincidence was too real, too close. Once again, his breath caught, his lungs closing in fear. Where was she?

Panic seized his heart and his mind spun in thousands of directions. He couldn't think straight, much less function, locked up in images of her death. "Clara."

"Michael." Archie sat beside him. "If you thought it was Clara, he might have too. Maybe now he thinks she's dead…"

"I don't know. He was a lot closer than I was." Mike ran his hand through his hair and shook his head. "Send a telegram to David. Tell him we'll be heading to Sacramento on the first train out of here in the morning. I want to stay here tonight, keep watch for him in case he tries to take a train out."

Archie nodded and stood. "I'll be right back."

Michael stared at a spot on the floor, taking several deep breaths. Where was she? Why hadn't she told him her plan? Let him help?

The only thing he knew now was that the woman who had died tonight was not Clara. He prayed she was all right, that somehow she'd succeeded in whatever she'd planned to do.

"Clara, where are you?"

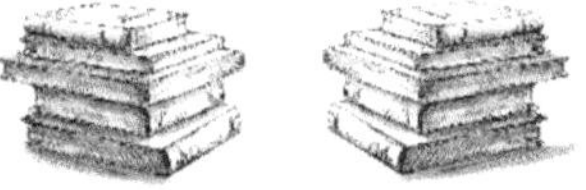

He that's secure is not safe.
–Benjamin Franklin

The slosh of water permeated each beat of the phrasing. "'Thy fate is the common fate of all; into each life some rain must fall, some days must be dark and dreary'."

"Jane?"

"Yes, Arthur?" Jane didn't pull her gaze from the water. She couldn't. If she did, the boys might see how terror had seized her heart in a grip close to deaths. Arthur would, at least. The little one had his arms braced around her waist and had fallen asleep the moment the ferry started moving.

"Where are we going?"

"I'm taking you across the bay. There is another stop on the rail line. You're going to get on a train and go to Sacramento. Michael should be there."

"You're coming too, right?"

The panic in his voice pulled her attention away from the water. She shook her head. "There's still something I have to do."

"You can't just leave us alone! What if Michael ain't there?"

Jane reached out and grabbed his hand. "He will be. I told him to be."

"But you don't know! Please, Jane…you can't leave us alone. Ya can't go back there. Please don't go back there. He ain't right."

"He has answers. I need answers, Arthur."

"We need you."

Tears filled Jane's eyes and she looked away. Torn between her duty to care for these children, and her desperate need to know. She had no idea what was right any longer. The world was upside down, and the small child clinging to her like she was his mother and he knew it threw her more off-balance. Did he know? Had she known? "I've got to go back."

"He ain't right. He'll hurt you," Arthur whispered. "And Jesse needs you."

Wiping at a tear, Jane sniffed and looked down at the sleeping child. "Jesse."

"He can talk. He just never let the bad man know it. He said his name is Jesse." Arthur looked down at him. "You've gotta keep him safe. You know that."

In that instant, the world righted itself. Life and his own mother had failed the child many times over. Answers were important, but nothing was more important than this child and getting him home to his pa. "Yes, I do. Clara didn't keep him safe. I have to."

"Jane?" Arthur fidgeted. "Is he really yours?"

"I believe he really is David's son. I don't know if he knows me. I don't know if I..." She choked on the lump of emotion that formed, clearing her throat. "What matters is that we get him back to David."

Silence settled between them again and Jane took a ragged breath. The pain from her foot and the presence of the young child kept forcing tears she didn't want. She hadn't expected to find the boy with Arthur and it had made her all the more determined to get them back to Dominion Falls.

It had all happened so fast she hadn't had time to think or feel. In the quiet, she relived the moment and the fear and panic was growing. She'd taken a carriage and bribed the hotel clerk for the correct room. Another bribe had gotten her a key, leaving her low on funds.

Both Arthur and Jesse had been terrified when the door opened and she could see why. The ropes that tied Arthur were still strewn on the floor and his arms and feet were still numb. She'd rushed them out to the carriage and headed right for the ferry.

Every street they'd turned on to, she'd panicked, fearing seeing him a step ahead of her, but they'd gotten to the ferry without incident. Now she just had to find her brother and send the children on their way.

Could she? Now that she was away from the city, she wondered if she should. She knew she shouldn't. There was far more that needed protection than the two children in her care now.

She hadn't realized she'd started crying again until Arthur's hand rested on her shoulder. With a shuddering breath, she dabbed at the tears and smiled. "Sorry."

"You ain't like him."

"He seems to disagree. According to him, I'm just like him."

"He's wrong."

The ferry was slowing and Jane turned her attention to the small boy wrapped around her waist. "Let's go, Arthur. We haven't much time if we're to make it to Sacramento tonight."

Arthur stepped up next to her, wrapping her arm around his shoulders. "Ya been limping bad. Are you all right?"

"I haven't been using my crutches." She shifted the sleeping boy, holding him tight. On the way toward the depot she allowed Arthur to help her along. "Once I can sit down, I'll be better. Don't worry. I'll be fine."

Arthur looked far from convinced, but stayed blessedly quiet. As soon as they got to the depot, she purchased the tickets and got them on the train. Jesse had woken up and insisted on walking himself, and she didn't deny him.

Once they were settled on the train, Jane stared out the window. There was no conversation and both boys fell asleep again under the gentle urging of the train. Sighing, Jane leaned back against the seat and forced aside her own exhaustion.

By the time the train whistled their arrival in Sacramento, it was dusk. Both boys stirred at the sound of the whistle and Jane took a deep breath. The pain in her ankle was severe, but she was more concerned that she couldn't feel her toes.

Sighing, she forced herself to her feet once the train had shuddered to a stop. Taking Jesse's hand, she nodded to Arthur to take the other before they made their way down the aisle. She had to let go of Jesse's hand to get off the train, using the rail and the conductor's hand to help herself down.

Resuming her hold on the boy's hand, they started through the depot. She searched for any sign of Michael, growing more concerned with each passing minute.

"David!"

Jane spun in surprise at Arthur's call, quieting him. "Don't shout. Just to be safe, please."

Arthur didn't acknowledge her, just started walking faster before releasing Jesse's hand. "David!" He rushed the final foot and threw his arms around him.

Jesse was holding back, so Jane squeezed his hand. "It's all right, Jesse. David will take very good care of you. And Arthur will be with you the whole time."

David's arms grew slack, his focus on the small boy. Wavering, he dropped to his knees in front of him. His voice cracked when he finally spoke, "Jesse?"

The tears formed again and Jane could barely manage a nod. Sniffling, she brushed at a tear. "That's what Arthur tells me."

Searching the boy's face, David remained silent. When he turned toward her, he shook his head. "Is it really?"

"Yes, David."

"It's okay, Jesse. See. David's real nice." Arthur smiled at the boy when he clung to Jane. "He'll make sure we ain't hurt."

David nodded. "No one's gonna hurt you, Jesse. Not ever again."

"Go ahead," Jane urged, pulling her hand free of Jesse's. She straightened up. "I need to go. Train is pulling out in a few minutes."

David stood and grabbed her hand. "Where do you think you're going?"

"I have something to finish."

"Don't go back, Jane!" Arthur protested. "Please. If it ain't safe for us—"

"It's okay, Arthur. I'll be all right. I told you I would see you in Dominion Falls again. I meant it."

David's grip on her wrist tightened. "You can't go back."

"I know you want to arrest me for whatever crime you can, David. I assure you that you'll get your chance. But I have to finish this."

"He thinks you're dead." David hissed in her ear.

"What? How? Why on earth?" Jane pulled back and searched his eyes in shock. "What happened?"

"I don't know. Michael and Archie said they'd been delayed," David started to explain.

"What do you mean, Archie and Michael? They're in San Francisco? Nobody was supposed to go there."

"You're staying here until they get here," David said firmly. "Then you're coming back to Dominion Falls."

Jane took a few ragged breaths and held his gaze before looking over at Arthur. Her anger faded the moment she saw his face and she nodded weakly. "Fine."

David kept his hand in Jesse's and pulled Jane along with him. "I can't believe that you did this. Then again, maybe I can. I never knew you."

"Oh, David. Wait." Jane gasped, her steps faltering under his fast pace. When her leg went out under her, she was surprised to find Arthur there. She smiled weakly at him and whispered, "Thank you."

Arthur nodded and looked back at David. "We should probably get outta here quick. He ain't gonna be happy when he finds out we aren't in that room."

"He could already be on their trail," Jane said quietly. "I did the best I could to cover our tracks, but I don't know if it was enough."

"She's real good at it," Arthur tried to assure them both.

"Yeah. Deception was one of her finest qualities."

If there be hell upon earth
it is to be found in a melancholy man's heart.
-Robert Burton

The boys were finally asleep.

With Arthur's help, Jane had managed to get Jesse bathed and ready for bed. Soon as the younger boy was in bed, she'd had Arthur follow right behind. Exhausted as he was after his ordeal, Arthur had put up no fight at all. Now the two boys were tucked safe in the bed behind curtains, and she was alone.

David had left to send a telegram and get food and supplies. After threatening her if she even thought of leaving, he'd disappeared. Of course, she couldn't go much of anywhere any longer. She wasn't about to leave the boys alone, and even with the aid of a crutch she wasn't sure she'd get very far with her ankle bad as it was.

The incessant throbbing pain got the best of her, so she sat on the couch and lifted her foot onto a pillow. In a painful, slow process she removed the bindings. By the time she got to the last layer, tears poured down her cheeks. She couldn't stop the sob that escaped at the deep purple, yellow and green hues spread across her foot and leg.

She exhaled a deep breath and braced herself on the couch, pushing up onto her good foot. Every hop toward the tub jolted the injury, but she bit her lip to avoid making any further noise. She drew up her skirt and sank the ankle into the now cool water, hissing through her teeth.

"Clara." David's voice was thick with concern.

She whimpered as he drew close. When he touched her arm, she brushed away his comforting hand. "Don't."

Against her request, his arm went around her waist, one arm under her knees. He lifted her from the water and carried her back to the couch. Once David set her down, he placed an extra pillow behind her head before pulling aside her skirt.

Her whole body jerked when he touched her ankle. She sat fast and swatted his hands away. "Stop. Don't. Please, David. Don't."

"You've been walking on that all day?"

"No. I've been walking on it for two days. I wasn't sure how much he knew of my injuries. I wanted to be sure I drew no suspicion."

"Why would you do this?"

"I had to get him back!" Jane shoved him away again. "This was my fault, Arthur being kidnapped was my fault. I had to make it right. Now stop. Don't worry about me. Don't fuss. Just don't. Keep being angry. Stay angry. That's what Clara deserves."

A long sigh escaped him and he shook his head. "The bone wasn't set before you did this. You just broke it in the accident."

"Well it isn't set now for sure. I'm fine. I'll live."

He moved toward her foot and she fought him off again. Tears poured down her cheeks as the pain battled with her own self-loathing for what he'd done and the fact he was still trying to help her. His frown deepened. "Jane."

"Damn it, David. Don't do this to yourself. To me."

"You're right. I almost forgot."

In an instant his concern faded away and her heart sank like a lead cannonball into her stomach. She swiped at her tears, trying to be strong. This was what she'd wanted, for him to hate her. It's what she deserved after what Clara had done. "Don't forget. Ever. It's dangerous to forget. I'm finding that out more every day."

"I sent the telegram. Mike and Archie'll be here tomorrow. You and the boys will stay here until I get back with them."

"All right."

David pushed himself to his feet and walked away, grabbing the satchel he'd dropped. He sat down on the chair by the couch and pulled it open. "I got some food so you don't have to leave the room tomorrow."

"You'll trust me to stay here?"

He held up a set of shackles. "Not on your life."

"Oh, that's lovely and won't scare Jesse one bit." She was being snide, but she didn't care. It was ridiculous to think she'd go anywhere now. She couldn't walk, much less run away.

David's head drooped and he caught it with his hands. He buried his fingers in his hair, shaking his head as he sighed. "Jane, I don't know what to do here. I want to hate you. I want to blame you. I know I should, I know how bad I'm hurting, how angry I am. But I forgave her so long ago, forgave you. We've got a son together."

"He's your son. With Clara. I'm not her. It's best that I'm not. She was stupid. She left. She didn't have all the facts and she left. She ended up living a life of lies and deception. She was a horrible person."

"I've had lots of time to think on it once Mike told me everything. She was hurt."

"Not by you." She studied him as he sat there staring at his own feet. "She took the easy way out. She gave into fear."

"She didn't trust me."

Jane sighed and twisted her hands in her lap. "She hurt you. She hurt herself. She hurt that little boy. She doesn't deserve your sympathy. Neither do I."

"Why'd you do it?"

"What? There's so much I can't explain."

"Go after Arthur. Alone."

"I had to."

He moved, dropping his hands. After a moment he rose and moved close enough to sit on the edge of the couch. "No. You didn't."

"You've blamed yourself for seven years over something you could not have possibly known, something that wasn't your fault." She stared at the ceiling, twirling a lock of hair. "This all was my fault. Whether I remember it or not, in some way it was caused by me. I blame myself and I wanted to make something right."

"Amnesia won't make a lick of difference in any court."

"I'm not expecting it to and I never planned on using it as a defense. There is no defense."

"Clara." When she refused to look at him, afraid of wavering, he cupped her cheek and dragged her eyes to meet his. "Jane."

"I told you, hold onto that anger. Hate me, hate her."

"I got every right to be angry. Part of me is. But damn if I don't still care about what happens to you."

She couldn't believe he was saying these things. The whole thing was so ridiculous she couldn't stop the snort that burst out. "You are a weak man."

"You always said so."

She drew down her brows and studied him in confusion. "What? Clara did that?"

"Yeah. Of course, you didn't mean it then. I think you mean it now."

"Not so much." She smiled weakly. For all that had happened, she thought David might be the opposite of weak. She was the weak one.

His thumb brushed along her cheekbone as she kept her gaze lowered. He remained silent until he had her attention again. "You're right."

"No, I'm not."

"You don't want to know what about?"

"Not particularly." She closed her fingers over his hand and pulled it from her cheek. Last thing she needed to do was encourage his affection in any form. He'd forgive her too easily. Plus, the pain in her ankle was starting to deepen; her focus was wavering. "Don't be nice to me. I don't deserve it."

"Sure you do."

"Damn it, David."

"Didn't you just say that you aren't Clara?"

She squeezed his hand, careful to not squeeze too hard and reveal her pain. Her head ached with her efforts to hold back the pain. Her voice came out too strained for her liking.

"You agreed with me a few weeks ago. You said you'd know if Clara was still in here."

"Clara took away my son. But you, Jane, you brought him to me."

"You need to make up your mind, David."

"I'm still mad. Mad at Clara." He shook his head, his fingers running along her neck to her shoulder before giving her a gentle squeeze. "But mad as I am, I still love her."

"David, please."

"I'm never going to forget that you were once her. There's still enough of her in you, I can't help it. I'll go through with the divorce because I let Clara go years ago, but part of her is still here. I was angry as hell when I realized how deep Clara's lies went. But then you went and saved him, risked your own life, to bring him to me. You make it damn hard to stay mad."

She sighed. "David."

"Will you let me talk?"

"David, I would love to have a deep, philosophical discussion with you. About the strength of true love and the weakness of the mind. Or who lied to you and who I am. Even debate what there is left of Clara and who I am as opposed to her, but I can't. Not right now."

"Why not?"

"Because I can't focus."

He ducked his head as hers drooped to maintain eye contact. "What?"

"David. I can't feel my toes. I can't—my whole leg hurts by now. Something must be done about my ankle."

"I'll get a doctor."

"No!" She slapped a hand over her mouth at the volume of her protest. After she checked her tone, she spoke again. "It's not safe to have anyone come or go. You have to help me."

"I don't know, Clara."

"You've helped set bones on the trail. You told me so yourself, there wasn't always a doctor around to fix up the guys, you all had to make do. You can do this."

"I'm not so sure about that."

"The longer we wait, the worse it will be." She grasped his hand. "I trust you."

His brows knit together and he opened his mouth in a hint of protest. After a moment his shoulders sagged. "All right. I'll try. If it doesn't work, we're getting a doctor."

"Fine."

"Then let's get you set up."

Jane nodded and did her best to move. They worked together in silence to get her ankle propped where he could easily reach it. Once she was in place, she reached over her head to grab the arm of the couch.

David paused, and then unhooked his holster and stripping the holster from the belt. He handed the strap of leather to her. "You're going to need something to bite on."

"Thank you." She set the strap in her mouth, and it squeaked under the pressure of her teeth. With her eyes closed, she gripped the arm of the couch and held on tight. A whisper of a touch to her leg came moments before a white hot flash of pain. Somehow she squelched the shriek, spitting out the belt and taking short breaths against the pain.

"That didn't do it. I'm going to have to try again." David's voice was quiet. "I'm sorry, Clara. There's still no color in your toes."

She nodded fiercely, breathing out low and slow against the pain shuddering through her limbs. "Just give me a moment." She might have been embarrassed over the tremor in her voice, but she couldn't care just then.

With shaky hands, she grabbed the strap of leather again. Once she'd set it in her mouth, she braced herself for the next attempt. This time there was no warning, only pain. She couldn't stop the scream or the fresh influx of tears.

The hum of David's voice lacked solid form. Whatever he said swam through her head without making sense. She caved to the pain moments later, slipping into the welcome black. Another sharp spike of pain brought her back.

Colors danced before her eyes when she blinked them open. A quiet groan welled from her belly as spikes of pain shot from her ankle up her leg. "That hurts."

"Really? I thought it tickled."

She laughed through the pain and forced herself to sit as he finished wrapping her ankle tight. When he finished and sat beside her, she cupped his cheek. "Thank you."

"Think you're going to live?"

"Until the noose is around my neck."

"That isn't funny."

"I'm not joking."

He pulled her close, resting her head on his chest. His hand ran along her back. "You did a lot of things wrong. I just can't believe you murdered anyone."

"It doesn't matter what you believe. In the end, it won't be up to you." She took a deep breath, relaxing in his arms. It was more comfortable there than she expected it to be, almost familiar. With a deep sigh, she wrapped her arms around him.

"You going to give up?"

"No. Not yet. I have to know what happened. I need those answers. The why, and what did I actually do? I'll find a way to learn what happened."

"Jane," David pulled back from their embrace and searched her eyes, "what if you don't?"

"You said it yourself. Amnesia is not a defense. It will never hold up in court. Not knowing if I committed a crime does not pardon me from having committed it when I was Clara. I may not be her, but this body was hers."

"How can you be so calm about this?"

"Because I have to be." She leaned her forehead against his and clasped his face in her hands. "For what it's worth, I'm sorry. I can never make up for what I did to you…but I am sorry."

"I know you are." His hand closed over hers. He kissed her wrist before holding it against his chest.

*Permanence, perseverance, and persistance
in spite of all obstacles, discouragement,
and impossibilities:
it is this, that in all things distinguishes
the strong soul from the weak.
—Thomas Carlyle*

"It's not your fault."

Michael didn't move a muscle outside of what the rocking of the train forced on him. His face buried deep in his hands, where it had been since he'd told her what happened to the woman in San Francisco. He sat opposite her without saying a word, shoulders sagging.

They'd stayed in sleeper cars from Sacramento to Denver, but now they were in a passenger car. Soon they'd be in Dominion Falls and this was the closest Michael had come to her since he'd seen her in Sacramento. She'd spent most of the trip asleep rather than face her pain, and he'd avoided her the few times she'd been awake until David had forced them together. "I mean it. It's not your fault."

"I didn't know you sent her. I shouldn't have called out. I thought it was you from a distance, and then he killed her."

Jane had hired the woman Johnny had killed. She'd been a vagrant Jane had run across in Denver, one that had looked somewhat similar to her. The moment she'd seen the woman, Jane knew what to do.

The reason for the veil had been simple: beyond body type and hair color, the vagrant looked little like Jane in the face. Her face was rounder, and the eyes were the wrong color, the similarities were hardly enough to fool an evil, clever man like Johnny.

Her instructions to the woman were simple. Drop the bag, wait for his approach, and then run like the dickens to the nearest police officer or safe place to remove her hat. She wasn't to stick around long enough for him to look in the bag. All Jane had needed was the temporary distraction to get into the hotel room.

The last thing that was supposed to happen was her death. Jane hadn't expected Michael to do anything different than she'd asked. Now the woman's death weighed as heavily on her own conscience as it did Michael's.

"Calling out to her was foolish. Going to San Francisco was foolish. I told you where to go. The simple fact is there is a lot that should be different."

"If I hadn't called out."

"If I had never left David. If I had never gotten involved with Johnny. If I hadn't told Cole everything. If I hadn't left you out of my plans."

"That's a lot of *ifs*."

"That's right. I have plenty of my own in my head. I have little room for yours. Please be pleasant or take your guilt elsewhere."

"Who was she?"

"A vagrant. She looked a bit like me. The differences could be covered with the mourning veil. I didn't believe she would fool him. That's why she wasn't supposed to allow him to get close to her. I told her to run before he ever touched the satchel."

"I confused her by calling out to her. She didn't know which man was the right one."

"Most likely."

"There was no money."

"He didn't know that. Not at first." A frown turned down her lips. It felt like a permanent resident. She stared out the window and shook her head. "Too many deaths. Too much pain. There's no way to make this right, is there?"

"It would appear not."

A phrase rose in her mind, and unbelievably she laughed. "I'm on the wrong side of things."

"How's that?"

"Syrus says 'the remedy for wrongs is to forget them'. Well, I have forgotten them. Too bad no one else has."

Michael chuckled. "Yes, the forgetting is supposed to be done by those that were wronged. Not the other way around."

She wiped an errant tear and focused on the passing scenery. "I'm not going to get out of this, am I?"

"Probably not with your neck the length it is now."

The corner of her lip twitched. How odd he would make such a comment right after she'd done the same with David in Sacramento. Of course, she'd been more blunt and less poetic about it. "What a pleasant way to put it."

"I'm serious, Clara." He dug into his pocket and pulled out a square of folded paper. Crinkling filled the silence as he opened it.

She didn't want to see it and her eyes closed involuntarily. When the rough paper crunched in her hand, she braced herself and opened her eyes. Studying the crude image, she shook her head. "This is a very poor likeness."

"But it could be you."

"Yes, I suppose it could. That madman said I was wanted for murder. Although this names the woman accused. According to this the name of the murderess is Constance Pinot Querney."

"Murder."

"Of a Mr. Jake Querney. I see. I can read."

Michael left his bench to sit next to her. "This says the murder happened here in Colorado."

"She was sent to an asylum." The blood drained from her face. Her fingers went cold and jerked, crinkling the edges of the paper under her grip. "Where she escaped. Wanted for murder, fraud. It would seem you're right. Hanging would be the sentence for either crime."

"How can you be so calm?"

Her hand shook and she clenched it into a fist. Within her hand the crude drawing disappeared into wrinkles. "What choice do I have? None. Once I had an idea I might have committed crimes, I knew what had to be done. I don't want to die, Michael, but I knew it was likely to happen."

"But you don't remember. Any of it."

"It's not a defense. I don't have a defense and I'm not even certain I want one." She placed her hand on his. Over the many silent hours she'd spent alone she'd had time to think about it. Though she'd not seen the posters in Denver thanks to her distraction, she'd thought many hours over what the madman had told her. "Just because I don't remember committing any crimes does not make me any less responsible."

"I can't watch you go through that, Clara."

"Then don't. Once whatever sentence I'm given is given, walk away. Clara left seven years ago. This will just make it permanent."

He shook his head and clasped his hand over hers. "I hate this."

"It isn't my favorite way to look at the future, but facts are facts."

"You were always far too logical."

"Not always. If I were, I wouldn't be where I am now, facing this fate."

"Clara." David's voice was quiet. He slid onto the bench Michael had abandoned and reached over to tap her knee. "How are you holding up?"

"I'll be better once we're home unless…" Jane offered a weak attempt at a smile. "Are you here to arrest me, Sheriff Schaffer?"

"No. Don't know that you committed any crime." David shrugged. "Until I do, or I'm told you arrest you, it's not going to happen."

"Someone certainly thinks I committed a crime." She waved the wad of paper in her hand. "I don't want you bending the law."

"Near as I can tell, that poster looks a little like you, but not enough to convince me. It's also looking for a Constance Querney. The only person I see is Clara Schaffer, turned Jane Doe."

Michael squeezed her hand. "We just need time, Clara. We'll find a way to prove you didn't do this. We're going to use every minute of time we have to find the answers."

"What if the answers only confirm what we've been told?" A shuddering breath rattled through her lungs. She shook her head against the rising fears. "Besides, just how do you propose we find those answers? No one but a maniac seems to know where I was for seven years."

"Let me call Tommy," Michael started.

"No."

"Tommy? Your brother?" David's eyebrows rose. "That might not be a bad idea, Clara. If anyone can help, it might just be him."

"No." Shaking her head, Jane leaned against the smooth wood framing the window. "I won't let any other family know. It's bad enough the two of you found me, only to face the possibility of me dying again. I won't do it to anyone else. I cannot torture another soul like this. It isn't fair to any of you."

"But, Clara. Tommy is a—"

"*No*." She hit the seat with her fist, unleashing as much of her panic as she could. The town had just come into view and all she wanted to focus on was that. Sanctuary. Home. Cole. Managing to find some of her voice, she whispered, "No more family."

"I really think you should reconsider." Michael wrapped his hand over her fist. "If we can stop this, we need to try."

"Why?" The train whistle blasted, interrupting Michael's reply. Within seconds, the boys and Archie appeared and sat down. Jane couldn't help but focus on Jesse, still silent but excited. His legs swung under the bench and his smile grew when Arthur whispered something in his ear.

Her hand dropped to her stomach and a tear slipped down her cheek. The fear she'd been trying to keep at bay gained strength again.

By the time the train shuddered to a stop, she was shaking and gripped Michael's arm tight. There was no discussion around her, but David scooped her into his arms. She wrapped her arms around his neck and buried her head in his shoulder, breathing deep as possible to keep from losing her weak grip on control.

Every step he took brought her closer to tears. By the time he stepped out onto the busy train platform, a few tears leaked out.

"Give her here." Cole's voice knocked her fragile hold on her control out of the way.

A deep sob echoed from her depths, acres of fear in the simple sound.

David held tight to her, his lips pressed to her temple. "Goodbye, Clara."

She hugged him, letting him say goodbye, as he hadn't been able to before. "She loved you. She was young and foolish, but she loved you."

"I know." David held on for another minute before his hold loosened and his lips left her temple. David cleared his throat. "She needs to see Daisy. I tried to set her ankle again, but I'm not sure it's set right."

"I'll take care of her." Cole hovered at the edge of her vision. "Don't you worry."

"He always worries," Jane said at the same time as David spoke.

"I always worry."

Even Cole managed a smile. "Give her here, Davie."

"Take care of her." David stepped forward and in moments, Cole's familiar strong arms held her close. With a shaky smile, David nodded. "I'll see you tomorrow, Jane."

"Tomorrow." Jane lifted her gaze to Cole and touched his cheek. "Now what?"

"We get you healed, and then we find your answers."

"Sounds like a plan. Just one question."

Cole's brow lifted. "What's that?"

"Can I sleep first?"

*Cease to inquire what the future has in store,
and take as a gift whatever the day
brings forth.
—Horace*

Jane draped her arm over her eyes. If for no other reason than to hide how much the doctor's examination hurt. Of course, Cole's nearby pacing didn't help her patience any.

"Daisy, you're hurting her," Cole snarled near her ear.

"She has a broken ankle. She's hurting, period." Daisy didn't sound the least bit flustered by Cole's venom. Jane supposed after three years as Cole's favorite whore, Daisy would be used to his temper. The knowledge that Cole no longer owned her contract probably helped bolster her temperament as well. A sharp pain shot through Jane's leg when Daisy applied pressure. "Can you feel that, Jane?"

Jane released the tight grip her teeth had on her cheeks. "Quite."

"I know it seems the opposite, but that is a good sign. It looks like David set it well, considering the circumstances." Daisy's fingers didn't stop their poking and prodding of the offended ankle. "In a hotel room, biting on a belt? Could you try to explain again why you didn't call a doctor?"

"With a maniac running around murdering people that looked like her, what do you think?" Cole's hand gripped

Jane's shoulder tight. The pain didn't compare with what was shooting along her leg thanks to Daisy's ministrations so she kept silent. Cole's voice rumbled on in her defense. "She got the boys back, didn't she?"

The boys. Jane's trip to San Francisco had been a tentative success, with both Jesse and Arthur rescued from the clutches of the madman Johnny. The cost of her already broken ankle now worse seemed worth it to have both of them in relative safety. More importantly, that Jesse was with his father—a place he should have been all along. If only Clara had not been such an idiot. Once again Jane's stomach churned over the disgrace of a woman she'd once been.

"Y'all right, Jane?" Cole's harsh tones softened as his voice hovered close in her ear.

"Yes. How is Jesse?" Jane pulled her arm away from her eyes. Jesse, her son. The son she couldn't remember any more than she could anything from her life before she'd waken in Dominion Falls six months before.

"He's well. Malnourished and still won't speak to anyone but Arthur." Daisy turned to grab the wrapping for Jane's foot. When she turned back her features tensed in a stern glower. "Once we're done here, Jane, I want you off this foot until I say otherwise. You're very fortunate I don't have to amputate."

"I know." Jane gripped Cole's hand as Daisy wrapped the ankle tight. He winced before she did when her nails broke his skin. "Sorry."

"No problem." It came out in a grunt, but Cole offered no real protest. His frown lingered as the wrapping continued. When he spoke again he changed the subject abruptly.

"What's gonna happen to the Silver Saddle now that Guy's dead?"

Jane blinked. She'd not had time to think about that. With Daisy still treating patients in the hotel, she probably should have thought of it sooner. She chalked it up to one of those times Cole managed to surprise her. Though now that they were on the subject, another question brought itself to the forefront. "Do we know who killed him?"

"According to Arthur, he heard someone with Johnny say he was dead. Not sure if this other man did it, or what exactly happened, but Johnny clearly knew about it." Daisy finally finished her torture and tied off the wrapping. "As far as the hotel, I don't know. Rumor has it Jackson is trying to buy it."

Both Daisy and Jane shuddered at the same time. Jane wrinkled her nose. "I do hope for your sake, Daisy, that such a thing never comes to pass."

"You could always come back." Cole helped Jane sit. He grinned at Daisy, the playful shine in his eyes returned now that Daisy wasn't abusing Jane's injured ankle. "Still ain't managed to replace ya."

Jane pursed her lips to cover her own smile at Cole's playful jibe. "I sincerely doubt Daisy would appreciate returning to performing services at your saloon any more than she wishes Jackson to own her contract."

"Hey, anyone would treat her better than Jack. Even me." Cole winked.

"You couldn't buy my contract anyway without someone to sell it." Daisy glared at Cole, the teasing humor lost on her. "So don't concern yourself with it."

Cole shrugged. "Suit yourself."

"Now, Jane, I know you needed your rest, but since I didn't get to see you yesterday, is everything else all right?" Daisy set her hand on Jane's knee, a meaningful lift of her brow and nod of her head the only elaboration to the question.

Jane didn't need to ask what she meant—the pregnancy she had yet to tell Cole about. She offered a subtle nod. Despite the turmoil of the past week, she didn't believe any issues had arisen, none that she could tell. "I believe so. I'm just still very tired."

"She's done nothing but sleep since she got off that train yesterday, so don't give me that look." Cole folded his arms across his chest, taking Daisy's pointed frown as a personal affront. "I didn't keep her up for nothing."

"Easy." Jane set her hand on his arm. "She was just asking."

A knock interrupted any further protest. A gruff voice sounded through the door. "Janey. I got to get that trunk—"

"I'll handle Norman." Cole strode from the room, most likely glad to have something to do other than fret.

Daisy's shoulders relaxed, and she moved closer. "Any signs of trouble from the baby? Bleeding? Cramps?"

"No. Everything seems to be fine. I'm just tired, is all." Jane cast a glance at the shut door, the reminder of the trunk bugging her as it had in San Francisco. "I don't know what made me get that trunk. It just felt like mine."

"What trunk?" Daisy checked the flexibility of Jane's sprained wrist. There was hardly any pain as she bent it back and forth.

"In San Francisco there was a room with abandoned luggage. I saw a trunk that I just knew had to be mine. I even knew the name Annabel Lee was carved into the bottom."

Jane twirled her wrist once Daisy released it. "Feels much better."

"Looks just about healed. Now, as for the trunk, was it a memory?"

By now Jane should be used to the hopeful look people got when they thought she might be remembering something from her past. Amnesia was no fun, especially when you might have forgotten a great many crimes. The look rankled every nerve she possessed, no matter how many times she saw it. She sighed. "No. Not exactly. I would call it more like an instinct. A feeling."

"It's been six months."

"And for the first time, you don't sound hopeful my memory could return." Jane fiddled with the edge of her bodice, not sure how to feel about Daisy's apparent concession to the depths of Jane's amnesia.

"I thought it would have returned by now, is all." Daisy patted Jane's shoulder before stepping over to clean up the tray of supplies. "I don't know what to think."

"She's just plum lost her mind." David Schaffer's voice filtered into the room, accompanied with a smile to them both. "Sorry I didn't knock. Cole said you were done and to come on in. He's going with Norman to pick up something at the depot."

"I suppose it's all right. You are still technically my husband." Jane attempted a smile and found success once David laughed out loud. She'd been struggling to figure out how to handle a husband she couldn't remember, but who remembered her clearly. Somehow they'd managed to form a friendship, and she still couldn't believe he'd forgiven her after the revelation of Jesse's existence. "Where's Jesse?"

"Playing with Isaac." David sat on the edge of the examination table and took her hand. "I still can't believe he's real. That we managed to have a child together all those years ago."

"I'm sorry it took so long for you to meet him."

David wiped a tear from her cheek. "We don't know why Clara did what she did, and odds are we can't know. Much as I want the reasons, I want all those answers, for now having Jesse here is enough."

"For you." Jane cleared away the lump in her throat. "I'm sorry. I just still can't believe I did that to you. You're a bit annoying, but you are a good person."

"I'm annoying, am I? Who's the one that doesn't know how to be silent when the need calls for it?"

"That would be Jane." Daisy smiled at them both. "I'm going to get these things put away. David, will you be sure she doesn't use that foot for one second on her way back to the saloon?"

"Yes, ma'am." David saluted Daisy. "I don't want to have to set it again. I think she busted my eardrums with her screaming."

"I didn't scream." At least, Jane didn't think she had. The pain had been so blinding at the time. The children hadn't been awake when she'd come to, so if she had, it couldn't have been overly loud.

"Ready to go back? You still look tired."

"I am. Exhausted, really. My life is exhausting."

"Ever think of just sitting back and relaxing?" His lips twitched in an attempt to cover laughter.

She smacked his chest and snorted. "If I did, we wouldn't have Jesse or Arthur back now would we? Besides, there's still seven years that I haven't a clue about what happened to me. I'd like to figure that out."

"First, you need something more than that maniac's word."

"I know. Trust me, I know."

*Mystery magnifies danger,
as a fog the sun.
-Charles Caleb Colton*

Cole's room was flooded.

Piles of fabric spilled across his floor like the rolling waves of the ocean, covering the once-empty surface in a pool around Jane. Her clothes—but not her clothes. She sat amid the sea of material, staring into what now appeared to be an empty trunk from what he could tell.

Her skin was pale as milk, but he couldn't be sure if it was from fear or the pain in her ankle. For some reason she continued to stare in the trunk, unmoving. Her fingers gripped the edge, knuckles white.

He waded through the materials of her past to crouch beside her. She didn't look like she'd slept or eaten much since before the nightmare had begun at the train celebration. He hated seeing her this weak, this lost. Without a response to his presence at all, he slipped a hand around her narrow waist and tried to get her to stand. "Come on. Ya need rest."

Her hand on his stopped him. She gave his fingers a gentle squeeze before she reached into the depths of the trunk. "I don't believe it."

"What?"

"*The Works of the Late Edgar Allan Poe.*" Her hand shook as she withdrew the book from the depths of the chest. "The same book we found with the horse carcass months ago."

"Why would ya have two of the same book?" Cole didn't bother to try to hide his confusion when he sat on the floor next to her. After all, he didn't understand the purpose of onc book, much less more than one of the same thing. He took the book when she passed it off. He couldn't read it, but one thing was immediately clear. The other book had been well worn, cracked and peeling leather on the spine, the words fairly rubbed off the cover, while this one was near as new as one on the shelf. "This one ain't as broken."

"No, it's not. I wonder if the notes are the same."

"Notes?" He was completely lost now.

"Yes, notes." She dug through the trunk, her head shaking. "Newspapers, periodicals. These aren't being used as lining. They're stacked neatly."

He grunted when she dropped a stack of newspapers in his hands. A frown formed as she lifted another stack from the trunk. He dropped the stack he held on the nearest plume of petticoats. "Jane."

"Why did I have these?"

"Hey." He cupped her cheek and pulled her face toward his. Her features were pale, her eyes wide and glittering with some odd emotion that took her over every time she tried to face the past she couldn't remember. "Ya got that look in your eye again."

"What look?"

"That crazy look."

The flash of her eyes was all the warning he had before she shoved him away. "That is not funny. I am *not* crazy. I'm not insane. I'm not. I wasn't. I can't be."

"That ain't what I meant."

"Constance, or me, or Clara. One of us was sent to an asylum. An asylum. She never went to trial because they put her in an asylum." She shuddered, not that he blamed her. Asylums were nightmarish places to be. He knew all too well. "She escaped. What if…oh, I would rather be hanged than sent to one of those places."

"You ain't gonna be hanged."

"You have no way of knowing that. All it would take is one telegram, from Graham or someone else who dislikes me, and it's all over. They could very well hang me. Or send me to…don't let them send me to an asylum. Cole, swear it to me. I can't. I…" Her already stilted breath came in ragged gasps. Her eyes grew wider with every word. The panic on her face was all too familiar, but she usually wore it when the renegades attacked.

"Jane." He grabbed her wrists so quick she yelped. Before she could panic further or fight he yanked her close. Like a startled deer, she froze in place, stiff in the circle of his arms. Then a small gasp of air burst out and she sagged into him.

"I'm sorry," she whispered. As almost always happened when he pulled her fraught body close, she molded against him until their bodies were flush. One arm wrapped around his waist, the other hand rested on his chest right over his heart. "My head. It's racing. I no longer know what to think."

"First off, stop worryin' yourself about Graham. He ain't sending no telegram nowhere."

"You don't know that for certain."

"Sure I do. After Mikey broke his nose, he shut up real fast." Cole laughed when her head dropped back, her jaw open wide. As amusement took over her features, it warmed him all the way to his toes. "Yeah. Graham went running his mouth the day ya took off. Michael beat on him real good. Graham got knocked out cold."

"Michael?" A laugh flittered out of her. "He's half Graham's size. Goodness, he's barely bigger than I am. How did he do that?"

"He said something about five brothers and a mean older sister."

She shook her head with a sigh. "That is no guarantee, Cole. He could just be biding his time until he has something to get me on. He doesn't care for me, you are quite aware of this."

"Let me worry about Graham." He tugged her close again until she was settled in his lap. "Now ya got some stuff here that you gotta go through and it's all reading and words. Lots of words. That should excite ya."

"You know what, Cole? I am not excited. Not even a little bit. The more I learn about myself, the more trouble I appear to be in. I really am at a point where I do not care anymore."

"That doesn't sound like the Jane I know."

She snorted. "No one knows me. Not even me."

"Bull."

"I'm not in the mood for arguing with you."

"But arguin' is what we do second best."

"Cole."

He grinned at the twitch he noted at the corner of her mouth despite her scolding tone. "And much as I'd love to remind ya what we do best…I don't think you could handle it right now."

"Please."

"Besides, if we got ourselves hurt again because of our…best…Daisy would be awful mad." He chuckled when her smile broke free and in response she turned her head as far away as she could in an attempt to hide it. "But that ain't ever stopped me before."

She squealed when his hand slipped under her skirt and along her thigh. Swatting at his hand, she playfully beat at his chest when he leaned in for a kiss.

Her lips were warm and inviting. He hadn't realized how much he'd missed her touch until she was there. He pulled her close and traced the seam of her lips with his tongue. She opened to him so fast it took his breath away, and he shifted to lay her down on the floor.

She planted her hands on his chest and pushed him back. "Wait."

His low groan filled the space between them and he frowned. While he didn't like the idea of hurting her with their coupling, being interrupted was a worse sin right then. His whole body ached as she kept him at bay. "Why?"

"I want to finish going through the trunk."

"It'll still be there."

"Cole. You are the one that not one minute ago told me I should be excited about this, and now you're telling me to wait? Are you going to make up your mind?"

"Right now, there's only one thing on my mind." He should have been madder when she pushed him farther away, but she had a point. He had told her to be excited, and he knew the question of her past hurt her bad. He'd put aside his own discomfort for now; he had for months after they'd first met, after all. He chuckled, not willing to drop it without a proper protest. "Ya don't play fair."

"I know." She slid away from him, keeping her injured leg off to the side. Her head ducked back inside the trunk. She banged around inside, hitting the bottom of it.

"What are ya doin'?"

"It's empty. I remember reading that some people put in false bottoms. I was hoping that perhaps I was that smart. Apparently not."

Cole hopped to his feet and grabbed the bottle of whiskey and glasses perched on a shelf nearby. He dropped back down next to her and shoved away some clothes to pour them both a glass. After a long sip, he frowned as she kept poking through the trunk. The more he thought about it the more she had a point. "Can't believe there ain't nothing but clothes and papers."

"Maybe there's something in the papers, but otherwise, no answers."

"Find that hard to believe. Girl smart as you not leaving nothing."

"I think we've seen Clara wasn't always of sound mind." She frowned, tapping her thumb against the trunk. "Then again, maybe it was smart. Johnny doesn't give me the impression he leaves much leeway."

He straightened and peered into the trunk. The whole piece was one of the fanciest he'd seen, complete with a lining and shelves she'd already removed and set aside with all their gaudy jewels. "What about the lining?"

"What about it?"

"Well. Ya got nothing in the trunk. Maybe you hid it."

She waved her hand dismissively and downed her whiskey in a gulp. "If I'm so smart I probably figured I would just remember. Joke was on me."

"If you're so smart, ya probably had a backup plan."

"Oh yes. I'm quite brilliant." Sarcasm laced every syllable.

"I really hate it when ya give up. Makes you look weak."

She pursed her lips and blew out a huff of air, the noise a dismissal itself. Ignoring him, she poured herself another glass.

He frowned as she downed two more glasses faster than he'd seen her drink in a while. Before she could pour another, he set his hand on the bottle. "Ease up. Don't wanna drown yet. I ain't done with you."

"Maybe I'm done with you."

"Don't believe that for a minute." He winked when she huffed a weak protest. While she grumbled and flounced back into a pile of clothes he turned back to the trunk. He ran his hand along the edge of the lining. "Musta been making good money with that guy. It's a nice trunk."

She snatched the bottle and poured another glass. At his leer, she lifted the glass in a mock toast. "Have at it. I'm going to waste my time with these newspapers."

He moved the stack of newspapers closer to her when she struggled to grab them. As she grabbed the first paper, he snatched the knife off the floor where she'd left it. Along one side of the trunk he found a hitch in the fabric where small stitches held it shut.

He made the first cut there. Along the top edge of the trunk he sliced through the fabric. Every time he reached a corner, he ripped back the lining. Nothing showed up, not even where the stitches had held the lining in place. With a frown he studied the lining in the lid before taking the knife to it as well.

This time as he pulled the fabric away from the wood he hit pay dirt. Something was carved into the wood. "Well. What do ya got here, Jane?"

The glass fell to the floor with a clunk and she was beside him. "What?"

"This." He ran his finger over the wood, the woods carved into it catching on his rough fingers. The little schooling he had helped him recognize a few letters, a 'C', and a 'D' as well as several others. "What's it say?"

"It's an address. C. Hodgkins. Yankton, Dakota Territory."

"Someone you know?"

"Good question."

"Jane?"

"Once again, it's more questions, no real answers." She sighed and picked up one of the newspapers. She flipped through it with a tilt to her head, leaving it open and setting it aside. Then another paper earned the same fate, followed by a magazine.

"Jane?"

"Poe."

Cole poured another glass of whiskey, mumbling a few obscenities. He pushed himself to his feet and stretched out his back. Most of the stitches were gone, but the skin was still pulling and sore. "When you come back, let me know."

"I'm right here."

"No you ain't. You're wrapped up in them papers."

"Every single one of these has a piece by Edgar Allan Poe. All of them. That can't be coincidence."

"So what's it mean?"

"I have no idea." She stirred, turning toward him when he sat on the bed. With a sigh, she smiled. "Sorry."

"No. I told ya to be excited. My own damn fault."

Chuckling, she gripped the edge of the trunk to try to pull herself to her feet.

He wasn't about to make her struggle for it. It would have been amusing, but the thought of having her in his arms was more tempting. Flying to his feet, he grabbed her under the arms and lifted her up.

"In a hurry?"

"Yeah."

"Haste makes waste." A playful wink preceded her smile. "And I'd hate for this to be a waste."

"Sure you're up for it?"

"Why do you think I had a few drinks? The pain isn't quite as bad right now."

"See, if ya hadn't said that, I mighta let you." He scooped her up with a grin. "But now I can't. You need healing first."

She pouted. "I hate when you think you're smarter than me."

"Just don't go getting all down again. It ain't a good look on you." It was good to know she was up for a mock-fight, at least. To him it meant she was still fighting, and that's all he needed to know just then.

"No?"

"No."

"Oh." She tugged him close when he set her on the bed. "Then I suppose I'll need some inspiration to see the bright side of things. I do have a probable hanging in my future."

Cole hated to be reminded of the wanted poster they'd found in Denver. The poster had a woman that appeared to be an awful drawing of Jane—but it named Constance Querney as the wanted woman, not Jane. Wanted for murder. He frowned. "You ain't dead yet."

"I'm not?"

"Sure don't look it." He chuckled. "Don't feel it neither."

"Really? Maybe I just need a little reminder."

"Think I can handle that."

"I'm sure you can."

He who does not fear death
cares naught for threats.
-Pierre Corneille

Jane rested on the bench in front of the church. Service had ended. The parishioners spilled into the meadow. They mingled in small groups socializing and, she dared guess, gossiping. Reverend Greene had welcomed her back into the church with nothing but kindness, which brought her great relief.

Mike had tried to convince her to join him as he conversed with the others, but the thought of standing for long made her ankle throb in protest. She'd begged off so she might sit with her foot raised. He'd fallen for the mild exaggeration of her pained state. If she were completely honest, Mike's accusations of her being skittish were part of the cause. The treatment she'd received ever since the disturbing suggestions of her criminal past had come to light led to her feeling shy for the first time ever.

A few curious gazes still fell on her, several not-so-kind ones too.

A young boy crept around the skirts and bustles of the women. His blond head darted under a man's cane in a display of quick reflexes. He paused near a wagon hitched up at the corner of the church. Wide hazel eyes remained trained on her and her alone.

Jane's nerves tingled in concern. She was afraid of startling the boy away and yet afraid of his coming anyway. She still wasn't certain how to behave around the child that had proven to be hers from a life she couldn't remember. Part of her screamed that he was her son. She berated herself for her hesitancy to allow the maternal feelings and concern that surged every time he had held her hand or clung to her on the journey home.

Fear kept her attempts to remain distant and detached firmly in place. What right did she have to claim a child she'd led into a life such as the one he'd lived?

Jesse snuck closer to her. Blond curls shone and bounced when he ducked behind the bench next to the one she sat on. She guessed the suit he wore was Isaac's, a last minute outfit for Jesse to wear to church. It was much too short in the legs, but so large in the waist he had suspenders holding them up and a belt cinched tight around his belly.

Amusement bubbled despite her efforts to keep her cool. Jane turned her attention away. The attempt to curb her laughter made her ribs ache beneath her corset. She set her hands at her ribs and tried to gather herself. Out of the corner of her eye, she could see Jesse reach the end of her bench.

His head popped over the top of her boot before he sank slowly back down. Jane snickered in spite of herself. Her hand flew to her mouth to try to drown the sound, but it was far too late. The laughter welled, surging forward just as Jesse appeared again over the top of her shoe. His eyes fixed on her.

Jane cleared her throat. Careful to keep her eyes averted from the approaching child for fear of scaring him off, she focused herself on other tasks. Though in the general public eye she might not have minded a note of indecency, she always took care to be respectful in front of the church. Her position attending to her ankle had shifted her skirts so that her leg was slowly being exposed, so she pushed her skirt around to cover the limb.

As she fussed, Jesse's curls inched along next to the bench. She could have sworn a quiet giggle came from the boy, but with the steady hum of conversation and laughter of the other children, she couldn't be certain.

"Miss Jane." Just as Jesse's hazel eyes had appeared, Mrs. Kilmurry spoke nearby.

Jane gasped in surprise, her hands slapped to her skirt when they billowed out with Jesse's speedy race under the bench. The drape of her skirts gave him good cover, but her stomach churned when she realized he thought he needed to hide. She tried to push her frown aside in favor of a smile. "Mrs. Kilmurry. Good morning."

"It's good to see you out an' about." Mrs. Kilmurry stopped in front of Jane, her soft Irish brogue lent a cheerful note to her words. Her unruly red hair peeked from under a carefully placed hat. She had yet to be successful at a Sunday visit to church with well-managed hair.

"It's wonderful to be out enjoying the day and a good sermon, even if I am rather useless at the moment." Jane laughed. It was a relief to note how many whispered glances her direction had stopped with the approach of the leathersmith's wife, Mrs. Kilmurry. She wondered if the whole situation had been like a large game of chicken. "I'm just glad I have Tempest to help me around. The crutches are a pain."

"Aye, but a necessary evil. Where are they?" Mrs. Kilmurry's gaze cast about in search of the items in question. At a movement of Jane's skirt, Mrs. Kilmurry's eyes widened, and a grin spread across her features. When Jane cleared her throat and shook her head, Mrs. Kilmurry nodded and winked.

"Mike left the crutches in the wagon. When he's around he is my support. I don't mind as church doesn't require much wandering about." Jane shrugged. It didn't bother her that Mike was wandering about mingling. She rather enjoyed the quiet and if she were truthful, the possible chance to speak to Jesse again.

"Nessa, what are you up to?" Mr. Kilmurry stepped out of the crowd. "I've been looking for ya—oh, hi there, Janey." He grunted when Nessa elbowed him. "Sorry, my dear. Good morning, Miss Doe."

"It's all right," Nessa soothed.

Jane chuckled and bowed her head. "Good morning to you, Mr. Kilmurry. I trust life has been treating you well?"

"Aye. It has. The Mrs. and I got ourselves a storefront on Second Street. It is simple, and Hammy canna begin work until spring, but it is ours, and we'll be moving in before the first snowflake falls." Mr. Kilmurry's chest puffed out in pride.

"That's wonderful to hear. I'm sure it will be far easier to live within your shop. It will also be easier on your wares." Jane nodded. "Congratulations to you both."

"Thank you." Nessa smiled and held her hand out to Jane. "We ought to get home. We'll see you soon, lass."

"See you soon." Jane shook the extended hand. Once they were out of sight, another familiar face came into view. David's features were twisted with panic as he looked under a wagon. She waved until she got his attention and pointed down toward the bench.

David's shoulders sagged as he trudged over. "Everything good here?"

"Just fine, Mr. Schaffer." She patted the bench beside her. "I just had a visit from the Kilmurrys, and there is some creature that keeps messing with my skirts. So everything is quite lovely, thank you for asking."

"Thank goodness. I thought I'd lost something very important myself." His hand shook when he patted hers. "I never want to feel like that again."

"I'm sure you never will. At least, that's what I hope for you." She smiled and sighed. "This sitting around while all the world chats is going to get quite tedious."

"You've survived worse."

"No, this is far worse. Forced immobility? I realize it's probably a just punishment after all I've done, but I swear, it's torture comparatively." She draped her hand over her brow dramatically. "My world shall end in boredom."

David snorted. "Of course it will."

"Jane? Is something wrong?" Mike appeared, his hands on his hips. "Did you do something to your ankle again?"

"No." Jane huffed. "I've done nothing but sit here like a good little girl."

A smirk twisted Mike's lips. "Do you even know how to do that?"

Jane's eyes rolled up as she pondered the question. She tapped a finger to her chin. "No. No, I'm not quite sure I do know how to do that."

"Didn't think so." Mike shook his head. "Should I get the wagon ready? Or can you survive a while longer over here?"

"Go, be social. I'll behave. Just bring me back good gossip since I can't very well create any sitting here nice and quiet." Jane sighed.

"Gathering gossip at church? Jane, really." David nudged her shoulder and rose. "Do you have everything handled with—"

He didn't finish that statement as Jane followed the path of his finger to her skirt. A handful of curls poked out from behind it, only to disappear a moment later with a giggle. She nodded. "Yes, I think I'll be just fine here. If there's any problem, I'll alert you."

David touched the tip of his hat before departing. He didn't go far but hovered at the edge of the crowd where he could keep an eye on things.

Jane sighed and wrapped her fingers around the edge of the bench. She drummed her fingers along the underside of the wood. "Such a beautiful day. The trees are starting to change colors. The sun is shining so bright. Whatever will I do, sitting here by myself?"

Something—or rather someone—got their fingers between hers and the wood. She stopped her tapping to trap his fingers there for a moment. He tugged once, and she released him after a brief moment to resume her drumming.

Jesse crawled out from under the bench and sat on his bottom behind it. With his knees pulled up, he rested his forearms on them.

Jane smiled. "Ah. There you are. Are you hiding from someone?"

He shook his head.

"No? Oh, good. I'd hate to ruin a game of hide and seek." She bit her lip. "Well, then what could have brought you over here? It wasn't just to say hello, was it?"

A one-shoulder shrug was his only reply at first. A small smile started to form, but he still didn't lift his gaze.

"Well, that's a lovely thing to do. You're very kind." She leaned down and rested her elbow on her thigh. "I hope you're having fun with Isaac and Arthur."

He began to nod again, but then his eyes grew wide and he scrambled away.

"What? What is it?" Jane's brow furrowed when he darted to David's side. A thump on the bench behind her made her back straighten. The hair on the back of her neck rose.

"Well, well, well." Jackson Krenshaw's voice slithered over her skin like a snake. "Look at you. Holding court once again. You do so enjoy this, don't you?"

Her nose wrinkled, but when David took a step toward her, she shook her head subtly. She couldn't stand the man, but she wouldn't give him the pleasure of running away. "Mr. Krenshaw, how lovely to see you again."

"Oh, Jane, false platitudes don't suit you at all."

She turned to face the man beside her. Dressed in a suit and gloves, a tall hat, his hands rested on a silver-tipped cane.

Jackson flaunted his wealth in the obscenest way possible. "I'd say the same, but I daresay they are all you know."

"Tut-tut. You ought to be careful who you upset." A sly smile curled his lip. "After all, rumors do have a way of getting around this town, you know."

She wrinkled her nose and turned away. It had to be the lesser of two evils to have her back to him rather than have to sit there watching him look down his nose at all the good people milling in the meadow. "So I've noticed."

"I'm sure you have." His chuckle wasn't light or friendly. "You appear to revel in it, actually. Makes me pleased all over again that we didn't follow through on my proposal."

"We?" Jane just couldn't help herself. She scoffed. "I flat-out refused. There was never a *we*; it wasn't a mutual decision. You are deluded."

"The first of many mistakes. You forget what power I hold."

"In this town, you hold none, remember? Outside of your wealth, you have no position in government. Most of the citizens despise you; your mineworkers get jobs elsewhere as fast as they can. Your belief of your power is as deluded as your memory."

His head whipped toward her, and his nostrils flared. For just a moment she thought he might lose control of his demeanor. Just as quickly, he settled down and the shifty smirk returned.

The flash of anger she'd been thriving on began to fade under his calculating gaze. The last time she'd seen that look he'd bought the house she'd wanted out from under her and used rumor and reputation to ruin her chances at a mortgage through the only bank in town. Some scheming and trickery of her own had placed the homestead back into her ownership, but Jackson could have another ace up his sleeve. Not that she knew what it could be.

"Latest gossip has it that Clara Young is a criminal."

At least he hadn't made her wonder long. Although Jackson with that tidbit of knowledge and the money he could use to get answers, or do worse, only added fuel to her sudden jump in nerves. She forced her voice to remain steady. "Rumors are just that, Mr. Krenshaw. Unfounded, and usually exaggerated tidbits of truth."

"I think most of the town by now has realized that in your case, rumors are usually truth."

She kept her focus elsewhere so he wouldn't see the words had an effect on her. In truth, she would rather know that the rumors did stay only from a morsel of truth. To that end, she'd taken pains to make sure her associations beyond Cole were now far less suggestive of sinful deeds. She'd even avoided going to the Army camp to check on the ailing Major Webb.

"A little money goes a long way with certain groups, you know. More than law enforcement, in some cases."

Jane saw no reason to add any assistance to his cause. Instead of protesting or questioning, she let him have his fun. If dragging out his point made him happy, it was no skin off her nose. If only she could get her stomach to believe that, so it would stop twisting into a knot.

"Have you heard of a group called the Pinkertons, my dear?"

The insinuation sent a cold stab of fear to her heart. If she'd had forethought, she would have hired them herself months ago, but she admitted to being fearful of doing so. There were too many tales of the Pinkertons' skill and brutality, not to mention many of them would turn loyalty for a higher payment. Her trust in others wasn't strong enough for that. With a hard swallow against the solid lump in her throat, she offered Jackson a nod.

"Oh, good. I had thought to offer you their services back when we first met, but since you were so averse to assistance so early on, I didn't think you'd care for it. Perhaps now the time has come to send a note to Joe."

"Joe? I assume that means you have your very own Pink in your pocket. Convenient."

"It can be. What do you think, Jane?" Jackson leaned toward her. "Shall I make the call?"

"What is it you want, Jackson? You wouldn't be so bold to make threats on a Sunday without wanting something. I find your veiled threats tiresome." That was as close to a bald-faced lie as she'd come to tell yet. She did find him tiresome, yes, but the threats still made their mark. Recent weeks had left her shaken and less confident in her ability to get out of trouble this deep.

"I don't want anything, Jane. Not from you."

Jackson's whistle cut through her tense nerves enough to make her jump before he strolled away, swinging his cane. Not once did he bother to smile or nod to anyone he passed. The days of winning this town over appeared to have passed for him.

That might have been the most frightening realization of all.

Mike wandered through the thinning crowd toward her. The closer he got, the more his brow pinched in concern. "Everything all right, Jane? What did Jackson want?"

"To remind me he hadn't forgiven me yet for the embarrassment I've caused him." Jane gripped his arm to pull herself upright. "He's an ass making empty threats."

"Are you certain they're empty threats?"

"Not at all." She messed with her skirt to hide her shaking hand. Once it was supposedly lying flatter than it had been, she tucked her hand through his arm to use him for support. "What can I do about it, though? Nothing but try to get answers before he does."

"We should keep an eye on him. If he does find something, we'll want to know whatever it is he knows." Mike wasted a dark glare on Jackson's departing carriage.

"You know what they say, better the devil you know than the devil you don't know."

"I don't think that applies in this case."

She released her hold on him to grip the edge of the wagon. "He won't do anything yet. Short of start the process. I won't lie and say I'm not worried about him, but I'm more concerned about the man that does know everything and has designs to use it. Johnny, or whoever he is, and my past are the priority over Jackson at this moment. If Jackson manages to uncover something, then we'll worry."

"I'm always worried at this point."

The weight of the world crushed her shoulders until they sagged. The pain and torment she'd caused her brother was horrible, and she wished more than anything she could take it away. The fear, panic and guilt welled until she spun fast to throw her arms around her brother's neck. "I know. I'm sorry I put you through this."

"Hey." He hugged her back. "Jackson really got to you, didn't he?"

"No," she mumbled against his shoulder. The chuckle he gave in response let her know how unconvincing she sounded. She sighed in acquiescence. "Maybe a little."

"Then let's get you home. Bet Cole's waiting on you."

She nodded and let him help her into the wagon. After the dust robe had been tucked in around her skirts, she straightened her shoulders. It wouldn't do her any good to linger on the worries. There was work to be done. Not that she knew where to start.

"Yes?"

"What?" Jane turned to her brother in surprise.

"The way your mood changed and that look on your face—you can only be scheming."

"Not exactly scheming," she hedged. The sideways look he gave her didn't quite bring laughter, but she did smile. "I mean it. I'm trying to figure out how to help myself without quite the amount of expendable income as Mr. Krenshaw."

"What about the trunk?"

She sighed. "It appears to be a bust. We found the name inside, but otherwise, it's just newspapers, magazines, a book or two. Nothing noteworthy."

"Books? Didn't you say there was strange writing in one of them?"

"Yes, the first book we found. One of the books in the trunk was identical but in almost pristine condition. Clara only marked a few passages here and there."

"Huh." He balanced the reins in his hands, keeping the horses at an easy walk. Her house was in sight, but he took his time. "Maybe you should bring the trunk home. You'd have much more room to go through everything than Cole's room."

"And you would be able to stick your nose in easier." She snickered when his cheeks darkened. "That's what I thought."

"You can't say there's anything wrong with being curious. You're just as bad."

"I didn't say there was anything wrong with it." Already, the fears sparked by Jackson were fading into the background. Present, but nothing she couldn't handle. She grinned. "Just telling you the subterfuge was unnecessary."

"Noted."

"You're late." Cole's voice reached them before they'd arrived at the door. "Don't you got better things to do than jaw away your morning?"

"Absolutely not." Mike pulled the wagon to a stop so Cole could get to her side and help her down. "Just because you find people and relationships useless doesn't mean the rest of us have to feel the same way. I find them extremely useful in most cases."

Cole shook his head. "She's supposed to be taking it easy, not spending hours wandering around chatting."

"Oh, stop fretting. I sat on a bench while he wandered and chatted. I did no wandering of my own. Had a nice conversation with Mrs. Kilmurry and a far less pleasant one with Jackson." She squawked when his arms tightened fast around her.

"What did Krenshaw want?" Cole's eyes narrowed.

"To make threats." Mike was out of her line of sight now, but his voice was dark. "Scared her pretty good. Crazy woman hugged me like she was about to die."

"Thank you, Mike. Now you've got Cole up in arms." Jane sighed. "It's fine, Cole."

"It's not." Cole shook his head. "But we'll talk about it once you're inside."

"I'll get some ice from the icehouse for you while I'm back there putting up the horses, Jane." Mike clicked his tongue, and the wagon rambled around the side of the house.

"I don't like it," Cole mumbled. He carried her inside and set her on the sofa. Once her foot was propped up, he sat on the floor beside her. "Jackson don't make idle threats."

"I know. There's not much we can do about him except beat him at his own game. We have to find answers before he does." She set her hand on his. "We have to believe we will."

"We got no clue how."

"And therein is where our worry should be. What do we do now?"

With the past I have nothing to do, nor
with the future. I live now.
-Ralph Waldo Emerson

"I was sixteen."

Jane stilled at Cole's sudden introduction to his past. The fingers she'd been using to tease along his chest froze in place. Cole never spoke of anything beyond his years in Dominion Falls. For a moment she wondered if she dared let him go on, unsure where the story he told would lead. Afraid of the remaining pieces of her heart she could lose to this man.

"My pa decided he'd make a killin' in the gold rush, damn fool that he was. Took us all out to California. He didn't find one nugget, but we stayed. Ma made him. Only thing she ever got him to do, and she regretted it." His thumb ran up her spine, but he stared at the ceiling, his eyes not flickering away from their focus.

She didn't say a word, afraid to interrupt. Instead, she wrapped her arm around his chest to give him a reassuring squeeze.

"I met Ella when we went to town a few months later. Got sweet on her straight away. Took a job working with her pa at the general store so's I could make some money to court her right. We got hitched a year later."

When his hand stilled on her back and he grew quiet, she nestled closer. The moment was ripe with tension and yet so calm, she was afraid to breech the quiet but couldn't stop herself. She'd seen the images, and there was more than a wife, there had been a child. Fears about the life growing inside her made her blurt it out, "And Lydia?"

"Ella was carrying Lydia right quick. We weren't married a year before she was born. Everything was good. Real good." His voice trailed off in a sigh.

"Tell me about her," Jane whispered.

"Ella was a good woman. Serious. Not real schooled, but smart about practical things. She took care of our home real good. Not silly like most girls. Not…spirited like you are. She was lovin'; a good Ma. I was real proud to have her as my wife."

Maybe she should have been jealous, but Jane could only smile at the affection in his tone. The fact that he was capable of love stirred something in her heart, deep warmth bound tight in a cage of fear.

His thumb brushed along the small of her back again in soothing circles, though she was certain that the action was more soothing to him than to her. "We never knew what happened."

The sudden influx of pain in his voice twisted her stomach in knots. She took a ragged breath against her churning insides. "Lydia?"

"Yeah. We put her to bed one night. She was gone by morning. No reason. No nothin'." His jaw clenched. "Ella. She weren't ever the same after. Losing our girl changed her. She did nothing but stare at the fire all day and night. Her pa wanted me to put her away. Said she weren't right. I couldn't. I could take care of her, and I did. Until one night."

The emotional turmoil refused to let her remain still any longer. She pushed herself up on her hands to focus on him. The odd stillness of his features displayed none of the depths of torture his tone carried.

"I was near asleep. Trying to stay up with her and help her all the time was wearin' on me. I couldn't keep from feeling asleep." His eyes closed under her intense stare. "I shoulda listened to her pa. I wasn't strong as I thought. When I fell asleep, she got a butcher knife. I didn't hear her until she was right above me."

Her gaze darted to the long scar seared across his stomach. From the time she'd first seen it, she'd wondered at its origin. She reached out with a tentative hand and trailed her fingers along the white ridge of skin. Tears filled her eyes before she could stop them. She wanted to tell him to stop, that his story was too much to bear—but he'd lived it. He was the one that had borne it all these years, and continued to bear it.

His hand closed over hers and held it still right over the reminder of his wife. "She was wild. Like I never seen her. Stronger than I ever seen her. I had to fight her off. It all happened so fast. I was hurtin', and bleedin', and then…"

Jane couldn't move, couldn't breathe. The tight grip his hand had on hers transferred his old panic and fear right to her heart. There was only one direction this path led now, one path that would lead him to shut everyone out. Her soft gasp whispered through the room, and she wiped at an escaped tear. "You had no choice."

"I didn't mean to hurt her. I was just trying to get the knife."

A small splash of salty sorrow landed on his stomach and curved along the lines to the bed beneath. "Cole."

His hand cupped her cheek, and he pulled her close. "Her pa wasn't gonna see me hang for it. He knew I ain't never meant her no harm, he knew what she was like. He gave me the money to run."

"But you ran from more than the law."

One gentle tug pulled her lips to his, and he caressed them gently. He rolled with her until she was on her back. Hovering above her, his finger trailed along her cheekbone. "Ain't let no one in since. Graham's closest I got to a friend. I was with whores, but in other beds, never in here. You're the first person 'sides me that's ever been in here."

Every fiber of her being screamed *why me*? She couldn't form the words; ask what her heart wanted to. A deep aching fear settled into her soul. Fear of the pain they could cause each other. Fear of what the future held. Fear of how he would handle another child after what he'd gone through before.

No words came, and they appeared to be failing him as well. The intensity of his gaze pulled on her fear. She was sure he knew she was holding something back, willing her to confess. Her refusal slipped out in a tear that he gently caressed away with the pad of his thumb.

His hand slipped down her neck, coursing over the soft contour of her breast without pause, down along her waist to her hip where it lingered. His thumb trailed along the small swell that had started to form on her abdomen.

Did he know? How could he? In the week she'd been back, he'd never seen her ill. She hadn't felt ill. There'd been no clue allowed to escape. He couldn't know.

Just when she was sure he might have guessed, his hand moved again. It brushed down her hip to her thigh, and he gave a gentle pull. She followed his suggestion easily, lifting her leg to wrap around his waist.

She pulled him close. His mouth closed over hers as their bodies joined again. His tongue searched her mouth with careful precision, the slow dance of their lips mirrored in their bodies.

Tears escaped with each quiet and loving moment, until the walls started to build again between them. Abandoning the surrender of loving for the familiar frenzied need, they clung to each other until they were both sated.

Breathless, she gasped when he rolled onto the bed next to her. A smile tugged at her lips when he turned toward her and pulled her close. Before they could get comfortable, her stomach let out a loud growl.

His chuckle rumbled in her ear, drawing a giggle from her.

"Apparently satisfying one appetite has raised another."

"Ya sure that the first one is really satisfied?"

"Oh, that's never satisfied." She rolled onto her side and chuckled. "I'm afraid it will have to wait until I've eaten. Besides, it's just about time for you to open the saloon. I'd hate to keep you from business."

"Wouldn't mind if ya did."

"I'm certain you wouldn't." She laced her fingers into his hair and pulled him into a slow kiss. The moment she pulled back, she sat up. Her first awkward attempts at untangling her uninjured limb from his were thwarted. "Would you mind letting me go?"

"I would."

"Cole."

He laughed loud when her stomach growled again and released his hold on her. "Seems like you're always leaving me in search of food."

"Seems like you're always making me hungry. One cannot enjoy pleasures so often without a little sustenance. You wouldn't starve me, would you?"

"Guess not. Need help?"

"Unfortunately, I always do these days. I'm looking forward to my ankle healing so that I'm not so dependent on others." Without another argument, she felt him rise from the bed. Before she knew it, he'd helped her dress and had gotten clothes on himself.

She sat on the edge of the bed while he finished putting on his holster. Taking his offered hand, she let him lift her up onto her good foot. He wrapped his arm around her waist and half-carried her to the door. Letting out an annoyed huff of air while she waited for him to open the door, she frowned. "This is getting annoying."

"You can't be trusted to stay off it if you use a crutch. Plus, it would annoy you if ya had to hobble everywhere. It would take too long."

"Stop throwing my words back at me."

He grinned. "No. I'm gonna do it when I can. You don't leave much chance that I can pick on ya for much else."

"Just help me downstairs—oh." She yelped when he tossed her over his shoulder. "Cole."

With a laugh, he smacked her on the ass before turning to carry her to the stairs. "You said to help ya downstairs. This is the fastest way. Best stop fighting so hard or I might drop ya down the stairs."

"Cole Mitchell. You put me down."

"No."

There was no stopping the laughter when his hand slipped under her dress and pinched her. She beat on his back without much force, somehow managing to push herself up enough that she started to slip back over his shoulder.

He paused at the top of the stairs to let her finish her attempt and grinned when her foot was on the floor. "You shoulda waited until ya were down the stairs."

"Not on your life." Still laughing, she allowed him to scoop her up in the more comfortable cradle of his arms. In just a few seconds, he had her outside at her horse and on her foot.

"Ready?"

"Just a second." She shifted inches closer to Tempest and nodded. "Ready."

His large hands circled her waist and lifted her toward the saddle. He held her steady until she'd swung her injured foot over and stayed close until she settled in. "Want company?"

"Mike will be giving me plenty of company. Much as I would enjoy your companionship, Mr. Hamm is waiting for you to give him the thumbs up. I will see you later, Mr. Mitchell."

He winked before stepping away to handle Hammy.

Jane nodded to Hammy and turned her horse away to start the short trek through town. Along the way, she felt the lingering suspicious stares mixed into the friendly greetings she got from others.

It was a reaction she was becoming accustomed to. Despite her brother and Cole's blatant anger at the situation, she understood. Not once had she lied to any of the people looking at her in suspicion, but how could they know it? It would take time—time she didn't have a lot of.

The ride through town only lasted a few minutes, but it would have taken almost half an hour with a crutch. She was all too glad to accept assistance on and off her horse if it meant she could get around as expedient as she always had.

Within moments of pulling up to the hitching post in front of Turners, David tied off her horse. He offered his support on her way down. "Mike already ordered you some food."

"Good. I'm starving." Jane grinned and took his arm. The careful negotiation of the steps took no time at all. The smell of food made her stomach rumble again, but the conversation took her immediate attention.

"I don't know what's going to happen." Daisy pushed her food around her plate with a fork. The frown she wore creased deep lines in her forehead. "I know Jackson was trying to get full ownership. I definitely don't want that."

"Well it makes sense. He was already part owner." Cora sighed. "I just feel sorry for anyone that has to work with him."

Jane took a seat, thanking Cora when she poured some coffee. "What's going on?"

"They're trying to speculate who's going to take over the hotel. What will happen to the Silver Saddle with Guy gone?" Mike shrugged. "Apparently, there's no better gossip right now."

Jane shook her head and dove into her food. "There's plenty of gossip. It's just interesting because some people have stakes in what happens. Not to mention the article in Rusty's last paper that suggested a bidding war."

"Who else would bid on it?" David took a sip of coffee. "Not that I'm complaining. Jack's got too big a piece of this town already."

"Outside of Daisy, who really cares?" Jane felt Michael's focus on her when she grabbed some food from his plate. Giving him a dirty look, she returned to her own plate.

"Don't you care?" Daisy blinked and looked at her. "You had a contract too."

"Ah, but my contract was with the man, not the business." Jane shrugged and ate another large forkful of her meal. After she'd nabbed another bite from Michael's plate, she smiled. "Therefore with his death, the contract became null. I'm essentially without a source of income."

Michael swatted at her hand when she went to take another bite from his plate. He leaned in with a shake of his head. "What has gotten into you? You hate beans. Why are you eating all of mine?"

Daisy sighed. "I'm not so lucky. My contract is with the Silver Saddle. Now my fate is at the hands of a stranger."

"Maybe not." Rusty walked up with a bright smile. "Just finished today's paper. I thought Mike might want to see the first copy."

When Michael took a copy, Jane gasped at the visible headline. "What?"

Michael chuckled and nodded. "Perfect, Rusty. Thank you. I appreciate the warning. Not sure Jackson is going to be so pleased with this edition."

"Michael," Jane smacked him on the arm, "you bought the hotel?"

Mike winked and grabbed Jane's mug to take a sip of her coffee. "What? You think I left Wyoming so I could start ranching again?"

"You bought a hotel? How?"

"You think you're the only one with a brain, Clara?" Mike still wore a smug smile. "Thought you were good at reading people?"

Daisy stared across the table. "You now own my contract?"

"It's open for re-negotiation. All staff is, effective immediately." Michael leaned back, resting his arm across the back of Jane's chair. "Although I do hope you'll stay on staff. I have plans—and your services as a doctor will be a part of those."

"You couldn't have told me?" Jane admonished.

"Didn't want to say anything until I was sure."

"I won't work for you."

"Wouldn't dream of asking you."

*Nothing is more honorable than
a grateful heart.
-Seneca*

"Miss Doe." An exceedingly young, round faced corporal stood at her leg beneath where she perched on her horse. A bright smile lit his baby-face.

"Corporal." Jane smiled back down at the young man. "I heard word that Major Webb has been returned to the camp. I was hoping I might be able to see him."

"He has, ma'am. I'm sure he'd be real glad to see ya."

"If rumors hold true, the general is due to arrive at any moment. Perhaps as early as tomorrow."

"In this case the rumors are mighty true."

"Wonderful." She shifted her weight onto her good foot and grabbed the pommel. "Would you be so kind as to assist me down?"

"Of course." He waved over another soldier to grab the reins before he reached for her. "Help inside the tent?"

"Yes, please. Thank you so much." She leaned on the corporal's arm the few feet to the tent. Right inside the flap she stopped short as she spotted Al lying on the cot the Army provided him. A shirt draped across his chest, his arm hooked in a sling. Al's cheeks were sunken; a full beard now covered his once youthful features. His skin was sallow and new lines creased his eyes. This man was a distant echo of the one she'd come to call a friend.

"I don't look that bad." There, finally, he was. Al smiled and the simple action brought life and color back to his features.

"You look like hell."

"And you can't walk. What of it?"

Jane laughed out loud. The man had a point. She nodded to the corporal and let him help her the rest of the way. She sat in the chair next to the bed, taking Al's hand in hers as the corporal left.

The man had risked his life to rescue her and Arthur and received no reward beyond a near-fatal wound and weeks of recovery. She didn't know how to express how much what he'd done meant to her, so she chose to focus on something that wouldn't draw her completely to tears. "You really don't look all that good."

"I'm alive. You're alive, and so is Arthur. Of course, I hear that's because of your efforts and not mine."

"Well, someone had to help him while you were off being lazy."

"Touché."

"I'm sorry." Her efforts for light conversation were lost in a sharp crack in her voice.

He set his hand on hers. "You aren't the one that shot me, Jane. You've got nothing to apologize for."

"It was my past actions that led to this." Her voice shook but she struggled through and did her best to sound strong. "Guy is dead. You were shot and almost died. Arthur could have been killed. All because of Clara."

"Like you said—because of Clara. Not Jane."

"You're one of the few people that see it that way, Al."

"I know I've not seen you in a few weeks, but I don't remember you being so whiny. Or is this Clara coming out?"

She pursed her lips and glared at him. "You sound like Cole."

A low chuckle brushed aside her frustration. "How is the bastard?"

"The same. Jealous, possessive, short-tempered."

"Should we give him something to actually be jealous of?"

Giggling, she moved herself over to sit on the edge of his bed. She propped her hand on the other side of his waist and hovered over him. "Have we ever?"

"You have."

"I have never been anything but honest with Cole. It is not my fault that he has failed to ask the appropriate questions." Jane poked him in the side. "Like the rest of the town, he assumes I've kept you and your men well-satisfied."

"And the fact that he assumes it doesn't bother you?"

The weak hold she had on her smile faltered so quick she had to look away. Of course it bothered her that Cole assumed she gave herself to any man that turned her way, but she had no room to talk. Not once had she asked if he was still enjoying the comforts of his whores. Like him—she assumed—she'd prefer for him to tell her, she had no desire to pry such truths from him.

"So it does bother you."

A subject change was sorely needed. The last thing she wished to do was reveal her innermost truths that she didn't dare reveal even to herself. If they continued on this line of conversation, she might just open up on things best left unsaid. She cleared her throat and drew her hands into her lap. "So the General will arrive tomorrow?"

He took the change of subject in stride. "Yes. We're working out the final details of the treaty. David and his friend have been quite helpful."

"David told me that part of this treaty means you will release the Indians you have in custody. Is that true?"

Al hesitated. "Jane."

"I wouldn't ask, but everyone is town is talking about it, Al. The fact that David's friend is yet another Indian you've dared to place your trust in has people in a tizzy. Worse is the idea that the worst punishment most of the Indians will receive is being sent to a reservation."

"Believe me, that's plenty of punishment."

"For killing innocent men and women?"

"Jane, what do you know about what happens on the reservations?"

She twisted her fingers together in her lap, unable to shake the sense she was about to be lectured kindly. "To be honest, not much. I tend to avoid the subject of Indians altogether, most definitely the reservations."

"Most men don't think like I do. I know what reservation they're going to and I know the man in charge. They'll receive random punishments bordering on torture for the simplest supposed crimes. I don't like sending them there."

"They're criminals."

"So are you," Al's voice was direct, but kind, "if rumors hold true."

She straightened her back and lifted her chin with what little strength she could muster. "And I fully expect to be hanged for those crimes. I've never once expected any less of a sentence, or special allowances for my situation."

"Would you rather be tortured or see a quick death?"

"I am being tortured," she muttered without censor. Rather than face what she'd said, she skipped subjects. "What of Martha?"

"General Bryant will be escorting her to Washington after my men and I transport the Indians to their destinations. I'll be reporting to Washington with them." He tapped her arm. "If Starbird is among the Indians that turn themselves in and you identify him, he'll also be taken to Washington as a traitor."

She set her hand over his and squeezed. After so much time on the subject, she had to change it. "What will become of you once Martha's trial is over? I assume you will not be returning here."

"By the time all of my responsibilities in this matter are concluded, I will be close to the end of my term. I'll be working at a desk until that time comes."

"You won't re-enlist?" Jane was both surprised by and understanding of the revelation. While she knew from their conversations he was tired, but he was also so dedicated.

"No. I think I've done my job. I did what I could here to make this whole process as peaceful as possible. I wasn't always successful, but I'm proud of the job I've done. I'm not willing to do it again."

"Will you return to North Carolina?"

He shifted, wincing before settling back against the pillows. Once settled again, a little paler for his efforts, he sighed. "I haven't decided yet."

"You haven't been home since before the war." Jane pulled herself out of her own misery to study him. "You should go see your family. Your home."

"Jane." With a grunt of effort, he sat up again. "If you go to trial—"

"You mean *when* I go to trial." She wasn't a fool. From where she stood there was little chance of her avoiding her fate.

"*When* you go to trial, I can put in a word. Maybe it will keep you from the gallows. You don't need to suffer for her crimes."

"If I avoid the gallows, I would be in prison for a long time. That is suffering. That is torture. I choose a quick death." She cupped his cheek to stem his protest. When he fell blessedly silent, she placed a chaste kiss on his other cheek. "But thank you for offering. I should get home now. I only wanted to see that you were doing well. You're still healing, so I won't tire you any further."

"I'll be busy with the general's arrival for the next few days. I hope you will indulge me with supper once everything is settled."

"I look forward to it." She pushed herself to her feet. In that moment it struck her how very long the tent was when you had but one foot. She pursed her lips at the lack of supportive furniture between the chair she'd sat on and the door. "Now to get back to my horse."

"Corporal!" All called out before he chuckled. "I admit it would be amusing to watch you struggle your stubborn way across my tent, but I'll be nice this time."

"You're too kind, Major." Jane laughed and shook her head at him, glad his spirits were well enough for teasing.

When the corporal entered, she accepted his assistance back to her horse. Soon as she was settled back in the saddle, she turned toward town and took off.

She had no plans to stop, her mind already back on the magazines and papers she'd found in the trunk and the mysteries they contained. The past week had been filled with enthusiastic reunions with Cole; enjoying every moment with him she could while she could. Her fears of what he'd do once he learned of her condition left her grasping at every moment together, and left little time for solving riddles.

While she'd thoroughly enjoyed every moment in Cole's arms, the pressing need to learn the truth took precedence. Soon enough she'd be unable to deny to him what was happening, the child inside would be obvious. In her heart she knew Cole wasn't ready for another child, and likely never would be. He wasn't even ready for a real relationship.

As much as she treasured his support and caring in the past weeks, she would need to start pushing him away. She had no other choice. If she gave him freedom now he couldn't accuse her of trying to trap him.

A sharp whistle pulled her from her thoughts. She slowed Tempest to locate the source. Before she could focus on what was happening, Cole had leapt into the saddle behind her. She gasped, yelping when he grabbed the reins and spurred the horse into a much faster clip than she was comfortable with. "Cole!"

He didn't say a word, just raced down the road toward her house.

"Cole. What are you doing?"

A tug on the reins pulled them to a stop in front of her house and he swung out of the saddle. The moment Jane shifted to get herself down, Cole reached for her.

She tried to protest the impulsive move. "I'm not—"

His lips captured hers, sealing her protest with searing heat she felt to her core. Without clear thought, her body responded to his insistence eagerly. He tugged her body tight against his and backed toward the door.

She gasped for air when he released her from the brutal, claiming kiss. Her protest morphed into a sharp yelp when he scooped her up and carried her toward the bedroom. She tried to push against him, and when he laid her out on the bed she hit him hard in the chest. "What in the hell are you doing?"

"You gotta ask?" He sucked in her lower lip and nibbled at it. She didn't want to respond, for she knew what she needed to do, but her nerves sprang to life against her better judgment. His lips trailed down her chin to her throat.

She couldn't help but arch into the warmth of his lips. Her brain spun in circles, alive from the fire of his touch, though she tried to force it back to calm. After all, this action wasn't of affection, it was of another emotion. "Acting on your jealousy?"

"I ain't jealous." He found the sensitive patch of skin beneath her ear. His capable fingers popped open the buttons of her bodice faster than ever.

"Laying claim to me again? Marking your territory?" The bitter words tumbled from her lips before she could stop to think, but his possessive claiming wounded her pride. The words hit their mark, and he froze above her. She tried to still her nervous, rapid breathing.

His smirk twisted into a grimace. Nose to nose with her, he remained still for several moments before forming a reply. "No one could own ya."

"It's good you know that." She'd stilled her breath and dug deep into the pain of what she knew would be their upcoming downfall to force venom into her words. It should have been more difficult, but his ministrations had made her ache for him. Unsatisfied libido had always made her grumpy, and forcing herself to say the words she knew would anger him made her even more so.

In one slow, painful gesture, he pulled the weight of his body off hers. He planted his hands on either side of her head, and the anger of her words had settled in his eyes. "Always did."

"Good. Always remember." Her heart twisted when he stood and walked away. Why was she torturing herself? Why couldn't she just tell him? End the grief. Let him make the choice she knew he would. Her heart would break either way, why not do it faster rather than slower? "Cole."

His footsteps stopped somewhere in the next room. Silence fell, wrapping around her heart and squeezing it still.

"I'm pregnant." There. She'd said it. Surprisingly, she wasn't panicked or giddy, or much of anything. A calm acceptance settled inside, perhaps because she'd already run through every possible outcome of this scenario in her head. The persistent silence ripped through the calm she'd felt until a tear trembled up and escaped down her cheek. She clung to a small vestige of the rare feeling of hope that he might, perhaps, not do as expected.

"Who should I congratulate? Or do ya even know? Could be anyone's right?"

That lingering smidgen of hope shattered into a million pieces, each one shearing through her already bleeding heart with razor sharpness. The pain pooled into a dark pit of growing anger. How dare he?

She flew to her feet, ignoring the shooting pain in her ankle to storm to her bedroom door. All set to yell at him, the fear in his features shocked her silent. None of his angry accusation matched the deep creases of fear lining his face.

Dread and hope curled into a pained grimace as he dragged his normally strong, fierce gaze from hers. When he couldn't even look her in the eyes, she knew. He wanted her to agree with him, he needed her to; he was too weak to face the possibility of having, and losing, another child.

Tears filled her eyes, but she dug down deep to give him this one last thing before she released him. Her hand gripped the door – pain, fear, loneliness, and revulsion racked her body as she forced forward the first outright lie she'd ever told him. "Yes. It could be anyone's."

Turmoil rode through the curves of his features, hardening them into pure fury. "Just like I thought all along. Been getting comfort of your own on your visits to the Army camp. How many has it been?"

"I don't have to answer to you. I've released you. Now get out." She couldn't stop the flow of her tears; the pain wouldn't give into the anger any longer. Nothing could stop the pain anymore.

He turned his back on her, one hand gripping the back of a chair so hard his knuckles were white. She couldn't see his face anymore, but his voice was strained. "I knew you was holdin' something back."

"Stop. This is not your problem. It's mine and mine alone. I'll deal with it."

"What's that supposed to mean?"

"Get out." She turned away this time, but didn't hear him move one foot toward the door. Exhaling slowly, she forced her voice to calm. "You don't have to worry about me any longer, Cole. Go back to your cold comforts and keep your distance from everyone. For I no longer have to worry about you either."

"I won't do it again. I can't. One kid was enough."

"Get out!" She slammed her door and locked it, sinking to the floor. She bit down hard on her thumb, directing every inch of physical and emotional pain at the innocent digit. It was an eternity before the smash of the front door told her he'd left.

She'd known he'd leave. She'd hoped he wouldn't. "Now what do I do?"

*My grief lies all within.
And these external matters of lament are
merely shadows to the unseen grief that
swells with silence in the tortured soul.
-William Shakespeare*

Jane stood on the top step of the church while Michael remained behind by the door talking with Reverend Greene. By a stroke of luck, the crisp and cold month of September decided to grant the perfect day. After a bitter cold snap, in the last days of the month the sun shone bright and the temperatures soared into almost hot weather.

The past few days had been rough, and Jane had used the excuse of the cold and her aching ankle to remain at home while she coped with her inner pain. Michael knew that she and Cole had parted ways. Jane had yet to tell him the root cause, and Michael was beside himself with doubt that it could be over.

He'd also sworn to make Cole pay for hurting her, but she had managed to talk him down. In as close to a clear head as she could, she'd explained that it wasn't Cole's choice. In a way, she supposed it wasn't. He couldn't help the pain that overtook his soul from his past anymore than she could help the pain that consumed her from her missing past.

Though she hurt, ached, and mourned the loss of what she'd weeks ago admitted was her love, she held no malice toward him. In some ways she wondered if it wasn't better this way, better that he'd not have to be so entwined with a life that could be taken on the gallows. He'd had enough pain and loss in his life; she would be relieved to not add this to it.

The pain welled again the longer she dwelled on the subject. Her hand fluttered in a nervous jump to make sure she hadn't erringly shed a tear. Finding her cheeks were dry, she released a sigh of relief.

She was glad today was Sunday, for it had forced her to leave the house. Being around others often had the effect of forcing her to act as if she was fine. Sometimes she actually believed she would be all right.

Mike's arm circled her waist. The action pulled her from her swirling depression of thoughts to face her brother's concerned smile. "All right?"

"Do I have any other choice?"

"There's always a choice, Jane. Please remember that." Pain lanced his words. "Clara forgot it in her pain, I can't see you do the same."

"Oh, Michael." She wrapped her arm around his waist and leaned into him. "That isn't what I meant. I meant I have no choice but to move on and face what's coming. To lean on those I care about. Figuratively," she glanced down at her wounded ankle, "and literally these days."

He chuckled quietly. "You have a point there. Sorry I panicked."

"I believe you've earned the right. Now speak of it no more, or I will not be able to smile in genuine happiness today."

"So long as that's your hope."

"It is my fervent hope." She did still have hope, one small bit of hope that none but Daisy and Cole knew of. The child inside kept her from completely collapsing and giving into fear. She hoped to leave it with something, some smidgen of truth to know she wasn't all bad.

"Jane?"

"Hm?" She jolted out of her resumed reverie to smile. "Sorry. I have so much on my mind anymore. It's easy to get lost."

"Well, then. Are you ready for your ride down the steps?"

Jane nodded and gripped the railing. She accepted Mike's help down the few steps onto the uneven ground. The wagon wasn't far, but she considered asking for her crutch.

Arthur ran up breathless, his hair disheveled atop his head. "You're joining us, right Jane? Ma made a picnic. We got lots of food. You comin'?"

"What did she make?" Mike flinched when Jane pinched him hard in the side. "What?"

"Ingrate. Of course we'll join you, Arthur. Are you sure there's enough food? Looks like you have a full blanket already." The blanket Cora had set out teemed with people. Jesse and David, Cora's cousin Lee, and Isaac were all there.

"Sure did. She made a lot of fried chicken yesterday, hopin' it would stay warm enough today for a picnic." Arthur waved at them both. "Come on!"

Jane chuckled. "At least you don't need to worry about cooking today."

"Or worry that you might cook instead and try to poison me." Michael's support disappeared in his efforts to escape her attack. He called back to her. "Not my fault you can't cook."

"I will get over there, and you will be sorry," she tried to yell after him, but her laughter made all attempts at anger fail. Now her dilemma stood in her lack of support. Believing she'd never use them properly, Mike had left her crutches in the wagon. After she'd used the ankle when Cole had been over last, she'd been very careful not to again without clearance.

Fortunately, her dilemma resolved itself with the help of David's approach. Right behind him, Jesse skipped along. David held out his hand. "Would it be improper for me to escort you since you've been abandoned?"

"Not at all. If you don't mind, I'd really like to hurry along. I'm about to commit fratricide and would hate to be delayed."

"Fratricide?"

"I'm going to kill my brother." Jane leaned into David's grasp. When a small arm circled her waist from the other side, she jumped in surprise. Spotting the wide-eyed boy, she laughed. "My heavens, Jesse. You startled me so. Are you going to help me as well?"

Jesse nodded, his curls bobbing as he did. A proud smile lit across his face. With his quiet voice, he replied, "I strong."

"You are the strongest boy I have ever met," Jane concurred. Secured between the two, though most of her support came from David, Jane made it to the blanket. She sank down to the ground and offered a glare to Mike. "If Cora wouldn't be upset with me for starting a food fight, I'd throw my lunch at you."

"You'll get me back. You always do." Mike grinned and took a big bite of chicken.

Jesse grabbed his plate and scrambled over to sit right up against Jane.

Jane met David's gaze, her brow wrinkling in confusion. At David's shrug, she took the plate he offered. Lunch proved to be both delicious and enlightening as David and Mike shared stories from their days on the trail and Mike's ranch.

While all the stories were kept appropriate for little pitchers with big ears, Jane began to suspect that many of the stories were told for Lee's benefit. By the end of the meal, Lee had an awed gaze on David.

Jane chuckled to herself and took a deep breath. "Amazing meal, Cora. Thank you."

Cora nodded. "I'm glad you could join us. You spend too much time hidden away."

"I know. I'll try to correct that. Going through all of Clara's things is so frustrating." Jane shrugged. "Today would be perfect. It's such a beautiful day, perfect for a quiet walk, don't you think, David?"

David did a double take, his brow puckering. "What?"

"Well, I'm no good for walking. I think I'll remain sitting right here and delight in the lovely weather and conversation. Perhaps you and Lee should enjoy the day with a lovely stroll." Jane grinned when both Lee and David turned bright red. "Someone should take advantage of this beautiful weather. My ankle is throbbing and I'm just going to relax here. Don't tell me you're going to let this day go to waste?"

His eyes narrowed, but the blush remained. David shook his head. "Of course I wouldn't."

"I should help clean up first." Lee's red cheeks wouldn't quit.

Cora chuckled. "She's right, Lee. You should relax and relish in the warm sun. You've been working enough lately. I'm sure Jane and I can clear up these dishes. Even with a bad foot, she can crawl well enough, can't you?"

"I do rather enjoy putting myself in undignified positions." Jane laughed out loud, joined by Mike and Cora both. "So, yes, of course I can help."

"Oh. I…" Lee rose and took David's offered hand.

Jane sat back and ruffled Jesse's hair while the pair walked off. "Don't you want to join that game of tag? I bet you're faster than all of them."

Jesse's enthusiastic nod threatened to shake his head right off his shoulders. "Fast!" He scrambled off and raced into the group of children playing. Arthur called for a time out and made sure Jesse got into the game.

"I think David might just strangle me for embarrassing him like that." Jane laughed and moved to gather the plates nearest her.

"They need a push." Cora scraped the plates Jane handed her. "Lee is concerned because David is still technically married and she's supposed to still be in mourning."

"Pish posh. I didn't wait to be divorced. Not that I knew I was married when Cole and I met." Jane lurched forward onto her knees to crawl over and grab another plate. The simple mention of Cole twisted her insides again. She cursed herself for bringing it into the conversation.

Mike watched the pair across the field. "David wouldn't overstep bounds either. Only time he ever did was with Clara.

He's a good man." Despite the earlier snit between them, Jane could have kissed him for the change of subject.

"Yes, he is. I always thought so, but I was with Kelly then." Cora set the cleaned plates in her basket. "I also think Lee's a little intimidated by you, Jane. Your closeness to David. She thinks you might want him back."

"Me? No. I do care for him. He's a good man and he's been very forgiving of me, and of Clara. Too forgiving sometimes." Jane sat back on her rump when her ankle throbbed again. "I'm not in love with him. I know he's still trying to say goodbye to Clara sometimes, and I allow him those moments. But I'm no real threat to Lee."

"It'll take time." Mike leaned back on his elbows. "But I bet they'd be good together. We all find someone when we aren't expecting it."

Cora gave Jane a knowing gaze.

Jane giggled. "Gee, Mike. You don't mean someone in particular, do you?"

"What?" He sat up fast. "I was talking about Lee and David."

"Of course you were. Why don't you go pick us some…*daisies*?" Jane squealed when Mike lunged for her, but couldn't move far or fast enough.

Mike pushed her hard enough to knock her over but rose to his feet. "You aren't funny. You and your imagination can go elsewhere."

"I can't go anywhere. So I guess you'll have to." Jane smacked his leg when he stormed off. "Child."

Cora snickered and sat next to Jane. "I thought I was the only one that noticed."

"Not at all. I've noticed it since before he bought the hotel. I almost wonder if that isn't why he bought it." Jane sighed. "It's nice to talk about other people for a change."

"Talk'll die down. Always does." Cora smiled. "Jesse was awful comfortable with you. It's good to see."

The knot of panic she kept a tight hold on twisted in her belly. Jane frowned and picked at a thread on her skirt. "David had better not be saying things he shouldn't."

"I don't think he is. Jesse is very good at understanding people."

"He had to be, the way he was raised." Jane clutched the blanket to cover her urge to run away from the discussion. Johnny, the man that knew what happened to her in the years since she'd left David, had taken the boy and sold him off to people and then kidnapped him back every time. Jane hoped to heaven she hadn't known. Already she hated Clara. If that were true, she might kill herself with self-loathing.

"He still carries scars. I've never seen silent nightmares before, but he has them." Cora set a warm hand on Jane's shoulder. "But he's warming up so nicely. He is very happy to be free of that life."

"Who wouldn't be?"

Time discovers truth.
—Seneca

David leaned on the fence next to Jane. He bumped his shoulder into hers. "How are you holding up?"

Though she had a good idea what he meant, Jane decided to plead ignorance. She picked at a splinter of wood in the fence rather than look him in the eye. "I don't know what you mean."

"Whole town is talking about it. Don't pretend you don't know." His hand closed over hers and effectively stopped her fidgeting. "You and Cole split?"

"Nobody is surprised by the turn of events, either. Least of all me."

"On the contrary. Quite a few of us are surprised."

"Then you're obtuse, blind, and every single one of you are fools."

"Defensive." He sighed and wrapped an arm around her shoulders. "I told you long ago, I know that look. You can deny your feelings all you want, but even though you aren't Clara, you get the same look when you're in love."

She had to divert the conversation for her own strength of appearance. Jane scoffed. "Love? No. Not love."

"Yes. Love."

"Please don't do this." An embarrassing quiver resonated through her words. "It's been three days. It's over, and I don't want to talk about it."

"For what it's worth, I'm sorry. I know you were happy."

Happy. Maybe in some moments she'd been happy. Maybe even peaceful. The inevitable end had been ever-present and ever-threatening, though. She took a ragged breath. "I also told you that when my time with Cole ended I would move on. Find another way to be happy. You need to give me some time first."

"You seemed happy today."

"Today has been a pleasant distraction." Out in the open air and around others, she found everything easier to push aside. When others were watching her, she didn't dare let them see how distraught she might have been over Cole. That's why she preferred company to solitude. "Lee is very sweet. I could tell she really enjoyed the stories of your manliness on the cattle drives."

"Jane," David groaned and buried his face in his hands, "why are you torturing me so?"

"It amuses me. You said you wanted me to be happy."

"Not at my expense."

"Oh, you poor thing. Falling in love with the adorable young widow. It must be so difficult for you."

"We're just getting acquainted. I wouldn't call it love." He stared out across the field where the children still played. "I think we'd both be happy with a subject change."

"Agreed."

"What about your trunk? Has it given you any ideas?"

"Nothing of much substance. The only things I can find written by Clara are pure gibberish. Nary a real word in the whole of her notes. Everything else in the trunk was clothes that aren't my style and Poe. Endless stacks of Poe."

"Clara always liked puzzles. Made them for her students all the time."

"I would prefer a puzzle I could figure out." She frowned and leaned her elbows on the fence. "And here I thought I was clever."

"You are clever. Sometimes annoyingly so. I'm sure you'll figure it out."

"Some days I don't feel all that clever. I can't even figure out my own past." She turned her back to the fence and sank to the ground. Once she'd maneuvered her injured ankle until it was settled comfortably out of her way, she leaned back against the fence.

David sat beside her. "Can I tell you something about Jesse?"

"What?"

"Jesse is my middle name."

What little was left of her broken heart twisted until it stopped beating. "No."

"Yes."

"How?" Surely it wasn't coincidence, but it made no sense. Unless Clara had known about the child. "No. Clara couldn't have—please tell me she couldn't have known."

"Arthur has said Jesse indicated the name didn't come from Johnny. Sure don't seem like he would have bothered giving him a real name anyhow."

"She told Mike she'd never keep a child from you. Ever. I can't believe, even with all of her lies, that she would have.

She was naïve and stupid, but she loved you." Tears slipped down her cheeks. "Maybe Johnny forced her, threatened Jesse's life."

"Used Jesse to make Clara do what he wanted?" Disgust added a note of hatred to his voice she didn't often hear. "But why wouldn't she reach out for help?"

"If Jesse were my son—"

"He is."

"I would do whatever I had to in order to make sure he lived. For you." Jane gripped his hand. "Clara loved you so much. You need to know that."

"Maybe she did. She still left."

"You should read her letters."

"I can't."

"Of course you can. I have them at my house." The words in one of Clara's letters came back to her in a rush. She groaned. "She never taught you to read."

"We never got around to it."

"You need to read them."

"Maybe you can read them to me."

"No." Jane resituated herself so she could face him dead on. "Clara broke so many promises, I can hardly count them. She broke your vows, your heart, and left you with unanswered questions. I want to make one of them right."

"Already have. You brought Jesse home."

"But there's more I can do, so much more. I can teach you to read. That way you can read Clara's letters yourself."

"I'd like that a lot." David lifted his head. His hazel eyes shimmered with tears. A sad smile lifted his lips, and he brushed a finger along her cheek. "It wasn't just you, you know. I broke my share of promises too."

"Forgive yourself. Clara loved you, but she was a naïve and a bit foolish."

"You should forgive her."

"I can't, not yet. Not until I know what she did. Why she did the things she did. I have to believe the answers are out there."

"What if you never find them?"

She took his hand in hers and stared at the ground. "We both know I'm on borrowed time, David. We can't ignore the wanted poster much longer. I only hope I can find the answers before they come to claim me."

"I've sent out notices to surrounding towns alerting them to Johnny as best I could with his varied descriptions. I'd like to find Johnny before he can come after you or Jesse."

"Good luck. He changes his appearance so well." Each of the three times Jane had seen the man they called Johnny, he'd looked completely different. From a scruffy, filthy cowboy, to a cultured and portly French gentleman, to a trim businessman, Johnny was able to change his hairstyles and body shape as easily as one would change their clothes.

"And there's where the problem lies. We don't know what he'll look like or what he'll do next. I can't believe that he'd be happy just making you pay."

"With money? Or my life?" The harsh cold reality of his statement echoed her own thoughts in her darkest hours. Somehow she knew the maniac was far too clever and flat out evil to make things simple in any way.

"Yes." At least she wasn't alone in her dark thoughts. David squeezed her hand. "We won't let it happen. I can't let you hang."

"If Clara was truly a criminal, you're going to have to. And as Sheriff, you'll have to do it."

"Never. I'll make the marshal do it."

"See? Even you know it's possible." A laugh from the field drew her attention away from the morbid conversation. Jesse's squeal of excitement and his carefree play managed to make Jane smile. "As long as Jesse has had some happiness and found his pa, I can be at peace."

"That makes one of us."

She knew in her heart that was all that mattered now. The knowledge that Jesse was safe with his pa, and finding someone to care for the baby she now carried were the most important things. With those tasks complete, she would find the strength to turn herself in if need be. First, she'd have to tell someone about the baby. Perhaps Michael would care for the child when she was gone. Michael had enough heart to love her child like his own, but could she trust him not to speak ill of Cole, the child's father?

"Jane?" David's hand settled heavy on her shoulder. "Is there something else wrong?"

"Yes. No." She rubbed her forehead. There were some things she wasn't ready to reveal yet. The whole world would soon know of her pregnancy, she wasn't going to reveal it out of turn. "I think I'm just tired, is all. Could you get Michael for me? I'd like to go home."

"I think Jesse was hoping you'd join us for supper."

"I appreciate the offer, but not tonight. I don't feel up to it."

"All right. Soon, though. He likes being around you."

"Has he said he met me before?"

"No." He frowned and shook his head. "I asked, but he said no. Looked a little scared when I suggested it. I haven't wanted to ask him since."

That made his name make even less sense, if she'd never met him before. "Another puzzle I'm not sure I can solve."

"It's all right. We'll figure it out. Why don't I get Mike? You don't look well."

She didn't feel well. Suddenly her body ached and her head pounded. Everything piled up in her mind again, the confusion of unanswered questions begging to be answers. When David stood, she gripped his hand. "Will you come by the homestead tomorrow? We'll start your lessons right away. I can't break this promise. No more breaking promises."

"I'll be there. Three o'clock. That good?"

"Yes. Perfect. Thank you." She released his hand and sank back against the fence again. She screwed her eyes shut and tried to push through the headache pounding behind her eyes.

"Clarabelle?" Mike's hand touched her knee, concern making his voice thick. "What's wrong? Do you need to see Daisy? Is it your ankle?"

"I'll be all right. I just need to go home."

"What's wrong?"

"Jesse is David's middle name."

"I know." He helped her stand and half-carried her to the wagon. "You didn't know?"

"Of course I didn't," she snapped, wrenching free of his hold. She gripped the edge of the wagon, determined to get herself in.

Mike didn't wait for her to figure out how. He grabbed her waist and lifted her up until she could grab the seat and haul herself in. Once she was settled, he followed behind and climbed over her to his seat.

"What did Clara do?"

"I have no idea."

Learning is not child's play;
we cannot learn without pain.
—Aristotle

Jane stood on the porch of the closed library, staring at Mabel Greene's departing back. She shut her mouth the moment she became aware enough to realize it was hanging open. In her hand rested a set of keys, and in the other were the books she'd intended to return to the library along with one of the Poe books and many of the newspapers from the trunk. Her crutch rested against the nearby railing, but she couldn't find enough composure to move, much less need her crutch.

A wagon rattled along and drew to a stop beside her. "You ready to head back, Jane?"

She didn't move, still staring at Mabel's departing back, the keys in her hand a heavy reminder of the unexpected conversation.

"Jane? What's going on? Was that Mabel you were talking to?" Mike dropped to the ground nearby. "Hello?"

"Yes. It was Mabel." She shook off the surprise to face her brother. "She just offered me the position of librarian, if you can imagine such a thing."

"What? You being librarian? I can imagine it well."

"No. Mabel asking me."

"That is harder to imagine." He chuckled and leaned on the post. "I thought Mabel took the position over when the widow Teak died a few weeks back."

"She did, but doesn't have any desire to do so long term. When I was in there yesterday the place was a mess, not that the widow Teak kept it up much either, but she was old and it was entirely forgivable."

"Old? She was ancient." He set his hand on her shoulder. "You did want another job to help occupy your time."

"I suppose I did." She turned the keys over in her hand, a sense of excitement overriding her shock. "I still cannot believe Mabel would offer me the position. I'm almost certain the reverend put her up to it."

"Either that or she was desperate. I suppose stranger things have happened, though. Like you and Cole cooling off again."

She tensed, clenching the keys. "We've discussed this ad nauseum, Michael. Happy as Cole and I were to enjoy each other's company again, we realized it would not work. The decision was mutual and shall remain so."

"How long will it truly last? You have tried before, and it has never lasted long."

At least until the baby's born. She grabbed her crutch and moved to the door of the library. "It's permanent."

"You say that now, but it's only been a week."

"No. It's permanent."

"Jane."

"I will be adjusting the library's hours to have it open more. I'll be working Monday through Friday. I plan to open every day at one, and closing at seven." She took a shaky breath on her way to the desk. Books cluttered the shelves and the desk, some even scattered across the floor with no order or reason. She enjoyed the idea of fixing the library into something far more organized and enjoyable to be in. "And I can continue to try to figure out the point of my own notes while I'm working."

"Where are you in that?" Michael's frown was deep, revealing how unhappy he was with the subject change. It was of no consequence, because she wouldn't allow him to change it back. "Have you figured anything out yet?

"There are the books, of course." She held up the Poe book in her possession as she set the others on the desk. "The marks in the margin aren't anything I've been able to decipher. They look like scribbled nonsense. Almost as if she was bored with reading the same book."

"Let me see." He took the book from her hands and flipped through the pages. The concerned pucker of his brow morphed into a smile. "No. Not scribbles."

"What do you mean?"

He laughed. "I can't believe you dragged these out, Clara. Let's see, here you say '*his* insanity knows no bounds. I wonder if *he* can't decipher this, for *he* is as insane as this code'."

She snatched the book from his hands and scanned the margins. No matter which way she turned the book; she couldn't make out the phrase. "All I see is made up words. Letters mismatched, not a vowel to be seen. Not to mention the letters continually flipping upside down, which do have a pattern I've noticed."

"We swap vowels with symbols and reverse the alphabet, then turn the letters upside down every numeric next number, second to third to fourth and so on reversing after nine. Nick could never get the code memorized. His brain isn't fast enough, and he couldn't remember bible verses for church week to week, much less a code."

"So this says, 'I can't risk *him* deciphering. I have found another way. I pray *he* never learns what I did in Yankton'." Her loose hold on the book made it easy for him to take it away again. The statement brought to mind the carving in her trunk. "Yankton. C. Hodgkins."

"You picked the code up fast. You got that exactly right."

"You sound surprised. The passage you read to me contained all the vowels to determine their symbol and reversing the alphabet is easy."

"Nick would throttle you if he was here."

"I don't much care." She couldn't be bothered to think of a brother she didn't know and couldn't remember when Yankton sat at the forefront of her mind. "I have to find out what's in Yankton."

"Then send a telegram."

She blinked a few times, staring at him in surprise. "Well, that's so simple."

He chuckled low. As she continued looking through the books, he sorted through the newspapers she'd brought along. "Simple is best. It's usually the most effective. I do wonder why you keep capitalizing all mention of him."

"Avoiding a name?"

"Maybe." He lifted one of the papers. "Why is this passage marked? 'To repose confidence in the understanding or discretion of a madman, is to gain him body and soul'."

"In the same story she also marked, 'Why, as for that, a madman is not necessarily a fool'." When he'd set aside *The*

System of Dr. Tarr and Mr. Feather, she handed him the next paper with *The Premature Burial.* Still Poe. Every story appeared to be Poe. "The ones in this story that have been marked are a bit more disturbing."

"I see. 'I was lost in reveries of death, and the idea of premature burial held continual possession of my brain. The ghastly danger to which I was subjected haunted me day and night'."

Another highlighted passage she remembered hit her like a freight train. She gasped. "Oh, heavens. Correct me if I'm wrong, but I believe in that story there is another passage noted. 'I have no name in the regions which I inhabit'."

"Yes. It's right here. Why is that significant?"

"I have no name." She met his curious gaze. "He said that to me on the train—that he has no name. Of course it's ridiculous. He has to have a name. The problem is figuring out where in all of this mess it is."

"Do you think you knew?"

"I have no idea." Her legs wobbled. She sank into the chair. "Even if she did, she'd given up hope."

He sat in silence for a minute. "Why did she stay away? Why didn't she write me? Or Tommy? We could have helped. We could have gotten her and Jesse away from him. She wasn't stupid."

"I don't know. I ask myself the same question every day."

A shake of his shoulders stirred him out of his melancholy. He flipped through several pages in the book again before chuckling as he glanced at the papers again. "Uh, Jane?"

"What?"

"Did you notice a recurring theme? 'And neither the angels in Heaven above, nor the demons down under the sea, can ever dissever my soul from the soul of the beautiful Annabel Lee'."

"It's the only repetitive piece. Fifteen times, to be exact."

"I think the message is clear there."

"She was wrong again. Our souls were severed. I don't have the feelings for David she did." She straightened. "But that's what I need to do."

"What?"

"The telegram. I'll send it, signed Annabel Lee."

He set down the paper he held. A short nod of his head, and he grinned. "I think that's a good idea. Maybe it will get you the answers you need. That we all need."

"I just hope they come in time. If they do, maybe I can face the end in peace."

"That makes one of us."

She began to stack the papers in a neat pile. "I should go send that telegram. Then come back here and form a plan of attack."

"Jane."

"Hm?"

"We didn't finish our conversation." Mike grabbed her hand. "You know you can't keep things from me. What's going on with you and Cole?"

"We always knew he couldn't handle an actual relationship, Michael. I thought I felt the same. Somewhere along the line I started to want more. He couldn't give that to me. I was tired of wasting my time."

"No you weren't."

"I'm not having this discussion. It's over. Now let me go."

He released her hand and stood, walking with her to the door. "Do I need to throttle him for hurting you?"

"I'd really prefer you didn't. It's done. End of story. Leave it be."

"What about David?"

"Oh, Michael, do not even start with me."

"Up you go." he picked her up and set her into the wagon. After climbing in next to her, he picked up the reins. "Are you really going to continue to push David into the lovely arms of the widow Dynan now that you are supposedly not with Cole? You should answer. I know you like to feed gossip, and I can help spread it for you."

She held her crutch out at him in a threatening gesture. "You're beginning to annoy me today. Can we ride in peace?"

"No."

A frustrated sigh escaped, and she closed her eyes. "Boor."

"Love you too, Clarabelle."

Regret for the things we did can be tempered by time; it is regret for the things we did not do that is inconsolable.
-Sydney Smith

Cole leaned on the counter in the telegraph office and tapped his fingers impatiently. "You got it yet, Norm?"

"I'm comin'. Hold your damn horses, Cole." The curmudgeonly man bumped around in the small storage room behind the telegraph. "You ain't the only one receivin' packages, ya know."

"Well I'm the only one here," Cole snapped.

"You're such a bastard anymore."

Cole couldn't argue that fact. In the past week he'd been unable to do anything but grouse at everything and everyone in his path. Jane's revelation had thrown him for a loop he couldn't explain or get past.

Sure, he'd suspected a child. After all, it ain't like he'd never seen a woman with child. He knew every inch of Jane from head to toe, he knew when something changed, small though the change had been.

Still, he'd gladly denied it just to have her close for long as possible. If he'd had his druthers he would have denied it until the end.

Jane didn't let him. The woman had to do things her damn way. Every single time.

He wasn't allowed to continue the denial of the baby changing her shape into luscious, soft curves. She'd shoved the information on him hard and fast. No remorse, no time to stop her. Now way to even so much as cover his ears.

Trying to pin him, most likely. He couldn't be pinned, because he couldn't stomach the idea of another kid. Didn't even want to try to fathom such pain again. He couldn't. He wouldn't. No, he wasn't that stupid.

Norman finally appeared with his delivery, a fresh box of cigars. Best he could do now was take them back and keep on making do. That's all the past week had been since he'd last seen Jane, just making do.

"Wait, I got another somethin' for ya." Norman made his way back to the mail slots.

Cole tensed, wondering who he'd get to read the letter. Only a few people sent him letters, and they were ones he didn't want many people knowing about. Maybe he could get Graham good and drunk and have him read it. Damn fool wouldn't remember anything after that.

"Came in from Denver. Leanne somethin'-or-other. Hey, ain't she the little bit of a whore ya had a few years back?"

"She ain't a little bit anymore." Cole snatched the letter from Norman and shoved it in his pocket. Definitely didn't need anyone reading nothing from Leanne. He'd sooner go to Denver to see what she wanted before he let anyone read whatever nonsense she sent him. "Owns her own place now anyhow. Can't imagine what she'd want."

An all-too familiar, sultry voice interrupted Norman's reply. Jane's voice wove through his body and called him like a siren called a sailor. "Norman, I'd like to send a telegram."

Cole froze in place. Her gasp jolted him back to life. Out of the corner of his eye he could see her hovering just out of reach. Like a shadow, a ghost.

Norman's smile broke through his grump, the corners of his eyes crinkling as he focused on the door. "Sure thing, Janey. Let me just finish up with Cole. Where's it goin'?"

"Yankton."

He immediately thought of her trunk, the mention of Yankton. Could she have found answers? Did C. Hodgkins know about her past? Would she finally figure out who that maniac was?

No.

He didn't care, he shouldn't care. She wasn't his problem any longer. She had plenty of help and company to aide her futile search. Who cared if the maniac found her first? She wasn't his problem any longer.

Cole's grip on the box in front of him tightened, crumbling the edge. The mere thought sent a shockwave or horror through him. How could he live with that?

Digging deep he managed to bury all those worries and fears. He wouldn't fall into her trap. Not again. He nodded Norman. "Ain't no business left here, Norm. Gotta get back. Girls are waiting on me."

She stiffened, her pale features drawn. Her eyes wore dark shadows like skirts, and she appeared thinner somehow despite her condition. As her fingers gripped her reticule, and her lips tightened until they almost disappeared, a twinge of guilt struck him right where he'd buried everything.

No, he'd spent enough time allowing feelings he never should have. He wouldn't let her affect him anymore.

The simple act of walking past her stirred up enough air to fill his nose with the scent of her perfume. His heart plummeted to his stomach. So often that scent had wrapped around him. He glanced over his shoulder and found her eyes focused on him.

Caught, she pulled her gaze away and rambled on about her telegram. Though she'd turned away fast, he'd seen the tear on her cheek. The tear he knew he'd caused. He stormed from the depot, several colorful curses escaping under his breath. No matter what, he'd push away the emotions again. He had to.

There was no way he was going through the hell of having a kid. Not that he knew it was his. She'd told him as much. Just what he'd expected to hear. No, what he'd *wanted* to hear. What he'd *needed* to hear to make his escape.

He stopped in the middle of the street, feeling like he'd just been gored by a bull. She'd made it easy for him. Played on his anger. It had been so easy to leave. For him.

"Damn her." He resumed his fast pace through town. He'd told her everything; he'd let her in. She knew as well as he did he couldn't handle it. He couldn't bear to live through it again.

The pain. The destruction to his life.

The joy.

How could he have forgotten that?

Joy was gone. It was gone because he'd allowed himself to feel it. What a mistake it had been to let Jane in. To let her dig into his soul and open it up like she had. He'd never in his life felt the sort of things he did around Jane.

Not even his first wife had worked his emotions into such a frenzy. Jane had taken the anger and pain he'd lived in for years before she'd come and seen right past them. She'd always known he was more than such anger, had pushed and shoved until so much more had worked its way into his life. His heart.

She'd taken up residence in the place he'd guarded so hard. Because of that he'd seen glimpses of life. Of joy.

Now he was feeling joy wrenched away like it always was.

Wrenched away?

More like pushed away. He'd forced her hand, and she'd forced it right back. She'd shown his weakness in one fell swoop. With that, she'd let him have his out. She hadn't really been finding comfort in others, had she?

If she hadn't, the child was his.

The child *was* his. He knew it in his gut, maybe he'd known it all along.

"Cole," Graham barked.

He startled from his thoughts to glare at Graham. "What?"

"Why are you just standing there? We got a business to run. Them the cigars?"

"Yeah. Here." He tossed them on the bar and raced up to his room where he slammed the door. It was empty again.

The first thing he'd done that blasted day had been removing anything that made the room seem homey. All the little touches Jane put there. It had been a comfort to go back to what was familiar.

The barrenness.

Solitude.

Now it felt cold. Too empty.

He opened his nightstand drawer and reached inside. The book was hers. The first thing she'd left in his room. He'd never given it back. She'd never asked for it.

Whitman.

That's what she'd said it was, at least. He didn't know.

He sat on the edge of the bed, the book heavy in his lap. After a long sigh, he dropped back onto the bed.

There was no way he could go through it again. It was too much pain.

But not having Jane there was causing pain too.

It was too late. He'd let her in and there was no road now that wouldn't have pain.

He needed a way to make it right. To have her close again. If it was possible.

Would she even want him now?

Rumor grows as it goes.
—Virgil

"Have a seat and we'll see how you're healing." Daisy patted the exam table on her way past. At what used to be a dresser she picked up a tray already loaded with supplies to carry back to the exam table.

The once overly opulent lobby of the Silver Saddle was still as gilded and obscene, but now sat empty just beyond the door. Daisy had led Jane to a room once used by the whores for servicing men, but now had been obviously scrubbed clean with an examination table in the middle. A locked cabinet full of different vials and bottles gleamed.

The whole room now screamed 'clinic', all but the doctor herself. While Daisy had taken care to make certain her surroundings were proper, she still wore her whore clothes. Jane doubted it had much to do with that being all there was in her wardrobe. She had little doubt her brother would provide clothes if they were needed, and likely already had.

Jane edged her way onto the table and leaned her crutches against it. As Daisy finished getting herself ready, Jane hauled her foot up onto the table. "It still hurts a good deal, but it seems the pain isn't so bad. Then again, I could just be getting used to it."

"Pain like that isn't something you want to get used to." Daisy's words were softened with a chuckle. She cut through the binding and began to unravel the layers of wrapping. "Have you been staying off of the ankle?"

"As much as possible. Unfortunately, there have been some painful slip-ups. I've regretted each thoughtless one for hours. Most of them were purely accidental, one was motivated by an emotional response that left me without a clear thought." Jane winced when the fabric tugged. "Believe it or not, I am capable of following instruction."

"Considering how you ended up in this position, you'll forgive my doubts."

"I completely understand, Dr. Pearson. I am not an easy patient. I tend toward stubbornness, and I'm foolish and sometimes downright—*ow*." Jane yelped at the last tug of the bandage from her ankle.

"Sorry." Daisy flinched before she set the bandage aside. "My grip slipped. I apologize."

"It's all right." Jane sucked in air between her teeth. "It just caught me off guard."

"I would say it did more than that." Daisy set her hand on Jane's. "You really are stubbornly strong, too much so sometimes. You don't have to cover how much that hurt."

"I'd rather not sob all over your table," Jane spit out through gritted teeth.

"I'd rather you not kick me in the face because you react instead of sobbing while I'm seeing how you're healing."

Jane laughed outright and relaxed her shoulders. "Point taken. Sorry. I'm not one for giving into such histrionics, or rather I prefer not to be. I believe I have lost the battle a time or two."

"I think they call that being human."

"Heaven forbid." Jane smiled and squeezed Daisy's hand back. "Let's get this over with. Sooner we get through the pain of the exam, the sooner I can get it wrapped back up and left alone."

"Sounds like a good plan." Daisy set a hand on Jane's shin and gently pulled aside the splints. "The swelling has gone down considerably. It looks quite good. Let's see how well you're moving those toes."

Jane snorted. "You're joking."

"No, I'm not. I made you do this last week, don't act so surprised."

"I nearly passed out last week. I had hoped you would give me a week without."

"No such luck." Daisy moved to the end of the table. She pressed against Jane's toes gently. "How is that?"

Her lips pinched between her teeth, Jane managed to keep the yelp reined in and reduced to a grunt. She let out the breath she'd been holding as the quick, sharp pain subsided into an aching pulse. "It did not feel good, but it wasn't as bad as last week. I was expecting worse."

"That's a good sign. I'm well-pleased with your progress. You may be able to switch to a cane next week." Daisy pointed her finger and pinched her brows in the sternest expression Jane had seen her wear yet. "If you don't try to push yourself and keep doing as I've instructed. This is not an excuse to do more."

Jane held up her hands in surrender. "I understand. I promise to behave. I'd rather heal sooner over later. The crutches are really a hindrance to everyday life."

"Thank you. I'll believe your promise until I see otherwise." Daisy lifted Jane's foot with gentle care. She set out three strips of cloth before she set Jane's foot back down. As she set the splints in place and began to tie them on, she spoke low, "How are you feeling otherwise?"

"Quite normal, actually. I thought I might feel something other than tired by now, but I don't." Jane frowned. "Although my corset is growing tight, even when I wear it on the loosest lace now."

"Then stop wearing it. I'm surprised you still are."

"I feel quite out of sorts without it."

"No matter. If it's getting tight, wear it loose or forgo it all together. You can't stop yourself from growing at this point."

Jane bit her upper lip when Daisy began to wrap her ankle in earnest. At least Daisy was fast about it. Before Jane had real reason to complain or feel discomfort, Daisy was tying it off. "I'm well aware of that. I think I can handle more looks and whispers. I certainly get enough of them as it is."

"Word is that Mrs. Kilmurry has been quite vocal about those that still voice concerns about your supposed wickedness and criminal activity."

"I appreciate the effort, but Mrs. Kilmurry can't prevent everything." Jane sighed. The memory of Jackson's recent threats sent a shiver down her spine. "Sometimes people just need to see for themselves, I suppose."

"Isaiah seems to think you're going to run off if the law comes knocking."

"Isaiah is wrong." Jane didn't relish the idea of being hanged for crimes she didn't remember, but she wouldn't run. If she'd done wrong, she would take her punishment.

Daisy sat on the edge of the table. "I've been talking to Mike some. You know he'd clear you out. Says one of your brothers could make sure you weren't ever found.

The smile Jane managed to form trembled enough that she felt it. "Mike is a fool for suggesting it, and he knows it. That's why he hasn't said as much to me. I'm going to see this through to the bitter end. I can only pray I'll find answers before then so I can give some testament for what Clara did."

"Don't be upset, but I sent a telegram to Chicago. To Dr. Marcus. He's been studying hypnosis and written some papers on it. Maybe he can come help, or can recommend someone that can." Daisy set her hand on Jane's shoulder. "It's worth a try, isn't it?"

"I suppose it is." Jane wasn't sure she believed such a thing could work, but she did appreciate the effort. Plus, she would try about anything at this point.

"I'll let you know if I hear any word."

"Thank you." Jane grabbed her crutches. "I should get to work."

"Oh, yes. The library. How's that going?" Daisy cleaned the mess as she talked.

"Well enough, I suppose. It's slow going. Rearranging all of those books isn't easy on crutches. I'm doing things a shelf at a time; in most cases a book at a time, but I'm managing."

Daisy chuckled. "My goodness, you sound truly happy for the first time since we started talking. I think you're having fun."

"To be honest? I am. It's the perfect job."

"Glad to hear it."

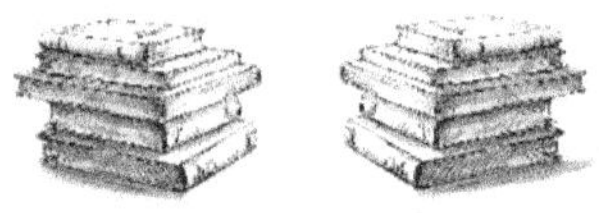

Reason can wrestle and overthrow terror.
-Euripides

"Jane." Lee's voice carried over the rattle of a wagon.

Jane stopped her slow progress toward town. When the wagon stopped beside her, she smiled up toward the seat. David sat nearest; Lee was half-standing in the wagon seat. "Good morning, Lee, David. How are you this morning?"

"We're fine," Lee answered for them both. A small frown creased her pretty features. "Why are you walking into town?"

"I should have clearance for a cane soon, but I don't see Daisy for another couple of days." Jane sighed. "Mike went into town early this morning to catch the train to Denver, something about meeting with investors. I thought I might be able to saddle Tempest myself, but it turns out that not even I'm quite that clever when I'm not allowed to use one of my feet."

David chuckled. "You do know that if you keep going at this pace, you're going to be late."

"Hush. I despise being late." Jane gripped the crutch she leaned on. At the rate she'd had to go on the uneven ground, she should have left at least half an hour earlier than she had. "And your pointless teasing is going to make me later."

"David." Lee cast him a disparaging look. When he appeared properly reticent, she turned a smile on Jane.

"Would you like a ride the rest of the way, Jane? There's plenty of room up here, and I had something to ask you anyway."

Jane hesitated, considering her own stubborn determination to do it on her own. She glanced down the path she still had to take; the length of road had never seemed so long before. That made the decision to allow humility in this one situation far easier than she expected. She nodded. "Yes. I would love a ride. Thank you, Lee."

When Jane made a move to hobble around the wagon to the other side, Lee gave David a good shove. "Help her."

"But it's fun to watch her struggle." David's laughing protest didn't stop his descent from the wagon seat. He held out his hand. "Come on, Jane."

Jane narrowed her eyes and pursed her lips. The man was having far too much fun with her struggle. After a moment she leaned her crutches against the wagon and set her hand in his. "You aren't as funny as you think you are, Mr. Schaffer."

"Sure I am. You just don't like admitting it. Someone might think you like me." He grinned and grabbed her closer before she could even protest. He spun her toward the wagon and hefted her in the air. "Ups-a-daisy."

He lifted her so fast Jane could only grip the wagon seat and haul herself next to Lee. The woman scooted further over, so Jane was able to sit and leave room for the still laughing David. Jane sighed. "Thank you for the offer, Lee. I hope I'm not delaying you in any way."

"Goodness, no. We just picked up Cora's supplies at the depot. A little side trip to drop you at the library won't set us back too much." Lee offered Jane part of the dust robe.

"Thank you." Jane gripped the seat when David's ascent rocked the wagon. "What is it you wanted to ask me?"

David got the horses moving again, and silence fell over the wagon instead of the conversation Jane had expected. When the silence lingered on, David pushed the matter this time. "Go on, Lee. I told you she won't mind."

"Sorry." Lee's cheeks turned a delicate shade of pink. "See, David told me what you two have been doing."

Jane quirked a brow. The only thing she and David had been doing was reading lessons. Granted, they were in private because it was no one's business but his. Of course, she truly hoped it didn't upset Lee in any way. In the past week since Jane had pushed David and Lee into a Sunday walk Lee had started to relax more about everything. Jane was relieved to have Lee less skittish around her. "Do you mean his lessons?"

"Yes." Lee's blush deepened. "I was wondering if maybe you could help me too."

"Oh." Relief relaxed Jane's shoulders and she smiled. This was a request she was all too happy to fill. She had no idea Lee couldn't read. "I'd be happy to. I'd offer to do your lessons together, but David already has a head start. He knew his letters and a few words."

"So do I. My mama taught me some before she passed. After she passed I had to go to work since she couldn't help Pa no more and I was the oldest." Lee fiddled with her fingers. She chewed on her lip. "I don't want to impose or anything."

"It's no imposition, I promise." Jane set her hand on Lee's and turned her smile on David. "I think there's room for one more. So long as David doesn't mind."

"Not at all." David pulled on the reins, and the wagon slowed to a stop in front of the library. "I sure wouldn't mind having you get frustrated at someone besides me."

"You still aren't funny." Jane elbowed him. She turned back to Lee. "David has a lesson this evening. Will that work?"

"It should." Lee's features had returned to their normal color and she gave Jane a bright smile. "Thank you."

"Don't thank me yet. You may dislike my teaching methods." Jane laughed and pushed herself to stand. "I'll see you both around six then."

David tapped the edge of the wagon. "Ready, Jane?"

"Yes." Jane set her hands on his shoulders to let him help her down. She took her crutches from the back of the wagon. Once she was ready to go into the library she nodded to them both. "Thank you again for the ride. I was just contemplating giving up and sitting down on the side of the road."

"Were not. You're too stubborn." David pulled himself into the wagon. Lee's laughter mingled with his. "Glad we could help."

Jane bowed her head to them, adding in a wave when Lee tossed one over her shoulder. The wagon sped down past the jail and turned right to head toward the other side of town.

The ride had been a wonderful distraction, the conversation occupying her thoughts. She made the decision right there and then to spend the night at the library rather than remain alone at the homestead.

Mike had already made arrangements for the livestock to be cared for in his absence, and then she wouldn't have to try to walk the mile and a half. Perhaps she could even spend the morning at Turner's store and restaurant where there'd be people around.

The idea of company brightened her mood considerably, and she unlocked the library still wearing a smile. If she had any sense of pitch at all, she might have hummed out loud. Instead, she contented herself with mental humming as she set about opening the library.

The shutters were pushed wide to let in the sunshine. She left the door open to let in as much light and air as possible. A stack of books remained where she'd left them Friday, next to a half-empty shelf. Her desk had books towered awaiting their new homes.

When she'd started, the library had been in disarray. Worse, books were lying in all manner of positions to hide how sparse the libraries resources were.

She itched to order more books, but first she wanted to have a full and complete list of what the library already contained. Then she'd not risk having duplicates.

Jane took a deep breath and rolled her shoulders. Anxious to start the day, she went straight for the desk to verify her list was complete. As she came around the side of the desk, she realized something sat on it, hidden behind the books.

Something that hadn't been there on Friday when she'd locked the doors.

A soft black hat with a pink ribbon and a small spray of feathers sat in the middle of the desk. The net of the mourning veil covered her book list. Jane recognized it instantly.

She took a step back as though it might bite.

In San Francisco she'd paid a vagrant well to pose as herself. Jane gave the woman clothes and a hat with a mourning veil to cover her features.

The vagrant had been killed; her throat slashed by Johnny—the very maniac hell-bent on making Jane suffer. Jane clearly remembered, as she did everything, giving the vagrant the hat that now sat on Jane's desk in what she'd thought had been her locked library.

"Back door," she whispered. Rather than take a straight path, she edged around the desk and made her way to the narrow back hall. The library had a small kitchen she never used, and that gave Jane pause. What if someone was in there?

Indecision kept her still until she realized it didn't matter. If he was in there, she had no recourse for escape anyhow. With or without her crutches, there was no way she could move fast enough to outrun a turtle, much less a man.

Jane took a deep breath to brace herself and edged down the hall. At the doorway to the kitchen, she paused. From what she could see, it was empty. The room was fairly wide open with nowhere to hide, not even a cellar to get into. The glass panes were still intact; there wasn't any sign of anyone ever being in there. She let out a deep sigh of relief.

She made it to the back door quick as she could, and found it locked as well. How the hat had gotten on her desk was beyond her. She leaned against the door, not sure she wanted to face the reminder so soon.

There wasn't any other choice. She had to. If only to verify it was the hat she'd given to the stranger along with a good portion of her savings.

The woman was dead. Mike had seen her body himself; there was no doubt. Johnny committed the murder—because he thought the woman was Jane or just to add to her guilt, she didn't know.

The hat still sat on her desk like a garish and horrific paperweight. Jane sat, hiding behind the stacks of books while she worked up the courage to touch the offending object. After a few minutes, she reached out to pick it up.

Her hands shook, but she turned it toward her. The veil draped down, revealing a large gash now that it hung free. At the edges of the ripped fabric was a substance she could only guess was dried blood.

As if that wasn't convincing enough, she kept turning the hat to find the small tear in the seam at the back brim. She popped it open easily with her nail, and her worst fears were confirmed. It was the same hat, and somehow it had ended up in Dominion Falls when she'd last seen it in San Francisco.

And it was in her thoroughly locked library.

Mike couldn't get back to town fast enough. She had to know if the woman had been wearing the hat when he'd seen her. If Johnny had taken it when he'd killed her or later somehow to torment her.

Not that it mattered. It tormented her either way.

Maybe she just needed Mike.

She dropped the hat into her desk drawer and tried to wipe her hands free of the memory. At least for now. She'd tell David and Mike when she saw them next.

The fear had to be swallowed. If Johnny was near, if he was watching somehow and she'd missed him, he'd want to see her fear. She couldn't give in.

She couldn't.

A heart that has truly loved never forgets,
but as truly loves on the close.
–Thomas More

Daisy had finally cleared Jane to use a cane. The increased freedom of movement and Michael's return to town had freed her up to take a ride. Michael and David were both fully aware of the hat she'd found in the library and warned her against excursions outside of town. Between Johnny's possible presence and the ongoing Indian negotiations, it wasn't as safe as it could be.

Johnny was more of a threat than the Indians at this point, but they could both be an issue if there was a rogue renegade out and about.

Once she'd made strong and deep promises to remain in sight of either town or the Army camp, Mike had begrudgingly agreed to let her go for a ride. He'd made sure she had her gun and told her to shoot first and ask questions later.

As she rode slow right outside of town, some nearby bushes rustled. Jane pulled Tempest to a stop. She grabbed her gun from its holster and leveled it toward the brush. "Who's there?"

No response came, though she heard whispers from the trembling bush. "Who is it? I'll shoot if you don't declare yourself."

Still nothing.

She fired a single shot at the base of the bush. The crack of gunfire echoed through the surrounding trees. Wildlife scattered. The shout and curse from the bush was definitely from a man, a white man at that. Jane called out, "Graham?"

"What the hell do you think you're doing?"

Jane slipped carefully from her saddle and hobbled toward the bush with her cane. "I could ask you the same thing. I asked who was there. You should have answered. The negotiations aren't over. I had no idea if you were friend or foe."

"You shouldn't be outta town then." Grahams bald head popped up, his round face twisted into a sneer. "If you can't handle a little fright."

"I handled it just fine. You're the one having a fit over the whole situation. Besides, I'm not that far from town. What in heavens name are you doing out here hiding in the bushes?"

Renewed rustling shook the shrub and Graham's shoulder jerked. He shook his head. "Just get the hell outta here."

"Oh. Not alone then? Why are you hiding out here? You've got comfortable—oh." Jane tried not to gasp when the small Chinese woman appeared before darting off toward town. Shock took over at the evidence of rumors before her. She stammered, "I didn't—I'm sorry, Graham."

She turned away as laughter bubbled forth, and pursed her lips to keep her amusement hidden. Rumors had been flying for months that Graham had his eye on the diminutive Linh Moon. Not a soul ever imagined he would manage to catch her, though.

"Don't you dare say anything."

Jane snorted. His face was beet-red from either embarrassment, or anger, or both. "Why would I? I'm not a gossip. I'll listen in on gossip, I'm more than happy to be the source of it, but I never spread it myself."

"Good. You better not."

"Or what?" Jane spread her arms in frustration. "What are you going to do? Are you going to do everything in your power to see that the entire town sees me as a lying jezebel? You already are. You want to ruin my reputation? You're sure trying, but I don't care. What could be worse than what you're already doing?"

"I'll wire the marshal."

"Go ahead." Jane felt a cold spark of fear in her heart at the threat, but also an odd sense of acceptance. Maybe she was ready, or something else. "I'm tired of waiting. So do it."

"Really?"

"I am not motivated to keep your secret, and you have no motivation to keep mine. The difference being I still don't hate you, no matter what you've done. I'm not going to spill your secret solely to cause you pain. I don't care who you screw. I certainly have no room to talk. I'm just surprised. I know Becky is aware of your saloon-related liaisons, but I didn't think she'd ever be all right with you and Linh. After all, this is a liaison of a different sort."

"Well, she can't complain. Not after all that time she's been spending with Cole."

The world spun and the blood drained from Jane's face. She leaned on her cane to steady herself. "They've been spending time together? I was under the impression that Becky couldn't stand Cole."

"Yeah. Imagine that. He went from one schoolmarm to another." A smug smirk crossed his face. "Not that I mind so much. It keeps Becky out of my hair, so that I can make some time of my own."

"Of course. It doesn't bother you at all." She caught the flash of anger on Graham's features before he squelched it. Her frustration blew away in his matching anger and she shook her head. "I should get back to town. I have work to do."

"You better not say nothing."

With a roll of her eyes, she turned her attention to regaining her saddle. She hadn't truly thought out getting back up without assistance. She made good use of the pommel and hauled herself to where she could get her good foot in the stirrup. Thank heavens Tempest stood still for the challenge.

Once settled in her saddle, she peered down at Graham. "I told you. I don't care who you screw. I'd simply suggest being careful. There are plenty of others that would love to spread this information around if they got a hint of it. Then you would for certain lose access to Becky's sizable dowry."

"Not about to do that."

"Didn't think you would." She turned Tempest back toward town and took off at a faster pace than Daisy would have approved of. Once in town, she slowed, spotting David in front of Turner's with Jesse.

The two were oblivious to the world around them, playing jackstones with intense focus. She couldn't stop her smile, glad to see them getting close. That was how it should be. They were a family. One she didn't dare try to be part of. Not with the future so uncertain.

"Jane." Mr. Kilmurry's voice interrupted her thoughts as it caught David's attention.

Jane turned her attention to the leathersmith and smiled as bright as she could. "Mr. Kilmurry. How are you today?"

"Doin' just fine. How's that holster work for you?"

"It's perfect." Jane ran her hand along the strap of leather that fit around her shoulders and secured under her bust. Soon as she'd obtained her weapon she'd placed an order with Mr. Kilmurry to make a holster that she could wear that wasn't a belt. Mrs. Kilmurry did the measuring and Mr. Kilmurry had made the beautiful piece that fit her perfectly. "So perfect that I'd like to order another."

"Really?" Mr. Kilmurry's smile lit up his whole face. "Sure ya need two?"

"I like to have two of everything. That way if I lose one, or it's damaged in some say, there's another on hand."

"Then I'll get right on it."

"Thank you. If you'll excuse me, I must get to the library. I'm running behind today." She gave him a nod and spurred on Tempest, moving through town to the library. The past two weeks had been difficult in many ways. The nights were the worst, when she couldn't help but feel how deeply she missed Cole. The days at the library gave her a reprieve, a distraction from all the chaos and pain hounding her.

For six hours a day she was able to lose herself in organizing the books and reading when no one was there.

She'd made every effort to keep distracted and out of town as much as possible. Avoiding talk and rumor of either her possible criminal past or of her and Cole.

She didn't even know if anyone had noticed she no longer wore a corset, or her increasing waistline. Apparently in some ways people were still too polite to infer such a thing as a delicate condition.

The whispers and rumors around her were ignored as best as she could manage in favor of retreating into her own grief. It felt unending and deep. A sort of grief that took years to get over. A sort of grief borne of love.

No matter she'd known long ago such feelings wouldn't be reciprocated, she'd lost herself to them, and to Cole. She'd been a fool. The terror of the train accident had given her the perfect excuse to ignore the face that Cole couldn't, or wouldn't, allow such feelings in.

The new knowledge of Cole's apparent attention to Becky threatened to break down her carefully built walls of false strength. Right then she needed the security of the familiar distraction in the library.

Quick as a wink, she had the library opened and set about putting away the books that had been returned. She'd been surprised and pleased at the amount of business the library saw. Until she'd started working there, she hadn't thought about those in the settlements that might come to town to help keep the place busy.

When a shadow darkened the door, she paid little mind. When it remained, she called out a brief greeting while she put away a few books. It wasn't until the footsteps stopped near her that she thought to pay attention.

The familiar mix of cigars and whiskey hit her nose and her senses came alive. A wave of pain thrust into her throat, sealing it shut when he stepped even closer.

Cole.

Of all the places she'd ever expected to see him, the library was dead last on the list. It hadn't even crossed her mind to imagine it. Yet here he was, and she couldn't even force out the words to tell him to leave.

"Jane."

A strangled gasp afforded her the air she needed. She shoved back against him when he drew up close enough to feel. She rushed to put the desk between them. Clearing her throat against tears, she slammed down the books she held. "Get out."

"We gotta talk."

"Talk? Now you want to talk? You hate words, you always have, but *now* you want to talk? It's too late for talking. Just get out." Her hands were shaking hard, so she pressed them into the desk. She couldn't deal with this now. Everything she'd done to convince herself she could move forward crumbled around her. The reserve of strength she'd been tapping into drained with every step he took toward the desk.

"That's it?" His large hands pressed into the wood opposite hers, inches from her own. "Don't seem right."

"There is no right any longer, Cole. You wanted out, you've got it. You can't jerk me around. It's better this way. I know it is."

"Then why are ya crying?"

"You hurt me."

His hand moved to rest on hers, clasping it. "I told you what I went through."

"Stop." Her eyes closed as she fought against the urge to cave. Much as she longed for the comfort of his arms, she didn't long for the doubt that he would stay. The constant wondering what would spook him again. If he came back in her life, she wanted to know he was there, not with one foot out the door.

"Why?"

"I can't handle this now." She should pull away, but couldn't find the strength to do so. The warmth of his hand soaked through the chill in her heart. Thousands of words caught in her throat until she couldn't manage to form one complete sentence. "Please."

"I told you. I don't know how to do this." Cole kept his voice low even though they were alone. His hand never left hers. It had been months ago when he'd told her he didn't know how to have any relationships outside of the whores he'd been with for years.

"Clearly." She snorted. Damn him. A smile teased its way through her sorrow. "I believe you're proving that quite well."

"You can't tell me this is better." He leaned closer, and she found herself drawn to him like a moth to a flame.

"All things considered." She stopped staring at their joined hands and met his intense gaze.

"What things?"

"Johnny, or whoever he is, is out there waiting to strike. If he doesn't, Jackson digging into my past will bring the law to my doorstep. This is better. You're free."

"What if I don't wanna be?"

Those words. She'd longed to hear them, and dreaded hearing them. For they were everything she wanted to hear and the last thing she ever wanted to hear. The joy of hope and pain of loss wrapped into one simple sentence. "You need to be. You don't need this."

His eye twitched and he dropped his gaze. She couldn't read the emotions from the top of his head, but his fingers tightened around her hand. "What about the kid?"

"I'm going to ask Mike to take care of it. Or perhaps send it to Clara's family."

He jerked back and twisted his body as though he'd been burned. She no longer had the anger in her to be offended that he might be upset over her choice. She'd always known there were emotions that ran deeper than anyone in town realized. Right then what she hated most was that he was hiding them from her.

With his back turned, he didn't speak. He ran his fingers through his hair. In the past few weeks it had grown longer than she'd seen it yet, until it brushed his shoulders.

She reached toward him, but drew her hand back before she made contact. "What is you want, Cole?"

"I dunno."

Her first instinct was to ask him why he'd bothered coming by then, but she knew it had to be an impulsive move. She laughed weakly and looked back down at her desk. "Everyone will soon know that I'm with child. It's inevitable. Some will likely suspect it is yours."

The unasked question lingered in the cool, still air. His fingers threaded together behind his head and he kept his back to her.

"Most will assume as you did, that it could be anyone's. You won't be culpable in any way."

"Are you saying it's my kid?" He spun and leaned closer again, ever closer to her face. "You said I assumed. That mean I was wrong?"

"It means that you assumed. I gave no assertion to your accuracy."

He all but growled. "Jane."

"Do you really want to know?" Jane fought against the rising fear and anger. She had to know if he wanted to know. The last thing she needed to do was run away because she was scared *he* would run away again.

"What if I do?"

"That's not an answer." She straightened her spine to appear as strong as possible. The flicker of his gaze toward her corset-less and larger waistline wasn't lost on her. "Do you really want to know the truth?"

"All things considered?"

"Yes. All things."

He took a deep breath, and his hand moved toward hers again. While he held his gaze steady with hers, indecision puckered his brow. It was an eternity waiting for him to speak, an eternity she wasn't sure she had.

The door opened with a loud creak. David's voice broke through the moment. "Jane? I wanted to—oh. Everything all right?"

Jane closed her eyes and dropped her head. Sometimes fate had the worst timing. Or maybe it was for the better. At this point she no longer knew what was better, so she strongly doubted Cole did either. "Everything's fine."

"Just fine." Cole's voice was gruff, still so quiet.

"Should I come back?" David moved to her side in a protective stance.

Jane smiled and shook her head. "I said I was fine, David. I meant it. However, you don't need to leave. Cole was just leaving."

"Jane." Cole didn't move away from the desk where his hand gripped the edges tight.

"You don't have to choose right now. I never asked you to choose right now." She wished it could have been that easy, but her life didn't tolerate *easy* any longer.

Cole's brow furrowed. "Ya sure?"

"Yes. I'm certain." Jane was glad David remained quiet beside her. Cole might have lost his cool if he hadn't. "I have an appointment with David anyhow. You know how to find me should you make your choice."

Cole's fingers brushed along hers before he straightened. After a brief nod, he turned on his heel and left the room.

Jane dropped into her chair and buried her face in her hands. It was almost too much to hope that he would listen. Hope was such a rare commodity these days, she wasn't sure she had any to spare on this.

David rested his hand on her shoulder. "Are you all right?"

"Of course I am. At least I will be. It's fine, I told you that. There was no fight, he just talked." She sighed. *He gave me hope.*

"I'm thinking this is a bad time."

"There's no such thing as a good time. Not lately. I'm guessing you got the divorce papers from Lloyd?"

"Yes."

She squeezed his hand. "I know this is difficult for you. You know it's best."

"I understand why. That's the only reason I'm making it so easy for you." He chuckled and winked. "Plus the fact that you've been far more fun when you aren't thinking I'm going to try to make you Clara every time we're together."

"You're far more enjoyable to be around when you aren't looking at me all love-struck every minute of every day." She slapped his arm when he batted his eyelashes at her. "Thank you for helping me smile."

"You're welcome. I just got one thing I want to go over before we worry about those papers."

"Should I be concerned?"

"Jesse."

"I can't, David. No." Shame and regret slowed her heart once again. The fleeting joy she'd felt flew the coop. She couldn't allow anything close to caring with that boy. Not with a noose possibly waiting for her. She'd hurt the child enough. She folded her arms across her chest and gave an emphatic shake of her head. "I can't."

David rested his hands on her shoulders. "I think you should. Get to know him."

"I can't," she reiterated. "It's not right."

"You didn't know he was—"

"No." Jane's eyes closed and she shook her head. "I…I think it's wonderful that you can get to know him. That he will know his pa. He should."

"Is it because you say you don't like kids now?"

"No. Although I do still wonder how I tolerated a school full of them—that isn't it. He is a sweet boy, I saw that—I see that."

He tucked a finger under her chin. "Tell me."

"Look at his life. He's never had a home. A family. Anyone he has been around has been taken away. The man that claimed him sold him to the highest bidder."

"Clara…"

"He deserves to know you. To know his pa."

"He should know his ma too."

"We can't make-believe forever, David. Right now it's easy. There is enough to deal with recovering from what we've been through. But sooner or later we have to face facts. Someday in the not-so-distant future, you will have to put me behind those bars."

"Not if—"

"Yes."

His jaw clenched, but he nodded. "He still deserves—"

"I will not do that to him. He does not deserve to know a mother that he will have to look at through those bars. That he will have to know was put to death for crimes akin to the man that put him through such horrors."

"You're his ma. That's all that will matter."

"No. What matters is that he has something real. Something that will not be ripped away from him again."

David smiled. "You do like kids."

"David."

He kissed her forehead. "I still say he should know you."

"You have to stop pretending. You have to face facts." She cupped his cheek. "Even the most difficult ones."

"Are we agreeing to disagree?"

"No. We're agreeing that I'm right. This is best. Just like our divorce."

"You're not always right."

"Yes, I am."

Life may change, but it may fly not;
Hope may vanish, but can die not;
Truth be veiled, but it still burneth;
Love repulsed, - but it returneth.
-Percy Bysshe Shelley

The depot bustled with activity. Norman's office overflowed with people, each one trying to get their mail, their next train ticket, or send a telegram before he closed for lunch. Rather than wait standing up or push herself to the front of the line, Jane took a seat on the bench outside on the train platform.

The cool October air filled her lungs. She sighed and rested her head back against the building. Since his brief appearance at the library the week before, she'd seen neither hide nor tail of Cole. If she were honest, she hadn't expected anything. He had a lot to think on and, unlike herself, had the luxury of choice. Knowing what he'd gone through with his first child, she didn't blame him for his fears.

She cursed herself for not putting a time limit on his decision, but if she had it would not have been a real choice. It would have been forced. The tragedy he'd been through had changed his life on every level. He deserved the chance to think it through all the way without pressure from her.

In the end, though it would break her heart, it would be easier for Cole if he chose freedom. His pain would be brief then, without the lingering suffering of what might have been. He wouldn't have to watch her die, thinking she might love him.

A shuddering sigh coursed through her and she let her eyes fall closed, soaking up the cool heat of the October sun. She hadn't realized she'd drifted off until the dream started. It was the man, the mangled and dead man of her nightmares, and he was very much alive.

"You are her. You have to be." His hand clasped hers tight. "I don't understand."

"He wants you to believe that. This is what he wanted all along, and I didn't see it soon enough. I am not Constance. I never was. I cannot let you or her family suffer. I can't suffer any longer. That is why I'm telling you this now. Your life is in danger."

"It's been so long. It's so easy to believe you're my wife."

Clara nodded. "I know. I think that's why he's tolerated me so long. I've only just begun to understand the depths of his madness."

"We're going to Georgia. You have to tell them. Her parents." He flew to his feet. "Now."

"Jake, wait. We can't just run out of here." Her fingers dug into his arm to hold him in place. "He'll kill me, or you, or worse. We have to be smart about this. He doesn't yet know that I know what I do."

He wiped at a tear on her cheek. "Constance."

"My real name is Clara. He wanted me to forget. To become Constance. I see it now. I was so foolish, so naïve.

Now that I understand his plans, I have to stop them. I have to save my son. Please. You have to help me."

"You have a son?" He shuddered and sat. "Constance. She was pregnant when she disappeared. Are you certain?"

"That was ten years ago. My son is only six. I didn't even know he was still alive until last year. Please, Jake. I'll do whatever you want, go wherever you want, tell whomever you want me to the whole truth. First, I have to save my son from that monster. I have to get him back to his father."

"Why did you lie to me?"

Her lip trembled, and she sank to the floor in front of him. "To get alone with you. He was watching. If I made any mistakes, he would have killed you then. We must be careful. Very careful."

"Why should I help you?"

"To get justice against the man that took your Constance. Your wife and child. I will help you, but you have to help me. If we move too soon, he will kill my child. Please. Will you help me?"

He pulled his face from his hands. "What do we need to do?"

"Do you have money?"

"I always travel with it."

"A lot. We're going to need a lot of funds. I can pay you back every penny. I have an account. I took a great deal of his money and secured it away right before we sent for you. It's too far away to access right now."

"Where is it?"

The room shook and dimmed around the edges. The man's visage grew blurry and faint. Jane sobbed. "Wait."

"Jane?"

Jane reached toward the retreating image with a desperate gasp. A hand grasped her arm moments before she tumbled off the bench. "No. Wait. I was about to remember."

"Jane, you all right?" Norman's weathered features replaced Jake's. He kept a tight hold on her arm like he feared she might still fall. Gruff though he was, concern puckered his brow. "What were you about to remember?"

"I don't know." She wiped at her cheeks, though she'd managed to keep her tears hidden. "It was a dream, I think. I didn't realize I'd fallen asleep. I'm fine, truly. Just a little disoriented."

"Ya sure?"

Jane smiled. The remaining tension eased away when Norman's face wrinkled into a bright smile. "I'm certain. I didn't realize I was so tired. I just came by to see if there'd been any response to my telegram yet."

His smile faded and he shook his head. "Not a word, Janey. I can resend it if you want. It's been a couple weeks since ya sent it."

"No. If there was going to be a response, it would have already come." She tried to cover her disappointment. The telegram she'd sent to C. Hodgkins had gone unanswered. It had been her best hope for answers. The notes in the book had yielded little else by way of information.

Her hand fluttered to her stomach. Though her best hope for answers, the telegram had not been her last hope. She still held out some hope for the life inside. She'd finally concluded that Michael would be the best person to ask to care for the child once it was born. If she was going to be hanged, that is.

"Jane?"

Norman's voice pulled her back from her thoughts, and her cheeks grew warm under his gaze. She'd totally forgotten he was there. "Sorry. I'm still not fully awake. Go on to lunch, Norman. I think I'll head to the library."

"If you're sure. I'd be happy to walk ya."

"You are very kind. I can make it all right. I have my cane and it's not terribly far." To prove her point, she rose and leaned on the cane. "Now go on. I'm going to be slow and enjoy this beautiful day."

"All right. Good day, Jane." He tapped his hat and started toward town.

Jane moved at a slower pace behind him. He was long gone down the street before she'd reached the corner of the building. A twinge in her abdomen gave her pause. She set her free hand against the depot as the pain stretched into a dull ache.

She grunted against the cramp, taking a few deep breaths. As it passed, she leaned her forehead against the building. Concern bubbled up and she wondered if she ought to see Daisy. With each passing moment the ache both faded and lingered.

"Falling asleep against the depot?" Laughter trickled through Al's voice as he hopped down from his horse. "I know you said you weren't sleeping well, but if this is the case, I have to tell you it isn't the most effective way to rest."

She breathed out the last pain and strained against the lingering tense lock of her jaw until she forced out a smile. "I have to take my rest where I can get it. After all there is no rest for the wicked, you know."

He offered her his arm, smiling when she took it. "Well, I don't know about that. You aren't nearly as wicked as you've been made out to be."

"The rumors do have me painted as quite a soiled dove."

"Not that you discouraged them in any way. I do recall several occasions that you came to my tent in the middle of the night."

"To talk. Play cards."

"Poorly."

She smacked him in the arm. His words held a ring of truth that made her laugh when she tried to glare at him. "So I'm no good at poker. Doesn't mean I can't have fun playing the game."

"No, but you lost quite a few bucks to my men."

"And to you."

"I tried to let you win it back. You just kept losing—Jane?"

She gripped his arm when the pain returned with a vengeance. The worry she'd been brushing aside blossomed into fear. Her heart stilled. Something was wrong. This was stronger than any ache she'd had yet. "Oh."

"What's wrong?"

"I think I need to see Daisy."

"Is it your ankle?"

A shock of pain tore through her and her knees buckled. The next wave shot straight to her back. Al's arm wrapped tight around her waist to hold her up as she doubled over. "Al."

His shout rang in her ear, but she couldn't make out he words. Colors swirled in front of her eyes, trying to drag her into blissful oblivion. She was scooped into the air, the acting turning her stomach. She groaned, her head falling against a padded shoulder. A soft cry grew into a whimper. "Hurry."

"I'm going fast as I can," Graham snapped. "What in blazes were you doing?"

"Walking." She groaned. "Why did you—"

"Webb can't pick you up. He's still recuperating. I was right there." Graham wasn't at all careful with his steps, and every impact ripped through her.

Her head swam. "Hurry."

"I'm right here," Daisy spoke quietly. After shoving Graham out of the room, she took Jane's hand. "What happened?"

"Something's wrong. Baby. Pain. Help."

"I'll do everything I can."

The thing we fear we bring to pass.
—Elbert Hubbard

Cole couldn't stand still for nothing. He paced the length of the porch in front of the Silver Saddle, ignoring the three men seated on the bench by the door. They didn't matter. No one mattered but the woman in that building.

Al's shout of her name had been the first thing to draw him out of his saloon for over three days.

The agony creasing Jane's features had shocked him. He'd gone completely numb, unable to move. Graham had done as he should have and hauled her to the makeshift clinic.

Now he stood locked outside, not knowing what was going on.

Only that something was terribly wrong.

In his soul he knew, but still denied the truth. The suggestion it had been her ankle passed muster as an excuse.

It had to. Anything else was unacceptable.

Jane didn't deserve that pain. He'd never wanted her to have such agony. He couldn't live it. Not again.

"Would you stop?" Mike flew to his feet. "You're making me insane with your pacing. Why don't you go back to the saloon? You don't care anyway."

"Excuse me?" Cole spun on him. The man had no idea what or how he felt No one did. No one but Jane—or did she?

"You're not deaf. Do you really think that after the hell you've been putting her through, treating her like—"

"Mike," David set his hand on Mike's shoulder, "now isn't the time."

Somehow David's words made Mike back down, but Cole was far from grateful. At this point, he was more than up for a good fight. He had a lot of energy and frustration to burn off.

Mike had no idea of Jane's condition. Far as Cole could tell, Jane hadn't told anyone. They all looked lost, confused. They were all certain that she'd somehow hurt her ankle again. Not one of them had suggested anything else.

Cole knew.

Every beat of his heart ached. He'd waited to give her an answer, so he could be sure. He hadn't wanted to betray her again. To say he was fine only to leave.

Now this.

Daisy cleared her throat, making everybody on the porch jump. She wasted the time to glare at Cole before turning her attention to Mike. "She's doing better."

"Daisy?" Mike moved closer. "Is she all right?"

"She will be, I think." Daisy cleared her throat. "It was her appendix. It's very tender. I'd like to keep her here for a day or two to make sure I don't need to operate."

Mike stared hard at the woman in front of him. His usual adoring features when he looked at the former whore hardened. Whatever Daisy had said, it had angered rather than reassure the shrimp. "It can't be. It's got to be something else. Examine her again."

"Michael," Daisy pleaded. She glanced at Cole for help, but after her earlier sneer, he felt no such urge. The woman could suffer her lie alone.

"She doesn't have an appendix. The doctors removed it when she was twelve. It kept causing her pain."

Daisy flushed a deep red. Cole knew she'd been caught in the lie. The familiar flutter of her hands belied her riled nerves. Her calm poker face she usually wore as a doctor disappeared in the anger of her would-be suitor. "You should speak to her, Mike. She's in surgery. Go on in."

Mike didn't wait to be told twice. In a flash, he was inside, leaving the rest of them on the porch.

Cole folded his arms across his chest. He glared down at the woman whose contract he'd owned a few short months ago. He didn't care that she glared right back. All he wanted was answers. "Daisy."

"Not now, Cole."

"Walk with me."

"No." She planted her hands on her hips and lifted her chin. "In case you forgot, you no longer own me. I owe you nothing."

Cole met her gaze without wavering, needing to know. "Is she really gonna be all right?"

"She'll be fine. Go back to the saloon. There's nothing for you here."

David frowned. "Daisy. I know I haven't known you long, but it doesn't seem like you to make a mistake like that. Was it her appendix?"

"All I can tell you is that she's going to be fine. I'm sorry." Daisy frowned when Cole stepped closer. She pointed her finger at him. "Go."

"When can I see her?" Cole touched her arm. No charms would work at this point. All he had left was his desperation to know the truth.

"You can't."

He caught the pain, balled it up tight, throwing it right back into anger's hands. He snorted his disbelief. "Can't?"

"She doesn't want to see you. I think it's best."

He didn't believe it, couldn't. "Why?"

Mike stepped out of the clinic, pale. He cleared his throat. "She doesn't want to see anyone—not even me."

Daisy set her hand on his arm. "She's exhausted. Check on her after a while. I'm sure she'll want to see you then."

Mike nodded absently, glancing back when she disappeared inside.

David's brow furrowed. "Michael? I thought you said—"

"I did."

Cole frowned. "What the hell—"

He never saw it coming. Before the words had fully left his mouth, Mike was in arms' reach. White spots blasted across Cole's vision when Mike's fist connected with his nose. Blood poured out of his nose.

"You bastard."

The question is not, "Can they reason?"
nor, "Can they talk?"
but rather, "Can they suffer?"
—Jeremy Bentham

Mike didn't have time to think, not that he really wanted to. Within seconds of punching Cole, the man retaliated. Drawing on the years of fighting with his brothers, he countered and swung back with ease.

The few blows he took didn't reach through the anger, the pain, the blinding fury. He wanted Cole to suffer like Jane was suffering. They flew over the hitching post into the street, knocking over Kilmurry's cart in the process.

A splinter of wood drove into his arm, but he ignored it in favor of delivering a solid kick to Cole's kidneys. His arms were grabbed, but he was far from finished. Pure venom shot from his throat. "You aren't a man. You never were."

Cole was being held back by Graham and a soldier, fighting against their grip with a deep growl. "She never had any complaints. Kept comin' back for more."

"Stay the hell away from her."

"Mike." David's voice was strained as he fought to keep hold of him.

"She'll be back. She won't be able to help herself." Cole fought an arm free only to have it grabbed again. "Just tell her to stay away. See how she takes it."

With renewed fury, Mike fought against David and Archie, trying to get free and have at the man again. "Bastard. You didn't deserve her. You didn't deserve—"

"*Michael.*" Daisy's shriek stilled both men for the briefest moment. She ran in between them with a glare for each of them. It landed at last on Mike, her disapproval clear. He'd almost revealed Jane's now-lost pregnancy to the whole town. An unneeded embarrassment now. "Jane wants you both to stop acting like children. Cole, go away. She doesn't want you."

"I don't believe ya." He shoved off the soldier easily. "Let her tell me."

"You son of a—" Mike lurched forward.

"Stop it." Daisy planted herself in front of Michael. "Is this really how you want to deal with this? What would Jane say?"

"That it's high time I made that bastard pay for what he's done to her."

"Go to hell." Cole broke free and stormed forward. This time it took four men to hold him back.

"Cole," Daisy stayed close to Mike, trembling despite the surety in her voice, "right now is not the time to deal with this. Jane is in no condition for visitors. Your nose is broken; I can see it from here. Let me patch it up."

"Don't bother. You don't owe me nothing, remember?" Cole fought against the men holding him. His voice rose. "There ain't no one that owes me nothing."

Mike tensed when Cole broke free once more, braced for another attack. The chance never came as Cole turned and strode back to his saloon. Moments later a shot was fired, and people scattered from the building.

Graham rubbed his hand over his face. "I got his damn nose, Daisy. He ain't gonna let you near him now."

"You don't say? I never could have guessed." Daisy rolled her eyes and pulled up the straps of her dress from where they'd fallen. "Make sure it's straight. He gets mad as hell if you set it crooked."

"We'll see." Graham pushed through the dissipating crowd.

David was apologizing to Mr. Kilmurry, but Mike couldn't find the urge to do the same. He pulled some money from his pocket and held it out in silence. He had no idea who took it from his hand; it didn't really matter. Nothing much mattered at the moment.

With the disappearance of Cole, his anger lost its power, crumbling into the depths of despair again. Jane's pale features creased in turmoil filled his mind again. The strength that had filled his limbs gave way to trembling.

A touch to his forehead jolted through him, the sharp sting of the wound Daisy inspected brought him back to the present. He wrapped his hand over hers and pulled it away. "I'm fine."

"Funny. I thought I was the one you were paying to be a doctor. You need stitches, Michael." Daisy sighed. "Come inside and let me stitch you up. David's taking care of Kilmurry. Any more time out here and you'll have the rumors flying more than they are already. That's the last thing Jane needs."

Mike dropped his head, the truth of her statement hitting home. He didn't fight the pull of her hand into the Silver Saddle. In total silence he let her lead him into the rooms he'd turned into a clinic for her. He frowned. "Where is she?"

"I had Ike help me move her to my room. I don't want her going home tonight, especially since she'd be there alone." Daisy kept her back to him, gathering the supplies she'd need. "Provoking Cole was a bad idea."

"Thinking wasn't exactly my strong suite at that minute."

"I noticed. What would Jane say? Getting into a fight and getting yourself hurt?" Daisy set the tray beside him and dabbed at the wound. Her forehead creased, pained worry filling her green eyes. "Cole could have really hurt you."

"I've fought against bigger men. I'm not worried."

Her frown deepened, pinching her brow into a delicate little V. "That isn't the point."

"I know." He sighed and closed his eyes. Rather than argue further, he let her work. "As to what she'd think, she'd be mad."

"No, really?"

"But maybe she'd finally understand. He's no good. She deserves better."

"She might not think so."

"Well she does."

"He's not as bad as you might think."

He grabbed her wrist again, and held her gaze. "You can't mean that."

"I know. He owned me, and ordered me around, but he was always...I can't explain it. I've seen what Jane's seen; I think all his girls have. That's how he reels us in, and why we're so happy to come along." She shrugged. "Just no one has seen more than that. No one but Jane, I don't think. He sure hasn't hung on to anyone this long before. She got under his skin something fierce, like nothing I ever saw."

"He got under hers, too. I thought that was why she was hurting so bad, I didn't know about the baby. If I'd known."

"She would have told you in her own time, she couldn't have avoided it." She cupped his cheek gently. Her sad smile faltered and she pulled her hand back, stepping a foot away. Clearing her throat, she threaded the needle. "Do you really believe it was Cole's?"

Mike couldn't deny the disappointment he felt when she pulled away. In the past weeks he'd watched her grow more confident every day she'd been a doctor again. The doubt lingered in her dress and in her occasional attempts to tell him he'd made a bad choice. He stared at her delicate hands threading the needle, responding to her subject change with little emotion. "She seemed certain. I only saw her for a few minutes though."

"She never told me for certain whose it was. Not that it would have made any difference. I couldn't have talked to him about it even if I'd wanted to."

Michael grunted in agreement and pain when the needle pierced his flesh for the first stich. "I don't know if he knew. If he did and he—"

"Stop." Daisy continued stitching, keeping her focus there. A frown curled down her lips and pulled her brows down low. "It's bad enough that she's in pain, physically and emotionally. Now she has to see you bleeding and broken, thanks to a fight that was supposedly over her honor."

"What else should I have done?"

"Curbed the impulse. You're intelligent enough to not run on pure emotion."

"Well, it would have been pointless to have a battle of wits with him. It's just not fair to do that to someone so unarmed."

Daisy was fighting the twitch of her lips, he could tell. Despite every attempt, a small laugh escaped. "Michael."

"It was stupid. I'm not usually one to do something like this, Daisy. Just when I saw him, I got so mad."

"I did too."

He stared straight ahead, still trying to comprehend what had just happened to his sister. The pain she must have been going through dealing with her condition all on her own. Now this? He took a shuddering breath. "She didn't tell me. She tells me everything."

"This was intensely, deeply personal, Michael. Her situation is…unique."

He glanced at her out of the corner of his eye. "What do I do?"

"Don't go around beating up Cole for every wrong. I'll run out of thread."

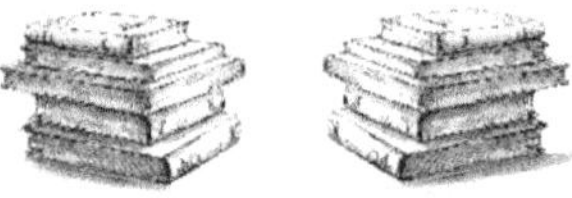

He jests at scars that never saw a wound.
–William Shakespeare

Cole growled to hide the yell when his nose popped under Graham's beefy hand. He hadn't expected Graham to be gentle about it, but it always hurt like a bitch when he had to have his nose fixed.

The physical pain was so much easier to deal with than his racing thoughts, so he fought to keep his focus there. He grunted when Graham threw a towel at his face.

Graham wiped his own hands, eying Cole with a dark glare. "What in the hell was that mess about anyway?"

It was easy to lie to Graham. The idiot only saw what he wanted to. Easy as a two-bit whore, Cole pulled the lie out. "Damned if I know. The bastard jumped me and started beating on me. Don't know what the crazy bitch told him. Don't much care anymore."

"He went nuts like that just because she hurt her damn ankle again?"

"Nah. Daisy says it's her appendix." A total lie. Any doubt he might have had was erased with Mike's blatant attack and the words he'd said. Cole's lips curled around his teeth in another growl when he thought of what had to have happened. "I woulda done him in if you hadn't stopped me."

Graham snorted. "Sure. You're more messed up than he is. The shrimp's got a good fight in him. He would've floored you."

Cole closed his hand over the bottle of whiskey he was using for a painkiller. His fingers slipped along the blood he'd dripped when he lifted it to his mouth. The look on Jane's face when Graham had carried her to the Silver Saddle…he knew that look. He remembered it. He'd lose her for this, just like he'd lost Ella.

Jane had always been a damn strong woman. The mere thought of her losing that fight turned his stomach something fierce. Emotions warred within him.

He wanted to go to her, comfort her. Keep her as far from that pit of despair that had done in his wife as he could.

The other part was set to run. Far and fast. Even Jane wouldn't be strong enough for this. He couldn't stand to watch her disappear into the madness.

He realized Graham was still looking at him, his comments ignored. Cole curled his lip toward the man.

"What? He floored me. You really think he can't floor you?"

The misconception amused Cole, and he turned his grimace into a cold smirk. "Don't misjudge me, Graham. I wasn't out yet."

"'Course not."

"Don't matter nohow." The whiskey burned a hot trail down his throat, killing the lump that threatened to shut it off. He'd find a way to see her once more. After this he had to be done. She had to know he was done. For good. He'd gotten in too deep. He couldn't handle it again.

Hell, he hadn't handled it the first time. All he knew was that of all the women in the world, he knew he couldn't lose Jane. He couldn't watch that strong, incredible woman disappear into an empty shell.

"Why not?" Graham's voice grated on every nerve as it distracted Cole from his dark thoughts. The burly man slugged his whiskey down. "You aren't seriously going to let him bully you around?"

"No." Once again, the lie tumbled from his lips without a stumble. Graham was hardly a man he told anything to. Even though he called him friend, he didn't trust him worth a lick. "I was done before this. I ain't going back. Ever."

"Right." Graham chuckled and dropped his empty bottle on the counter. He shook his head and tossed his bloody towel in with the linens. "Of course you aren't."

"I mean it."

"You always do. You always go back. It won't be any different this time."

Cole didn't need to lie this time. The amber liquid in his bottle taunted him, burning his throat and turning his stomach before he ever tilted the bottle. It wasn't the whiskey. It was her again. No, a lie wasn't needed. "It's different this time."

"Sure it is. Every time you say that, you still go back. The day you stop going back is the day she's swinging."

Before he could stop himself he was on his feet. The implication of Jane hanging for crimes she didn't commit wrenched another gaping hole in his already torn soul. He grabbed Graham by the collar. "I told you to stop saying that. She ain't gonna swing."

"Like I said, you'll go back." Graham peeled Cole's hands off his collar and wiped at the blood that had dripped from Cole's freshly bleeding nose. "You always do."

Pure rage coursed through him when Graham closed the door. He emitted a frustrated yell and threw the basin of bloody water across the room. The shattering of the vessel and spray of water did nothing to dissipate the anger or pain.

She was suffering. He couldn't watch her go through it. He didn't have the strength to do it again. So why did he want nothing more than to bully his way into her room? To hold her. To have *her* tell *him* it was going to be different for her.

Worse, why did the knowledge it wouldn't happen, that she'd never let it happen, kill him worse than the idea of her disappearing?

When had she taken him over so completely? How had he let her?

Every way forward was paved with pain and loss. One way or another he'd lose her.

Then again, he'd already lost her. Long before this.

Maybe she was right, he didn't need this. Didn't need to see her suffer and possibly die.

All he had to do now was make sure it stuck. Then get out. Away. Maybe he'd leave and set up shop elsewhere.

And never let anyone in again.

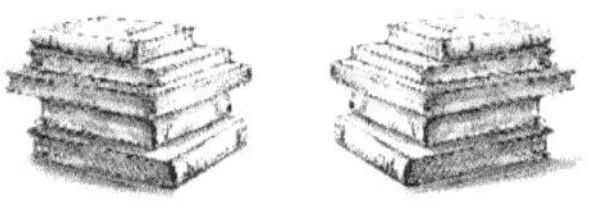

What is deservedly suffered must be borne with calmness, but when the pain is unmerited, the grief is resistless.
—Ovid

"Jane?"

David's quiet knock filled the dark and silent room. She wanted to tell him to go away. She couldn't deal with him. She couldn't deal with anyone. Not now. Not when her last glimmer of hope poured out of her.

A sliver of light creased the room, growing larger before darkness fell again. Silence. He was in the room, but not moving.

She made no move to turn up the lamp. The dark was soothing, enveloping. It was where she wanted to be. Alone.

There was no comfort now. There never would be again. But then his hand folded into hers. With a shaky breath, she found her voice. "David."

The lamplight grew brighter, illuminating his features lined in worry. He brushed some hair off her cheek, and she was grateful she'd been unable to cry. Explaining the tears would be too much. She wouldn't be able to without a reasonable explanation.

"Are you all right?"

The answer to that was too complicated, too messy, and too painful. She didn't dare answer. All she could manage was to pull his hand close to her chest and soak in the little comfort it offered. She managed a weak nod. "I'll be fine. I'm only tired now."

"You look more than tired."

"Is that the polite way to say I look like hell?"

"Yeah." His lips turned up in a smile that trembled and threatened to crumble. "I guess it is."

A weak laugh got tempered by a whimper. "At least you're honest."

He sighed. "Jane…"

"Not now," she whispered. "It's nice just having a hand to hold. Please."

"For as long as you need it, it's yours."

If you would weep, you must first of all feel grief yourself.
—Horace

The tree bent and swayed outside the bedroom window. An approaching storm whipped the leaves from the trees, tossing them aside without any care. Jane's tears welled again, and she sniffled against them when Daisy pulled the sheet back over her legs.

The snap of Daisy's medical bag cracked through the room like gunfire, but Jane hadn't the energy or care to jump. Daisy's quiet sigh twisted Jane's heart, the sigh of finality. The pregnancy was gone; her bleeding eased enough to convince her of that.

Jane didn't like pity, but she felt so deserving of it. Despite Cole's reaction to the news, the baby had given her hope.

"You're healing well. I wish you wouldn't stay here by yourself. It isn't just the physical side that needs to be healed." Daisy set her hand on Jane's shoulder. "At the hotel, Michael can help."

"I'm doing everything you told me. I've been taking all of the medicines. I stayed in bed for three days. I'm not pushing myself. I haven't even gone to the library. It's been a week. I need to get back into life. That is how I'll be helped."

"Pretending like it never happened?"

"Make no mistake, I will never forget that it happened. I have been mourning in my own time and in my own way. I will not have Michael hovering over me fussing and worrying. That won't heal me. I doubt there is anything that would heal me now."

"All right." Daisy patted her hand. "I'm sorry."

Jane closed her eyes against the fresh well of tears. If only she could get out of the house so she'd have distraction. Then again, outside the house she'd see Cole.

"You still haven't told me, is there anyone we need to inform?"

The indirect nature of the question made Jane snort. For so long everyone had been dainty around the suggestion she was sleeping with many men to her face, while being rather lude behind her back about it. Now not even her own doctor thought she could ask the question directly. "Just ask. Be direct about it, I am so tired of subterfuge."

"You were so distraught, and in physical pain. I wasn't sure if your utterings were true. Neither was Michael." Daisy cleared her throat. "So the father was…"

"The father is, no was, Cole. By the gash on my brother's forehead, I'm assuming Cole already knows. There is no one else to inform."

"Oh. You are certain, then."

"Appearances can be deceiving. For all intents and purposes, you still look like a whore. Yet here you are with a medical bag, treating my maladies. You are the town doctor.

You should know better than anyone that not all is what it seems. Not everyone is as they seem."

"I'm sorry. I shouldn't have asked."

The only laugh Jane could muster was weak, without much feeling behind it. "Why not?"

"It's rather nosy of me."

"And it's not of the whole town to spread rumor and gossip about my activities? You might have asked, but even you couldn't ask me directly, so why answer anyone directly? Not even Cole bothered to truly ask. He simply assumed I'd slept with every man in the Army camp, not to mention my soon to be ex-husband."

"Jane."

"I didn't dissuade him from the notion, though I could have." Honestly, Jane had been about to, but Cole had never come back to see her. To ask her directly. He'd had three days before the miscarriage. Of course, there still was no sign of him, although she was far less surprised by his absence now. The loss of the baby would only serve to remind him of the fear that had kept him away—the memory of his dead wife and child.

"Why not?" Daisy squeezed her hand. "I mean, if he was the only one."

"He was the only one." Her lips trembled against her will, and she tried to stop their betrayal of her emotions. The grief threatened to surge forward again. She'd lost Cole, and now she'd lost the last piece of him she'd been clinging to with all her might. His child. His absence had been far more tolerable when she still had a part of him with her.

Jane laughed again, a short barking sound that startled both herself and Daisy. "This town's tendency toward gossip helped form the assumption. I knew it and encouraged it. There were times I'd ride out to camp in the middle of the night."

"Why? Why encourage such rumors if they weren't true? Why keep up the appearance of ill-repute if there was none?"

"Why wouldn't I? People would talk either way. Cole and I were about nothing more than sex." Jane wrinkled her nose against the lie. For her they were more, but he hadn't made any similar admittance and had run at the first sign of a tie between them. Even if he'd run from his past and not her, the pain still cut deep. "As to the Army camp, I went to play poker. I listened to their stories, kept them company as a friend, never anything more."

Daisy shook her head. "So there was nothing to the rumors. But did you really think that you and Cole were nothing more than—"

"I seem to make friends with men easier than women. Yours and my pitiful attempts at something akin to friendship prove that." Jane changed the subject quick. She wasn't about to discuss her real feelings with Daisy. The depths of her feelings were too unexplored. She hadn't even been able to tell Cole, she wasn't about to tell the woman before her. "That doesn't mean I take them all to my bed. Cole was the only one."

"Oh, Jane…"

"He was the only one." Jane turned away to avoid seeing the pity as clear as she heard it. "He's infuriating. Maddening. A brute. But he was the only one that made me feel— anything."

"I'm so sorry."

"After everything, when I realized that I was…that there was a baby. It—it changed something." Jane steepled her fingers as the emotions threatened to block the right words from her. She took a shuddering breath and faced the woman beside her. "I was still facing everything I was before: jail, a hanging, an unknown past, but…"

"But what?"

"For a few short weeks all of that—it was still there, it was still terrifying, having a child was terrifying—but for the first time, I had hope."

A tear slipped down Daisy's cheek.

"But there's no hope now." A knock on the door interrupted Daisy's attempt to protest, and Jane jumped on the distraction. "Come in, Michael."

"I'm not interrupting, am I?" Mike's head poked into the room. "Just wanted to see if you wanted some more tea."

"If I did, I could get it." Jane huffed and banged her head against the wall. "I'm not an invalid."

Daisy stood. "I was just finishing. She's doing better."

"You didn't tell me when I could go back to work."

"Wednesday." Daisy's brows pulled together in a frustrated frown. "If you promise to keep taking it easy."

"Any other orders?"

"Take laudanum and lie down if you start to hurt." Daisy waited until Jane grumbled an agreement before nodding. "Then Wednesday."

"Thank you." Twirling the lace edging on her bodice between her fingers, she fought against the new sting of tears.

"Help yourself to some tea." Michael lowered his voice when Daisy stopped next to him. "I'll be out shortly."

"Take your time." Daisy squeezed his arm before she slipped from the room.

If Jane had been feeling much of anything besides her own misery, she might have smiled at the gesture and resulting smile it put on Michael's face. Now that Daisy had started to feel less sorry for herself, Jane was starting to like her more. Not to mention she was glad Michael had something to distract him from her miserable life.

"Care to explain this?"

All Michael's amusement had disappeared, the almost annoying levels of concern had hardened into anger, and Jane had no idea what could have caused it. Until a pouch landed in her lap to reveal the source of his anger. The second she saw it she knew what it was, and her hand flew to her mouth to cover her gasp. "Oh, no. Michael. It's not what you think."

"Snakeroot. It's the whore's tea." He turned his back to her and pressed his hands into the door. "I found it in the pantry, Clara. Did you do this?"

"No. No. I swear it. I couldn't. I wouldn't. I never took any." Her voice quivered uncontrollably as she shoved away the pouch as far as she could. "I got it, yes. I thought about it for about five minutes after…"

"After what?"

"After learning I might be hanged, for what child deserved to have the yoke of my misdeeds on their shoulders?" Jane's tears couldn't be stopped. She spoke the truth, for not even learning of Cole's past had made her consider ending the pregnancy. Only knowing her likely fate had been enough to frighten her into considering taking such a tea. "I got the tea, but I couldn't do that. I couldn't. I couldn't."

"Don't lie to me."

"Look at me. I'm not. I swear. I meant to dispose of the tea, but then things got…" She sat straighter and reached for his hand. "I didn't want this. God, this hurts so much. I never wanted this. I wanted to do it right this time. My child wouldn't have had a pa, but I couldn't get rid of it. I loved it. More than I ever knew I could."

He sank onto the bed next to her. After a moment, he wrapped his arm around her. The attempt at comfort was weak, but she appreciated it. He kissed her temple. "I believe you."

The tears erupted, gushing like waterfall down her cheeks without a break. The pressure of Michael's hold increased, his tight grip assured her with every heaving sob that she wasn't alone in this.

Somehow Michael pulled her into a full hug, and his chin rested on her head. The brush of his fingers along her arm soothed her as his soft whisper reached her ears. Over and over he repeated, "It's all right, Clarabelle."

The tears eased enough for her to catch a breath. A weak chuckle erupted only to be choked away a moment later. "You want to know what's so ironic? After everything that's happened, I actually thought that I…"

He squeezed her gently. "Were getting another chance?"

"Something like that. I was scared. I was worried that I would be hanged and not a part of his life. I worried that Cole would never come around, and the child would be without both parents. But I still had hope."

"You still need hope."

"With Jesse, oh Clara was so horrid. It was wrong to feel the way she did, to consider ridding herself of a child for as long as she did. I knew it the minute I had that tea in my pantry." If Johnny were right, she'd still considered it in labor months later.

"Clara was scared."

"So was I." She pressed her tongue against her teeth while she considered her words. The mild twinge of pain kept her present, away from the depth of tears she wanted to wallow in. "Jesse has been through hell, yet he survived. She ran from David, from the possibility, and yet Jesse is still alive and so loved. She was afraid to love her own child. I did nothing but love mine."

He was silent, his jaw clenched tight. A single tear had escaped and now shimmered on his cheek.

She wiped it away. "This time I loved this child with everything I had. Even given my situation. Even knowing that Cole would run. I couldn't help it. I loved our child. I don't know how it's possible, but I did. Now it's gone. Everything is gone."

"It's not your fault. This didn't happen because of anything you did."

"Are you sure? After all that Clara did, you don't think this is just desserts?"

"It doesn't work like that. It's not a barter system."

She rolled her eyes to the ceiling and her body trembled with restrained tears. "It feels like it is. I am alone. It's so fitting. 'To be left alone, and face to face with my own crime, had been just retribution'."

"Longfellow. He also said, 'Look not mournfully into the past. It comes not back again. Wisely improve the present. It is thine. Go forth and meet the shadowy future without fear and with a manly heart'."

"Go away."

A shaky smile crossed his lips and he kissed her forehead. "I'll be back for supper. Cora is making several meals for you. I promised her I would bring them by tonight. We will finish this discussion then."

"No, we won't." She forced a smile and squeezed his hand when he laughed as she'd wanted him to. In truth, she was surprised he'd agreed so quickly, but then she remembered Daisy was still there. He didn't want to argue in front of her, and that's exactly what they would have done if she'd had the energy for it.

"I'll see you at supper."

Jane nodded then closed her eyes when he left. The rising sob made her clamp her hand over her mouth to silence it. She gripped her stomach and bent over, trying to keep the fresh eruption of sorrow at bay until she'd heard the front door close.

The minute it did, she dropped to her knees on the floor and again let the grief free. The brief presence of others couldn't keep it at bay for long.

The aching emptiness had taken hold. The sense of life that had sprung from the knowledge of her pregnancy had moved so far away she could barely remember it.

She'd loved the child. More than she'd thought possible. So many hopes for its future, a future she'd likely never see. A lifetime of memories she'd never know. She'd wanted the child to have so much.

Cole had been right; it was all too much to bear. He'd been right to run, and run far. This pain was too great, and she hadn't even held the child in her hands. He had held Lydia.

Yes, he'd been so right to run. It was too much for a person to bear.

Her wails bounced off the walls, returning to twist the knife deeper in her heart. Each hiccup and sob revived the physical pain, strengthened the knot in her soul until she was reduced to a trembling ball on the floor that welcomed the shelter of sleep.

The oblivion couldn't save her. Dreams as deep and dark as her thoughts tormented her. The fitful throes of sleep created aches that deepened into pain until she woke with a gasp. A glance at the clock told her she'd grieved and slept for hours.

She grabbed her cane to push herself to her feet. With one hand tight around her waist, the other gripping her cane, she walked to the pantry. The gleam of a whiskey bottle caught her eye, and she snatched it close.

The fire of alcohol burned down her throat. After taking several ragged breaths, she took another long drink. It wasn't the medicine or tea Daisy had prescribed, but it would do. Maybe getting drunk would help her forget.

By the time she'd taken several more gulps her tears were dry. Anger pushed its away ahead of layers of grief. Why did this have to happen? Was it because she hadn't pushed David to allow her punishment to come?

She pondered wiring the marshal herself. It certainly was an interesting idea to her clouded mind. After all, why put it off now? There wasn't much else that mattered. If it were possible, her life was a bigger mess than Clara's had been.

A knock on the door startled her out of her misery, and she cleared her throat. Testing herself against the aches of her body, she was pleased to find the whiskey had made most of it tolerable. With a nod, she stepped from the pantry and wiped at the remnants of her grief still dampening her cheeks. "Come on in, Michael."

When the door swung open, her knees buckled at the sight on the other side. Of course Michael wouldn't knock, this was his house too, but it couldn't be Cole. No. He wasn't supposed to be here. It would be easier without him. Wasn't it?

"Don't need to come in. And I ain't Mike."

"What do you want?"

"Just making sure you know that I'm done." The words were harsh, his eyes dark. As she swayed and tried to maintain her own strength, his glower faltered. His brows turned down in a grief that echoed her own. "I won't do this again."

"I didn't need clarification. Your absence has made it quite clear." The whiskey rushed through her and filled her with false warmth, driving the heat of her anger. Her heart bled at her actions, but the fire of alcohol kept despair tamped down.

"You lost it, didn't ya? They won't tell me nothing, but the kid's gone, isn't it?"

The anger flew away at the frank assessment. Her mind faltered into a muddy mass of useless words. "Yes."

"I told you it was too much."

She was sure her mind was playing tricks on her. For a moment she would've sworn his voice cracked, the harsh tones of anger fading. A sob rose against her will and she gave in. Her hands slipped from the back of the chair as collapsed into the welcome black oblivion again.

This time her dreams afforded her a brief respite. In them she could feel his arms around her again, holding her secure and safe in a sanctuary she'd thought long gone. She clung to the dream, to him, wishing it could last forever.

"I'm here." The smooth tenor of his voice eased her nightmarish trembles.

"No, you're not." She hung on to the warmth of her dream, curled tight into what she was sure was a pillow. "You're not real."

"Just sleep, Jane. Sleep. You gotta be stronger than this."

"I'm not."

"You gotta be. You've just got to."

She whimpered and buried her face further into the dream of his chest and wept until she could weep no more. While her dreams would let her, she soaked in his warmth, the soothing touch of his hand on her back.

But as always, he was gone, and the nightmares returned.

There was no safe haven. The end would be all too soon.

The serpent may, without being poisonous, raise high its hood, but the show of terror is enough to frighten people--whether he be venomous or not.
-Chanakya

"Are you certain you're ready for this?" Mike held the door to the library partially open, as if ready to close it again at the first sign of doubt from her.

"Yes. Stop badgering me, please." Jane set her hand on his arm. Though his hovering did bother her, she appreciated the concern more than she cared to admit. "I know you're worried, but Daisy said I could go back to work."

"I'm not worried about your physical ailments."

"I know. Thank you." She gave him a kiss on the cheek before she pushed the door open the rest of the way. "But I won't continue to appreciate it if you harass me constantly. I promise if I have any trouble whatsoever, I will send for you directly or go down the street to see David."

"Does David know?"

"No." She started across the room rather than face his worry any longer. "You, Daisy, and Cole are the only ones that do know. Hopefully it will stay that way. David has not pushed me for further information, and I'm grateful for that."

"Have you seen Cole?"

"No. Not since he stopped by to ask if I'd had a miscarriage." She didn't know whether to be relieved or upset over his absence. Truthfully, she didn't know how she felt about anything most times anymore. "Is my inquisition over?"

He chuckled and hugged her. "Sorry. I am allowed to worry."

"Yes, but not here. Please, Michael. Not here." The last thing she needed was more fuel for the gossip mill by having her brother publicly worrying over her every action.

"Right. You've got work to do. How about I bring supper?" He held up his hands in surrender when she glared at him. "It's an honest gesture. I'm not snooping, I swear."

"Well, I suppose so." She wouldn't mind the company away from her own thoughts anyhow. "Long as it's not snooping, I wouldn't mind."

"Good. I'll stop by around six. We'll eat, and I'll help you until you close."

"Sounds perfect. Thank you." She pushed him toward the door. "Now go."

Once he'd left, she sank into her chair. The one difference between the quiet at home and the quiet at the library was the distraction of work and the occasional other soul perusing the shelves. If she let it, the everyday humdrum of work would be her saving grace.

And she intended to let it.

Without further ado, she hauled herself back to her feet and began to pull books from shelves, sorting by genre and then alphabetizing. With only the occasional interruption by someone looking for a book or simply checking on her, the afternoon managed to past faster than she'd thought it would.

Before she knew it, the clock chimed five. Her body ached from the work, but she was glad for it. Soon enough Michael would be along with some food, and she'd be able to relax and let him work while he kept her company.

"It's so nice to see the library open again." Jackson's smirk carried through his tone. "I don't believe the town has been quite the same without its *demure* librarian."

So much for relaxation. Jane remained seated while he strode across the room. Somehow she had to remain calm. Last thing she needed was Jackson's smarm, but here he was. She had to suffer through and not let him see a hint of her inner turmoil. "I've never once seen you in here before. Why should its state of being matter to you now?"

"Well, I was concerned for your welfare, of course. Such talk swirling around town of the way you collapsed into the arms of one of your lovers."

"Major Webb is not a lover." Goodness, that felt good to say outright after all this time. She should have done so sooner. Of course, she wished the first person she'd said it to hadn't been Jackson. She remained stock-still and seated proper as he circled the desk. "And I hardly collapsed into his arms."

"Of course not. Your denials are a little late, don't you think? I believe you'll find a few deaf ears for such things." He leaned one hand on her desk, the other on the back of her chair. "I guess you should have thought of your reputation sooner."

"It is not my reputation that is my concern, Mr. Krenshaw." The hair on the back of her neck stood on end when he leaned close. She wrinkled her nose at the moist heat of his breath along her ear. "None of this is any of your concern. What are you here for?"

"If your reputation isn't your concern, what is? The law, perhaps?"

She wasn't quite certain how she managed to remain almost still with her hands flat on the desk. The only movement she was unable to contain was a small twitch of her hand toward her head. She kept the misbehaving limb in place even as her insides roiled against the implications. "I told you. Rumors are just that, rumors."

"Rumors don't have wanted posters."

"Certainly, they do. It is called presumption of innocence."

"Still." Finally he stepped away. On his circuit around her desk, he causally kicked her cane so it clattered and rolled away.

"Once again you tax me, Mr. Krenshaw. I do enjoy good wordplay on most occasions. However, this is just you dragging out what you think is your ace in the hole. Why don't you show your cards so I might decide if you are worth any amount of panic?" She only prayed he couldn't see she was already panicked by his statement.

He pulled open his jacket and slid out a roll of paper. "This arrived for me a few days ago. I'm sure you could only imagine my surprise to see such a familiar face on it." He unrolled the paper to reveal the familiar wanted poster she herself had seen on the train.

She had no idea if she had any visible reaction, but she finally moved in hopes of hiding any tells that might sneak into the open. Her hands pressed into the desk, and she shoved herself to her feet. "I am not sure what you mean, Mr.

Krenshaw? I look in the mirror every day and from what I can tell, that picture has only a passing resemblance."

"You're too modest."

"And the name on that poster is Constance Pinot Querney. I am entirely unsure who that could possibly be. I have never heard of her, and all reports are that my name before my amnesia was Clara Young Schaffer." She bent to pick up her cane, upset to find her hand shaking.

"My man is looking into it. I'm certain we'll find some tie between you and this name."

"We. Impressive. You fancy yourself a sleuth because you have hired a man to do the work for you?" She stood again, pressing her hands firm onto the cane to hide their trembling. "You, Mr. Krenshaw, have found nothing. Nothing for me to be frightened of. Not that you much care, as you are after nothing else but torment."

"No. I'm looking for justice."

"No. I don't believe you are."

He chuckled, a dark sound that sent the familiar slithering shiver down her spine. "I suppose we'll see. Here," he set the poster on her desk, "keep it. I have several more copies at home. Perhaps they'll go up around town, see if anyone knows this Constance?"

Jane clenched and unclenched her jaw. As she'd been contemplating her next suggestion herself, the only pain she felt in it was that it was being made to a man bent on destroying her quite thoroughly. "If you believe anyone might. I'm sure the marshal of the territory would appreciate assistance in apprehending this murderess."

"I'm certain he would. Marshal Lewis shouldn't be bothered until we're certain though, should he?" He smiled.

"At least now you have something to go on in your search for truth. You are still looking into your past, right? Or did you give up when you found out you were a criminal? I'm sure most people would understand if you did."

"I haven't given up. I dare say that I'll find the real truth before you do."

"Oh dear. You haven't got the resources, or if you do, you aren't using them."

She pinched her brow together at the last comment, trying to imagine what on earth he could mean. At the moment, it didn't matter, what did matter was getting him out of the library. She needed time to digest it all. "I appreciate your attempt at candor. Now if you please, I do have work to do."

"Of course. Good luck, Jane."

Jane remained by her desk as he left, staring at the wanted poster. Once the crisp steps stopped reverberating off the floorboards, indicating he'd made it to the street, she rushed to the door fast as she could. She stood on the porch to make sure his departure was thorough. When he rounded the corner by the saloon, Jackson tipped his hat toward the porch.

A few moments later, Cole stepped around the corner, a deep frown on his features.

"Jane." David's voice reached her the same time Cole turned away. "Is everything all right? What was Jackson doing here?"

"More threats. I'd almost think he was in league with Johnny at this point, but he doesn't have enough information."

"You sure he doesn't have more than he's telling you?"

"Not completely, but Jackson isn't good at keeping things close to the belt. He's been anxious to show me the wanted poster for days, but I haven't been at work."

"Did he tell you what he's up to?" He gently touched her elbow and led her back into the library. "So we know if there's anything to be concerned about?"

"He's looking to see if there's any connection between Clara and Constance." Jane sighed. Back at her desk, she sank into her chair. "Which we've already done."

"And we found nothing solid linking you two. A young woman, daughter of General Pinot. She was married to Jake and disappeared when she was pregnant. According to the papers, she was never found, and they didn't know who did it."

"But we suspect it's this Johnny." She rubbed her temples. "Based on what I remember Clara saying to Jake, it sounded like Johnny was obsessed with Constance."

"Which doesn't help us since we know Johnny isn't his real name, and official records of any sort are difficult to come by."

"Precisely. What wasn't burned in the war was buried by Confederates with more power than a simple Colorado Territory sheriff." Jane smiled. "The question is: will a Pinkerton have more luck than you did?"

"Only if he had sympathy for the south in the war."

"Well then, I hope whoever Jackson has in his pocket is a thorough Yankee."

Never despair;
but if you do, work on in despair.
-Edmund Burke

For nearly two whole days she'd been back at work. The normality of the routine and the intensity she'd been focusing on the rearranging of the shelves helped distract her from everything. Nothing could take away the gaping hole she thought might never leave, but at least it kept her busy.

When she wasn't at the library, she spent every minute with David, Michael, or out at the Army camp with Al. Anything to keep from returning to her empty house. The memories contained with it. The incessant dreams of Cole's arms around her, his strength pushing her toward healing she didn't feel ready for. She had to stop thinking about him. Somehow, she had to stop.

Michael's constant fussing dragged her down so much she'd finally yelled at him to stop. Instead, he now prattled ceaselessly about the bevy of town gossip that continued without her shenanigans. He told her Rusty had taken on Arthur as his apprentice at the newspaper.

Through him she learned of the arrival of Martha's sister, Katherine. A woman with a reputation of her own, vibrant red hair, and an apparent personality to match. He also told her she wandered about town in pants like a man.

Of course, he confirmed the rumors of Cole spending time with Becky, Graham's fiancée.

She was certain he'd thrown in that bit of news out of pure spite, and a misdirected sense of protection. He wanted to be positive she wouldn't return to Cole's side. Right then she didn't need the help. As much as she longed to turn to Cole, her pride wouldn't let her, and neither would he. He was done. He'd said as much himself.

She suspected he simply couldn't handle the pain after the death of his first child years before. Instead, he ignored it. The result being she suffered alone.

Truly alone in so many ways seeing as none but Daisy and Michael knew what had happened to her. Every step she took through town was careful, a mask of happiness she didn't feel plastered in place. A joy she'd once known and felt now a mere echo in the depth of her private grief.

Writing carefully in the book in front of her, she blew on the ink to dry it before setting the book aside and working on the next. She couldn't explain how comforting the smell of the library, all book dust and ink, had become for her. When she walked in the door every morning it washed over her and relaxed her. She'd even considered sleeping there.

It was a ridiculous idea of course, but she had to admit the idea of putting a bed in the unused kitchen of the library was far more tempting than it should be. Even with the negotiations with the Indians close to over, Jane still harbored a sense of unease being outside of town when Michael stayed in town.

Perhaps it was the negotiations, or the fear that Johnny would return, or pure, simple loneliness. Whatever it was, if she didn't consider it wasteful to not use her perfectly good homestead, she'd spend every night right there in the library.

In just a few days she would be faced with the warriors who were turning themselves in to the Army to be sent to the reservation. Al had warned her in advance, asking if she'd feel strong enough to identify the man who had shot her.

She was nowhere near strong enough for everyday life, much less identifying the man who had shot her. However, as she did every second of her life any longer, she'd do it anyway. If it meant an end to part of her turmoil, she'd be happy to do so. To see the memory of her shooting buried with so many others where they belonged. Where she could handle them. In her own time, in her own privacy.

The door opened, and Jane closed the book in front of her before looking up. The smile she'd put on strained to remain in place as she took in the proper young woman that had entered. "Afternoon, Miss Becky."

"Miss Jane." Becky nodded stiff and with a smile as taut as Jane imagined her own to be. "I was hoping we had a certain book in the library. It isn't one I've had occasion to look for before, so I wasn't sure."

Jane nodded as she pushed herself to her feet. "I've also added some of my own books since I started building on what was here. What is it you're looking for?"

"*Leaves of Grass*."

"Whitman. My favorite." Jane's voice cracked, and she cleared her throat. The book she'd left at Cole's once again. She'd yet to get another copy for herself. It was simple coincidence. She had to stop taking everything to heart. "There is a copy here. I made sure of it."

"Oh, good. I need it for, um, something." Becky rolled her hands together, a bright smile crossing her features—a fake smile that didn't reach her eyes. "Well, I suppose it doesn't matter why I need it now, does it?"

"Of course not." The heat rose to her cheeks fast, so Jane turned to the shelves. In her rush to avoid the woman she'd left her cane at the desk so she had to limp, but went straight to the book. She pulled it from the shelf and ran her hands over the cover with a sigh.

It was brand new. She'd not had the opportunity to take it out herself. Most people preferred Whitman's tamer words, not the vibrant, sensual book she now held in her hands. She hardly thought Becky was the kind, but then again, she'd not thought her the kind to make time with a man like Cole.

Her heart twisted as she carried the book back, fighting tears she didn't want Becky to see. With easy elegance, she wrote the date in her ledger and held it out to the woman across her desk. "Sign here. Might I suggest *I Sing the Body Electric*? It's one of my favorites."

Bright red hues crossed up Becky's bosom straight to her cheeks and her hand shook as she signed her name. Becky made no bones about her station in life and would never do anything to cross lines of impropriety on most occasions. Jane wondered if the woman had ever been kissed.

Most likely she hadn't received more than a chaste peck in her time. The woman's father was strict as they came, and near as she could tell not even her courting with Graham had been more than ceremony. The two were hardly together.

How on earth Cole had wrangled her from the clutches of the man was beyond her, but then again, Cole was good at many things that were surprising. She inwardly flinched at her thoughts returning to him. She really had to stop it.

A deep frown creased Becky's features. "I don't think that will be necessary."

"You'd be surprised." Jane fought the welling levels of pain. She'd kept it at bay for days. The simple presence of the priss before her wouldn't make her give into it. Rather than let herself feel it, she took a wicked twist to make the woman uncomfortable again. "The words are enough to have a strong effect on men that claim to have no appreciation of poetry."

"I'll keep it in mind," Becky mumbled. "Miss Jane."

The clock chimed, and the tension flew from Jane's shoulders in an instant. She was saved from further torment with that one chime. "The book is due back in two weeks. If you'd like to keep it longer, please let me know. For now I must close. I have an appointment."

"Yes, of course. I have one myself." Becky pulled the book close. With unnecessary care, she covered the title before darting from the building.

Jane let herself collapse into the chair, staring where Becky had disappeared. It had been childish to rile the priss, but she had little control over herself these days. Perhaps another day she'd bother to care, but not today.

The panes of glass distorted the town into wavy, murky lines, each flickering and jumping as the lamps were lit. For a moment she forgot her appointment, getting lost in the patterns and shadows that passed.

Not one of them knew. Pretending was so much easier when they didn't. David and Al suspected, but she wouldn't confirm or deny anything. They wouldn't understand, so there was no point in explaining. Plus, she could not stand the thought of any more pity.

One of the shadows grew closer and larger, and a hint of a smile tugged at her lips. Pretending was truly so much easier when there were others around. David's arrival was just what she needed to continue her distraction. She picked up the two books left on the desk to put them away when the door opened.

"David, you're right on time. Are you ready for this evening's lesson?"

"Ready as I ever am. Lee is relishing the idea she is further ahead than I am and can skip a few lessons."

"She should relish it. She's been working very hard while you've been lazy."

"I've been helping a friend." When she finally faced him, he kissed her forehead. "You're looking well. Much better than the other day."

"It feels good to do what I'm used to, to return to a routine. Jackson has stayed away for a few days." It wasn't a total lie; she just didn't feel perfect again. She felt better, though; better than she had at her worst for sure. "Let me get my things."

He picked up the books she'd strapped in leather and shook his head. "Nah. I'll get them. That way you can take my arm."

Somehow a genuine laugh found its way to the surface. "David. You look like a schoolboy carrying my books that way."

"Something wrong with that?"

"We're a bit too old for such things."

"Speak for yourself. I'm as young as a spring chicken. I'll be twenty forever."

Jane snorted as she locked the door. "Of course you are. I'm as virginal as Mary too."

"Jane."

She laughed and laced her arm with his. The muddy streets clung to their shoes and her cane, making their journey slow. "What?"

"Incorrigible."

"Always."

His chuckle was followed by a squeeze to her hand. "There's a storm heading in tonight. Why don't you stay at Cora's? Then you wouldn't have to worry about weathering the storm alone."

"I don't know. We'll see how I feel after supper."

"Oh good." He flashed his teeth and winked. "Then I can make sure to enlist Arthur to help me convince you."

"Now that isn't fair."

"Maybe not, but it will work."

She pursed her lips and turned up her nose, huffing a grunt of displeasure. He was right. Arthur would be able to convince her, despite her reservations about staying under the same roof as David and Jesse.

Several greetings from friends slowed their pace further, and by the time they got to Turner's, it was nearly dark. The good news was that the supper rush would be almost over. The bad news was it made David's argument to stay in town that much stronger.

They weren't two steps in the door when she stopped short. She'd managed to avoid seeing Cole for two days. Now he was there, sitting very close to Becky, at a table nestled in the corner.

Their conversation was focused, intense, the Whitman book open between them. They kept their heads huddled together, intent on each other alone.

Jane felt a lump rise in her throat and moved to leave, but David's hand closed around her arm. "Don't let him get to you."

Jane took a ragged breath and tore her gaze from the pair. "I'm sorry. You're right. After all, he's just a man, right?"

"Never thought much of us before."

Her lips twitched as she tried to hide the laughter, but it escaped quickly. "True."

"So come in. Sit and eat. Cora said she was making venison stew."

"Yum." She squeezed his arm and leaned up to kiss his cheek. "Thank you."

"Don't thank me. I'm just stating facts." He held out a chair for her and set the books down before heading back toward the kitchen.

Jane let out a long breath as she took in the situation. After a moment she chuckled to herself. David had sat her with her back to the corner. Sometimes he was smarter than she gave him credit for. Of course, her position didn't prevent her from hearing Cole's loud laughter.

Her stomach twisted and roiled, threatening to erupt. Maybe she couldn't do this. Not yet at least. Then again, he knew it was hurting her. The last thing she wanted to do was give him the satisfaction of running from the scene.

Taking a deep breath, she opened her purse and pulled out the envelope that had been inside it for days. It was addressed to the marshal. She hadn't sent it yet, and had no idea why not. Didn't she want the interminable wait to end?

Cora and David's laughter danced out from the kitchen, lifting her spirits a little. No, she wanted to live first. Right now she wasn't living. When she remembered how to live, then she'd be prepared to face the end. To accept whatever fate had in store for her.

First she needed to live.

Couarge is fire, and bullying is smoke.
—Benjamin Disraeli

Cole slowed Faro at the bottom of the hill. The road before him wound its way through the larger homes of the wealthier settlement. Homes much larger than the families they held were a stark contrast the wild country on the mountains that served as their backdrop.

His nose wrinkled, but he spurred Faro on up the road. The largest house at the top of the hill was his destination. For its one occupant, it was the most obscene display of wealth. Once upon a time, it had been the Daugherty's home, as had all the land now filled with houses.

Back then the home had been smaller, and well suited, if a little too big, for a family of four, then three, then two. When the Daugherty's had left for Denver, Jackson had bought the home and land, then sold the land for far more than its worth. He'd made a killing and built onto the once grand but simple home until it was a monstrosity.

The amount of staff Jackson needed to run it left Cole thinking the man had to be insane. All Cole wanted or needed was simple. One room was enough. No one ever cleaned it for him. He did what was needed. Staff was a pointless waste of money.

When he crested the hill, the dirt road gave way to cobblestone. Another display of wealth.

Cole wondered what in the hell he was doing. A man with this amount of money wanted nothing from Cole. All he had in his hand was threats.

Threats he was more than happy to make good on, but he doubted that mattered to Jackson.

The door opened before Cole had stopped. A man stood shadowed in the doorway. It wasn't Jackson; that was all Cole could tell.

The guy was tall and skinny, and when he stepped onto the porch, there was no way to describe the man but bored. A long sallow face with jowls that wagged when he spoke in a low drone. "Mr. Krenshaw is not receiving."

"Too bad." Cole hopped down from Faro. He wrapped the reins around the banister. "'Cause I'm delivering."

The bushy gray eyebrows twitched, as did the large nose. The butler sniffed and lifted his chin. "Your attempts at humor aside, Mr. Krenshaw is still not receiving."

"Who's gonna stop me?" Just before Cole charged up the steps, the door opened again.

Jackson frowned. "It's all right, Godfrey. I'll handle this."

The butler bowed to Jackson before going inside.

"What do you want, Cole?" Jackson folded his arms across his chest and peered down his nose. "I don't have time for the likes of you."

Cole's temper flared. He hated being looked down on, especially by someone like Jackson. He climbed the steps two at a time until he towered over Jackson. "But ya do got time to harass Jane?"

"Coming to the harlot's defense? If I didn't know better, I'd think you were being noble."

"You don't know nothing."

"I know enough, Mr. Spencer."

Ice ran through Cole's veins at the name. No one knew about the name Spencer, not even Jane. The one person that should have known was her. Not this bastard. He wasn't about to let Jackson think it meant a damn thing. He curled his lip and leaned toward Jackson. "I don't know what you're talking about, Jack. What I wanna know is why her?"

"Why not? She's a criminal, although you know all about that yourself, don't you? I guess the pair of you are a better match than we thought. Not that it matters any longer if the rumors are true." Jackson's lips curled into a snake-like smile. "What was it I heard? She went with the major again? Or was that her husband?"

Cole's hands curled into fists. If he wouldn't find himself in jail for it, he'd deal Jackson a few good blows. Cole's own wonderings over Jane's behavior aside, he'd made mistakes since her pregnancy. A lot of them. The hole he'd dug was so deep he didn't know how to get out. The reminder he'd pushed Jane away, maybe into another man's arms was enough to make him want to pound someone. Preferably Jackson.

Jackson laughed low and slow. "Well, well. The dunce is speechless yet again. Maybe you should go back to school and learn some proper English. Or is that you're doing with Miss Carmichael? Or are you just feeling up to the task of sullying yet another reputation as you did Miss Doe's?"

Like I would touch Becky Carmichael. Cole snorted. "Are you trying to make me feel bad 'bout something?"

"No. Not at all. Just giving you a friendly warning."

"You don't scare me, Jack. Not a lick." Cole took a step toward the bastard. It amused him to see the man step back. For all his bluster, Jackson was still the same simpering wimp he'd always been. Cole wasn't scared of him, no matter what he thought he knew. "There ain't nothing you can do to me. I got nothing to hide."

"Somehow I don't believe you." The ass kept going with his bravado. Jack straightened with a smirk. "Jane, though. She's got plenty to hide, doesn't she? One simple wire to the right person and—"

Cole saw red when Jackson mimed being hanged. Before he had time to second-guess himself, he grabbed Jackson by the throat and slammed him into the side of the house. Panes rattled in the windows. "Leave her be. She ain't done nothing to you but embarrass ya. Most the men in town of guilty of the same."

Jackson's eyes bulged when Cole squeezed tighter, but somehow the man still smiled. It made no sense.

"Cole," David hollered from below him, "let him go."

Now it made sense. Cole narrowed his eyes. After another long second when Jack's lips took on a blue color, he released the cretin. He stepped back two whole steps, ready to move again at the next bit of threat toward Jane. "Son of a bitch."

"Sheriff," Jackson squeaked and rubbed his throat. "I'm relieved to see you got my wire. This man came to my house and assaulted me for no reason."

"No-account bastard." Cole clenched his fists.

"Cole, don't." David, for his part, didn't sound at all demanding in the request. It cut through Cole's anger to realize the sheriff sounded downright bored and lazy with the order.

"Did you know I have a telegraph in my office, Cole?" Though his voice was rough, and he still rubbed his throat, Jack managed a smarmy grin. "It's most convenient for a man such as myself, in my powerful position, to have easy access to communication. I called for the sheriff before you ever dismounted."

"Leave her be." Cole narrowed his eyes. "Don't matter none what you think you can do to me. Just let her be."

"Noble. Pointless and weak, but noble, I suppose." Jackson cleared his throat. When he spoke again, he raised his voice so David could hear him. "I want him arrested, Sheriff. For assault and trespassing."

"I know. You already said so in your telegram. Funny how you knew he'd stoop to assault." David climbed the steps. Rather than grab Cole, or place him in shackles, he merely touched Cole's arm. "Let's go, Cole. Only thing you'll accomplish here is more time in jail, and neither of us wants to be around each other that long."

Cole jerked his arm away from David's reaching hand to stormed down the steps. He ignored the resulting conversation on the porch. Jackson was toying with them, and somehow he'd learned about Cole's past. Cole knew that by the simple fact that Jackson had used his given name, one Cole himself hadn't used since he'd left California.

"Let's move before you do something else stupid or Jackson comes up with something else to throw at you." David hopped up into his saddle. When Cole didn't immediately respond, he frowned. "Don't make me force the issue, Cole. Just come peacefully and you'll be out of jail in a day or two."

Cole muttered every curse he knew but pulled himself into his saddle. He urged Faro to follow David's horse. When David slowed, Cole tried not to notice.

"What were you doing at Jackson's? He'd find any reason to throw you in jail; you do know that, right? Any reason at all. He loves to play powerful. Was this about Jane?"

"None of your damn business." Cole fought the urge to spur Faro into a run and leave David in the dust. It would be so easy, but he knew better. Besides, if he ran now, he'd leave Jane more alone than he already had.

If Jackson had thrown his threats and money into the ring, Cole had to find some way to compete with that. Jane was too busy figuring out what she'd done and trying to find Johnny to have to worry about what Jack was up to.

That was it; Cole had to get some power behind Jane. But how? He didn't have much money to spare. All that he had was earmarked for his usual responsibilities.

What he did have was a few favors he might call in.

Nothing here. It was too close to home and under nosy Jack's eyes. Plus, if that crazed maniac was anywhere around, he needed to think anything Cole did wasn't for Jane. He frowned. That meant holding off his apologies longer. Not that apologies would do any good at this point.

If rumor were true, she was finding solace with Major Webb, or Davie himself. Cole grunted, wanting nothing more than to believe that wasn't true. Then again, didn't she need comfort? The baby was gone, and he'd seen proof of her grief himself.

Comfort. The idea of the kid being his and once again taken from him turned his stomach as fresh as it had the day Graham had carried Jane to the clinic. The only comfort he had now was making sure Jane didn't suffer for Clara. He didn't deserve comfort any longer.

Damn, he was a bastard. He snorted. "Bastard."

"Cole?" David cast him a sideways look. "You going to give me trouble? Or go in nice and easy? I'm not in the mood for a fight."

"I ain't fighting you, Davie. Bastard knew you were coming. Didn't take much to rile me up. Just don't expect me to like it."

"I wouldn't dream of it."

*All that is necessary for the triumph of evil
is for good men to do nothing.*
—Edmund Burke

Obtuse.

The lot of men and women. Completely obtuse.

Once again he'd managed to insinuate himself in the mining town of Dominion Falls. All he'd had to do to avoid detection was stay clear of Clara and her brother. They were clever enough to spot him. No one else was. Ever.

Even now as he sat in the saloon of Clara's lover, right in front of the man, he wasn't recognized. He'd had to place black wax on some teeth, lose every bit of extra weight, and adopt a vernacular of the crudest form. A few days' work in the mines without a bath left him filthy enough to mix in with the local riff raff.

Child's play, really.

Cole looked right at him, served him beer—and nothing.

So very easy.

Of course he knew Clara and the idiot behind the bar had parted ways. No one in the town balked at gossip. They thrived on it, and he was all too happy to listen.

To his great luck, Clara appeared to be highly distracted. And ill. The woman that had challenged him on the train, and tricked him in Frisco, now couldn't be bothered to notice the new miner in town. Most of the time she holed up in the library.

An easy target.

All he had to do was complete his perfect revenge.

Make her suffer.

Until she begged him to take back his money and leave her alone.

Not that he would ever let her be.

No, Constance needed to be where she belonged. Where she could no longer haunt him.

She needed a reminder.

One that left no mistake he hadn't forgotten her. He'd never forget, and she shouldn't either.

He'd taunt her for a while.

Tease her with threats she wasn't expecting. Threats that didn't need words.

She'd let loose the insanity he knew she held.

Until she had no defense against him or anyone else.

Then set the law on her.

Once he did that, she'd cave. Run for the hills. Right into his waiting trap.

Sometimes I dream of running. If only it could be so easy to escape. Naïve enough to fall into his trap, too smart to be foolish enough to think I could extricate myself from it.

Jane pinched her lip tight between her fingers as she studied the paper before her. She had to connect the lines somehow.

The simple piece of paper in her hands was almost completely covered in ink. Every word Clara had written in the margins of the Poe book now covered it. Lines of text filled the space, written compact and tight. There seemed to be no common thread except the man she'd found herself tied to. Most of the sentences were simple, clear mentions of the insanity and cleverness of Johnny.

Then there was the text about wanting to run. Different than the others. She didn't dare hope it meant Clara wasn't a criminal—but perhaps she'd been unwilling.

Most hopeful of all was a small bit of text, buried so deep in the binding she'd almost missed the handful of words.

What happened? I only remember pain,
but not birth.

If Clara didn't remember the birth, what could have happened? How did Jesse receive David's middle name?

"You missed supper." Michael's voice reverberated through the empty library.

Jane lifted the bucket beside her, not bothering to comment as she set it down. The words before her, the puzzle they presented, were far too important for distraction.

"Eating on the job, then? What are you doing?" He tapped the top of the paper. The only thing that saved him from having his hand smacked was that he didn't try to pull it away.

"I have a meeting with David shortly. Was there something I could help you with?"

"Another meeting with David? That's almost every night the past few weeks. How does Lee feel about that?"

"Oh, Lee's coming as well." She waved off his teasing concern and assumptions. She hadn't the time for subterfuge any longer. "I took all the things Clara wrote in the Poe book and wrote them down trying to make sense of the whole thing. There appears to be no sort of timeline to it, so I'm not sure if there is any rhyme or reason."

He flipped through the Poe book casually. "Sure doesn't seem to be. Almost looks more like you used the book as a random confessional."

"Not enough of a confessional, I'm afraid. None of these outbursts say anything of significance." She pinched the bridge of her nose and blinked against the blurriness in her eyes. She'd been deciphering and staring at the words all day long. Even if she had them memorized, she couldn't stop reading them over and over.

"You've got these remembered, right?" As if he'd read her mind, Mike repeated her thoughts back to her. "So why don't you let me have the paper and I'll look it over tonight. I knew Clara like I know myself."

She snorted at the irony of his statement. "Of course you did. That's precisely why you don't know where she was for seven years."

"Bitter and unnecessary."

"Sorry."

He laughed at her grumpy tone. "No, you're not, but I appreciate the sentiment. Let me give it a go anyway, will you? I thought you'd learned that you don't have to shoulder this whole thing by yourself."

"I hate feeling like I'm not in control. It's all I've felt like lately. I thought maybe for once I could control this. But I can't. Clara won't let me in."

The bucket clattered across the floor, and Mike's hand rested warm on her back. "You have done nothing but focus on this for weeks. Maybe it's time for a break."

"No!" She sat up so fast her head hit his arm. If she didn't focus on this, she'd have to focus on other things: her impending divorce, Cole, the baby that never was, Johnny – who could be anywhere. Her lungs stopped working, and her jaw clenched tight against the sudden pressure of the emotions she'd buried.

"All right. I'm sorry."

"The Indians." The words came out choked and weak, but she forced the change of subject forward. Something, anything but the pain.

"What about them?" He took the change of subject in stride, but slid the paper she'd written on off the desk.

"They're signing the treaty soon. Next week, right?"

"That's the word. David and his friend Black Moon are working on some issues with the treaty." Mike sat across from her, slipping the now-folded paper into his jacket pocket. With its disappearance, her muscles relaxed. "But you already knew that."

"Perhaps. Al and I might have discussed it."

"How is Al? David's the one that deals with him most of the time. I'm so busy with changing that hotel over and deputy work I don't bother worrying about the Indian news except what David tells me at the office."

"He's healing remarkably well. Like any man, he doesn't believe his recovery is fast enough."

"Any man? Does that make you a man?"

"No. It makes me stubborn." She stuck her tongue out at him playfully. "As I was saying. He's not up to full strength or able to fully use his arm yet. With the shot so close to his shoulder, he's not certain he'll regain full use of it again."

"I suppose that is a possibility."

Jane leaned on her desk. "Now what are you doing with the Silver Saddle? Only people I have seen go in and out are patients."

"I can't see any good in opening a hotel that disgusts me with its décor." He chuckled. "So I'm ripping out all of the garish decorations Guy used to represent wealth."

"And?"

"I haven't fully decided yet. I have a few ideas."

She stared him down until he squirmed. "Don't play games with me, Mike. You're the one that said I needed distraction—so tell me already."

"I've considered the health resort and spa route. I've visited a few and seen what draw they have, and Dominion Falls is a strategically secluded town for such a thing. However, the location of the Silver Saddle is horrible."

"I imagine not. It is in the center of town."

"The way the building is set up doesn't allow for much expansion, either."

She twisted her lips as she thought it over. "No, it doesn't. You could certainly build more walls downstairs to allow for the appropriate rooms, but that would close off your reception area."

"Exactly."

"While the style of the hotel was horrendous, Guy was right to leave it wide open and put in so many windows."

"And to white wall the interior."

"Precisely." She tapped a nail on the desk. "That doesn't leave you with many options, not with your existing building. What are you going to do?"

"Before I bought the Silver Saddle, I got a piece of land near the foothills. Soon as those treaty talks began the land office expanded its offerings, so I jumped on it."

"You didn't tell me that."

"You were a little busy." He had a point. For so long she'd been distracted or distraught, or both at the same time. Some days simply getting out of bed was the battle, other days she felt almost normal.

Almost.

He shrugged. "Not only that. I honestly had no idea what I'd do with the land. We have a house near the depot, so I had no need to build. I just thought I should buy it before anyone else had a chance to. It's a nice area. There's even a small waterfall back in the woods."

"Perfect for what you want to do—if you have the capital to build something like that. Would you sell the Silver Saddle to get it?"

"Don't want to do that."

"You need capital."

"But it would make a perfect clinic with all those rooms."

Actual amusement rose to the surface, unlike she'd felt in weeks. Jane had to close her mouth when she realized she'd left it hanging open. She fought against the smile. "I see."

"Jane."

"No. No, you're right. It really would. It does."

When her laughter escaped, he grabbed a small stack of letters from the desk and threw them at her. "Stop it."

"No. I think it's adorable."

"Jane."

"Michael. Don't. Don't you dare." She held out her hand and her chair screeched back when he started toward her again. With a shriek, she leaped from the chair and darted across the room.

He held the mug of water she'd left on her desk threateningly in the air. While he remained just out of reach to touch her, the water would certainly hit her. "I don't want to hear it."

"I didn't say anything."

"You'd better not."

"I wouldn't dare. But if I did…"

"Don't."

I have great faith in fools –
my friends call it self-confidence.
–Edgar Allan Poe

After a visit with Al, Jane made her way across the Army camp to a well-guarded tent. She nodded to the sergeant guarding the door as she passed.

She pushed aside the canvas flap and poked her head inside the tent. As her eyes adjusted, she saw no sign of the prisoner inside at first. That seemed odd since Al had just told her Martha had been pretty stagnant since she learned the renegades would be turning themselves in. She stepped inside and let the canvas drop with a sharp slap. "Martha?"

The blankets on the cot moved, and one arm reached into the air. When Martha sat up, a huge yawn stretched her mouth. "Yes? Oh, Jane. I didn't expect to see you again."

"I would have come sooner, but—"

"You've been busy." Martha pushed aside the blankets enough to sit on the edge of the cot. "I'm sure you wouldn't be surprised to hear that rumors carry fast and far. Even to the isolation of an army prison tent."

"How could I be surprised? Rumors in this town travel faster than currency." Jane sat on a chair near the bed. When Martha ran a hand along her well-swollen belly, Jane's heart twisted. While she certainly hadn't forgotten Martha was pregnant, she'd hoped she'd be far more able to handle it. She'd been wrong, so she diverted her eyes rather than face it. "How are you holding up?"

"I still don't even know if Lewis is alive. Or, if he is, what the renegades did to him."

"Word is that we'll all know soon enough."

"He didn't shoot you."

"I'll know it was him, Martha. If it wasn't, I'll say as much."

"I know you will." Martha sighed. Her shoulders drooped as she tugged the blankets back up to her chin, hiding the child she carried. "Things were better before the general arrived. He isn't as considerate as Major Webb."

"He doesn't appear to be, from what little I've seen." Jane leaned on her knees. "Has Lloyd been able to help you at all?"

"He's tried to do what he can. Unfortunately he can't come to Washington with me. There might be an associate of his that will work on my case. If my mother has any say in the matter, she'll be hiring some high-priced lawyer in Washington to work the case."

"Good. I doubt the charges will stick."

"I'd rather win knowing my lawyer cared more about me than my parents' wealth and status." Martha frowned and picked at some dirt under her nail. "Especially since those parents disowned me when I married Lewis."

"You said yourself a child changes your perspective. Perhaps your mother wants to know her grandchild. Maybe time has changed her." Jane sucked her lips between her teeth to cover her grin at Martha's snort.

"The only thing Mother does is get more proper. More uptight. Everything is always about what others think. Impressions over truth.

"Interesting."

"What?"

"Here I always thought you were the uptight one. You've always been so concerned about what everyone thought." Jane smirked. "Like mother, like daughter?"

"I'm *nothing* like her."

"You aren't?"

"No." Martha sat straight and lifted her chin. "I resent the implication."

"For months you tried to tell me how proper women act, and then derided me for being nothing like a proper woman. You judged my relationship with Cole before it was anything more than friendship. You yelled at me for uncovering my legs when I was lying in bed recovering and hotter than blazes all because you felt it was indecent."

"I was trying to make things easier for you. I'm sure you've well noticed by now. People around here talk."

"I don't care what people say. They would talk if I was a saint." Jane shook her head and looked away. This wasn't going like she'd hoped. Then again, she had no dog in this fight; she was just trying to be decent.

Jane sighed. "You'll never see it as I did, but for me it was just as you have described your mother. Someone looking down their nose at me for not being a proper woman. I don't care for proper. I'll be satisfied with good-hearted."

"Is that enough?" For once there was no sign of disdain in Martha's tones or features. All Jane could see there was simple curiosity.

Because of that, Jane answered with a nod. "For me it is."

"Then you are lucky."

"If you say so."

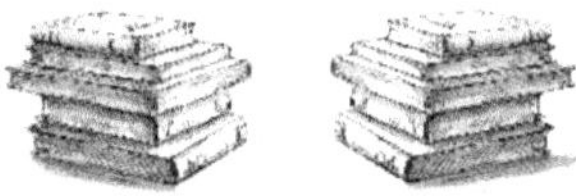

No calculations of interest, no schemes of policy can do the work of love, of the spirit of human brotherhood.
—William Ellery Channing

A day in jail had given Cole nothing but time to think, which turned out to be exactly what he needed. The minute Lloyd managed his release, Cole was at the depot sending telegrams to connections he had in Denver. There was one in particular who he knew would help no matter what he asked.

He'd bought his ticket for Denver the same day.

It hadn't brightened his day to see Becky boarding the same train. From what he could tell, Graham hadn't been too pleased either. Cole had no idea why. Graham knew Cole couldn't stand the uppity woman. What was more, Graham didn't like Becky any more than Cole did. He was marrying her for a dowry, not affection.

In Pueblo he'd had to switch trains, and at the station Becky had tried to get his attention. Cole ignored her and hoped that would be the end of it. He had far too much on his mind to worry about Becky and whatever harping she had in mind.

Unfortunately, his attempt to ignore the woman had the opposite impact than he'd hoped it would. She dared to step out of her plush cabin and in with the common folk in the passenger car. Cole knew better than to feel honored.

"Mr. Mitchell, we need to talk." Becky dusted the seat across from him with her kerchief. Once the imagined dirt was gone, she edged into the space between the seats and perched on the edge of the seat she'd just cleaned. With her back straight and hands folded in her lap, she kept her prim and proper look too well.

Cole scoffed and looked out the window. "No. We don't got nothing to talk about."

"I'm afraid we do. Our little arrangement is going to need to end."

"What?" Cole snapped around so fast Becky gasped and backed away. "No. We had an agreement. I paid you in full, and you're gonna finish the job."

"It's not possible." Becky dabbed her neck with the handkerchief. "Do you have any idea what the folks in town have been saying? About me?"

"You knew what you were getting into. I told ya what would happen straight off." He leaned back and smirked as her nose wrinkled. "You said no one would dare speak of you like that. It ain't my fault you didn't believe me. You took my money quick enough, so you finish what you started."

"It upsets Graham."

"Like you care."

She flushed bright red. "Of course I care. He is to be my husband."

"Because none other in town with any sort of standing would have ya. No matter what sort of dowry your pa threw out there. Graham's just the first one stupid enough to believe your money's gonna make him happy."

"Your view of our relationship is inaccurate and bolstered by your own warped views."

"Suit yourself. You still gotta follow through."

"Well then at least let me tell Graham what we are doing. I do not need him acting jealous for no reason."

"No." Cole glared at her. "Nobody needs to know I'm learning to read. It ain't none of their business anyhow."

"Are you embarrassed?"

"No." He wasn't, really. Most people in town knew he couldn't read by now. He just wanted to be sure the first person that learned what he was doing was Jane. Problem was figuring out how to tell her since she wasn't speaking to him. At least he didn't think she was. He still hadn't gathered the courage to try. Cole grinned before Becky could question further. "But you are."

"What woman wouldn't be? You know what they're saying about us."

Jane wouldn't be, although now both of them were facing some consequences to their more outlandish acts. "And anyone that believes I'd take you to bed belongs in an asylum. They'd be right plumb-crazy."

"Well." She flinched and her lips twisted in what he would almost call offense. "I could say the same."

"You really wish you could." Cole chuckled when she flew to her feet. He gripped her wrist before she could storm off. "We had a deal and you've been paid."

"I think you've learned all you can."

"That so?"

"Yes." She twisted her hand free of his grasp. "We're done, Mr. Mitchell. If you want to learn more, I suggest you ask Miss Doe."

"So I ain't done learning."

"I'll return half your money to you. I will not let you continue to embarrass me."

"I ain't done nothing to embarrass you. That was all them and their rumor and gossip. All I did was get reading lessons. Not my fault ya let talk bother you." Cole smirked when she flounced away. If Becky wouldn't help him, that didn't just leave Jane. Kat was back in town. If she stayed long enough, maybe he could get her to help him finish his learning. At least that half-crazy woman still spoke to him.

He sighed and rubbed his hands over his face. Nowadays it seemed like he couldn't even say one word to Jane. Never used to be a problem, even though he was never good with words. He was a man of action. But he knew that wasn't close to good enough for Jane. Not this time. She deserved more.

And he planned to give it to her somehow.

If only he could figure out how.

Since there is nothing so well worth having as friends, never lose a chance to make them.
-Francesco Guicciardini

Michael turned the book over in his hands. As Jane sat in silence, he lifted and tilted and turned it several more times. His brows knit together and he shook his head. "I don't understand. What is it?"

"It isn't another code?" With that hope out the window, Jane rested her chin on her hand with a pout. "I couldn't make sense of it for anything. I was hoping you'd have some idea, as you claim to be the puzzle master."

"Har, har." He brought the book close to his face. "Well, it is your handwriting."

"You don't say?"

His glare held no amusement. "I could go back to work."

"Of course you could, but work isn't nearly as interesting as this puzzle."

"Maybe it is."

With a smirk, she shrugged and reached for the book. "Fine."

"No." He tugged it close and turned it over again. "You've written over every word about five times. Only a few letters stick out. A few numbers, too. How on earth did you expect to decipher this? The ink has practically soaked the back cover."

She didn't bother to lift her hand while he continued to scour every inch of the paper lining the back cover of the Poe book. Instead, she rested her cheek against the tablecloth. After she'd deciphered every bit of code in the one book, this last piece of paper was her newest mystery. Never before her days in bed recently had she bothered to pay attention to the back cover.

Before she'd merely glanced and thought the paper was part of the cover. Upon closer examination she'd discovered paper so covered in ink and words that it matched the black leather of the cover. She'd discovered the deception through the few sections of paper not so covered, the letters and numbers Michael had just pointed out.

Under straight moonlight she'd found the layers of graffiti intriguing. Words stacked on top of each other with such intensity that in some places the paper had shredded. The few letters that could be considered clear were barely legible, the words wouldn't ever be.

For a week she'd tried to make something out of it, anything really. In the spare time she allowed herself, her focus had been on that page. She was certain it held some message, but her inability to decipher what the message might be was beginning to make her mad.

"There's a one, a four. I believe I see a three, maybe an eight? An A; is that an N?"

"Goodie. You've found the same letters and numbers as me. I could shout for joy."

"Jane."

"Sorry." She dragged herself to a sitting position, but propped her chin on her hand again. "I should have known better than to hope you would have an idea. I couldn't help myself, though. You are the closest thing to Clara I have."

"Besides yourself, you mean."

In total frustration, she stuck her tongue out at him. She was exhausted with the ineffable puzzle that filled her every moment. The lack of answers made her wonder if she'd ever find the answers David, Michael and even Jesse would need. Even if the puzzles were a distraction and a weak attempt to fill the hole in her heart, the whole matter was becoming more cumbersome than the hole itself.

"My, my. Childish ways enter in?"

"'It is the ignorant and childish part of man that is the fighting part'."

"Emerson."

His smile managed to lighten her mood and she returned it with only a smidgeon of effort needed. She nodded. "Yes. Emerson."

"So what are you going to do now?"

"Send a letter to the marshal."

"What?" Michael flew to his feet and leaned toward her. Fury and pain twisted his features into a tortured grimace. "Are you insane?"

Heat rushed to her cheeks and she dropped her hands and gaze to her lap. She twisted her handkerchief in her hands. Then out of nowhere, a giggle burst forth. "According to certain reports, yes. I was in an asylum after all."

"Clara Louise."

She snorted, unable to stop the rush of laughter at the absurdity. Another giggle ripped out into the air before the full-on laughter of the ludicrous notion followed behind. Her body trembled as she tried to contain it, her mouth fighting against the tight line she used to hold the braying laughter back.

His eyes were wide, his hands still planted on the table. When her laughter showed no sign of ceasing, he sank into his chair again. He shook his head, a small chuckle erupting between them. He rubbed his hands over his face and moaned. "Clarabelle."

The muscles of her stomach started to ache, and she wrapped her arms around her waist. Small tremors of laughter eased their way out when she leaned her forehead on the table. His hand rested on her head, and she sighed out the last of the amusement until it dissipated into the floor. "Oh, Michael."

"It wasn't that funny."

"I must laugh. I have to. Otherwise I'll spend every minute crying, wallowing in misery. This is all too much. I don't want to do it any longer. If I send for the marshal maybe we can find some measure of resolution."

"Please don't. We need more time."

"For what? Answers? We aren't finding any, in case you hadn't noticed." Jane sighed and pulled the book away from him so it was back in front of her. "And it will never be enough time for you, even if it took fifty years. Why drag it out? It will be worse in the end. I've accepted my fate. I advise you do the same."

"I can't. You aren't a criminal."

"Perhaps not. But Clara was."

"No." When her hand came to rest on his, he gripped it tight and shook his head. "Clara isn't a murderer. I won't ever believe it."

Tears blurred her vision and she held his hand as tight as he did hers. She took a ragged breath. "I don't believe she was either. I think perhaps she was a criminal, but I cannot believe she was a murderer. She'd told Jake everything. She was worried for his safety. From what I could tell he was going to help her."

"She didn't kill him."

"I don't know. I don't remember the moment of the murder much as I've tried. So I can't say for certain. Maybe Jake backed out. Maybe he changed his mind and she retaliated. Maybe she was insane by then."

"Jane."

"We just don't know."

He pulled her close and hugged her with his free arm. The weight of his chin on her head completed his now-tight hold on her. "I do. Clara couldn't. You couldn't."

"But I did. To save Cole's life I killed that Indian. I didn't even think about it, I just fired. Are you certain that to save Jesse's life, Clara wouldn't do the same?"

"Then she would have killed the monster. Not a total stranger."

"You're far more certain than I am." Her eyes closed, and she relaxed into his shoulder. For a brief moment her mind was blessedly blank, but then the chaos started again. Thoughts swirled too fast to catch, ripping at her current calm state of mind.

Michael backed off when she jumped to sit straight. "Why don't we head over to Cora's and get something to eat? Maybe we just need to take our minds off this."

"No. I think I'm going home. I still have some food left from the overly large basket Cora sent for me when I was laid up." She grinned at him. "You'd think she was feeding an army for two weeks and not just me for a few days."

"I noticed. All right, then. I'll get back to work. When do you need to go out and take a look at the Indians?"

"Tuesday. Al said that they are due to turn themselves in on Saturday. They're going to need a couple of days to get them all organized. Then I am to report to the camp and see if it was Starbird that shot Kelly and I."

He took her hand when she moved to stand. "Will you be able to know without the war paint? It's been months."

"I looked right into the eyes of the man that shot me. Of all the things I've forgotten, that will never be one of them. Just like I will never forget the face of the maniac that helped destroy Clara's life, no matter how much he changes it."

"You want me with you?"

"Al will be there. I won't be alone." She kissed his cheek and offered a small smile. "But I do appreciate the offer and may still take you up on it. We'll see how I feel on Tuesday."

"I'll remember to keep business light, just in case."

Her reply was interrupted by the sound of a gunshot. The screams the followed stilled Jane's heart. It couldn't be an attack. Not so close to the end of negotiations. The crash of glass and shouts echoing through the street squelched her panic fast.

It wasn't Indians.

"What the hell?" Michael flew to his feet and toward the door, with Jane close on his heels. They both stepped onto the porch in time to hear the next crash of glass.

"Graham. Ya bastard."

Another scream came from the direction of the saloon, and Jane rushed down the street. Cole was not there to guard his bar. She'd seen him get on the train that morning. One of the whores appeared in front of the boarding house, and Jane ran for her. "Heather."

"Jane!" Heather grasped her hands. "He's out for blood. We ain't done nothin'."

Another crash echoed out from the saloon, and Jane cringed. Heather ducked along with her even though nothing came from the building. Jane shook her head. "What happened?"

"Word got out 'bout that Celestial. They were all laughin' at him."

"Oh no." Jane spotted David pushing through the crowd toward the saloon and pulled her hand free of Heather's grip. She shoved her way through the thick crowd of bodies, ignoring all the shouts, laughter and talk.

With a gasp, she burst out of the crowd where it stopped almost ten feet from the saloon. Broken glass littered the street and porch, and the door hung from its hinges. The trough was shattered and Wills lay sprawled in the muddy puddle, Daisy hovered over him cleaning blood from his arm.

Jane gathered her skirts and started for the door, barely darting aside in time when a barrel of beer shot out the entrance. The door flew off its hinges as the barrel shattered in the street, spraying beer over the jeering crowd.

"Jane," Michael caught up to her, "let David handle it."

"He's drunker than I ever seen him before." Iris wisely stood off to the side, clear of the windows. The older whore twirled a ribbon on her bodice and tapped her foot. For a moment Jane thought she saw a glimmer of a smirk before Iris ducked her head and gave the ribbon a sharp tug. "And that's sayin' a lot."

Jane took Michael's hand when another crash shattered through the chaos, followed by a shout from David. "I'm going in there, whether you like it or not. He's destroying the place. They just finished rebuilding it."

"No, you're not."

"You should go in." Jane smirked. "After all, you're deputy. David needs help."

"Let go of my hand."

"Not on your life."

Michael's eyes narrowed. "Jane."

"You're wasting time." She shouted over the renewed yelling from inside. The shake he gave to try to rid himself of her did nothing, and she snorted when he grumbled a few curses before storming toward the doors.

She released his hand soon as he crossed the threshold, and slowed to almost a stop. David faced off with Graham, and Michael moved to flank him. She glanced around at the damage while they dealt with him.

The bar was half smashed, and sprawled on the floor beneath the damage, and Mac lay out cold. Tables were tipped and broken, it appeared very little had made it past Graham's wrath. She pushed off the wall with a frown.

"*You.*"

Jane froze when Graham's beefy finger pointed at her, but then took a few steps closer. His anger didn't bother her so much, as she'd done nothing wrong. "It wasn't me that said anything. I told you, I have no reason."

"Then how?" Graham's finger shook, his round face was red as a beet. His lips curled over his teeth in a snarl. "I knew you couldn't be trusted."

Jane stepped gingerly over a tipped table, taking note of how David and Michael were circling now that she had Graham's full attention. It hadn't been planned, but it was working remarkably well. She sighed. "Graham, I would be the last person to tell anyone. I know what it's like to want to be with someone that everyone thinks is a bad choice. I wouldn't have told. I couldn't have."

"Becky heard all about it. She's making threats. Then she went off with Cole today on that train." He sneered at her gasp. "Yeah. They both got on, didn't you know? She said it was all coincidence. I don't believe her none, do you?"

Her jaw clenched, but Jane didn't move. She hadn't known that much. While she'd seen Cole heading for the train with his suitcase in hand, she hadn't witnessed him board. Had no idea Becky, of all people, had gone with him. She swallowed to refuse the tears that made her brows twitch and her nose itch. "But why destroy the bar?"

Behind Graham, Michael stealthily grabbed a chair and crept forward.

"Because of that bastard and all of them. Them no-account fools." Graham waved absently toward the door. "All of them out there. They were all laughing. I don't get laughed at. Not by a bunch of miscreants."

Jane shrieked when the chair hit Graham square in the back of the head. Stumbling out of the way, she toppled over a felled table and crashed to the floor. Her head bounced slightly and she groaned as aches she'd managed to push aside thrust back to the forefront.

"Jane, are you all right?"

The impact had awakened every pain she'd begun to recover from, and added a few more to the mix. Despite all of that, she knew she hadn't suffered any serious damage. She closed her eyes against the creeping headache. "I'm fine. I just need a minute. Keep doing what you need to."

"Good," David grunted. "Bastard is fighting us half asleep. Daisy! We need something to calm him down."

Footsteps pounded along the floorboards. The wood under her head reverberated as a pair of feet stopped near her.

"Sure you're fine?"

The feminine voice surprised her, but the amusement in it made her smile. Jane cracked open an eye, blinking to open them both when she saw ankles instead of skirts. Shaking her head and blinking a few more times, she looked up to see the slim line of pants in place of a skirt. The woman wore a feminine blouse and a jaunty hat atop her fiery red hair.

Michael's previous mention of Martha's sister and her penchant for pants clued Jane in to who stood before her. Her smile spread open, and she chuckled. "You must be the infamous Katherine Daugherty."

Red curls bounced in agreement. "I'd hardly call myself infamous, but you got me. You still haven't answered my question, though. Are you sure you're fine?"

"A little sore here and there, but I suppose it's better than being trapped under that beast."

"Makes you wonder how Linh managed, doesn't it?" Katherine held out her hand with a flash of teeth. "Come on."

Jane accepted the hand and help to her feet. Once all the way up, she groaned and stretched out the soreness. "I'm Jane, by the way."

"Good to meet you. So sorry he blamed you when it wasn't even your fault. I was the one that blabbed."

"Even if he'd known, he would have blamed me." Jane sighed as Graham was dragged past them, unconscious. She glanced around the building at the damage as she rubbed the back of her neck. The extent of damage made her heart sink. "They just had to rebuild a few months ago thanks to the renegades. Now this."

"They'll manage. Always do." Katherine set her hands on her hips. "But I guess I should help clean up. It's appropriate penance for causing it."

"You really blabbed?"

"Yes. I thought it was quite an amusing combination, and so I shared it with Hammy."

"That was your first mistake."

Katherine's musical laughter filled the room. "Oh, so true. He's as big a gossip as they come. I don't know that there's a bigger one in town. Not even my sister."

Coughing to cover her giggle, Jane nodded. After a moment, she frowned and glanced away. She'd almost forgotten this was Martha's sister. The contrast between the two women was so startling. "I'm sure your sister had plenty to say about me."

"She sure did. Didn't seem to like you much in general, but was appreciative of your attempt to help once she was in jail."

"The feeling's mutual. We tolerate civility." Jane felt heat rising to her cheeks, not wanting to upset the woman. It was the first woman she'd met that she'd instantly liked. Whether it was her bold pants-wearing nature, or the persistent smile. "Not that your sister isn't a good person. She let me stay in the boarding house rent-free for some time."

"No need." Katherine held up her hand. "She's judgmental. Quite the hypocrite when she wants to be, really. She's my sister, I know. However, that's how I knew I'd like you."

"Oh, really?"

"Really." Katherine brushed down her bodice. "Well, I'd better get to work. See if I can't get some of those lousy drunks to help."

"I'll help. I'd also bet I'd be able to get a few of those drunks to help myself."

"I know why I'm cleaning up. Why are you?"

Jane kept her eyes diverted, bending to pick up a chair and right it. "I have a sick need to keep helping Cole."

"Oh. We're going to get along just fine, Jane. Just fine."

*The power of a lawyer is in the uncertainty
of the law.
—Jeremy Bentham*

Cole fought the urge to tug his collar, though he gave in to the discomfort enough to tilt his head and stretch against it. For several hours he'd been dressed in his finest, first waiting for the lawyer in front of him, and now waiting on the man to speak.

The lawyer appeared deep in thought, pulling on a pipe while he considered his own notes. Cole's closest contact in Denver, Leanne, had assured him that this lawyer was one of the best. She'd had a good enough relationship to get Cole in without any loss of funds. It helped that Leanne still owed him a lifetime of favors.

Finally the lawyer lifted his head and narrowed his eyes. "You do realize the only reason I agreed to speak with you at all was because of how interesting the case seemed. An amnesiac with a criminal past was too intriguing."

Liar. A whole mess of bribery had been involved, too. Cole may not be the smartest in the lot, but he was no fool. Rather than ruin what little progress they'd made, Cole nodded. "That's what Leanne tells me."

"I only wish I could offer you more of substance. I have very little to go on here. No real facts. I'd like to meet Miss Doe for myself."

"But that would require more favors."

"A trip to Dominion Falls? An appointment? Yes, yes it would. I'd be happy to do it, of course. With the right incentive to get me on that train."

Cole pursed his lips and rose. "Well, I gotta talk to her first. See what she says."

"Very good. Send a telegram if my services are required."

Cole strode to the door, a snarl curling his lip. The lawyer wanted nothing more than all the favors he could cash in. He'd given Cole no real information or hope for Jane's case, granted he had very little information.

Problem was, Cole was more than willing to cash in all his favors if it meant keeping Jane away from the gallows.

Every single favor from the lifetime he was owed was a fair price to pay to see Jane live. Even if she lived on without him. She didn't deserve to die. She didn't deserve the pain she was already in. Never had. Not even the pain he'd dealt.

"Mr. Mitchell." The feminine voice that hit him the moment he left the room was familiar. He just couldn't place it.

Once he'd closed the door and turned, he knew why it was so familiar. None other than Kathy and Martha's mother stood before him. "Mrs. Daugherty."

"I must say I'm surprised to see you in the offices of Greenburg and Stein. So surprised that I've spent the past hour speaking with Miss Perkins here while I waited for you to finish with Mr. Stein." She rose from the chair she'd perched on like a queen. Kat and Martha's mother had always been good at acting like royalty. She took her role as town founder with far too much seriousness. Her once-red hair now shimmered silver, and she was dressed to the nines, even at midday. Unlike Jackson, though, she wore her wealth with style instead of crass.

"I had some questions." Cole gave her a nod. "Best be off."

"Just a moment, please." Lillian wove around the chair between them. "Would you be so kind as to escort me to my carriage?"

"Why?"

"Because it's polite. You do know how to do that, don't you?"

As he was already annoyed after his appointment, it took considerable effort not to respond with curses. He smirked. "Thought you didn't mix with the riff-raff."

"You cleaned up well enough, I suppose. Now offer your arm like a proper gentleman."

"Ain't nothing proper about me, Lil." He offered his arm anyway.

"I learned that long ago when you chose to bed my daughter." Lillian didn't sugarcoat things. It was one thing he'd always liked about her and her younger daughter. "Not that you were the first or last, I suppose. That one was always uncontrollable."

"Kathy's got a good name. She's a wild-cat."

"I know all too well. At least Martha learned to settle down, even if it was with an Indian, much to her father's disappointment."

"That why you're seeing the lawyer today? To try to keep her from swinging?"

"I have many reasons to visit lawyers. My wayward children are only a small portion of that." She waited for him to open the door. Even though they were now free of the building, she took his arm again. "None of my reasons are as interesting as yours, I must say."

"How would you know?" Cole kept walking down the street, away from the waiting carriages. He began to wonder when she'd let him go.

"Stein's secretary Miriam likes to chat. She told me. An amnesiac with a possible criminal past? I'm surprised Dominion Falls has become so interesting."

"You should visit. There's a lot that'll surprise you—especially what Jackson has done to your old house."

"I've heard tell of a monstrosity." Lillian sighed. "Such a shame too. It was a nice home. What does he think of this woman?"

"He liked her well enough at first. Proposed marriage to *help* her along."

"So he might seem charitable, hmm?"

"That's what Jane said." Cole stopped short.

"Of course. I take it by your tone that he doesn't feel so charitable any longer?"

"Not since Jane went and embarrassed him. Showed him up a time or two. Got his name off the election ballots and got him so fired up he landed in a pile of manure."

"She sounds delightful." She chuckled.

"Why are you so curious anyhow? You don't visit no more. Not even with Martha in jail or Kathy back flouncin' around town."

"Katherine is there?" Lillian's eyes widened. "Which means she once again came right through Denver without a bye or leave. I think perhaps you're right, Mr. Mitchell. A visit may be long overdue. I'd like to see my daughters and meet this—Jane, you said?"

"I did. Jane Doe."

"How original." Lillian's dry tone was betrayed by her smile. "Sounds like plenty of excitement is happening in our little town. I should come to visit."

"I'm sure Jack will be thrilled to see ya."

"I'm quite certain he won't. There's my carriage." She held out her hand to him. "Good day, Mr. Mitchell."

Cole eyed her hand until she wiggled her fingers. With a quirk of his brow, he took it and gave it a good shake.

"You enjoy playing heathen, don't you?"

"Always did." He winked. Once she'd settled in her carriage, he tipped his head and watched it depart with a frown. Lillian coming back to Dominion Falls could spell trouble, or a hell of a lot of chaos and fun.

He chuckled. Not once had he run into Lillian on his frequent trips into Denver. Of all the times for it to happen, this had been a good one. He couldn't wait to see the sparks fly when she got back to Dominion Falls.

Not that it solved the problems he'd come to Denver to resolve, but at least it would serve as good distraction on his return.

No, on his return he didn't need distraction. He needed to figure out how to talk to Jane. If she'd only take the first step, it would be so much easier. She was better at words than he was.

Damn it. He was a man. He'd stop being a coward and talk to her.

She just better not ignore him.

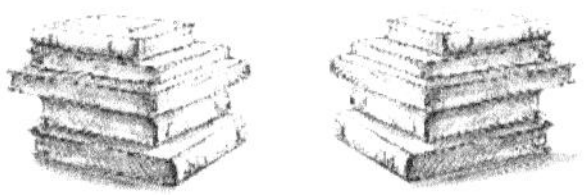

Let us live for the beauty of our own reality.
–Charles Lamb

Their glasses clinked together, and Jane lifted hers to her mouth. She had to grip the edge of the table to toss it back lest she fell over. A night of no sleep, an empty stomach, and about a third of the bottle of whiskey made her a wee bit unsteady.

Both glasses slammed down simultaneously, and Jane chuckled, placing her hand to her forehead. She exhaled until the spinning stopped and sat back. "Well, I do believe we should have gone to bed hours ago like everyone else."

"If we had, we wouldn't now know everything about each other. After all, much of what you've told me is top secret."

Jane nodded her agreement, then met Katherine's gaze with a smile. "So, will you admit it now? You came back here to be with Norman, yes?"

"No. Yes." Katherine's cheeks got as red as her hair, and she poured another glass for them both. They'd spent the entire night cleaning up the saloon and had decided to use whiskey instead of coffee to keep them awake.

It might have been a mistake – but it sure was a fun one.

Jane scoffed. "Uh-huh."

"I don't know that it could ever work. He is a few years older than I am."

"No. Really?" A giggle quickly descended into a pig-like snort, and Jane clamped a hand over her mouth. Norman was nearly twenty years older than herself, and Kat had to be about five years younger at least.

"Well, sometimes experience counts for something."

"Ah yes, but age does not wisdom bring. Are you certain you have the right man? You did sleep with Cole too." Both of them burst into laughter, clinking their glasses again before drinking them down.

Kat shook her head against the burn of the whiskey and shook her finger at Jane with a giggle. "Don't underestimate Norman. He's got strong fingers from working the telegraph."

Lips pursed taut to try to force back the guffaw, Jane put all her effort into stopping the laugh. Her failure was complete as it burst from its seams to echo through the empty saloon. She clasped Kat's hand. "Oh goodness, I am glad to have met you."

"I am just happy you don't hold it against me that I was with Cole."

"It wouldn't be my place. Besides, it was five years ago. Every time you've visited since, you've made your time with your strong-fingered friend."

Kat poured another two glasses full of whiskey, unable to stop her stream of giggles. "And my relationship with Cole was pure sex. Unlike yours."

"That's all ours was," Jane said too quickly. Kat's knowing wink brought heat to her cheeks and she tossed back her whiskey to buy some time. Though they'd had help at first cleaning the place, by about three in the morning they'd been the only ones left cleaning up Graham's mess.

They'd passed the hours talking, and Katherine had proven to be as interesting as she was supportive. Before she knew it, Jane had revealed the entire sordid story of her relationship with Cole. She'd even told her about the baby.

In return, Katherine had shared her own history. The arranged marriage she'd run away from, her sordid relationship with the man who'd taught her about sex, the loss of a dear friend, joining the temperance league, and traveling the country with the ladies until their more violent methods in the name of God disagreed with her for the last time. She also revealed her brief fling with Cole, which had ended when she started growing close to Norman.

Now Katherine knew just about as much about her as Cole did. Jane had instantly trusted her and was relieved to have a confidante without the complication of it being yet another man. That was the last thing she needed.

The problem was that Katherine was too perceptive. She'd tried to corner Jane into admitting just how deeply she cared for Cole. Jane could hardly admit it to herself, much less to Katherine; and certainly never to Cole.

"So should we add this bottle to Graham's bill?"

The change of subject was a welcome relief, and Jane was able to find a genuine smile again. "Yes. It is his fault we were up all night and had to supplement sleep with whiskey."

"Mornin', Jane." Iris yawned and stretched, leaning against the wall. "Girls wanna get some extra sleep since we ain't gonna be open straight away."

"Is that so?" Jane couldn't keep the amusement from her tone. The liquor made her far too giddy, and Kat's sniggering sure didn't help. Oh well, it couldn't be helped. That didn't mean she would let this slide by. "What makes you think the saloon won't be opened?"

"We got one table, and you're usin' it. Bar's half broke. Graham broke up most of the whiskey, and you're drinkin' some too." Iris shrugged. "Nothin' to open with."

Katherine couldn't hold it in, despite the hand clamped over her mouth. Her laughter overrode Jane's initial attempt at a reply. By the time she'd settled enough, Jane was fighting over her own laughter.

Her hand pressed to her chest, she forced her breath steady. "No such luck, Iris. Right now Hammy's getting estimates on tables and supplies from Cora. When he gets back, I'm going to have him shore up the bar until it can be fixed or replaced."

"Ain't no way we'll get tables in today, and tomorrow's Sunday."

Jane stood, leaning into the table when the floor tilted under her feet. Was she really trying to be commanding while drunk? She could only imagine how ridiculous she looked. Not to mention she was certain Cole wouldn't appreciate what she was doing a bit. Not that it mattered. She was still determined to help. "You're all going to be working when Cole gets back. Or do you really want to deal with him if you're not?"

Iris straightened, her brows furrowing. "I guess not."

"Good. Now go clean up. I can smell you from here. Make sure all the girls are ready. Once we get some tables in here, Cuddy is going to open up. Without tables, hopefully all of you will be occupied to make up for some of the loss."

Kat leaned back in her chair and propped her feet up on the table. "You do know I'm going to tell Cole all about this."

"No, you won't." Jane sat down. "Katherine, this isn't anything."

"Janey."

"Cuddy." Jane grinned. Cuddy carried two crates into the saloon, stacked high enough he could barely see over the top. "Good. Cora had two cases? What about the beer?"

"Cora only had one case." Cuddy dropped the crates on the ground with a grunt. "Your brother gave us the other. He said we could have a beer barrel too. Won't hardly last a night, but it'll help."

Jane rose and crossed the room when he pried the top off the box. "What about glasses? Where's Hammy?"

"He's comin'. Had to get a wagon for the rest of it." Cuddy pulled out a few bottles of whiskey. "Cora wrote down everythin' for ya. Said you could have it at cost until she realized it was for the saloon."

A snort scrunched Katherine's freckled nose. "So? She's known Cole longer."

"Exactly."

Jane laughed. "It's of no matter. Graham will be the one paying for it. Katherine has a running tally. At the rate he's going, Cole could buy him out for two dollars based on what he owes."

"It ain't that bad, is it?" Cuddy smirked. "This place isn't fancy."

She clapped him on the shoulder before bending to pick up a couple of bottles and carry them behind the bar. "He did plenty of damage, Cuddy. Not just to property but to people too. We've put down the charges for medical care for Wills and Mack."

"I always knew Graham was a bull." Kat hopped up and started to help put away the whiskey. "I just never realized one drunken fool could do so much damage."

"If he only hit, it wouldn't be so bad. Unfortunately, he's a thrower."

"Of people and things." Nodding in agreement, Katherine set the last bottle in place. "Word is that it was Mack's hard head that broke the bar."

"Then he shouldn't be too damaged. That man has a thick skull. To this day he still gropes me every time he passes." A huff of air blew the bangs from Jane's forehead. "One of these days, I will do worse than slap him."

"Miss Jane." Boards clattered to the floor to help announce Hammy's arrival. He pulled off his hat and slipped his fingers along the brim. "I brung some scrap wood like you asked. Got my men headin' over to help."

It was impossible not to smile at the man. Jane found him endearing despite his regular drunken state. Except on very rough days he was never anything but polite, and the man never seemed to have a rough day. "Thank you very much, Mr. Hamm. Did Cora give you a list?"

"Sure thing, Miss Jane. Right here. Said the tables ain't gonna get in for three days. Lent four tables to you until then." The paper trembled when he handed it out, and he slipped his hat back on. "Guess four is better than nothin'."

"It is. That will give us five. Unless you can help." Jane squeezed his hand, her smile straining her cheeks when he blushed. "Do you think you can make tables and chairs out of some of your scrap wood?"

"Aw, gee. We can sure try. Don't know how fast, though." Hammy stuffed his hands in his pockets. "There's an awful lot ya want doin'."

"Well, Mr. Hamm, look at it this way. The sooner we get it done, the sooner the saloon can open and you can get your beer."

That perked him up. A grin formed. "True. Guess I best get on it. Will you be stayin' here?"

"I would, but I need to go see Graham at the jail. Then I need to help Reverend Greene with his deliveries." Jane kissed his cheek. "We're low on beer, but I told Cuddy that you got priority. Your beer is on the house at least until Cole gets back."

"Weren't necessary, but I'm much obliged." He tipped his hat again and shuffled his feet. "I best get on it so's the saloon can open."

Jane nodded, turning to head outside.

"Jane, wait." Katherine caught up quick, lacing her arm with Jane's. "So what's this about helping the reverend?"

"Well, after your sister and Mabel's little adventures, the congregation didn't want Mabel continuing the runs. So Reverend Greene agreed to take them over." Jane shrugged. "He wanted help, and I offered. We go out on every Saturday with supplies to the camp."

"Camp?"

"In one of the attacks, ten homes were burned down in the second settlement. Not to mention a few of the homesteads on the outskirts. A base camp was set up." A frown tugged at her lips, her mood getting darker. Most of the families had been living hand to mouth, and now winter was adding to their current state.

"Goodness. I didn't realize that many families had been misplaced. How many lives were lost?"

"Total?" Jane sighed. "In the settlements and homesteads, there were fifteen losses. Quite a few cattle were stolen, and other livestock. If you want to include the loss of lives in town and the railroad workers, it was much greater."

"I don't know whether to be upset that I didn't come sooner, or relieved." Kat's pace slowed. "I was here in March, but hadn't had the opportunity to come after that. I was trying to come out every few months to see Norman."

"It isn't like there was much you could have done. Your presence wouldn't have stopped the attacks." Nudging her with her shoulder, Jane grinned. "Much as I would love to control the actions of others, even I know it's impossible."

"Very true." Her forehead relaxed, and Katherine allowed a small laugh. "However, this town is important to me. Do you think the reverend would mind if I offered my assistance as well? A penance for my absence during difficult times."

"I'm certain he would appreciate the help. Penance not required."

"Good. Now are we really going to see Graham?"

"Yes."

"Why? Or is it just to explain to him about the list we've compiled?"

Jane pursed her lips. "That's part of it. He should know the amount of damage he's done. However, I also want to make sure he's thinking clearer now."

"Graham never thinks clear."

"I know. That's the problem."

"What was that you said about controlling the actions of others?"

"He's Cole's friend."

"Ah. I see."

Feeling the heat rise to her cheeks again, Jane cleared her throat. "Depending on how long David decides to jail him, it could get ugly. He's a drunk. Without a drink, it could be bad for him."

"To be honest, I don't think Cole will mind."

"Neither do I. Not right now."

"So I ask again, why?"

"He's a brute, and an idiot. He did something very stupid and should pay for his mistake. That doesn't mean he should suffer. I would hope that when I pay for Clara's crimes, it will be fast. I don't think anyone should suffer. That isn't justice. It's cruelty."

Wherever there is a human being, there is an opportunity for a kindness.
-Seneca

Graham gripped the paper Jane had handed him. His large hands shook hard, crinkling the paper with each jerk. "That's a lot of money. It can't have been that bad."

While Kat lingered outside the cell, not daring to get near Graham, Jane sat next to him on the cot. She squeezed his wrist. "Yes, it was." She and Kat had taken several hours and a few pots of coffee to sober up before daring to run their errands. Now a headache lingered behind her right eye, but Jane felt more clear-headed.

"I just managed to get us help on that damned place. Secured an investor to make up what Cole couldn't get together for the repairs. We're supposed to turn it into a real hotel, not use the money for more repairs." Graham dropped the paper and ran his hands over his bald head. He leaned his elbows on his knees. "With the Indian attacks over, I don't have as much dead bodies to care for. Just what I always had from the mines, and they've been real careful lately. Business is slow. I don't have the money for it."

"And Becky sure won't pay for it for you." Kat leaned on the bars. "So what are you going to do?"

"What are you doing here, Kat?" Graham flew to his feet, almost knocking Jane to the floor.

"I made the list you're complaining about. I figured you'd argue so I came to defend it." Despite her bravado, Kat backed away several steps. "Everything on that list is at prices Jane or Mike managed to finagle for you. Many of the prices would have been much higher if they'd known it was for you. You should be grateful it's as low as it is."

"Nosy little whore."

"Graham." Jane resituated herself on the cot. She wasn't about to let him see how his angry outburst had shaken her. "It's because of Kat's help that the saloon is even open today. Just because you don't remember the level of your drunken idiocy doesn't mean you should take it out on Kat, or me."

"You're the one that told. Got all of them laughing at me." Graham turned his fury back on Jane.

Jane shook her head, both to argue with Graham and dissuade Kat from confessing the truth. All Kat's confession would do was rile the already volatile situation. "I did no such thing. In the end it doesn't matter who became the official snitch, the two of you weren't exactly being discreet."

"Were too."

Kat snorted and covered her mouth, which turned into a failed attempt to curb the laughter that shook her shoulders. "Please. I've been in town for three days and I knew. You are no stealthy paramour."

Jane's lips twitched, but as Graham's dark glare remained fixed on her, she didn't let her laughter loose.

"I got your list. Get the hell out, Kat." Graham still didn't move, but his fists were clenched threateningly at his sides.

"Barrel-fever Graham is even more unlikable than every day drunken Graham." Kat shook her head. "He's unreasonable, Jane. Let's go ahead and leave."

"Go on outside. I'm going to stay." Jane smiled at Graham's shocked jaw drop. After his angry outburst, she liked gaining the upper hand. It could be all that saved her. If it didn't kill her. "I'll be fine. I want to let him have his chance to have it out with me. He's been wanting to since as far back as I can remember."

"Your funeral." Kat shrugged.

Jane waited until Kat stood on the porch with David before resting her hands back on the cot. "Well. Go ahead then."

"I don't got nothin' to say to you."

"So, technically, you have a lot to say to me, then?"

His brow furrowed over her dark eyes. "What?"

"You said that you don't have nothing to say to me. By not having nothing to say, that means you have a lot to say." The rising bubble of humor made her wonder if she was as sober as she'd imagined she was. Graham's continuing confusion only added to the building inappropriate giggle.

"You make no sense, woman." He gave a frustrated growl and stormed across the cell. "Everything was fine."

"Until what?" The possibilities were numerous, after all. "Until me? Until the Indians blew up the saloon? Or until your drunken stupor?"

"Yes."

She sighed and tilted her head to stretch her aching muscles. "Do you love Becky?"

"I'm marrying her."

"That isn't what I asked."

He dropped into the chair, the wood creaking under his weight. Rather than respond, he stared at his hands. The silence lingered as he picked at the bandages spread across his bloodied knuckles.

"All right. Do you love Linh?"

"What? No. I—"

"Ah."

"Do you love Cole?"

"If this was about me, maybe I'd answer." Jane sat forward and picked the paper up off the floor. "You've got some choices to make, Graham. A lot of them. First is the business."

"It'll earn the money back. I'm not worried. I got another business."

"Exactly." She pursed her lips. "You do. Cole doesn't. This business is all he's got in the world right now. And you almost destroyed it just a couple of months after the renegades blew it up. You've just managed to get the place repaired a few weeks ago. In turn you helped Cole out, found an investor."

"And he sold Daisy."

Before she'd left to go after the boys in San Francisco, Cole had admitted that was why he'd sold Daisy's contract. He'd told Jane that in the end it hadn't been enough to make all the repairs and they'd had to find an investor. How Graham managed it, she'd never figured out. He was no better a savvy business man than a stealthy paramour. "Right. But now what? You could sell to Cole cheap and leave the responsibility to him now. He's going to be furious with you anyway."

"Don't want to." The words emerged with the pout of a petulant child. He must have known it, too, for he straightened his shoulders. "I like having it. Dead bodies all day ain't exactly fun."

"Then you're going to have to stop being an ignorant fool and start acting nicer to Kat. She might be the only one left in town that can get you back in Cole's good graces, or at least where he won't kill you soon as he'd look at you."

"Could ask Becky, since they're so close now."

Jane's heart flopped into her stomach at the reminder, but she kept it to herself. "But you won't. Becky will be mad enough that this happened. I get the impression she doesn't care for embarrassment much."

"No. She don't." Graham leaned back in the chair. One leg stretched out, and he fixed a stare on her. "He'd listen to you. He isn't done with you. I knew it all along. Don't know what you did to him, but he's not the same."

"I don't think I'll be talking to him. He's made his opinions quite clear, and I've made mine clear."

"He'd still go back to you. Bastard's a fool."

"Takes one to know one." She leaned forward. "And changing the subject isn't going to distract me. You also have to figure out what you're going to do about the women in your life. It's clear you have somehow managed to develop feelings under that thick wall of brute—and they're directed at Linh."

"You're crazy."

"Maybe I am. Doesn't make it less true."

He chose to ignore her, glaring toward the door when laughter sounded from Kat and David.

"If you want to continue on with Linh, you'll have to be more discreet. I can help you with that." She smirked at his guffaw. "Just because I chose to be indiscreet doesn't mean I don't know how to be when the need calls for it."

"Why would you help me?"

"I have no idea. But know this. I'll only help you until your marriage. If you choose to marry Becky despite whatever it is you feel for Linh, I'll be done helping you."

"Hypocrite."

"If you're talking about David and me, our divorce plans have been decided for a long time. I made my choice, and it was Cole at the time." She didn't want a loveless marriage, and as dear as David had become to her, it wasn't love. They both knew it, and had for some time.

"Becky probably won't even want me anymore." Despite the grumpy words, his tone didn't match.

"Don't sound so hopeful." Jane's tone was dry and drew a chuckle from Graham.

Miracles did exist if she was having a companionable conversation with Graham. She certainly wouldn't count on it lasting too long.

"I mean it, Jane. He's a fool when it comes to you."

Jane glanced his way, trying to come up with something to say that wouldn't make her start crying. Digging deep, she found a smile. "Be careful, Graham. I might start to think you care two figs about me."

"Can't have that."

"No, we certainly can't."

"Reverend's here." Kat stood in the doorway with a sour frown directed at Graham. "You ready, Jane?"

"I'll be right there." Jane walked to the cell door. "Think about it, Graham."

"Janey."

"What?"

"He'd take you back. He'll be back."

"Perhaps. Doesn't mean I'd take him back."

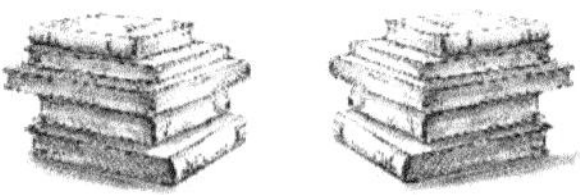

Teach this triple truth to all: A generous heart, kind speech, and a life of service and compassion are the things which renew humanity.
—Buddha

"I never imagined." Kat arched her back in a stretch before wiping her wrist on her forehead. "I mean, you told me the numbers, but this isn't what I pictured."

Jane smiled as she shoved down on the crowbar to open the next crate. Once open, she counted the bags of flour. Just enough for one to each family. She nodded and took in the cluster of tents spread out before them. Laughter rang through the camp as children darted in and out of tents, racing between them in a tremendous game of tag. "At least it's something."

"Not enough for some." A woman about Jane's age with hair so blond the sunlight made it seem white set down another crate from the wagon. Mrs. Broder sighed and set her hand on her hip. "We got two more families pulling up and leaving on Monday."

"Oh dear." Jane frowned. "Who is it this time?"

"The Abbotts and the Stantons." Mrs. Broder hefted a bag of flour and handed it off when someone approached. "They both got young ones. With the weather getting so cold, they can't hold out for a house."

"There has to be something we can do." Kat picked through a crate of clothes, separating them by age and gender. "Or everyone is going to leave."

"I wonder." Jane spun in a circle to survey the whole camp.

"She has that look." Mrs. Broder chuckled. "I've seen it before when she managed to gather these tents for the families. I'm sure she swiped some from the Army."

"I stole nothing." Jane shrugged. "They were offered. Al was very generous, as were many in town."

"Of course they were. What with your unique sort of persuasion." Kat's loose hair fell across her face in a gust of wind. She shoved it aside. "So what are you thinking now?"

"The tents are too cold to last all winter. With the men still working in the mines most of the week and the unsure nature of donations, the replacement homes are being built one or two at a time. They'll never all be finished." Jane bit her lip, work put aside while she pondered the possibility.

"One blizzard and this camp would be in trouble." Kat's folding ceased. Worry lined her brow. "But even if I open up the boarding house to them, that's only three families, or four squeezed tight."

"No matter what's done, it'll be tight." Mrs. Broder sighed.

"Yes, it would. Still, I wonder if tight with walls wouldn't be better in the long run. Four walls, a roof, and a fireplace. Even if it's a squeeze, it might convince more families to stay." Jane smiled. "Someone should talk to Mr. Hamm."

"About what?" Reverend Greene sat down with a sigh. "All the wood has been delivered. The men are putting it to use already. Now what's this about Hammy?"

"I was wondering if he might donate some time and materials to build a lodge for the families before winter hits." Jane pointed to the edge of camp. "Over there closer to the hill so one side is protected. Of course, in the spring, it can be torn down and the materials reused for houses."

"If anyone will talk to him, it should be you. After all, he's sweet on you." Kat ducked when Jane took a swat at her. "I saw him this morning when you asked him to help. He was all ready to say no, and you just smiled, and he turned into a drunk little puddle at your feet."

Mrs. Broder handed off another bag of flour. "Whoever talks to him should do it soon, before the men use all the wood for the Brownes' home."

Jane's train of thought burst at a giggle behind her. A smile crept across her lips, and she dared to glance over her shoulder. A flash of a small skirt was all there was. Another giggle to her other side and she spun with the same result.

By now Mrs. Broder and Kat were both bright red in attempts to contain their laughter. Reverend Greene had far less success, a rich chortle sounding before he made his escape to help hand off more supplies.

The game continued for several minutes, and Jane was happy to let it. Then she moved to go right, but turned the other way and caught the child around the waist. She spun fast until the girl squealed and Jane herself felt dizzy. When she stopped, a set of gangly legs wrapped around her waist.

Jane grinned. "Lizzie Broder, what sort of trouble are you trying to get into?"

"None, Miss Jane." Lizzie's blond hair shimmered as white as her mother's. She leaned in to whisper. "I wanted to show you something."

"It's difficult to show me something hiding behind my skirts." Jane set her down. "Mrs. Broder? Do you mind?"

"Not at all. We've got things handled here for a little bit." Mrs. Broder returned to work alongside Kat.

Lizzie tugged Jane's hand and half-dragged her to the tent she shared with her family. "Hurry."

"I'm hurrying." Jane stepped inside with Lizzie and followed her back to the small curtained-off area with her cot. "So, how are you doing?"

After she'd scrambled onto the bed, Lizzie shoved her hand under the pillow. "All right, I guess. The wind is scary still."

"It scares me sometimes too. My house gets awful quiet at night, and when the wind is really strong, it whistles in my stove's chimney and rattles the windows." Jane touched the canvas. "I bet out here it sounds like howling animals."

Lizzie nodded and drew out a piece of paper from under her pillow. "I drew the pictures for the poem."

Together, Jane and Lizzie had created a silly poem for when the girl was scared. The drawing was simple, but displayed it all very well. "So, I see. Apples and bananas."

Lizzie pointed to the next picture. "Monkeys in a tree."

"The monsters cannot get you. They only come for the flea."

"The dark is naught. The stars still shine above."

"No evil enters a home so filled with love." Jane touched the last picture of Lizzie and her parents, the sadness Jane kept so well hidden raced up out of nowhere. "You draw very well, Lizzie. I didn't know that."

With a shrug, Lizzie set aside the picture. "It doesn't have any color."

"No, but it's very nice. I bet if you visited me at the library sometime, I might be able to find some paint you can use to color it."

"Really?" Lizzie brightened. "You don't mind?"

"Not at all. Jesse, Isaac, and Arthur will be coming to visit on Monday. Maybe we can ask your ma if you can join them." Jane leaned in to whisper. "Now are you still having trouble with your math?"

Lizzie ducked her head with a sheepish smile.

"Get your slate. I can help you for a few minutes."

*When anger rises,
think of the consequences.
-Confucius*

The train whistle signaled their arrival back in Dominion Falls. Cole remained in his seat while everyone around them bustled toward the doors. He didn't have a lot of motivation to move. The trip to Denver had been unsuccessful on all fronts.

It wasn't like he needed the added frustration. Jane still wouldn't speak to him, not that he blamed her one bit. He'd been an idiot and his lack of skill with words meant he'd never made it right. She'd also been spending a hell of a lot of time with that husband of hers. It made him wonder if they were still getting divorced.

His teeth ground together with a click, and he punched the seat in front of him. The past month's hard work might be for naught if he couldn't tell her what he'd done.

"Sir?"

Cole jolted out of his internal misery at the conductor's voice. The rest of the train car sat devoid of passengers. He hadn't realized he'd been sitting there so long. With a short nod to the conductor, he rose and strode off the train. Much as he was loathed to admit it, the weeks without Jane had been miserable.

Never in his life had he second-guessed his decisions. Once he'd made up his mind, it was final. Now that woman had him second-guessing everything. He knew he'd been a fool—not to mention a heartless, cruel bastard after she'd lost the baby.

He'd offered comfort, but only after he'd hurt her. He wasn't even sure she knew, she'd said he was a dream. He might have stayed and faced things, but her damn brother came home again, and he wasn't about to have it out with the shrimp before he'd faced Jane herself. Jane was the only one that deserved his repentance, not her brother or anyone else.

Over the hiss of train brakes, a familiar laugh rang out.

"Kathy?" Cole spun, his body going numb when Jane's laughter mingled with Kathy's.

A wagon raced out from around the back of the train. Both women whooped and laughed as they drove so fast a hat flew off.

"Now them two are gonna be such trouble." Norman lifted his hat and scratched his head. "Ya know, they spent all morning in my kitchen chattering away and drinking all my coffee. I swear I'm going to be deaf from their noise."

"Kathy and Jane?" Cole shook his head. Those two fiery women together would be a dangerous mix. "When did they meet?"

"Why, yesterday of course. When Graham..." Norman's wrinkled features twisted in a grimace. "Aw, gee. I forgot. You don't know."

The anger Cole had managed to tamp down with shock bubbled up again. Every muscle went rigid and he spoke through a clenched jaw. "What did Graham do?"

Norman's weathered features turned beet-red. After a moment of stammering, he spotted someone entering the depot. "I'll be right there, Mrs. Kilmurry. Excuse me, Cole."

Cole narrowed his eyes at Norman's quick escape. Something bad had happened for sure. He stormed off the platform toward the saloon. The wagon with Jane and Kathy parked down the street in front of the library, both women still wrapped up in animated conversation.

They spotted him at the same time. After a whispered exchange, Jane darted into the library. Kathy, however, headed right for him.

She rushed up and threw her arms around him. "Cole. So good to see your smiling face again! How was your trip?"

"Outta my way, Kathy." He gripped her waist and peeled her off him. After he set her aside, he resumed his path.

Kathy wasn't about to be ignored. She laced her hand through his arm and sped her pace to walk alongside him. "Since you're being a stubborn ass. I guess someone already told you what happened, then."

"No. Just know Graham did something stupid."

"Well, yes. He did. Jane and I have taken care of things as best we could."

"You and Jane? You and Jane?" He spun on her and advanced until she was forced to back up against the railing of the bank. "Why are you so chummy with her anyhow? She ain't none of your business any more than I am. And why are ya sticking your nose in again?"

"Well, well. Aren't we testy?" Kathy lifted her chin. Rather than show a hint of fear, she smiled at him instead. Damn woman knew he'd never hit a woman. "Jane is a lovely person. Very funny, and rather daring and bold. I can see why you like her."

"I don't."

"Of course not." She pushed him back a few inches. "Now are you going to keep yelling at me, or shall we proceed to the saloon?"

He clenched and unclenched his fists. Kat wouldn't leave him be. She was as stubborn as Jane. He released a growl of frustration and turned away to head toward the saloon again. This time when she tried to take his arm, he yanked it free of her grasp.

Once he got close enough, the damage became all too clear. Worst part about it was, he was still outside. The doors were gone, the windows on one side boarded up, the railing on one side pushed out and splintered in the middle, the trough below it gone.

The repairs from the renegade attacks had only been completed a few weeks before. Even with the money from the investor Graham had scrounged up, he couldn't afford more damage like this. He didn't have another ace in the hole like Daisy to sell.

"Come along now." Kat tugged his hand. "No sense standing there with your mouth hanging open. Might as well see the rest."

"I'm gonna kill that bastard." Anger was easier, always had been. He had to focus on that above all else.

"You'll have to wait until he's out of jail. I'm pretty sure David is going to keep him locked up until Monday." She stopped inside the doorway when he refused to budge any further.

Cole's stomach sank to the floor. The familiar surroundings of his saloon now stood in ruins. Makeshift tables and chairs littered the floor along with several he recognized as Cora's from her restaurant. The bar itself drooped on one end with a few beams of wood propping it up. Two lone bottles of whiskey stood on the shelves behind the bar. The mirror behind the shelves had been shattered, and only one sliver remained.

"We've made a cost estimate of all the repairs, and Graham is prepared to pay them."

"Damn straight he will."

"You have more beer and whiskey arriving on Monday, and a few more tables." Kat leaned against the door. "The girls thought they could take the day off, but as the main source of income until the booze comes in, Jane wouldn't have it. She went head to head with Iris. Pretty impressive."

"I know." He'd always found her handling of the whores impressive. Hell, he'd always found Jane impressive. He shook his head to rid himself of the thoughts. Now wasn't the time. "What the hell happened?"

"Graham was drunk, as usual. Word is he was already hot-tempered about you spending time with Becky."

"Why? He don't give two figs about her any other time. Besides, we ain't nothing."

"But you are spending time with her." In response to his glare, she shrugged. "Anyhow, the men thought it would be a grand time to tease him about Linh. He wasn't too happy about it. Started throwing things, and people, around. Mack's head is what messed up the bar."

"I'm gonna kill the bastard."

"You've said that already." Kathy moved behind him. Her hands pressed firm into his back. She grunted when he didn't budge. "Stop being stubborn and go have a drink. You're a miserable human being when you want to be."

After he'd let her struggle another minute, he moved to the bar. He did need a drink, after all. The few souls that had braved entrance into the saloon kept a wary gaze on him.

"So, after they managed to haul Graham off to jail, there was this to deal with. Jane and I wrangled a few bystanders and got the place cleaned up. Most everyone left after a few hours, but Jane and I worked through the night, and some of the next morning to get this set up like it is now. Jane somehow got Hammy to make the tables, and Cora to donate some and give you a deal on re-purchasing supplies."

"Why'd Jane do anything?"

Kathy sighed, and her head dropped forward until it thumped the top of the bar. "Idiots. The both of you. Such idiots."

Cole ignored her comment. After everything they'd done to get the saloon up and running and all the talk of making it more of a hotel, Graham went and pulled this. He poured the drink she'd told him to get and tossed it back.

"According to Jane, Graham wants to make amends."

"Well, he can't." He slammed down his glass, and half the room jumped. "I'm done. Not going to put up with his idiocy any longer."

"I guess that's your choice."

"It is."

"But he's your best friend."

"No, he ain't." Not since Jane came into Cole's life. Not once had Graham bothered to act like a friend to Cole. Rather, he tried to sabotage Jane at every turn, and sometimes Cole had let him, idiot that he was.

"Stubborn."

"Why did you bother coming back here again?"

"I came to see Norman, remember? I'm glad I did, too. Meeting Jane has been a wonderful turn of events. If I'd known she was here sooner, I might have come out of pure curiosity." Kat leaned on the bar. "Of course, she had a few startling revelations about you. What on earth were you thinking pushing her away like that?"

"None of your business."

"Cole. I know everything."

He spun the glass on the bar, wondering at how after apparently one night Kathy could know everything. When he met her gaze and found her more serious than teasing, he knew she had.

"If that's really the reason you pushed her away, you aren't as smart as I gave you credit for." She didn't flinch when his fist hit the counter. "Do me a favor and get a new bag of tricks sometime. Jane deserves better. So do you."

He flinched at the last words. After all he'd done in his life that was one thing he doubted. "Not sure I do. Go play with your old man, Kathy. I got a business to run here. What's left of it, anyway."

"Fine. I'll leave you to cope for a while, but I'm not done with you."

"I wouldn't dream of thinking you were." Cole downed another whiskey. Realizing his stock was probably low, he shoved aside the glass. He rubbed his hand over his face and tried to get his thoughts together.

Everything had been going so wrong. Something had to go right soon.

It just had to.

The anger of lovers renews their love.
-Terence

David's kind, hazel gaze studied her with intensity. The din in Cora's restaurant around them kept their conversation private. Even so, he lowered his tone. "Are you going to tell me what's been going on?"

Jane kept her fingers laced tight with David's, and she fought against the rush of emotion threatening to claim her. They'd just signed the divorce papers and they were now tucked away in the basket beside her. The whole thing should have been such a relief. Instead, emotions she'd managed to keep buried the past few days thanks to many distractions were bucking against her carefully placed façade.

"Jane?"

Of course, now she had Cole glaring at her from across the restaurant. He'd returned Saturday evening, but she hadn't seen him since. Not until just then. As she'd tucked away the signed papers he'd stormed passed her and taken a seat in her line of sight. So much had been going on, she'd been relieved to not see him, and Kat had done much to keep her occupied.

But now he was there. She found life so much easier to bear when he was holed up and she wasn't forced to face the reminder of her unresolved pain. She was happier pretending she was all right. David's finger brushed a lock of hair from her cheek, and she couldn't stop herself. Before she let out the welling tears for the entire world to see, she spun and buried her face in his neck, holding tight to him until she could regain control of herself.

"Hey. If I knew it would upset you this much, I wouldn't have let us get divorced."

His stab at humor forced an unenthusiastic laugh from her and she shook her head. His hands ran along her back in a soothing gesture she was grateful for. Even if he suspected what had her such a wreck anymore, which she was sure he did, she could never tell him the truth. "It's not that. I'm sorry."

He squeezed her arm. "No need to be sorry. Been worried about you."

"I know. I'm trying. Some days are just harder than others."

"Is it Cole?"

It was everything. Cole. The baby. The hangman's noose. Some days it was just more than she could bear. Right then she wanted nothing more than to get away from Cole's dark glare and curl up in bed. "Not really."

Her voice cracked, which made David chuckle. His low laughter rumbled through his chest, helping to warm her mood. A soft kiss was placed to her temple. "You say I'm not a good liar. Neither are you."

"I wasn't lying, exactly. It's not just him." With a sigh, she pushed away but kept her hand on his chest. "Although he's not helping my mood right now."

"So talk about something else."

"Like what? I haven't got much that isn't bleak." While she had good days, today wasn't one of them. The dark depression clawed at her more strongly than she could fight against.

"That isn't like you Clara." He set his hand on hers where it remained on his chest. "It isn't much like Jane, either. You're always finding the silver lining."

"Sometimes there simply aren't any. Even the richest mines can be emptied."

"Clara."

"I'm sorry. I need to go." She gave him another quick hug. "I'll bring you Clara's letters tomorrow."

The moment his arms relaxed she pulled away, grabbed her basket, and rushed for the doors. Her ankle was sore and still throbbed in protest, but she pushed on as fast as she could. She had to get home. Away from everyone.

Like every other moment of her life anymore, fortune was not on her side. All the way down the street nearly everyone stopped her to chat. From Mr. Kilmurry, to Hammy, and even Mabel stopped for conversation. It was a never-ending stream of dialogue all the way down the street.

She wanted it to stop. She needed it to stop. When Arthur ran up to her she nearly screamed in frustration. Home. Safety. Sanctuary. There, no one could see her cry as she had in the restaurant. There she was free.

There was no comfort there, but she didn't want comfort. Any sense of comfort had left with Cole, with the child. In truth, she shouldn't have comfort, peace, warmth. None of it would be deserved.

"Jane?"

"What? Oh, I'm so sorry Arthur. My mind is elsewhere today. Can I look at your article later? I think I need to go lie down."

"Yeah. Sure. Will you be at supper? Ma's makin' fried chicken."

"No. No, I'm going to stay at home until I have to get to the Army camp tomorrow. Stop by the library after school tomorrow." Not today. She couldn't take anymore today. "I'll look at the paper then."

With relief, she made her goodbyes and headed toward home again. The pressure in her chest was building behind her eyes. Just a little while longer, she could release it again. In the quiet of her own home. Away from the prying, ever curious and judging eyes.

She was not one to mind causing scandal, but she'd be damned if she'd embarrass herself by bawling in front of them all. She'd rather show her more flamboyant and inappropriate side than any hint of weakness.

At the edge of town, a figure stepped from the shadows. A shriek tumbled from her lips, and she grabbed at her chest. She couldn't stop them now. The tears flowed as fast as her heart pounded. She hadn't made it home.

She dug in her basket for her handkerchief, trying to keep her head lowered so he wouldn't see. He was no longer the only one who could see. He was the one who couldn't. Wiping at her tears, she sniffed and cleared her throat. "What do you want?"

Cole didn't bother to answer, just walked past her in silence. Before she could stop it, a short laugh escaped. His footsteps stopped, and she clenched her jaw. "Scare the wits out of me and walk away. Nice. Mature."

"Was just passing by. Ain't my fault you're jumpy as a colt."

The sorrow railed against her, and she fought it off. Trying to force it into anger, frustration, anything but the aching loss she felt at having him feet away and not touching her. This wouldn't do. She couldn't go on like this. Her head hung low, and she took a ragged breath.

"So how's things with the husband?"

That was something she should have expected. It hit her and straightened her back. He was concerned about her relationship with David? Him? The one who'd been seeing an engaged woman. Meanwhile, he knew she'd been planning on a divorce. Grinding her heel into the ground, she spun on him. "You're an idiot."

"How's that?"

A growl of frustration was all she could manage. Spinning back around, she walked away from him. For half of the way home, she could have sworn she heard his footsteps behind her, but she never bothered to look back.

If he was following her, she had no idea why. He'd made his views quite clear. It was over. It had to be.

That didn't mean she liked it. That she ever would.

Only once had she made the mistake of admitting her feelings. She'd thought it was only a dream, so the words had spilled free without censor. He'd been gone in moments.

Then there was now. The recent weeks. When she'd needed him more than ever.

He hadn't been there.

She fought with the lock, trying to get the door open before it was too late. Not that it mattered. There was no one around. She was alone.

Alone.

The door flew open, and she stumbled into her house. She slammed the door shut and beat on it with a scream. It did nothing to dull the pain and frustration, but she didn't care any longer.

With a heavy sigh, she turned and leaned back against the door. "Bastard."

Her ankle began to ache from the abuse she'd just doled out on the door. Daisy would have her hide, as she'd just received a tentative clearance to walk without a cane. Jane grabbed the cane from beside the door and used it to cross the kitchen.

Halfway to her bedroom, a package on the table caught her eye. She froze, not sure where it might have come from. The only other soul with a key to the homestead was Michael. Since the incident at the library, she'd taken to locking every door and window at home as well.

Probably Mike. It has to be from Mike.

Hesitation slowed each step more than her ankle would have. The five steps took her several minutes, but once there she dropped her basket on the chair and snatched the bundle closer. She leaned the cane against the table and tugged on the twine holding the bundle closed.

The moment the ties came free, the burlap fell aside to reveal a bloody horseshoe with a letter pinned beneath. Jane gripped the edge of the table, unsure she wanted to see what the letter might say.

In the end, her curiosity caught up to the fear, and she tugged the paper out from under the shoe. The reminder of the stampede and what Cole had done to save her was enough to set her hands shaking, but the letter itself struck fresh fear into her soul.

Retribution runs red.

The words themselves appeared to be written in blood, crudely penned the width of a finger and stained red. Whose blood, she had no idea.

Her hand shook, and she dropped the letter onto the table and backed away. Air became thin, and her breath dropped to short gasps. She grasped at her shawl and ripped it off, trying to do the same with her bodice.

Under her trembling fingers, the buttons refused to release. Her vision began to dim and she tugged hard enough to that buttons pinged across the room. Somehow she stayed awake long enough to release the busks on her corset. Fresh air rushed into her lungs, and she dropped to her knees. She coughed and gasped for air until her breath began to steady.

All she wanted to do was give in. To let the torment of her past, of her present, of her losses and mistakes all win. The idea of returning to the desperate tears she'd released after the miscarriage tempted her more and more.

Instead, pushed herself to her feet. She wrapped the horseshoe and letter back in the burlap and placed it by her basket. She set her corset right and went to her bedroom to get another bodice. She'd take the *gift* she'd been left to Mike and then stay at the Silver Saddle.

If Johnny could get in her house, she'd not be so stupid to remain there alone. She moved fast on the unlikely but possible chance that he might still be inside. Soon as her new bodice was on, she grabbed her brush and perfume off her dresser.

She carried them back out to the kitchen. In a matter of minutes she had everything situated in her basket and grabbed her cane.

She'd promised she wouldn't let Johnny terrify her. It was a promise she was failing at. She hoped Mike had made some progress with the notes from the Poe book.

Otherwise they were still no closer to answers. Johnny had them all, and Jackson was trying to find them with more money and power than she had.

Jane locked her door and took a deep breath. There had to be a way. She just didn't know what it was.

*A mad devil and a dull spirit possess the
jealous at the same time.
-Johann Kaspar Lavater*

"Take your time, Jane." Major Webb's hand slid along Jane's waist. She leaned into him slightly to limp alongside him.

Cole noticed she now walked without the cane. Seemed too soon the way she limped now. Then again, he'd seen her walking a lot the night before. Racing, really.

Cole clenched his jaw, breathing out an angry breath. When Webb took Jane's free hand in his own, Cole ground his teeth together and a low growl rumbled out. The chuckle beside him ramped up his annoyance. "Shut up, Kathy."

"I didn't say a word." Her arms were folded across her chest, a bright smile remaining on her features even as she watched the pair move along the line of Indians. One step had her hovering close enough to speak low. With twitching lips, she laughed softly. "Of course, if I had said something…"

"Don't." Cole didn't want to hear it. Not when he had to keep one sharp eye on Webb to make sure he didn't take his supposed caring attention to Jane too far. He really didn't want to hear it from Kathy. She'd been a good lover and a better friend at one time, but knowing how close she'd gotten to Jane meant he didn't dare try to figure out what she wanted to say.

"It would have been that you two are stubborn fools."

"Kathy," he all but snarled. A sharp look from Jane shut them both up. If he were honest, the woman looked exhausted today. Come to think of it, she had yesterday too. Dark circles lingered under her eyes. The pleasant pink warmth of her cheeks was gone, replaced with an almost sickly pallor.

She'd lost weight, too. More than the temptingly plump weight she'd gained from the baby, she was now even skinnier than when she'd fallen into his saloon near dead.

Without even touching her, he could tell. He knew every inch of her better than he knew any woman. He'd spent hours learning every dip, every curve, ever soft inch of flesh.

Damn, he missed her. She was better off without him, he was sure. Once she'd healed from the loss of the baby, and she had to, she'd be better off without him.

"You failed to tell me you took her into your room." Kathy's voice was so quiet, he barely heard her under the low din of soldier conversation. The teasing smile was gone, and she kept a steady gaze on Jane as well. "An important detail to leave out, considering it's a first."

"Shut up." He couldn't tear his eyes away from Jane, or the way Major Webb held her tighter than necessary. Or was it? She didn't look strong. Considering the fear of Indians that had left her frozen in place at each attack, he imagined she wouldn't be very strong today.

"No, I'm sorry. It isn't him." Jane's voice shook, her hand gripping Webb's. "This isn't the man that shot me."

"Are you sure?" Webb frowned. "Take your time and get a good look."

"I'm telling you, it's not him." There it was, what he'd desperately hope still lingered. A hint of her fire. She was still in there. She hadn't completely lost herself. She'd been hurt in so many ways, tormented by life and man, but she was still fighting. "Let me keep looking."

"Jane, that's Starbird."

"Thank you for telling me. He's still not the man that shot me." For a moment, her back straightened with stubbornness. "Do you want me to find the man that truly shot me, or just name Starbird to help with the trial?"

"I don't want you to lie." Webb sighed. "Did you want to keep looking?"

"Do you want to know who it was or does it no longer matter since it was not Starbird?" Jane took a step back from him. Her hands set firm on her hips, her chin raised. Despite the strong stance, Cole caught the twitch in her brow. She was ready to crack. Beside him, Kathy took a step forward like she'd seen it too.

She turned to glare at him for a brief moment. Like it was his fault. Or maybe because he didn't move. He couldn't, though. Jane didn't want him. He'd hurt her too bad.

"Why don't you and I go with Corporal White?" Kathy rushed forward to Jane's side. "Take a walk along the line and see if you spot him. Then we can go back to town and far away from them."

Was it his imagination or did she relax more now that Kathy was near? Apparently Jane was in agreement that their friendship had become that deep that quick. Cole didn't think anything good could come of those two hardheaded women being so close.

He watched Jane carefully as she walked along the line. Unable to stand still, he kept fidgeting and shuffling his feet. He itched to go to her side and take Kathy's place. After her display with David yesterday, he'd seen red. Then he'd realized it wasn't his place to say or do anything about it.

In his anger, he'd gone after her. Unfortunately, he'd once again failed to find any sort of words to tell her what he'd been doing, what a fool he'd been. Words had never been his strong suit and he was the worst at eating crow.

Right then, though, he wanted to be the one helping her face the Indians to identify the one that had shot her. He wanted to be the one holding her hand.

She hadn't fallen apart. She was still alive, still strong.

Did she grieve? There had been tears when he'd startled her. He'd followed her home to make sure she made it all right. But was it over the baby?

The day he'd gone to make sure she knew he was done and hurt her so deep, she'd collapsed. He closed his eyes at the memory. He'd been ready to walk away and never look back, never face the pain. Instead, he'd picked her up off the floor.

The way she'd clung to him, he hadn't been able to leave. He'd held her close, letting her grieve against him. As she'd fallen into the depths of the pain, he'd beseeched her to be strong; she had to be. He couldn't watch her end up broken.

When she'd gone silent, he'd used her proximity to grieve as well. Until her brother had arrived he'd stayed. Then he'd slipped out of the window before Mike could know he was there.

How could he be done with her? He was in pain. He was grieving. For the first time in years he was feeling something. It was all her damned fault. No, he was far from done.

There was just one problem.

She was done with him.

His eyes flew open and stared at her retreating back. Not wanting to create more grief for himself, he'd hurt her. Now no matter what he'd done in the weeks to rectify the situation, she'd never forgive him. He didn't deserve it.

No, she should be angry with him. He was angry with himself. It was obvious she'd found ways to heal. Not one of them involved him.

Could he do the same? Heal without her?

He wasn't so sure he could.

"Cole."

Webb's voice restored the tension to his limbs, shoving aside the defeat he'd been feeling. Once again, the man had weaseled back into Jane's good graces. He was really beginning to annoy Cole. "What?"

"Did you want to see if you agree with Jane's identification?"

"Why? Did she have doubts?"

"Well, no." Webb frowned and adjusted his hat. "You're the one that first identified it as Starbird."

"Because of the war paint. Jane's the one that got the good look. Don't doubt that she'd pick one and mean it." Cole ignored Webb's next question to head back toward town. Kathy's words nagged him. What did she mean, they were *both* stubborn? Was it as hopeless as he thought?

Maybe he could bribe her to tell him what Jane was thinking. He sure wouldn't mind knowing what was going through that head for once. It wasn't something he got to do often. She was far too complicated for that.

Prideful. Giving. Evil. Loving. Damn her. She was perfect.

She was maddening. She was amazing.

She was…huddled with Graham? What the hell was that about? Her arm was partially wrapped around his stocky waist. They were close, much too close.

The anger he'd held toward Graham for destroying the saloon reared its head again. Initially, he'd only been upset, almost felt bad that Graham was so dumb to think he'd gone off with Becky. Then as the damage had revealed itself, he'd managed to get furious. Not even Jane's detailed list of damage and money Graham would have to repay had eased it.

It had taken a lot of whiskey.

But the whiskey was wearing off.

And Graham had his burly hands all over Jane.

Now he was seeing red. Graham would pay. For the way he'd run his mouth to Jane about what Cole might be doing with Becky. For destroying the bar. For moving in on his territory. On his woman.

Cole wouldn't stand for Graham's idiocy anymore.

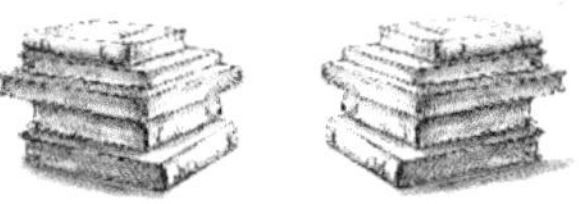

Anger is never without a reason,
but seldom without a good one.
—Benjamin Franklin

"Are you sure you're all right?" Cora set the teapot in the middle of the table and sank into the chair next to Jane. "I mean, if you're being nice to Graham, something has to be seriously wrong."

Jane let out a weak laugh she didn't really feel. "I'm still beyond annoyed with him. However, I don't like seeing anyone suffer. He hasn't had a drink since David locked him up on Saturday. It's starting to hurt."

Kat nodded. "I saw him when he called Jane over. He was shaking something fierce. Shouldn't he go see Daisy? I don't like the man, but someone should be with him when the worst hits. It'll get painful quick, it's an ugly thing to see anyone go through."

"He probably should, Daisy could give him a room at the clinic. Of course, that doesn't mean he will, the stubborn man. I'll try to speak with Becky today. I promised him I would. If I can get her to go see him and see what he's going through, maybe she can convince him to go."

"But he doesn't like her," Kat mock-whispered.

"But he wants her dowry," Jane whispered back.

Cora's hands tightened on her knees, her eyes wide. The trembling nerves were enough to get Jane's attention.

Jane had no doubt what was upsetting her, so she leaned forward. She rested her hand on Cora's. "It wasn't Starbird."

The woman's whole body sagged. Cora rubbed her hands over her face. "How did you know? I mean, are you certain?"

"Positive. I don't know anything about war paint, and none of them had it on. All I know is that it wasn't Starbird. I looked into the eyes of the man that shot me. I looked into Starbird's eyes. They were two different men." Jane took a sip of tea. "It was another warrior. He was in the group. Starbird had been beaten, or worse."

"By the soldiers?" Cora gasped. "Even before they had definite proof?"

"Al wouldn't do that." The saucer clinked from the force of Jane's cup. "He's not the type of man to do such a thing. It wasn't the Army."

"It was the Indians." Kat leaned forward and spoke low, though only a few tables were occupied. "Martha told me as much. She'd seen him at the village. They did it to make Martha help, and because he was a traitor to them in their eyes."

"I don't know. Kat and I didn't remain long enough to find out." Her nail ran along the flowered pattern on the side of her cup. Biting her lip, Jane concentrated on not shaking herself. Between the Indians and Cole's presence, not to mention her lack of proper sleep, she'd barely been able to stand up.

"You get 'im, Cole."

Jane flew to her feet at the muffled shout from outside. She raced across the restaurant to the front doors and threw them open to the cold air and the dull roar of cheering. Kat's hand gripped her arm, and Jane's heart caught in her throat. "Oh no. What is he doing?"

Locked tight in a battle stance, Cole and Graham rounded each other. An arm would break free to get a punch in before getting locked down. Then they tumbled to the ground, their shouts lost amid the cheers of the crowd.

Jane rushed down the steps, gasping when her arm was grabbed again.

"They'll kill ya, Jane." Mr. Kilmurry nodded toward the men. "It's been comin' a while now. Might as well let it finish."

"Well, that's just stupid. They'll kill each other." Jane turned back to the fight, cringing when Cole's fist connected with Graham's eye.

"Destroying the bar." Cole's fist connected again, but Graham's retaliating tackle knocked the wind out of him.

"You stole my woman."

"I saw you with mine."

Jane heard Kat's chuckle, and her eyes closed. "The anger is easier."

"It always is," Kat agreed.

David's shout broke through the sounds of battle, which turned the crowd's cheers to complaints of the sheriff's arrival. Opening her eyes, she gasped when Cole managed a harsh blow to Graham. Without thinking, she hooked her fingers in her mouth and blew.

The shrill whistle silenced the crowd and stopped the battle long enough that David and Mike could interrupt. The hard weight of Cole's glare tugged at her heart, but luckily, Graham's shout freed her from the bindings.

"Stay away from my woman."

"Which one?" Cole spat back, lunging toward Graham again.

"Becky, you bastard. She's mine."

"I wouldn't touch that harpy, you idiot." Cole wasn't bothering to look at Graham any longer. Jane's heart fluttered when he directed his attention to her. He wanted her to hear this, not Graham. "She's been teachin' me to read."

Kat yelped when Jane's nails dug into her forearm, and she pried the fingers off her arm. Grabbing Jane around the waist, she turned and dragged her back into the store.

Compliant, Jane followed in total silence. Becky had been teaching Cole to read? Like Jane had been teaching David? She'd thought he'd been jealous, but then she thought maybe he just hated her.

It had all been just one misinterpretation after another. She might have been amused if it hadn't been her heart hurting. At least someone found it funny. Kat was failing miserably at covering her laughter.

When Jane finally got the strength together to face the hilarity at her expense, Kat lost it. Clutching her sides, she bent over in laughter. After another whoop, she sat up and pointed at Jane. "Oh…oh my…he was…and you were…and you *all* were…and if you'd only…"

"It's not that funny."

"Yes, it is."

Her resolve cracking, a laugh burst out of Jane. "It's not funny. That fight…was not funny."

"No. No, it wasn't." Kat managed to compose herself "But…you were jealous, Graham was jealous, Cole was jealous…all for the same reason. Cole assumed you and David were…and so he propagated the continuation of your belief that he and Becky were…"

Jane pinched the bridge of her nose, shaking her head as they both continued laughing quietly. "Just don't tell Michael. He will think it's even funnier than you do."

"Oh, I don't think it's possible to find it funnier than I do." Kat smiled and sat down across from her. "Of course, you do know that all of this good humor could have been avoided. You are both so stubborn."

"Look who's talking," Jane shook her head. "You are just as stubborn when it comes to your feelings for Norman."

"Jane, you're a strong, intelligent woman. Why would you skirt around such a silly thing as an emotion?"

"Silly thing? Do you find it silly?" Jane wagged her finger. "It doesn't seem that way."

Kat sighed. "I just think you need to tell Cole the truth."

"I've always been honest with him."

"No. You really haven't."

*It is always the heart that sees,
before the head can see.
–Thomas Carlyle*

Jane cracked open an eye.

Darkness.

It was still dark outside, and darker in the all-too-quiet house. Once again she'd failed to sleep through the night. The nightmares woke her every time, the loneliness kept her wide-awake. A never-ending cycle of terror and solitude.

The empty bed mocked her insomnia, so she dragged herself from it and lit the lamp. In an annoyingly cheerful chorus of chimes the clock announced the time. Ten o'clock.

That couldn't be right. If it was, she'd been asleep for less than an hour. This would never do. She'd told herself she'd live again, but she was falling further into oblivion. She grabbed the gun she'd set on her bedside table and carried the lamp into the kitchen.

She's been teachin' me to read, Cole's words filled her mind. He'd wanted her to hear it. Why? He couldn't want her back. He'd made himself clear. Hadn't he?

Habit had her move the teapot onto the stove before setting the lamp in the middle of the table. Should she even try? Would he reject her if he did?

A knock on the door startled her from her thoughts. Who would be by this late? Other than Cole, who would rather sneak in than knock, no one would ever visit at this hour. Certainly not cold as the weather had turned.

Thoughts of the package she'd found yesterday crept forward, but though Mike had promised to come and stay the night, he had a key to get in. If it was Johnny, she doubted he would bother knocking. She eyed the gun she'd set on the table. "Who is it?"

"Kat."

She could swear she heard tears in her friend's voice and rushed to the door. "Kat, what are you doing out so late?"

The hug Kat caught her in knocked the wind out of her. "Oh, Jane. I was out trying to get fresh air. To think. I saw your light on. I had to stop. I needed someone to talk to."

"Come on in," Jane squeaked out, taking a deep breath when Katherine released her hold. "I was just making some tea. Sit. Try to relax. I'm more than happy for the company."

"I can't believe he did this." Katherine dropped into the chair. "It's so unlike him."

Jane jumped at the whistle of the teapot and disappeared into the pantry to get a second cup. Once she'd poured their tea, she sat across from Katherine, who'd dropped her head into the curve of her arm. Jane reached out and squeezed her friend's hand. "What happened?"

An envelope fell out of Katherine's fingers, landing on the table with a gentle *thunk*. "He said he can't do this anymore."

"Do what?"

Silence. Jane's brow pinched together, and she picked up the crumpled envelope. The moment the flap opened, a ring tumbled out. A small gasp escaped, but she saw the envelope wasn't empty. "A train ticket?"

"He said he's too old to keep doing this." Katherine groaned into the table. "He's tired of having me for only a few days at a time. That I was gone so long this time, he'd had plenty of time to think about it."

"Then why the ring?"

"That's my choice. I finally accept his proposal. Or I get on the train tomorrow."

"What? That's awful extreme."

"Is it? You said yourself, he's quite a bit older than me. We've been carrying on this way for five years now."

"But such an ultimatum. He knows you don't want to get married. You never have." Jane rolled the ring in her fingers. "Would he compromise?"

"He wasn't much in a compromising mood."

"He has always understood that you didn't want to marry before."

"I guess he thought I'd change."

"No, that doesn't sound like Norman. He's too smart for that."

Kat pursed her lips and danced her fingers along the rim of her cup before picking it up. With a sigh, she took a long sip. "What sort of compromise could I offer? I won't marry him."

"What's keeping you from staying on for a while?"

"I have business."

"Your job at the bank?"

"Yes. No." Kat shoved away from the table and started to pace. A lock of red hair tangled in her fingers, twirling through them.

"What's wrong?"

"Oh. You'll get so mad."

"Katherine?"

"Norman doesn't know. No one does."

The teacup rattled under Jane's sudden shiver, and she yanked her hands back into her lap. Her stomach did a little flip. "Kat, please."

"Staying here isn't so simple. I do have work, and it's very important, I do need to work in order to survive."

"But?"

"I have a daughter, Jane."

"All right. So why can't you bring her here?"

Kat stopped short, her lower lip lost between her teeth. "She's just about four and a half years old."

There wasn't anything she could say. Nothing at all. At that age, the child was not Norman's. Not based on what Kat had told her. It had to be Cole's.

Cole's child. With a woman he never loved, and who'd never loved him. Jane had loved him, perhaps still did, and their child was gone. Cruelly taken away despite that love, that hope. Tears filled Jane's eyes, and she gasped against the onslaught.

It was too much. Too soon. Jane shoved aside her tea. "I need something stronger." She darted into the pantry and slammed the door behind her.

The bottle of whiskey stared at her from the counter, and she grabbed it before pulling open the hatch to the cellar. Once she'd climbed down into the cold sanctuary, she let loose the tears.

She released her grasp of the bottle, and the shatter of glass echoed in her soul. It wasn't fair. To have lost her life, her love, and her child. She would have accepted the fact that she might never get to see it grow, but it never had a chance.

Now this. Kat was her dearest friend, but jealousy ripped at the bond she felt forming. Maybe it was just as well. She shouldn't have any ties to this life. It could end soon enough.

The cold dirt wall chilled her spine, and she stared up through the hatch.

She did have ties. As much as this pained her, Kat was still her friend. There was Michael. David. Jesse.

A choice had to be made.

On the one hand, she could cut herself off from it all. Refusing to live and accepting her fate would make the end easier to bear. Wouldn't it? It would spare so many others pain. Pain as deep as this.

Pain that cut through a soul until it bled. Pain that seemed to have no end no matter what she did.

Would a life unlived be worth it? There would be no pain to reflect on, to see in others' faces when she confronted her fate. It would be perfunctory, another body hung and buried.

There would be no joy.

No joy to reflect back on, to hold dear in her darkest days. Like Clara had disappeared into the void, as would Jane. As if she'd never existed to all but a few.

Perhaps she never had.

But that wasn't true. She'd lived so much in the past few months, so truly and completely.

She'd experienced joy. In between the horrors had been moments of great joy. Great peace. How could she live without seeing a few more of those? Should she not make what life she had worth it in the end? To live a life worth remembering?

What was the right choice? What would cause more pain?

She'd left Kat alone all this time. One way or another, she had to face her again. With a shaky breath, she wiped the remnants of her doubt from her face and climbed back up the ladder.

Kat hunched over her teacup, dabbing at her eyes with her handkerchief. Her shoulders shook with unrestrained tears. It wasn't right to take out her grief on Kat. Or Cole. Or Jesse.

It would hurt, but she had to make this right. Having them close gave her more strength, not less. If she allowed them to share in her grief. She couldn't make the mistakes Clara had. Clara had thought that loving David had made her weaker, because the pain was stronger.

Through Michael and Kat, she was learning that sharing the grief lessened its hold. She couldn't push them away. She needed them.

Taking a deep breath, she stepped out and sat down next to Kat. Immediately, their hands clasped together, and Jane had to clear her throat. "Does Cole know?"

"Oh heavens, no. If I brought her here, he would." Kat's grip tightened. "For me, I never had a doubt. Cindy is my daughter, not his. I had no emotional attachment to him, or him to me."

"That brings me little comfort."

"You have to stop being so stubborn, Jane."

"Speak for yourself." At Kat's laugh, Jane joined her and wiped at her tears. The laughter might not be heartfelt yet, but it felt better than crying. She would get through this. "So silly to be crying. One thing has nothing to do with the other."

"It isn't silly to still be crying. Not at all." Kat's hand smoothed along her hair. "It isn't like you stubbed your toe. You lost a child, one with someone you love."

"I don't."

"You do." Kat sighed. "Then I come along and I never loved him, and the child we created is growing tall and strong."

"Will you stay?"

"Will it hurt you?"

"Yes." Jane squeezed her hand. "But I still want you to stay. If Norman will accept the compromise. You can tell those silly abolitionists that you're taking a break from changing the whole world. You're going to focus on changing this little world."

Laughter filled the room, and Kat returned the squeeze. "That is as good a reasoning as I've ever heard. Changing this little world seems like a good idea. Starting with you."

"I can't let him back in." Jane's knuckles were white; her grip on Kat's hand was so tight. Tears filled her eyes, until one started a crooked trail down the apple of her cheek. He'd already lost too much. "I could be facing a noose soon. I won't put him through that. I won't do that to him."

"Pish posh." Kat waved her off. "You don't know what will happen. If that's true—then live NOW. Change this little world."

Jane looked back and laughed softly, squeezing Kat's hand. "I guess we both have something to think about?"

"How much tea you have?"

"If we run out, I have coffee."

"Good." Kat held up her cup. "A toast?"

"To changing this little world."

*What is uttered from the heart alone,
will win the hearts of others to your own.
-Johann Wolfgang von Goethe*

The walk to town had never seemed so long as it was that morning. After a long night of talking with Kat, Jane had managed to collapse into a fitful sleep. Kat stayed with her, and seemed to have as much trouble sleeping. While Michael had come home at eleven, he'd assessed the situation fast enough and left the two of them alone to their quiet discussions.

With a heaping dose of mutual convincing, they'd each agreed to do what the other thought best. Jane had agreed to make an effort to speak with Cole, and Kat had agreed to seek out a compromise with Norman.

They parted reluctantly at the depot with one last supportive hug. Somehow Jane had to face her demons, and she'd have to soon. Sooner than she expected, even. For despite the saloon not opening for another hour, Cole stood on the porch.

She lingered in the shadow of the former boarding house, trying to figure out how best to handle this. For weeks she'd avoided the man in a failed attempt to ease her pain. Still, the last thing she wanted was to have a confrontation in front of the saloon. No, this was too personal. An audience was very unwelcome.

After a deep breath, she squared her shoulders and picked up her chin. Eye contact. She'd avoided making eye contact for weeks. It was sure to get his attention. She wasn't disappointed. For as she approached and sought out eye contact, it had the exact effect she'd hoped for.

Before she'd made it past the saloon, he'd pushed off the hitching post and followed behind. Her hands were shaking. How could she open the library with nerves like this? She had to get Cole alone, but she couldn't even get the keys from her pocket.

She slowed in the middle of the street and turned to face him. Every pain, all her grief surged forward at the sight of him and beat against her best intentions. Instead of a calm, rational greeting, she snapped, "Yes?"

"Thought might be tryin' to get my attention."

"It seems I have."

"Well?"

Every inch of her quaked and trembled under his intense gaze, but she reached a shaky hand toward him. When his hand closed over hers, her whole body stilled. She closed her eyes and reveled in the contact. Somehow she found the ability to speak again. "I was wrong. About so many things."

He yanked her close. When he chucked his finger under her chin, she willingly opened her eyes again to meet his gaze. The leer that curled his lip didn't reach the confused, and she dare say concerned, depths of his eyes. "I ain't gonna—"

The last thing she was going to let him do was bark at her, deserved or not. She grabbed his shirt and closed the distance between them. Her lips caressed his until he responded. Soon as he relaxed, she shoved him away hard. The moment she did, she ached from the loss of contact, but stepped back.

"What the hell?"

A smile tugged at her lips and she took a few more steps backward. She'd hoped to see many emotions at war with him, and he didn't disappoint. Frustration, confusion, and she might have detected a hint of relief in his features. The rest of what she'd hoped for would have to wait for the quiet solitude of the library. Would he follow?

The sound of a step behind her after she'd turned confirmed he would, so she pushed on. Her hands still shook, but she managed to unlock the door and step inside. The nervous flutter of her stomach threatened to overwhelm her. To calm herself down she grabbed a few books to shelve, hoping the routine would let her keep her head enough to speak.

She had so much to say, and no idea how he would react to what she wanted to tell him. He could very well walk away again. If that were the case she'd have to accept it. She couldn't keep putting herself through such torture. It was just as likely he didn't feel the same.

One footstep. Two. The door clicked shut. Silence.

The book she held trembled as she shoved it into place. She couldn't let him speak first; she had to get out all she needed to say. "I thought this, whatever we had, had to be without attachment. I thought I was honest with myself. I thought I was honest with you. But it was all such a lie."

"What was a lie?"

"All of it. Everything. I fooled myself into thinking that I could do things how I thought you wanted. But I couldn't. I was happy, Cole. With you. Probably more than I should have been. It wasn't just having you in my bed…it was all of it."

She closed her eyes and leaned her forehead against the shelf in front of her. A slow, deep sigh pushed out some of her fear. "I was happy when I realized I was carrying our child. Maybe it was stupid to feel that way, but I was. But I couldn't show you, especially after you told me what happened with Lydia. I couldn't show you that you—you were the only one that made me feel."

A hollow laugh emerged at the irony. "The one man that made me feel everything and I could show you nothing."

His lack of response rattled her nerves. A tear slipped down her cheek. She pulled back from the shelf. After a deep breath that she exhaled slowly, she finally let herself turn toward him, trying to prepare herself for anything. "Are you going to say anything?"

"Crazy bitch."

Hope.

Right up until that very moment she'd had hope. Hope that Cole would feel the same. That she wouldn't have to live with the gaping wound.

Crazy bitch. The words rolled through her head over and over. That was it. It was all gone. Her knees trembled, threatening to give out. She turned and gripped the bookshelf, struggling to find her voice.

She croaked like a frog, her throat was so thick with emotion. "Oh. I see. That answers my question." She pushed off the shelf, but didn't make it a step.

His hand clamped on her shoulder, and he turned her toward him. He tugged her close and assaulted her lips.

She gripped his coat and pulled him close. A soft whimper of relief escaped her mouth as it opened under his unrelenting demands.

Urgent.

Need.

Fear, desire, longing, missing, searching.

Oh, how she'd missed his touch. Every muscle turned to jelly, quivering under his strong hands. He cupped her buttocks and started to lift, and she gasped.

Then he was gone.

Jane dropped to the floor with a strangled yelp. The shock of impact ripped through her exhausted body. "Cole?"

A scuffle nearby drew her attention. Michael shoved Cole toward the door. "You bastard. I told you to leave her alone." Michael took a swing at Cole.

"Michael!" Jane gripped the shelves to push herself to her feet. Before Cole could retaliate, she threw herself between them. "Michael, stop."

"I told you to leave her alone." Michael tried to get Jane out of the way. When she shoved him, he stumbled back at step. "Get out, Cole."

"Michael!"

"That's it. I'm done." Cole threw up his hands, stepping back.

"Cole." Jane spun around, holding Michael back. "Wait."

It was too late. He was walking away. She rushed to the door, but found she couldn't watch him walk away again. Her eyes screwed shut and she gripped the doorjamb. A hand settled on her shoulder, but she knew it wasn't Cole. She shoved Michael off and stumbled back into the library. "Get out."

"Clara."

"I'm not Clara. Now get out."

"Are you all right? He was—"

"Not doing anything I didn't want him to," she snapped.

Michael froze, his mouth hanging open. "You aren't serious."

"I'm very serious. I approached him, not the other way around. I wanted him here."

"After what he did to you? Clara, he hurt you."

"And I hurt him right back." She sighed and dropped into her chair. "I don't need him to live, to find happiness. I have had my share in between the pure hell I've been dealing with, but I want him here. I feel more with him around, the ugly and the good."

"I can't watch you suffer again."

"I won't have you being my defender. I don't need protection."

"You're my sister. I've seen how you suffered because of that bastard."

"No. Because of me. I've done this to myself. He may have helped, but I let him." She pressed the heels of her hands against her forehead. Each pound of her heart reverberated through her skull until she thought it might split open. "I don't need protection. Certainly not from Cole."

"Clara."

"Just go away. I want to be alone."

"I'm sorry."

His apology wouldn't bring Cole back. She didn't want to hear it. She waved at him, unable to find the strength to tell him again to leave. The second the door closed she dropped her head to the desk.

She groaned. "Damn it."

She couldn't let Cole walk away this way, but she had to work. Or not. The idea of closing the library was not without its merits. Right then the only thing on her mind was Cole. How it had felt to be in his arms again.

Whole.

For a few minutes she hadn't been broken. The pain was still there, but knowing he was there had eased it. Knowing he mourned with her.

He did, didn't he?

Or was he just there now because the baby was gone?

Her head popped up as her stomach performed a sickening flop into her gut. No. That couldn't be the case. Could it?

She planted her hands on the desk and stood. This time it had to be her. They had to be alone. Would he acquiesce? After what had just happened, she wasn't so sure.

It didn't matter. She had to try.

She left her things behind, rushing out so fast she almost forgot to lock the door. Once she'd completed that task, she rushed across the street.

She heard him before she saw him, talking to Wills. When she turned the corner, they were in an intense conversation, so she walked past. It would do no good to interrupt, but this was important.

With a frown, she stopped up short. It was too important. Whatever business he had with Wills could wait. She spun around, letting out a sharp yelp when she found someone right behind her. "Cole."

He didn't say a word, but his eyes were dark, penetrating deep into hers with an intensity that made her shiver. Was it anger? No. The hand that wrapped gently around her neck, the gentle brush of his thumb to her jaw, none of it came from anger.

"Cole, tell me this isn't because I'm no longer…"

"Been scrambling for a way to get ya back. I messed up bad."

"Yes, you did. But I don't care anymore."

The tips of his fingers ran down her arm, taking her hand and giving it a gentle tug. She followed without further question, back to the saloon. Neither of them stopped to acknowledge any greeting as they crossed the floor. Their hands gripping tight to each other all the way up to his room.

She wasn't sure what to expect once they got inside. Would he try to claim her again as he had in the library? Would he take the chance to yell at her? At this point, it didn't matter, as long as he was there.

When the door shut, he pressed her into it, but there was no force. Her breath grew shaky, her eyes closing at a whisper-light touch to her neck. For the first time, she didn't pull away from the tenderness.

She wanted to be loved. By him.

Her heart fluttered in her chest before it jumped into her throat when his lips brushed her neck. Gentle, tender.

This time when his lips closed over hers, they were soft and inviting. The last bit of tension in her body left as she ran her hands up his chest to circle his neck.

Their tongues moved together in a slow dance, searching without any urgency. She untied his tie and let it slip to the floor.

With the invitation open, they moved together, buttons popping open and clothes dropping to the floor in a rumpled trail toward his bed. Their lips never parted until he got to the laces of her corset.

His thumb ran along her swollen lips. A hint of a smirk played on his lips before he ran his finger down her chin and neck.

She trembled with a soft moan when his finger ran between her breasts and down to the corset ties. Biting her lip against the burgeoning smile, she let him struggle with the tight knot.

He looked up at her soft giggle and grabbed the lace, yanking her against him before just as suddenly spinning her around.

She gasped when the tight binding was released moments later and the corset fell to the floor. Grinning at the cut laces, she leaned back against him. His quiet moan and the feel of his lips on her shoulder were the only encouragement she needed.

He groaned as her shifting hips raised his desire, and his hands slipped along her waist to grip her and yank her back against him. He chuckled at her whimper and kissed a trail of hot fire up her neck.

When he nibbled her ear, her hands closed over his where they sat practically burning a hole through her chemise. Her body quaking with each touch of his lips, she spun around and pushed him down onto the bed.

His lips never stopped moving, continuing their steamy trail along her stomach through the fabric. Fiery fingers slipped up her waist and nudged the thin muslin out of his way.

A moment later, the chemise joined the rest of the clothes on the floor, and her drawers were kicked aside.

The feel of his lips against her skin, the way his tongue trailed lazy circles against her flesh sent the blood rushing through her veins chasing away the last of the lingering chill.

She let her fingers dance along the muscles on his back, feeling each one twitch and react to her touch. Curving her fingers, she dragged the nails back up toward his shoulders. Only a soft gasp escaped when he grabbed her and spun, pressing her down onto the bed.

He hovered above her, nose to nose as the heat of their bodies dragged them inevitably closer. When her leg slowly hooked around his waist, he still didn't move, holding her gaze intently.

Her breath hitched as they both hung in suspension, not quite yet willing to give in despite the screaming desire that filled them both. As she allowed her half-closed eyes to open all the way and meet his head on, she knew exactly what he needed.

She traced the outline of his lips with her finger and smiled. "You are the only man I've ever wanted. All I need is you."

Within moments, he complied.

Tenderness is the repose of passion.
—Joseph Joubert

Her head rested on his chest where his heart beat a gentle cadence against her cheek. His thumb ran up and down her spine. The comfort and peace of the moment drew a quiet sigh from her. She let her fingers dance across his chest, enjoying every second she was close to him.

Contentment.

There was still much to be said. Right there and then, in that moment, that didn't matter. They were happy to lie there and enjoy being together again. Soon enough the talking would happen. It was inevitable and highly necessary. Until the moment it was no longer avoidable, she wasn't going to move an inch away from his side.

For an hour she stayed there, not daring to say a word. A twinge in her stomach made her realize that soon she would need to eat. With great reluctance she moved, knowing it would break the spell.

She lifted her head to rest her chin on his chest. His eyes were closed, but the hand still running along her back let her know he was awake. It was good to know he was as content as she was.

She didn't even try to stop the smile the thought brought. When his eyes opened, she smiled brighter.

"What?"

"Not a thing." She widened her eyes to try to convey the innocence she was far from feeling. When he narrowed his eyes she giggled.

He snorted, and his thumb stopped its lazy trail along her spine. "Sure. What d'ya want?"

"I thought I already made that clear."

"Maybe you need to refresh my memory."

She shifted, nipping at his chest before moving up along him. After a soft kiss to his neck, she paused at his ear. "You. Every last inch of you."

"You already had that."

"Oh, I remember."

His chuckle rumbled through her. "Good."

Silence. The hesitation to breach the contentment was fighting with the need to do just that. Where should she begin? For once words were lost to her.

"I ain't sure I—"

Her fingers pressed to his lips. "Stop right there."

A frown formed under her fingers, and he sat up. One sharp tug from him and she sat across his lap. "Are you gonna let me talk, woman?"

"Sure you want to?" Giggling, she shifted closer and buried her fingers in his hair. "Your physical messages are always so much clearer. I'm sure it gets difficult to talk with that foot you keep lodged in your mouth."

Before she could think, he'd flipped her onto her back. He grinned when she shrieked and squirmed under his tickling fingers. Within moments he'd stopped, pressing into her until her laughter faded into a shaky breath. "I mean it."

All she could do was nod. Once again he was directing that intense, longing stare at her. She found herself lost in it. Not wanting it to end.

Now she could see the emotion behind it, and a flutter in her chest shivered through her. Her eyes closed as his weight lifted off her, but his warmth remained close at her side.

A single finger ran down along her waist until his hand finally settled on her hip. The silence lingered before he gave a gentle tug. Once she was facing him and had opened her eyes, he took a deep breath. "I ain't sure I like this."

Tension started in her belly, radiating through her muscles. One touch could easily send her to the ceiling.

What didn't he like? He'd seemed so relaxed. Had she been wrong? Somehow she kept silent, knowing he had to finish.

"What you been doing to me. It's not something I'm used to. It ain't like it was with Ella. It sure isn't like any of the girls." The light touch on her hip grew stronger. His fingers pressed into her flesh, until he released it as quick. "I ain't been with none of them since I picked you up off that floor."

Her gasp filled the silent air after his statement.

Had he really just said that? It wasn't possible. She couldn't lie still, but couldn't bring herself to move. The pillow filled her fist, her voice squeaking when she found it. "I didn't think…I…what?"

"I told ya. I don't like it."

"I'm sure they don't like it much either." The words had spilled free before she could stop them, followed by a nervous giggle.

His lips twisted in a grimace, and he smacked her hip. "Jane."

"Sorry."

"No you ain't." The fingers on her hip squeezed in a reassuring gesture. "It's not like I didn't have the chance, just didn't want to. Ain't a one of them I don't pity. Never pitied you. Not even when I was in that room with Daisy cutting on you."

"How could you not? I was hardly alive."

"You threw up on me."

Another giggle welled until it broke the surface. "I gave you the shirt I owed you for that."

He didn't crack a smile, but his frown creased his forehead deep. "Before you did that, you opened your eyes."

"I did?"

"Yeah. Looked right at me. Didn't look weak at all. Then knowing you made it far as you did near dead, I knew you weren't nothing to pity."

"Still. I never expected you to turn away your girls. I'd never ask it of you." Her grip on the pillow relaxed, and she moved her hand to rest on his chest.

"Was it mine?"

She sucked in air like it was running out. She sat up, turned away, and wrapped her arms around her waist. He still doubted? Why wouldn't he? She'd lied to him so he could run. A shudder ran through her, and her stomach threatened to revolt.

"It was."

"Yes." The trembling of her lips had to be stopped, so she sucked them in between her teeth. Hot streaks of tears slipped down her cheeks. She had to fight it off; she had to tell him the truth. "It couldn't have been anyone else's."

Silence.

A sob ripped from her gut, and she flew off the bed. She threw on her chemise, a rip of the fabric startling her. The creak of the bed let her know he was moving, and she stumbled to the dresser. Gripping the edge, she watched her knuckles grow white.

Why did this have to happen again? Damn him. "Damn you, Cole Mitchell. You made me lie to you. I never lied to you until that moment. How could you do that to me? How could you? I wouldn't have made you—"

His arms closed around her waist, and when she turned, his forehead pressed into her stomach. Locked tight in his grasp, she couldn't wrench away if she wanted. Her own grief rushed through her again. It had been unrelenting, but now his added to it. The silent evidence of it making her chemise damp.

She laced her shaking fingers into his hair, running soothing trails along his scalp. When his tight grip loosened just a bit, she joined him on her knees. She cupped his face in her hands; her thumbs wiping away the lingering sorrow.

Their foreheads pressed together, and then she collapsed. Falling into his chest, she gave in to the grief she'd tried so hard to keep hidden. Letting its salty bitterness spill onto his chest, feeling his pained tremors join hers.

Wrapped tight in each other, sharing their grief and pain, trying to comfort, they remained. When her tears slowed, his arms tightened around her. He pulled her onto his lap and them both against the dresser.

Her head nestled into his shoulder, her hand resting on his chest. With a ragged breath, she blinked against the exhaustion that was creeping in. "Damn you."

"I…" His voice cut off. A tight squeeze to her shoulder was the end of his attempt.

"You made me lie to you. I understand why. But I'm still mad at you."

"Forgive me."

"No. Forgive me."

His finger tucked under her chin as he lifted her face to his. "We both messed up."

"I was afraid." Tears threatened to spill over again, but she choked them back. She had to get through this. Closing her hand over his, she kissed his palm. "Afraid that if I let you see that you were more than just a passing fancy to me that you would run. I needed you too much to let that happen."

"I ain't ever gonna be like David."

"Thank heavens. I divorced him."

"What?"

"The papers are signed. I'm no longer married."

"So why all the friendly gestures?"

It was impossible to stop the smile, so she wiped at her tears and let it happen. "Why? Jealous?"

"I ain't jealous." A smirk crossed his lips when she giggled. "Much."

"Of course not."

"Jane."

"What?"

"I didn't want you to lie."

"Yes, you did. I told you what you wanted to hear." When he dropped his head, she brushed her fingers along his cheek. "I told you what you needed to hear. I knew you couldn't handle it, not after what you told me."

"I ain't weak."

"No, but you've been carrying that pain for too long."

He lifted his gaze. "Never wanted you to know it."

"I know."

"I was cruel. I wanted to be done To have ya hate me."

She offered a weak smile. "You came so close, but I kept dreaming of you."

"They weren't all dreams."

"I know."

He pressed his forehead to hers. "Weren't strong enough to do it right. I shoulda been."

"We both should have been." She took a shaky breath. "I have one thing I have to ask you to do for me. It is the only demand I'll make of you."

"What?"

"Don't ever make me lie to you again."

"You've gotta do something for me then."

"What?"

"Don't hide nothing from me. It's the same as lying."

Her lip trembled, and she nodded. "I know. I'm sorry. I promise."

"Then so do I." Pressing his fingers into her back, he pulled her closer. "So you ain't married no more?"

"No, I'm not. Does that mean I'm no longer intriguing to you?"

"Hell no. It's better that I don't gotta worry 'bout him. Do I?"

Jane snorted and shoved him. She stood and walked a few steps away with her hands on her hips. "Oh no. You're not jealous."

"Much." He wrapped his hands around her waist and pulled her back against him.

"David and I share a child. We're friends. Will remain so. But there's nothing more there."

"And soldier boy?"

"We play cards. Write horrible limericks. Just friends." She yelped when he scooped her up and set her on the bed.

A noise akin to a growl rumbled through his chest when she arched her body toward him. He smirked. "That's what you said we were."

"Oh. We are." She nodded, pulling him closer. "We are…friends…"

"And nothing more."

"Oh, there's something more…a great deal more…" Waggling her eyebrows at him, she chuckled softly. "And I feel it right now…"

"You do?" At her nod, he pulled her even closer and ran his fingers along her spine. He stopped just as his lips reached hers, their breath mingling. "Jane…"

"Yes?"

"Only *comfort* I want you lookin' for is mine."

"Yes."

"No more lies."

"None."

Fear is pain arising from the anticipation of evil.
—Aristotle

Cole didn't want to go anywhere. The last thing he wanted was for Jane to leave his arms for any amount of time in the near future. Jane's rumbling stomach and insistence that she needed sustenance to make it through the night was the only thing that got him moving. As it was, she was already in the hall, and he was still pulling on his boots.

He didn't go quietly either. The whole time he grumbled plenty of curses about the hassle.

They were far from done. Not even close, and he didn't just mean in bed. There was still a lot they needed to talk about. Words weren't his strong suit, never had been. They were Janes, but he knew he needed to do it; they needed to talk it out.

She was still in pain. For that matter, so was he.

Having her in his arms mourning with him had somehow been comforting. He found it strange to have them both so lost, yet somehow being that way helped. Knowing she was right there with him. She wasn't lost. She was his. They had time now for the rest.

Or did they?

With a possible murder charge hanging over her head, would they have time? Any day now that evil bastard could come back, or rat her out. He would have finally gotten her back only to have her taken away again.

Just the thought made every bit of his good mood fall away. He had to be close to her again. No more stalling.

She stood right outside his room, leaning on the railing overlooking the saloon floor. The moment he got close she leaned into him, and his mood improved. The saloon was busy, but not at capacity. It was still too early in the day for that.

The new tables had arrived and were now mixed in with the scrap-wood tables Hammy had put together. All thanks to Jane. He'd probably still be cleaning up the mess if she and Kathy hadn't done as much as they had. And at the time she'd been rightfully angry with him. Proof her feelings ran as deep as neither of them dared to admit.

Her lips brushed his neck, pulling him from his thoughts to follow her down the stairs. His hand lingered at the small of her back as if it were stuck there. The contact was minimal at best, but felt needed.

"What will you do?" Her voice startled him. Since he'd agreed to leave for supper she'd been unusually silent.

"What do ya mean?"

"I mean, what are you going to do about this? The saloon. The bar is still broken. Your tables are mismatched."

"I kinda like it like that."

Her delicious lips curved into a smirk he wanted to kiss right off her face. "I suppose it does have a certain charm."

He winked and tugged her close. "I'll keep business going. Got no choice. If anything's gonna get fixed, I need the money. Ain't likely Graham'll cough up the cash anytime soon."

"Don't count him out yet. I think he'll make good on the debt."

"I think I prefer it when you ain't friendly with him."

"Cole. He's your friend."

"Not anymore, he ain't." Not after what that bastard had done. Cole wasn't about to forgive him any time soon. He'd have to find a way to buy back his half of the saloon. "Not after this."

"You've been friends for years. This transgression might be egregious, but don't let it destroy your years of friendship." She placed her hands on his chest. Big blue eyes blinked sweetly at him, which worked his nerves more than his resolve. "Besides, without a partner, you'll be stuck working more often than not."

"Not working."

"Not at all?"

"No."

"Damn." She laughed and tapped his chest, not at all off-put by his hint of temper. "I still say you should talk to him. At least give him a chance to apologize."

"I got a question."

"Should I be scared?"

"Why'd you do this?" He nodded in the direction of the bar, and then glanced around the saloon. "Why'd you clean it up? Not just that, but fix it so I'd lose as little business as possible? Iris said you even got the girls moving when they didn't wanna."

"Like I told Kat, I have a sick need to keep helping you." Her amusement made her lips twitch, but there was something else there. Her need to help was more than what she claimed. Her eyes were soft with emotion; her teeth nabbed the edge of her lip.

He knew what it was. She'd said it once, and he'd been too afraid to face it then. Now it was something he wanted to hear. More than he thought he would. "That all?"

"Maybe." She focused on fixing his tie, her voice barely a whisper. All around them the saloon carried on business as usual. No one seemed surprised to have Jane among them after so long gone. For the moment, the bustle of activity didn't touch the two of them. She avoided looking at him, a faint pink tinting her cheeks.

No more hiding. He wanted it all in the open. "Maybe? What else?"

Her fingers fluttered along the edge of the vest, making sure it lay straight. After a few moments, she took a deep breath and peered up through her lashes. "I wanted to. For you."

"Why?" His hands closed over hers, holding them still on his chest. Under them, he knew his heart pounded hard, and he wondered if hers did too. Much as he wanted to hear, he was afraid to hear it. "Or are you not woman enough to say?"

A soft gasp flew from her tempting lips. The pink in her cheeks darkened and she gave a quick tug of her hands, but he had her trapped. Pursed lips preceded her glare. "Not the best way to get an answer."

"Tell me."

She leaned into him, her glare softening into something else. Her lips were parted like the words were hovering on the tip of her tongue. He held his breath, waiting.

"Lady Jane," Hammy's cheerful voice matched the mans gap-toothed grin, "what're ya doin' here?"

Cole could have cursed the old man right out the door for interrupting when no one else had dared. Jane didn't bat an eyelash, turning on the charm. She pulled her hands free without effort to give Hammy a warm hug. Cole's annoyance faded into amusement, for even after his friendly greeting, Jane's attentions still made Hammy blush and fumble.

In moments she had Hammy seated at the bar, a beer in his hand. Her vibrant banter didn't stop, even when she took a moment to say something to Cuddy. Without hesitation she excused herself from the two and weaved her way through the saloon as if she'd never left for a day.

On her way back to him she stopped at just about every table, taking a moment with everyone. She never stumbled for a name and edged on too friendly with them all. By the time she tugged on his hand to head for the door, he was chuckling low. "I still wanna know how ya do that."

"Do what?"

"You been here six months." Six months and she'd turned his entire world upside down. Had him wishing she'd tell him how she felt and longing for attachment to her. For everyone to know it, too. "You know them all. I even heard you asking about kids by name."

"I don't think there is a 'how' to it. It's simply something I do. It's polite." Her brows pinched together, and she wrapped her arms around his waist. "Now, you might believe I've forgotten, but I haven't. You changed the subject on me."

"You didn't answer the question."

"You changed the subject. Now what about Graham?"

Silence seemed a better answer than his rude retort. Two could play at this game. He wasn't about to answer her now. Not when she was going to browbeat him.

She ran in front of him to block his attempted escape. Her finger poked his chest. "I asked you a question, Mr. Mitchell."

"Mr. Mitchell?" He caught her, then tugged her close.

"You heard me."

"He destroyed my saloon, injured my customers. You put the numbers together. Ya know how much it's gonna cost to fix. He's out."

"What about as your friend?"

Cole snorted. "Friend?"

"Yes. He was incredibly stupid, and as much as it hurt your business, it hurt you more. It hurt you because he is your friend. His assumptions and his reaction spoke on his insecurities and displayed a lack of trust."

"I ain't Guy or Jackson. I don't pay you for your advice."

"No. You get this free of charge. Part of the price you pay for telling me you wanted no more lies." She grinned. She had him, and she knew it. "So you have to listen."

He fought back his laugh. It wouldn't do any good to bolster her belief she was right. All he offered her was a shrug. Once she walked off in an attempted huff, he let his chuckle free.

If this had been a real fight maybe he'd been upset, but he knew it wasn't. Instead, he followed the flounce of her skirts eagerly. If she were truly mad, he'd likely have a red cheek by now. By the time he caught up to her, she was in Cora's restaurant and a conversation with Michael.

His mood soured instantly. The shrimp was acting over-protective enough. Cole didn't want to have his nose broken again for nothing. Even so, he wasn't about to put up with Mike's bull.

Mike, for his part, looked entirely miserable as he was dragged by his arm. Jane didn't appear to care one way or another as she deposited her brother right in front of Cole. "Michael wanted to apologize. Didn't you, Michael?"

Mike's jaw moved in tense circles. "I suppose anything is possible. After all, Jane tells me you're finally going to start acting like a real man."

"Michael," she smacked his arm hard, "be nice or go away."

Cole shrugged. "Like I said. She ain't got no complaints."

"Oh my heavens." Jane threw her hands in the air. "Would the two of you knock it off? Put your pricks away. I am not territory to be marked and claimed."

Cole grinned despite the tension still coming from Mike. Jane's mood really had improved after their afternoon if she was up for this sort of argument.

Mike didn't appear too pleased with the turn of events. His lip curled and he pointed at Cole. "He isn't man enough to own up—"

Jane jutted her finger at her brother's face. "On second thought, do whatever the hell you want. When you're ready to act like real men, let me know."

Cole couldn't keep his eyes off of her for nothing. The way her angry stomping dissipated into an excited run. The tight hug with Katherine and their whispered exchange, both women bursting with a quick squeal before they embraced in another hug.

He could watch her all night. At least until he was sure he could get her home. They had a lot of ground to cover, and he was really looking forward to having her in his arms again all night long. It had been ages since he'd slept good. The last thing he was worried about was Mike.

Mike wouldn't stand to be ignored. "You hurt her bad."

"You broke my damn nose."

"Improved the landscape." Mike smirked. Bastard thought he was clever. He also wasn't afraid, like one sucker punch weeks ago gave him some sort of advantage. Cole jerked toward him, but the man didn't even blink. "I can still beat you into the ground if you dare to hurt her again."

"She knows what I am. She ain't walking away."

"She did once. She can again. From the time I got here, you've done more damage that the mad man out for her death. Clara deserves better."

Cole folded his arms across his chest. "You don't know everything you think you do, Mike. And she ain't your sister. Her name…is Jane."

"She is still my sister."

"Don't make her your property." Cole kept a sharp eye on Jane when Norman rushed in waving a letter. "She's got her own mind, always has long as I've known her. She knows what she wants."

"She also makes mistakes. Big ones." Mike straightened to get as close to Cole as he could. "And I swear that if you hurt her again—"

Cole reached out and gripped Mike's shirt, yanking him close until they were nose to nose. "Don't threaten me. I do what I like. And she ain't gonna get hurt again. Not by me. And not by that bastard. Not if I can help it."

Peeling Cole's hands from his shirt, Mike nodded. "You'd better make sure that sticks."

A shriek interrupted Cole's protest.

Across the room, Jane stood with the letter clenched tight in her hand. Her pink flush had faded into white shock. "Where's Jesse?"

Cora flew to Jane's side. "Jane. What is it?"

"I need to see him. Where is he?"

"He's with David." Cora tried to soothe Jane. "At the jail. Arthur and Isaac went too."

Kathy flew to her feet as Jane took off. "Jane. Where are you going? What did the letter say? Jane!"

Jane hadn't stopped for any of the questions. Cole raced out of the restaurant behind her until he managed to catch her arm halfway down the street. "Jane."

"I need to see him." She weakly tried to tug her arm free. The letter crinkled in her free hand.

"What the hell happened?" The letter she held out to him was short, but it was dark out. He had to get under a lamp to read it.

> *Did you think I wouldn't figure it out?*
> *You cannot deceive me. I know what you are.*
> *I made you. You will not succeed in saving*
> *him. Or yourself.*

By the time he was through, she'd disappeared into the darkness. She'd been too panicked to even let him read. After a short jog, he found her around the corner from the saloon in the middle of the street. Standing still. Staring at the jail in silence.

He set his hands on her shoulders and pulled her back against him. "He's fine."

More than fine. Jesse was laughing and playing jackstones with Isaac. At some point, the boy had started talking, at least around David, because now he was an endless stream of chatter.

A small sniffle caught his ear a split second before she spun fast and clung to him tight around his waist. He sighed and wrapped his arms around her. "David ain't gonna let nothing happen to him."

"I know."

"Jane."

She shoved away from him, stumbling a few feet away. Then she took off.

With a curse, Cole ran after her again. This was going to get old fast. Then again maybe not, if she kept making it easy for him. She was standing in the middle of the street, waiting for him. "What the hell?"

"I couldn't do this in front of the jail. They would have heard."

"Do what?"

"I can't do this, Cole. I can't have you running scared. I need you."

He took a step toward her, but she took a step back. "Jane."

"I don't know what he's going to do. I don't know when. I need to know you're here. Either you're all in or you're out. I need to know. I can't live in limbo."

This time she didn't move, and he pressed his forehead to hers. "I ain't gonna run. I'm right here. Can't promise to be perfect."

"Gee. What a surprise."

"We're gonna fight."

"We do it so well." She laughed weakly. Her hands clamped down on his neck. "I've needed you. I still need you I need to know you'll be there when I need you."

"You got me."

"All in?"

"All in."

*Truth is a gem that is found at a great depth;
whilst on the surface of this world, all things
are weighed by the false scale of custom.*
-Lord Byron

Jane could lie there all day long.

Cole lay flush against her back, his arms wrapped around her. She had no designs on leaving, but if she made any move, he held her tighter. Instead of objecting or teasing, she snuggled closer to his warmth.

She ran her fingers along his arm in a gentle dance before she laced them with hers at her waist. The past several days they'd spent every free hour they had together. They'd talked out all that had happened between them in excruciating detail, though they'd both still froze at the idea of saying those words, she knew he felt as deeply as she did.

Together they'd tried to come up with a plan to finish solving the puzzle of her past. They'd figured out nothing, and in frustration conversation had wandered from time to time. He'd even talked more about his past, in bits and pieces. Some things were still very private for him. Unlike her, he remembered his past. It was a lot more difficult to face when you remembered.

One of the things which had her most curious was the man he'd been then. The man before Cole. Before he'd come to Dominion Falls and gambled and borrowed his way to saloon ownership. Before the whores.

She sighed when he nuzzled her neck. The question rose so fast, she spoke without thinking, "What's your real name?"

Like a bull ready to charge, his whole body tensed. For almost two whole minutes he didn't move, barely breathed. She closed her eyes and exhaled. He wasn't ready yet or wasn't willing to tell her.

The idea he wasn't ready didn't bother her. Already he'd revealed far more of himself to her than he had anyone else. She could accept that easily. The rest would come with time.

She stretched against his tight arms so she could turn toward him. "Never mind."

"No. It ain't that." His eyes were closed, the tension dripped off of him. "Just been a long time."

She brushed her fingers along his cheek, into his hair. "It's all right. I can live without knowing. I was simply curious."

With every run of her fingers along his scalp, the tension he carried lessened. The clench of his jaw relaxed, and his arms loosened their hold. His ice-blue eyes opened to focus on her. "You're always curious."

"I like knowledge. Plato says that knowledge is the food of the soul. I agree."

"Knowledge, eh? That the only food for the soul?"

She chuckled. His tone and wandering fingers left little doubt to his meaning. "For the soul, yes. There are other hungers that must be fed. The heart. The body."

"I like that last one."

"I know."

"So do you."

"Damn straight." The rumbling of his laughter pulled her own free. She winked. "But one cannot exist on sweets alone."

He hummed against her neck, sending shivers right through her. "You sure?"

"Yes. That doesn't preclude one from trying though."

"Good."

It was so easy to be distracted when he did that. The tickle of his lips across her throat; his fingers dancing along her hip. Grabbing. Pulling her closer. Yes. He was very good at diversion.

"Really wanna know?"

She gasped, her fingers dug into his arms when he froze. At the precipice of total distraction, he'd pulled back. "Evil."

"Turnabout is fair play."

A groan made its way to the surface. She gave him a half-hearted slap to the chest. "I think you've been around me too long. That was a logical argument."

"You didn't answer."

"Yes, I do want to. That doesn't mean you have to tell me."

"Colton."

Her eyes closed when he punctuated the name with a kiss to her neck.

"James."

His lips moved lower, teasing and sucking. Her body came alive with excitement. She raked her nails down his arms to repay him a little in kind. Every attempt to focus on the names he was reciting flew away under his capable distraction.

"Spencer." With that, he'd revealed his full name, but she could no longer appreciate the depth of the revelation. He had her body humming in excitement with every touch of his lips, every teasing caress.

"Oh." She was far more intelligent than that answer. Yet she couldn't form any other words. He had her right where he wanted her, and she was fine with that.

The only thing that existed was his hands, his lips. Tender touches grew more insistent. Pulling, pleading, satisfying. Wrapped in each other, they let reality slip away for as long as they could.

Until the cold of the day, seeping in thanks to the long burned-out fire of the stove, made her shiver.

"Guess I should get the fire going again."

"You could. It wouldn't do much good. I still need to get out of bed." Jane curled closer to his warmth with a sigh.

"Nah."

"Yes, I do." She smacked him in the chest. When he started to pout, she laughed. "So do you. Cuddy won't be working tonight, so you have to. Otherwise, Hammy will moan and whine that you didn't open."

Cole groaned and rubbed his hands over his face. "Damn."

"I know. It's horrible to have to leave this room. I'll make it up to you."

"Promise?"

"Promise." With a wink, she nipped at his lower lip before scrambling out of bed. His reaching hands didn't stop her. She swatted them away. Each of his groans was punctuated by a giggle from her. "Hurry up. We might be able to eat before we need to work."

"That's what I was tryin' to do."

"Cole."

He growled when she slapped his arm. A wicked grin was her only warning before he caught her wrist. Before she could say *naughty,* his lips were on hers. He had her pinned tight against him and paid no mind to her struggle.

Not until she'd grabbed him in what could have been an intimate gesture, but instead squeezed him tight, did he stop. She smirked at his pained grunt. For the first time that morning it was she that had him right where she wanted him. He knew she could turn things either way with one little movement. "Is there a problem?"

"Not," he groaned, "nice."

"Neither are you." With a giggle, she released him and returned to scavenging her clothes. At least this time, as she dressed, he bothered to do the same, even if he did curse every time a new layer made its way onto one of their bodies. "Now be patient and maybe tonight I'll make it worth your while."

"You better."

"Trust me."

"I do." His arms went around her waist, not demanding. The gentle kiss to her neck brought a sigh. He really did know how to soothe the savage beast.

"Good. Because I trust you."

"Let's go get some grub."

She took his offered hand as he drew her close. "No, sir. We aren't having this argument again."

"But it's the funnest argument we can have."

"No doubt of that. I'm still not doing it. We both have duties to attend to. Now, hop to it, mister."

He pulled back to help her get her coat on before leading her downstairs. "Have you talked to Mike yet?"

"About your idea?"

"What else?"

"Oh, I don't know. I could talk to him about the weather. Jesse. You. His interest in Daisy."

"His interest in what?"

Jane laughed. "You heard me. What? You didn't notice?"

"She's a whore."

"Cole," Jane pursed her lips, "she isn't anymore. She's a—what in heaven's name is that?"

"What's it look like? It's an Indian."

"Don't be obtuse. Who is it, and why is he here? I thought Al's men were delivering them to the reservation and the northern territory."

"That's your former husband's friend. Think they call him Black Moon." His hand tightened on her hip. "And here comes Starbird."

Lewis Starbird stepped out of the boarding house, David right behind him. The three men stood there for several minutes speaking quietly. Jane didn't realize she'd been holding her breath until Cole pushed her into moving again.

She shivered and leaned against him. "Why are they here? How do you know and I don't?"

"Because when you're working, you're cooped up in that stuffy library. I got some of the biggest talkers in town." He chuckled. "That means I get to hear things. Outside of that, you been spending every minute with me, talking about what we're gonna do about you."

"So then tell me, oh wise saloon owner, what is he doing here? What is Starbird doing here?"

"Starbird got to stay. He's, uh…"

Jane bit her lip, trying to hide her smile. She cleared her throat. "Emancipated?"

"Yeah. That's it. It's his wife that's in trouble. The other one is free too. Archie and the council agreed that if he stays peaceful, he could stay in the surrounding area."

"They what?"

"Easy." He unpeeled her hand from his arm. "Thought you trusted David."

"Two Indians in town? We'd be better with none." The pressure in her chest had returned with a vengeance. The thought of the Indians panicked her more than she knew it should. Old horrors of a past she couldn't remember sure did like to exert themselves on her life now.

"You're the one that helped form the damn government. It was their choice."

"Don't remind me."

"What was that you were saying about tonight?"

"Trying to distract me?"

His low chuckle rumbled against her neck when he kissed her there. "Maybe."

"Good." She managed to find a smile, granting him a wink before slipping her arm under his coat. One squeeze to his buttocks and he was laughing.

"Jane."

Cole's laughter stopped the moment he heard Al's voice. Jane rolled her eyes at his grumbled curse. After another quick squeeze to his backside, she pulled away and rushed to give Al a hug. "You're back."

"Just got back this morning." Al held her for a bit too long—at least it seemed Cole thought so, for the second Al released her, Cole pulled her back to him. "Glad to see you're feeling better than when I left."

"I am. Very much." She grinned and jabbed her elbow into Cole's ribs.

After a grunt, he managed to grumble. "Get them Indians where they need to be?"

"The warriors are at the reservation." Al sighed. "Now I just wait on my men to return from the northern territory."

"Then you'll be in town for a few more weeks?" Jane's smile grew. "That's good to know. Why don't you join Cole and I for lunch?"

Al shifted and cleared his throat. "Don't think I can today. Maybe another time."

She couldn't see Cole's face, but the tension in his grip was enough. How could he still be acting jealous now? It was just ridiculous. She shook her head and sighed. "That's too bad. Why don't you join me for supper tonight? Cole will be working, so I'll be dining alone."

The grip on her arm tightened even more, and she winced. She stomped on Cole's foot and glared when he hopped away with a curse. "Pig."

"Crazy—"

"Don't."

Al replaced his hat. "Uh, Jane. Maybe it's best if—"

"Please, Al. I insist. Seven o'clock." Jane's grin grew when Cole's cursing stopped. "Unless you have pressing matters, of course."

"Can't say that I do." Al nodded. "Seven would suit me fine."

"Good." Jane hugged him again before heading to a table. The stares of the customers in the restaurant didn't faze her, she was used to them by now. When Cole limped over to sit, she folded her arms on the table. "I cannot believe that even now, you are still acting jealous. You are such a child."

"If there weren't no reason to be, he wouldn't have backed off."

"Thought you trusted me."

"I do."

"Then trust me and shut up."

"You hurt my foot."

She snorted. "I'll hurt worse if you don't behave."

"Yes, ma'am. That a promise?"

"Yes, sir."

"Good."

There are times when fear is good. It must keep its watchful place at the heart's controls. There is advantage in the wisdom won from pain.
–Aeschylus

Jane practically skipped across the street toward the saloon. Though her ankle still ached, Daisy had warned her that such a thing would likely remain for years. In fact, it could never fully go away.

"Jane." Kat joined her in the middle of the street, a frown creasing her usually chipper features. "Are you heading to work? Wait."

Jane stopped when Kat grabbed her arm. "What?"

"What has you in such a mood?"

"Daisy gave me full clearance to return to normal life. She said all is healed, well, all but my heart. That's on the path to recovery, though." Jane tugged Kat's hand. "What is wrong with you?"

"Nothing. Everything. Lewis is leaving for the Northern territory shortly. Of course, that means Martha goes to Washington all on her own." Kat sighed. "Martha says it was her idea and she plans to join him once the baby is born and she is free."

Jane frowned. "I won't claim to understand their reasoning, but I suppose I'm the last person that needs to judge anyone's relationship."

"There's worse news."

Never thought Starbird leaving town was bad news. Jane kept her thoughts to herself for a change. "What is it?"

"My mother is coming to town." Kat dropped onto the bench in front of the saloon with a dramatic sigh. After a moment she groaned, dropping her face to her hands. "Likely very soon."

"Oh dear."

"Exactly. She knows I'm here too. The telegram was addressed to me." Kat wove her fingers through her hair. "I'd planned on heading back to St. Louis next week to—"

"Settle your business?" Jane knew Kat wasn't ready to mention her daughter, Cindy, in public. The girl was safely ensconced in St. Louis with an old and dear friend of Kat's named Patrick. "Were you going to take Norman?"

"No, but I did tell him." Kat chewed on her lip "I had to in order to explain why I never stayed long. Patrick will continue to handle matters for me, he always does. Even so, I don't like being away so long. I could just send for my things, but there are other matters to settle as well."

"Of course. There is much to be done." Jane frowned. "How long will your mother stay?"

"As long as she feels is necessary."

"Then you'll meet her and go back to attend to business."

"You don't know my mother." Kat snorted. "If only it could be so easy."

"You won't have to face her alone." Jane sat next to her. "I hold no great fear for your mother. I'll help."

"I'm not certain even you can handle her."

Jane laughed, but it turned into a yelp when a loud crash sounded in the saloon. "What the devil is going on now?"

Kat turned to peer inside. "I can't tell."

"We just cleaned this place up. I'm not about to watch it get ruined again." Jane rose and stormed inside. She stopped so fast Kat bumped into her. "*Cole.*"

Only Cole's head could be seen above the bar. In the mirror they could see his back as he scoured the shelves for something. He flew to his feet and slammed his hands on the bar. "That bastard took it."

"What bastard took what?" Jane edged closer to the bar.

"When you cleaned up, did you find my horseshoe?" Cole turned his glare on Kat.

"What? No. What horseshoe?" Kat frowned. "All we found was broken glass and tables."

"Cole?" Jane was surprised at the squeak in her voice. She cleared her throat. "What horseshoe are you talking about?"

"Archie gave it to me after the stampede. Said I'd earned it by living. I kept it back here behind the bar." Cole's frown deepened. "It ain't here."

"Johnny." Jane gripped the edge of the bar.

"He was here. It ain't a coincidence, is it?" He hit the bar. "We gotta do something."

"Are you two saying that the horseshoe he left for Jane is the same one that you've been keeping from when you got caught in the stampede?" Kat wrinkled her nose. "And why on earth would you keep such a gruesome souvenir?"

"I don't know how it could be just simple coincidence." Jane dropped into a chair. "You didn't notice it was gone before?"

"Didn't think about it. Had it set back here outta the way. Never got around to hanging it up or nothing." He leaned on his elbows. "Until ya said something last night about the horseshoe he left you, I'd forgotten about it."

"Why?" Kat sat next to Jane. "What purpose would that serve? At the time you and Cole weren't together."

"I don't know. Maybe to show no one was safe. Or that he could be anywhere and I wouldn't even notice. I didn't even notice." Jane buried her face in her hands. "He could have done anything, and I wouldn't have noticed until it was too late."

"Jane." Kat's voice was quiet. She rubbed Jane's shoulder. "You can't be everywhere. Not to mention, you were going through something very difficult."

"He could have gone after Jesse. Or Cole again, or you, now that you're here. If he wanted me to not feel safe, he's succeeded." Jane ran over the past month in her head but couldn't place where Johnny might have snuck in. She dropped her hands and sighed. "Or maybe it's just Jackson being worse than we expected."

"He ain't clever enough." Cole turned the chair next to her and straddled it. "He's good at throwing around money, but he's not good at threats. He's had that poster for how long and done nothing with it?"

"True. If he wanted to torture me with it, it would keep showing up." Jane frowned. "You're right, Cole. We need to do something. I just don't know what."

"Well we need to figure it fast."

For what do we live, but to make sport for our neighbors, and laugh at them in return?
-Jane Austen

Jane wiped down the bar in front of Graham. She frowned when he just stared at the cup in front of him. "I'm not giving you whiskey, so don't even think of it."

"I'm allowed to think of it," he snarled.

"Graham."

"Is he going to come down or what?"

She set her hand on her hip and arched a brow. "Do you really need to ask? I'm surprised you had the guts to come in here so soon. Cole and I have barely been back together a week. I told you it would take time for me to talk to him."

"What's taking so long?"

"You do realize that he'd rather talk about what that maniac has in store for me, what torture and possible death I might face, than even mention your name."

He dropped his head into his hands. "So? I would too."

"You're real funny." She smacked him with the towel.

"I just want to apologize."

"He doesn't want to hear it. Not yet anyway. You broke a trust. Cole doesn't trust easily, you know that. We both do." She nudged his coffee closer. "Drink. You're here, might as well finish it. How are you holding up?"

"Better some days than others." His hands shook when he lifted the mug to his lips. Coming into the saloon had to be an absolute nightmare bad as she imagined he was craving. The thought deepened as he glanced at the whiskey bottles lining the wall behind her. "Worse most days."

"Do you have someone to help you?" Jane set her hand on his arm. "Is Becky offering any help at all?"

"Told me to sober up or the wedding's off."

"That's helpful." She couldn't keep the sarcasm out of her voice. Both Graham and his betrothed annoyed her to no end. "Especially seeing as you only care so far as that dowry goes."

"Hey now," Graham protested, but it lacked his usual ferocity. His shoulders sagged. "Yeah. You got a point."

"Anyone else helping?" She made a strong effort to keep her voice low. Not one head turned in their direction. That meant at least for the moment their conversation was being ignored by the nosey lot.

He made a check around the room himself to make sure no one was listening in. Once he was sure, he shook his head. "She's afraid of what Becky'll do. Gave me some funny-tasting tea, but that's it."

"It's only been a week. You're not going to make it without support." She sighed. "Which would you like me to talk to?"

His features darkened, and he shrugged.

"Fine. I will head out to their camp later today. I can't make any promises, and I expect you to handle the dowry on your own. That tells me your choice. If you change your mind down the line, I can't help you."

"So you keep telling me. Still don't get why you bother."

"I don't understand it myself sometimes." She patted his arm. "As far as Cole is concerned, he needs more than ten days to cool off. You know that."

"Guess so."

Jane sighed again and wiped down another glass. "I'll keep trying, but we'll see. You need to be sober first. That you'd better know."

"I do." He slurped more coffee.

Kat ran into the saloon, red hair flying behind her. Panic had her fair skin near white. "Hide me."

"What?" Jane threw down the towel.

"Hurry. Hide me. I'm desperate." Kat grasped her arm. "Where's best?"

"Icehouse is best." Jane gasped when Kat actually ran toward it. "Grab my shawl."

Graham's brow furrowed when Kat disappeared into the storeroom, the coat stand rocking back and forth with the force she'd used to grab Jane's shawl. "What in blazes was that about?"

"I have no idea." The door to the icehouse slammed shut, and Jane furrowed her brow. "I can't think of what Kat might have done to hide—"

"Katherine Marie Daugherty." A woman stood in the doorway, silhouetted by the bright early-winter light. She tapped a fan against her palm and surveyed the room.

"Well, I'll be damned." Graham chuckled. "If it isn't Mrs. Daugherty herself."

"That's Kat's mother?" Jane grinned. "That explains it then."

"It does?"

"Yes. It does." Jane nudged him. "You know her better than I. Invite her in, let's see what fun today can bring."

Graham hopped off his stool. "Mrs. Daugherty."

"Mr. Cooke. Where did my daughter go?" Mrs. Daugherty didn't step inside the saloon.

Jane tugged her bodice straight and stepped out from behind the bar. "She just ran right on through this room. Might have gone out the back, I'm not certain. Won't you come in? Stay a while and have a few drinks with your town's citizens."

Mrs. Daugherty turned her attention on Jane. "I'm not in the habit of drinking."

"We provide coffee, not just alcohol." Jane gestured to a full table. "I'm certain these gentlemen would be thrilled to spend time with their town's founding mother. Wouldn't you, Mr. Hamm?"

Hammy held up his beer. "To the Daugherty's."

Wills lifted his glass. "Good enough to form the town, but too good to join it."

Jane sucked her lips between her teeth to keep from laughing. It became far more difficult when Graham hauled Chauncey out of his seat to pull his chair out.

Graham made an elaborate show of removing his handkerchief and dusting off the seat. "Please, have a seat."

"Where is my daughter?" This time Mrs. Daugherty stepped into the building.

"Like Janey said. She came through just a minute ago." Graham shrugged.

"Said she didn't want to see you." Jane set her hands on her hips and walked right up to Lillian. "The last thing I would do is stop her. I really can't blame her for wanting to avoid you."

"Why on earth would she say that?" Lillian didn't back away. Clearly, she expected Jane to back down.

"My goodness, Mrs. Daugherty. I just can't imagine." Jane's hand flew to her chest in feigned shock. Graham's deep rumble of laughter almost tickled a smile out of her. She bit the inside of her cheeks to stop it. "Maybe it's because you told her she was a fool for wanting to be a strong and independent woman."

"Well. I never"

"Or maybe it's because of your behavior toward her when she tried to tell you that marriage was not for her. Or even the way you criticize everything she does—even when it's for the empowerment of women, something you should appreciate as a woman. You were one once, weren't you?"

"How dare you speak to me like that?" Lillian stepped closer. "You who—who works in a *saloon*."

"I don't quite work here, I help out a bit. My lover is the owner, after all. That doesn't make me a two-bit whore, if that's your implication. Of course, if you really want to look down your nose at me, I've also been divorced."

"And rumor has it you are a criminal."

Jane's eyes widened slightly, but she swallowed the fear. If word had reached so far as Denver, she might not be long for this world after all. "All of those things are just a part of who I am. Not that you would know based on your snap judgment. None of that matters anyhow. What does is you're in here now. You're welcome to stay and have a cup of coffee with the men that helped turn your tiny mining camp into a real town, or you can leave."

Graham still stood by the chair and waved toward it. "Mrs. Daugherty."

Lillian stood silent for a moment, her gaze never leaving Jane's. This woman was not used to being challenged. Whether she appreciated it or not wasn't clear. After several moments of silence, she nodded to Jane. "Coffee sounds wonderful."

"Good." Jane forced a smile. With the exception of the criminal accusations, she had rather been enjoying herself. "Have a seat. I'll be right back."

"Thank you." With stiff but graceful movements, Lillian made her way to the chair. She sat slowly, making a face at the dirty table.

Jane chuckled when every man at the table scrambled to offer to clean it with their dirty hankies. At least she wasn't the only one enjoying herself. She poured Lillian's coffee and carried it back to the table. By the time she set it down, Lillian had composed herself and appeared positively pleasant.

"I suppose this means that you are the Jane I've heard tales of?" Lillian took a sip of her coffee and waited for Jane to sit. "I must say I wasn't sure until you claimed to be Mr. Mitchell's lover. I saw him in Denver, you know."

"He failed to mention that bit of information." Jane maintained her smile while silently threatening Cole for leaving that detail out about his trip.

"From what I heard about the crimes you were accused of, you're likely to be arrested." As Lillian continued the conversation, most of the men left the table. They moved a respectful distance away as they always did when Jane's possible criminal past came up. As though not hearing about it would keep them free from culpability.

"It is a possibility," Jane demurred, unsure just how much Lillian knew.

"After Stein's assistant gabbed my ear off about you, I did some checking myself. It's an interesting situation you have yourself in." Lillian tilted her head. "I must say I wonder why you aren't behind bars already."

"I'm not certain you have that kind of time, Mrs. Daugherty. The story is long."

"And convoluted," Graham piped up. He took a seat next to Jane and nudged Jane's arm. "Go on, tell it. I'm sure Lil wants to hear it all."

Jane frowned. "It isn't a story I'm keen on telling again. Plus, I really don't think Mrs. Daugherty wants to hear it."

"You look afraid to tell it." Lillian set down her mug. "Considering your opinion of me, it shouldn't be too difficult."

"Or more so. I don't know if you are friend or foe. All of these men are friends, and they move away when such dark things are talked about." Jane sat straighter. "It isn't considered polite conversation."

"If you so revel in being impolite, what have you to fear?" Lillian lifted her chin. "If it makes you feel better, I despise Jackson Krenshaw and so I'm more apt to take the opposite side as he does."

Jane snorted. "Mutual dislike for a cad is hardly a basis for trust."

"I suppose not." Behind Lillian, a flash of red hair swept out of the storeroom.

"Then again, I suppose I don't know you well enough for you to be worth my fear."

"So I see." Lillian's brow quirked up, and she seemed to appraise Jane. "Then what is your decision? Are you going to share your story?"

"Lil," Cole's voice drew all their attention up to the balcony, "what are you doing?"

"Just asking Miss Doe about her criminal activities." Lillian lifted her mug toward him. "She seems rather close-lipped about it."

Cole tilted his head and frowned. "What's your game, Lil?"

Jane tried to keep her focus on the two, even as Graham slipped away from the table to help some of the patrons sneak Kat out the back. "That's what I'm trying to figure out as well, Cole. Apparently Mrs. Daugherty believes her status gives her carte blanche to ask me about anything and expect an answer."

"No. I rather thought you'd rise to the idea of being challenged," Lillian corrected. "I thought you were made of stronger stock."

"She's plenty strong. Don't mean she needs to go blabbing her business to anyone that asks. Not that she shuts up much." Cole smirked.

"Fine. If you must know, I have been curious since I saw you in Denver, Mr. Mitchell. I thought…if I felt the case was strong enough, I might help. You said Jackson was going after her. He's an awful big fish, and you're little more than bait." Lillian turned back to Jane. "And now having met Miss Doe, I'm even more curious and intrigued. She seems a strong woman."

Jane bowed her head at the compliment. "Coming from you, that's very kind."

Cole made his way downstairs once the saloon had cleared out some. He walked right past Lillian and set his hand on Jane's shoulder. "So you want to help?"

"I'm not sure yet. I don't know the whole story." Lillian looked at Jane. "Will you share now?"

When Jane frowned, Cole squeezed her shoulder and sat next to her. "Lillian pulls no punches. If she says she wants to help, I believe her."

"I'd prefer she say that if she can't help, she'll forget what she's heard." Jane folded her hands in front of her.

"I never forget, but I have many secrets, Jane. Yours would just be one of them." Lillian held her gaze steady while Jane contemplated.

"I appreciate your honesty." Jane sighed. "Then I'll start at the beginning as I know it."

"As you know it?" Lillian tilted her head. "What does that mean?"

"As Seneca says, 'Every new beginning comes from some other beginning's end'."

"That still doesn't answer my question."

"In order for me to live, someone else's life had to end. I don't remember her end, but I remember my beginning."

Let your plans be as dark and impenetrable
as night, and when you move,
fall like a thunderbolt.
-Sun Tzu

They'd just stopped, and already Jane missed the whistle of wind in her ears. The concentration and release their ride had encouraged dissipated with the reappearance of the town in front of them.

Jane slowed Tempest to a walk in an attempt to delay their return. With the treaty settled and the Indians on the way to their destinations, she and Cole had decided to take Tempest and Faro out for a run. It had, of course, turned into a race.

Neither of them won, as Tempest and Faro were good matches for each other.

Cole tugged on his reins, until their pace slowed even more. He quirked a brow. "Problem?"

"No. Not really. Just not eager to get back yet. It was nice to relax for a change." For the first time since their reunion, they hadn't even spoken of the baby or the dilemma of what to do about Johnny. Quiet peace and solitude.

He reached over to give her hand a squeeze. Now that they'd let the tenderness in, Jane treasured every moment he revealed it. In public, they were infinitely content to let the gossipmongers have a show. Scandal was fun.

However in quiet moments, when it remained just the two of them, true signs of affection filtered into every moment. They no longer dared each other to leave—instead they dared each other to remain.

After what they'd been through, they alone knew the truth. For as much as Jane had told Kat, even she didn't know the whole story.

"We'll go out again next nice day."

"Whenever that may be. According to the widow Dunbar, her joints are screaming in pain, which means cold weather is coming to stay."

Cole's laughter barked out, and he nudged Faro to the edge of the corral. "If you listen to that crazy old bird, you might not be as smart as I thought." He hopped down and opened the gate to let the horses in.

Jane slipped down off Tempest and nudged her into the corral. Once Cole made sure the stable hand had them handled, he shut the gate. She easily slipped under his extended arm and leaned into him. "I wouldn't mind that much either if she were right. Months trapped inside with only you and our bodies to keep each other warm."

A low chuckle rumbled through his chest. "Maybe you are smart."

"Maybe I am."

"Jane." Mike stood in the back door of the saloon as though he'd been waiting there for hours. Arms folded across his chest, somehow even short as he was, he managed to fill the frame.

"Well, Mike, you dared step foot in the saloon. Could your temper be improving?" Jane didn't flinch at his glare, choosing to kiss him on the cheek instead.

"I was worried when the library was closed. Should have guessed he would have distracted you." Mike jerked his chin toward Cole. "Thought you were determined to find answers, not see how long two people can remain in bed."

She sidestepped, planting herself right in Cole's path when he moved. She grunted when he impacted with her back. Despite a snarled curse under his breath, Cole made no further advance. One of his hands rested on her waist, just enough to let her know he was still in control. Jane smiled at Mike. "I'm not in bed, in case you hadn't noticed. Cole and I just returned from a ride through the countryside. Stopped by your land. It's really lovely."

"Jane." Mike's fists clenched, veins standing out in relief against his skin.

"Cole and I have spent the past week going over every single detail he missed while we were apart. Much as you love to paint me a total whore, I do have some self-control." Now it was her turn for anger, and she shoved aside her stunned brother to storm into the saloon.

The din of a busy day left her blessedly free of hearing whatever exchange might have gone down between Cole and Mike. When they entered, five minutes and three glasses of whiskey later, both looked angry, but undamaged. No fisticuffs then. At least there was some improvement.

Cole jerked his thumb toward the storeroom. Jane had the childish idea of ignoring him until Mike left. She had no such luck as Cole brushed his hand down her arm and gripped her hand. With a sharp tug, he half-dragged her to the storeroom.

She crossed the room and to the stove. After pouring herself a cup of coffee, she sat on a crate.

"Sorry," Mike mumbled.

"Noted."

Cole rubbed his hand over his face. "You got any bright ideas, Mike?"

"Just the one." Mike leaned against the wall. "Call Tommy."

"No." Jane set down her mug and rose. "No more of the Young family. You know what's going to happen. I won't put them through losing her again. I hate that you're going through it."

"Well, we need to do something." Mike's regret washed away in a fresh storm of anger. "Instead of waiting for the maniac to make a move."

"He'll make a move either way, most likely to my detriment." Jane's heart pounded against her ribcage. All the peacefulness of the afternoon flew away, replaced by white-hot anger and fear.

"I wish you'd let me—"

"No." She sat back down. "I'll send the telegram again. Try to get Hodgkins to reply. It's all I know that we can do."

"It doesn't feel like enough."

"I know."

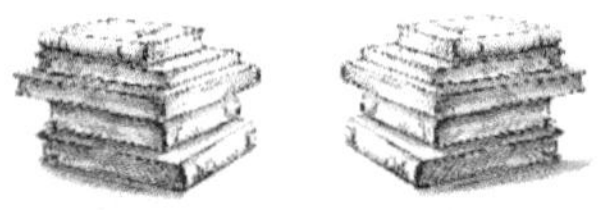

*This little reed, bending to the force of
the wind, soon stood upright again
when the storm passed over.
—Aesop*

All night long snow had fallen on the town of Dominion Falls. As morning broke, the snow continued, only easing about an hour before Jane was to open the library. Cole said he was surprised it had held off as long as it had. Normally snow fell well before November. Mike teased her for not remembering snow after all they'd faced growing up in Buffalo.

Of course, since she hadn't remembered, the first thing she'd done was run out in play in it once it was deep enough for such revelry. Until almost three in the morning the three of them had enjoyed the snowstorm. By then she'd grown chilled and her ankle ached.

She was grateful for the storm. It had helped eased the growing tension, as none of them had been able to hold onto anger when there were snowballs to throw.

Jane wanted to be out enjoying the day again rather than working in the library, but as she'd closed it the day before for their ride, she felt obligated to keep it open today. It was a shame, though. The streets were white with powder. Most of the town had stayed in all morning while it continued to fall.

"Faster, Pa. Faster."

Jane pulled her eyes up from the book she'd not been reading. The child's laughter reached a high pitch, racing by the library doors. Her chair clattered to the floor, and she ran outside.

Jesse held on to a sled for dear life while David ran through the snow with him. She gripped the railing when they raced past again, Jesse squealing with laughter.

"Stop, Pa. Library."

Jane closed her mouth from the gaping she'd been doing. Her heart beat double time as she continued to process Jesse calling him pa. "David, Jesse, are you enjoying the snow?"

"Pa goes fast." Jesse hopped off the sled. "Book?"

David caught her around the waist when she swayed. He chuckled low and gave Jesse a nod. "Yes. But don't make a mess in the library."

Jane's nails dug into his hand, and she sucked in a deep breath of cold air. "Pa?"

"I didn't tell him. He asked. He's very smart, Jane." He folded her into his arms. "Just like his ma."

"Shhh." She shoved him back. "Don't say that. His ma doesn't exist any longer."

His arm went around her waist and pulled her close again. When she shivered, he started inside. "I think you're looking at it wrong. What about when he's old enough to understand? Think he might be mad?"

"I won't discuss this with you again." Jane's frown was tugged away with a pull on her skirts. "Oh. *The Riddle Book.* What fun. Is your pa going to read it for you?"

Jesse shook his head. "You."

"I'm afraid I have to work. Although…" Jane grinned and took his hand. At the desk she sat and met his gaze. "Do you know what a riddle is?"

Eyes wide, Jesse nodded. "Tricks."

"Tricks of words, yes. Words can be very powerful. They can also be very silly. Do you want to try a riddle?" At his nod, she smiled. "My body is light, my head is white, with a cord I am laced around."

Jesse pursed his lips and narrowed, his eyes.

"I am beaten with sticks, yet not for bad tricks, but to animate by my sound." When his eyes widened, Jane straightened in surprise. "You know? The riddle is only half over."

"A drum."

"Very good. Your pa is right. You are very smart." She brushed a lock of hair off his forehead. "And you need a haircut. You should ask your pa to take you to see Lucky and fix it so it's not in your face all the time."

"Yes, ma'am." Jesse hugged her tight, holding on despite her gasp.

Jane looked at David with a frown. What had he told the child? His proud smile did nothing to soothe her racing heart. "Now go on. I have to get back to work."

"Jane," David leaned on the desk, "don't give me that look."

"What have you done?" Jane threw open her ledger and wrote down the title of the book. "I don't believe you."

"Why don't you get on the sled? I'll be right there." David pushed Jesse toward the door before turning back. "I haven't said a word. I told you I wouldn't. He's just smart."

"No one is that smart. How could he possibly know?"

"The same way you knew the second you saw him."

Jane slammed the ledger closed and rose. "Don't. Don't say anything. Let him be happy. You know what's coming, David."

"I can't do it."

"It has to be you. I need it to be you. I know it makes no sense, but having a stranger do it would be far more difficult. Not to mention, you're the sheriff and it's your job."

"I'll never forgive you."

"You should have never forgiven me to begin with." She rushed around the desk and hugged him tight. "Now go. Be with your son. He's ready for more sledding."

After he placed a light kiss to her cheek, he was gone. With another squeal of laughter, David and Jesse took off down the street. Jane ran to the door and closed it against the sound. A shiver led her to the stove.

The heat didn't touch her soul, and another shudder ran through her. It wasn't worth the effort, so she dropped back into her chair. She'd barely gotten back to pretending to read when the door opened again.

"Mrs. Daugherty?" Jane greeted the newcomer.

Lillian entered the library with as much grace and style as she had the saloon. Dressed in an understated but still exquisite dress, she wore her wealth with far more elegance than Jackson ever had. "I came to see how you were truly treating my library and its books."

Jane had to admit she was impressed that Lillian had toned down her dress now that she wasn't fresh off the train. When Lillian's words sank in, she did a double take. "Your library?"

"How do you think the town got one? I started the library when it was just a mining camp. Just because it was only a camp didn't mean it should be without some advancement of culture and knowledge."

"Admirable."

Lillian walked along the shelves. "There are far more books now than my visit last year."

"'Books are the treasured wealth of the world and the fit inheritance of generations and nations'," Jane said with infinite politeness. "I quite agree with Thoreau, and thus would never mistreat a book that touched these shelves or any other."

Lips pursed, Lillian raised her eyebrows and continued moving along the books. "So you treat paper better than you would man?"

"I cannot attest to the mistakes of my past. I make no excuses and I will face my punishment when it is brought to me. I told you as much three days ago."

"So I remember. I did think of one question I wanted to ask."

"Far be it from me to keep your curiosity unsatisfied."

"Why have you not turned yourself in?"

Jane pulled open her desk drawer and retrieved the well-worn envelope. "I've tried. I wrote this weeks ago. At first I didn't send it because I wasn't ready. A couple times in the past few weeks, I've tried to mail it. Every time I do it ends up back in my desk drawer."

"Is that so?" Lillian walked over and picked it up. "Addressed to the marshal. Why haven't you tried a telegram?"

"How do you think it keeps ending up in my desk? Norman won't send it. I don't know if it's of his own volition or if Cole is behind it, or even Katherine."

"Leave it to Katherine to stick her nose in. She is stubborn in her beliefs." The faintest of smiles crossed her features as she spoke of her daughter. "You have nothing to do with it? You are so adamant about your amnesia it makes me wonder if you don't find yourself exonerated in some way."

Jane stared at the envelope, leaving it lie where Lillian had set it down. "After our conversation, I cannot believe you are asking me this. Of course I don't believe myself exonerated in any way. I'm ready to face my punishment. My only wish is that I could remember what happened."

"To defend yourself?"

"No. I believe there is a proverb that says there is no shame in not knowing; the shame lies in not finding out. I want to know. What Clara did; what she didn't do. So that when my punishment comes, I can face it whole."

"You aren't whole now?"

"I am. In myself. My life is only six months old though. There are quite a few years before that I'm missing. It is someone else's life. I'm not Clara, and I'm trying to not make the same mistakes she did."

"'No change of circumstances can repair a defect of character'."

"Emerson." Jane smirked when Lillian's brows rose in surprise. "He is wise, but as Lord Chesterfield said 'Mankind is made up of inconsistencies, and no man acts invariably up to his predominant character. The wisest man sometimes acts weakly, and the weakest sometimes wisely'. Perhaps those seven years were the inconsistency. Perhaps this is. I would prefer to know."

"'Character is higher than intellect. A great soul will be strong to live as well as think'."

"More Emerson? Well, he also said that to be yourself in a world that is constantly trying to make you something else is a great accomplishment. You should applaud your daughter if you cherish Emerson's words so much."

"This discussion is not about my daughter."

"Every discussion is about your daughter. I'm her friend. That's why you are testing me. To see how much further I will warp her from your perfect image of a daughter. You've lost one to a treason charge."

"She has not been found guilty."

"But she has been ruined in this town. Even Starbird is making plans to turn tail and leave. Go to the northern territory. If found not guilty, will Martha join him?"

"I don't know."

"That means Katherine is your last chance to have a daughter. One you could be proud of. Perhaps already are, though you seem opposed to admitting it."

Lillian's brows arched, but she said nothing.

"I'm not going to turn Katherine against you. You've done that well enough on your own. I almost admire you, Mrs. Daugherty." Jane laughed at the double take Lillian did. "You helped form this town. You made sure it had a library and a church. You paid the reverend from your own pocket all of these years until there was an actual government and town funds to pay him with."

"But?"

"But you judge Katherine for being just as strong as you are. Certainly, she takes it to extremes you might never have, but she's not you."

"What of you? What will you do?"

"Continue to live. Cling to hope."

Lillian set down the book she'd been looking through. "How is it you believe you have hope? You seem defeated, saying you're going to face your punishment without a fight."

"That isn't defeat."

Lillian approached the desk. "Without a fight, you said. That is an earmark of defeat, is it not?"

"Perhaps. However, I thrive on truth. The truth of the matter is that Lloyd has found nothing that would help me win a case. The lawyer Cole saw in Denver had no advice without spending far more money than we need to. Even if we manage to find out some of Clara's secrets, we may never learn them all. She was in an asylum, and she had many secrets we have no idea how to uncover."

"'When you get into a tight place…'"

"'And everything goes against you, till it seems as though you could not hold on a minute longer, never give up then, for that is just the place and time the tide will turn'."

"Harriet Beecher Stowe." Lillian smiled. "One of my favorites."

"I doubt that I will see a long future."

"Never give up."

"I'm not, but like I said, I thrive on truth, and must face my future as I lived. I am proud of how I've lived in the short time I've had. I will continue to live to the best ability that I can. When I get into that tight place, I will pray for the tide to turn, but I do not expect it."

"You surprise me, Jane."
"I surprise myself most days too."

This is the true nature of home--
it is the place of peace; the shelter, not only
from injury, but from all terror,
doubt and division.
-John Ruskin

"Why, oh why did I do that?" Jane groaned deep and buried her face in her hands. In the heat of the moment the exchange with Lillian Daugherty had seemed welcome and appropriate. Upon reflection, Jane realized her impulsive retorts might have fueled a fire. "I actually like the woman, but I went on the attack. I must be insane."

"We all do it. We were raised that way. Ma made sure we knew how to debate, to pull on our own thoughts and the words of others. Every supper she broached a new topic for us to debate." Michael took a sip of his coffee. "You always had a mind for it."

"We'd spend supper in debate? That hardly seems appropriate."

"Always with respect to each other and the meal. Ma demanded as much. Pa rather enjoyed getting us riled up, though. He never took part, but he loved the show."

"So that's why I've always got these thoughts of others in my head?"

"Honestly, we don't know how you do it. Since you were a little girl, you had a knack for it. Ma had you reading at three, and from the first words you read, you had things memorized. Got under Nick's skin something fierce."

She rested her chin on her hand, trailing her thumbnail along the wood grain of the table. "Why wouldn't it? It annoys me most of the time."

"He couldn't ever remember something he'd read the week before. You remembered every word, every period and comma. Months. Years. Didn't matter." He laughed. "Although Ma did have to put you and Charlie on restriction."

"Why's that?"

"The two of you once had a two-hour long debate during which you spent the whole time citing others for your arguments. Ma made you both go to bed. The next day, she said we were no longer allowed to only use the thoughts of others. Debate did no good if you didn't have an original thought or idea of your own."

"Makes sense. Your ma seems a wise woman." She chewed her lip. "It still wasn't very good of me to do that. Kat will probably be upset that I annoyed her mother even more."

"Her mother needed to be annoyed."

"Michael." Her attempt at a chastising look was lost in laughter. "Be nice."

"You weren't. Why should I be?" He bumped her elbow with his. "Maybe you got through to her. You never know."

"Won't do much good if Kat won't speak to her." Jane sighed and sat back. She drummed her thumbs on the table.

"I thought Cole was joining us?"

She twisted her lips in a grimace. "He's sort of upset with me right now."

"Why?"

"I've been pestering him to talk to Graham. He's been arguing Graham is dead to him. However, I keep reminding him that they were the best of friends before my intrusion."

"I see." Michael's brow furrowed. He leaned closer. "Are you sure that's wise?"

"Not entirely, but they should at least talk. For the moment Graham is rather remorseful and being nice. It could change at any time. We shouldn't hesitate to take every advantage of the situation."

"Graham nice. That's new."

"Regret makes people do odd things." She sipped her tea. "Of course, I'm not all too happy with Cole either. Which leaves us both rather miserable and grumpy with each other."

"Not that I entirely believe you, but why?"

She pursed her lips and made a face. "The man flat out refuses to allow me to reside in my own domicile."

"I rather see his point."

"Not you too."

"Well, think about it."

"I do. I have." She huffed, her teacup clattering to the saucer with unnecessary force. "If I dare try to stay the night at the homestead he's either making Cuddy work extra hard or closing the saloon for the sole purpose of following me. He is in a panic."

"So are you." Michael closed his hand over hers. "You aren't really mad."

"I refuse to be terrorized."

"But you are."

She frowned with as much stubborn force as she could. After just a few moments, her shoulders sagged. "I refuse, Michael."

"I know." He wrapped an arm around her shoulder and tugged her close. Once she'd settled into the hug, he spoke. "We're all scared. You're allowed to be as well."

"I don't want your permission." She pouted but didn't pull away from the comfort.

He chuckled. "Too bad."

The clever retort she planned dissipated when two women stepped into the restaurant. Not just any women, but Kat and her mother. Together. Smiling. Arm in arm. "What in heaven's name?"

Michael straightened when she did. "Then I'm not the only one seeing it?"

Kat waved and walked toward their table. Her smile grew with every step. Soon as she was close enough, she swooped down to pull Jane into a tight hug. "Thank you."

"I didn't do anything." Heat coursed through Jane's cheeks as the elder Daugherty woman approached. "Except to be obnoxious to your mother. I do apologize, Mrs. Daugherty."

"Don't. I appreciate, and rather like, that you aren't afraid to stand up to me." Lillian smiled as she sat across from them. "Of course, once I realized that I liked you for such a thing, I realized maybe I should not hold it against Katherine that she does the same."

"But how?" Michael's gaze swung between the women. "I thought Kat was refusing to speak to you at all."

"She didn't have to speak, I just had to trap her." Lillian chuckled. "It took calling in a favor with Norman to get Katherine in a listening mood."

"I imagine we'll continue to have issues on occasion." Kat gave Jane a meaningful look. "But mother will be returning to St. Louis with me to help me get my affairs in order so that I might move back here permanently."

"It will be nice to have Katherine closer, even if she still refuses to join us in Denver." Lillian nodded.

"Oh—oh." Jane had to force her mouth closed and gather her thoughts. Lillian joining Kat meant the older woman would meet Patrick, Kat's former paramour and the man that taught her many indecent things, who now was her dear friend. Also, there was the situation with Kat's daughter. The trip would reveal the secret to the intimidating woman across from her. "Well, so your mother is joining you—in St. Louis. That's good. When will you go?"

"After Thanksgiving, I think." Kat frowned. "I wanted to go sooner, but with mother joining me there are other arrangements to be made."

Jane wondered how Kat would deliver the news of Cindy to Lillian. It wasn't every day a woman was introduced to her nearly five-year-old granddaughter. Jane almost wished she could go to witness the sight.

Lillian interrupted Jane's train of thought. "I'd also like to see how I can assist you while I'm here, Jane."

"What?" Jane shook her head. "Mrs. Daugherty, that isn't necessary."

"I know it isn't. Honestly, your story intrigues me, and if you won't take my help out of some semblance of kindness, then allow it for an old lady that wishes to satisfy this curiosity." Lillian smiled. "I'm afraid Mr. Mitchell chose the wrong partner to visit. Stein is not the best lawyer for this. I've invited Mr. Greenburg out to meet with Lloyd Kane and make sure you're receiving the best representation should the worst happen."

Michael squeezed Jane's hand so hard she winced. She gritted her teeth against the continual grip and smiled. "Thank you."

"No. Thank you."

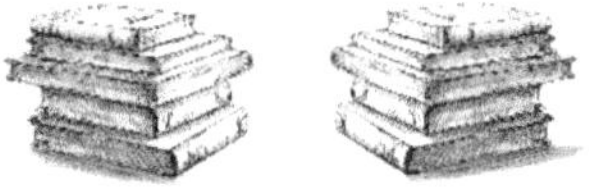

To fight and conquer all our battles is not supreme excellence; supreme excellence consists in breaking the enemy's resistance without fighting.
—Sun Tzu

Kat paced the length of the library. In her hands she held the paper Mike had held onto for several weeks. On it was every word Clara had written in the Poe book Jane and Cole had found months before. "I'm not seeing anything."

"Neither did I. Neither did Michael." Jane pursed her lips. She flipped through the book carelessly until she stopped on the ink-soaked last page. Something about the page filled with graffiti always drew her back. As if she'd be able to read every word ever written on it if she stared long enough. As always, only scribbles and a few letters answered.

"It almost seems like she turned this into a diary." Kat didn't stop moving to speak.

"That's not a diary."

"Hmm? What?" Kat lowered the paper long enough to look her in the face. "After all these little notes and confessions, why would you say that?"

"This was in the open. The code isn't so complex he wouldn't be able to figure it out. If Johnny or whatever-his-name-really-is was as brilliant as she claims, he could have figured it out with enough time. Considering she was with him seven years."

"He probably did."

"Right. I needed Michael's help because I wasn't looking at it as a code, which was foolish and naïve of me, but true." Jane leaned back in her seat.

"Soon as he clued you in, you saw it."

"And if you look at all of those carefully, none are exceptionally confessional as a diary might be. They're more moments of fleeting panic or brilliance. Like no other outlet was available." She chewed on her lower lip. "Except the mention of Yankton. Which makes me think the money isn't there. He likely already looked thoroughly if he read this."

"But he's still after you, so it likely isn't."

"Exactly. It's almost as though she wrote these when no other outlet was available."

Kat sighed. "True. The closest to a dangerous confession in here is the aforementioned Yankton reference, and when she began to wonder about Jesse."

Jane leaned on her hand again, intent on the last page. "Then there's this, which we still can't figure out. Was this the diary, and she just wrote everything on top of each other?

In some areas the ink is so saturated, the paper could rip if I'm not careful."

"There must be something else. Something we're missing." Kat slumped into a chair. She propped her feet on the desk. "Yankton?"

"It's the only thing I can think of. Clara took great pains to make sure the lining seam was sewn back properly after she'd carved that into the wood. The seam in the side Cole found was more obvious, but there was nothing in there." Jane drummed her fingers on the desk.

"Norman sent the telegram again, even though you didn't ask. Still no response."

"There's something there, but I don't know how to find out…" Jane's words trailed off when someone stepped onto the porch. The blurry image of a stovepipe hat gave her a good indication of who it might be. "Damn."

"What?" Kat dropped her feet off the desk and turned.

"Mr. Krenshaw," Jane said as both explanation and greeting. "Whatever could bring you out in such adverse weather when you have the heat of a dozen coal stoves to keep you warm high on your hill?"

Jackson removed his hat and carelessly brushed the snow right onto the bookshelves. Afterward he took great care to shake his scarf free of flakes in the same manner.

Jane clenched her fists, desperate to go mop up the snow before it could damage a single page. Unfortunately, the book in front of her caused her more concern. The last person she cared to see any evidence of her past was Jackson. She frowned and closed the book. As Jackson approached she grabbed the paper Kat had set on the desk and pulled it close to tuck under the book.

Kat crept toward the stove and grabbed a cloth. Jane breathed a sigh of relief when her friend moved to sop up the melting snow.

Jackson stopped in front of the desk. "I just wanted to see how you were doing, Jane."

Jane slipped the book and paper into her drawer when his gaze flickered toward them. She forced a smile and folded her hands before her. Though she was anything but, she tried to appear as calm as possible. "I can hardly imagine you would stoop to a simple kind and generous action such as that."

"You wound me." He touched his heart to add emphasis to his words. "Your wellbeing and lack of memory consume every bit of spare time I have."

"You must find a new hobby to occupy your time." Jane tilted her head. "Perhaps one of the whores you bring in every month can spare the time to teach you embroidery. I hear tell it is rather soothing. Although it can be brutal on your hands, and I imagine you need those for other activities, as I've heard word that not even the most skilled whore you bring in is able to get a rise out of you."

Behind Jackson, Kat's eyes widened. She clapped both hands over her mouth but wasn't quite able to cover her snort.

Jackson's eyelid twitched and his cheek developed a rapid tic. He rolled his shoulder and cleared his throat. "Insults from the town's two most notorious whores don't bother me."

"Jackson Krenshaw," Lillian's commanding voice echoed into the library. A hard edge Jane hadn't heard since their first confrontation the week before had taken hold. "My ears must be deceiving me, for I am quite certain you did not just call my daughter or Miss Doe a whore."

The transformation that took over Jackson's face was astounding and disturbing. The tic faded into an infinitely polite and false smile. Jane had to take a step back from the disturbing sight. Jackson turned toward the door. "Lillian."

Unlike when most men of the town greeted her, Lillian didn't extend her hand. When he took it anyway and kissed the back, her lips thinned. She peered down her nose at him as he rose from his bowed position.

"I'd heard word you were in town. It pleases me to no end to see such rumors prove true." Jackson's tone wasn't as joyous as his words indicated. "We've missed you and Henry."

Lillian extricated her hand from his. "Don't make me repeat myself, Jackson."

"Of course I would never suggest that your *lovely* daughter Katherine," Jackson's nose wrinkled as he said her name, "would ever be a whore."

"You don't lie well." Kat crossed the room to Jane's side. Their arms laced together immediately. "Jane, you have a far better memory than I. What was it Jackson called me the other day on the street?"

"Low-class, private whore." Jane filled in without hesitation. "I remember it quite well because I had to hold back Mr. Hamm, who so kindly rushed to Katherine's defense. Really, Jackson, isn't such language and crass behavior beneath your station?"

"There are many, many things and people beneath my station." Jackson sneered, but the pleasant façade returned a moment later. "I wasn't speaking of Miss Daugherty anyhow."

"No, I believe you were." Kat smiled as she laced her fingers with Jane's. "Because you'd already called my darling Jane far more colorful names before you accidentally bumped into me."

"It's too bad, really." Jackson's false smile grew as he faced Lillian. "For your own daughters both to fall into such depths of disgrace."

To her credit, Lillian didn't bat an eyelash. "Is that so?"

"First your Martha marries an Indian. Such a shame, we all grieved for you. We witnessed how it led to a life of savagery and then—treason." Jackson tutted and shook his head, though more glee than mourning lit his features. "You must be so disappointed."

"I can see how you might think so." Lillian's false smiled turned savage. "Considering how little value you place on humans as a whole, much less relationships."

"And then Katherine." The tic in Jackson's cheek returned, but he pressed forward. "Set to marry Jonathan Wright, which would have bolstered your wealth until you could have taken a position among the elite of Boston if you wished to."

"We still could," Lillian replied in a quiet tone. "If we wished to leave this beautiful territory."

"Yet," Jackson continued as though he hadn't heard Lillian. "She turned around and slept with more men in this town than any respectable woman should. Not to mention her affair with none other than Cole Mitchell."

"You say that like it's a bad thing," Jane interjected. She grinned over at Kat and winked. "I consider it far worse to have never been with a man of any considerable skill. One might look at their marriage bed as a duty rather than a joy, and shouldn't every woman be happy to lie with her husband?"

"Neither of you would know, would you? Or rather, Katherine wouldn't. Jane, I believe you do, although you still deny remembering your husband. Did you just prefer to stooping to the levels of common riff-raff than following propriety?"

Lillian chuckled. "Propriety, Jackson? You are a fine one to talk of such things. I know why you remain in Dominion Falls. You like to act as though it's far better to lord your wealth over the common folk as you do, but I know better."

"I haven't the faintest idea what you're talking about." Jackson tugged on his lapels. He tilted his head back and forth and cleared his throat as though perhaps he did know what she meant. "I remained while you fled so that I could see that this town became a town."

"And it only took another ten years to happen." Jane snorted. "You did nothing."

"You don't know what I've done." Jackson narrowed his eyes. "Now, Lillian."

Lillian lifted her chin, a wicked smile on her features. "Yes, Jackson?"

"If you wish to associate with criminals, that's too bad. I'd hate to see what your friends would think of such behavior." Jackson stepped closer. "Proper society doesn't care for—"

"Criminals? Yes, I'm aware. After all, that is why you remain here, isn't it? You attempt to deride me for associating with people that have the presumption of innocence on their side, when you yourself are the criminal?" Lillian crossed the room to Jane's desk. She offered Jane and Kat a warm smile before turning back toward Jackson. "I have the burden of proof on your crimes, Jackson. I have for some time. I'd hate to have to use them because you overstepped your bounds one too many times."

Jane grasped Kat's hand at the revelation, her smile growing more when Jackson's features grew slack.

"If you'll excuse us, Jackson. I have something to discuss with Jane." Lillian took a seat across the desk from Jane. She kept her back to Jackson and didn't speak again.

Jackson glared at her back for almost a full minute before he snatched his hat and scarf from the coat rack. He stormed from the room, slamming the door.

"I've always despised that man." Lillian sighed.

"Criminal activity?" Jane dropped into her seat. "I'm not surprised, to be honest. I'm just surprised that you have proof."

"Always know your enemy, Jane."

"Sometimes that's easier said than done."

They are like the clue in the labyrinth, or the compass in the night.
—Joseph Joubert

"When's that lawyer gonna get here?" Cole followed Jane right up to the library door. He was so busy eying the street around them that he ran right into her before she'd unlocked the door.

Jane grunted and pushed him back. "Tomorrow. Not that I expect anything of it. I think Lloyd is capable enough."

"*Enough* ain't enough. He's a drunk."

"As are most men in this town. He knows his stuff, and I've done enough research of my own." She finally managed to turn the lock and pushed open the door. "Now would you stop following me all over town?"

"You all went and made Jackson right mad yesterday. If he's paying a Pinkerton, he can have worse done to you than threats." He shut the door and went to the stove while she hung her shawl on a nail. "Not to mention the maniac keeps leaving things all over the place."

"You're just angry Johnny's been in the saloon and you missed him."

"You're just mad you ain't seen him neither."

"He rather is like a ghost." Jane sighed and dropped into her chair. "But I haven't seen hide nor tail in almost two weeks."

"Biding his time. Making you fret." He set a hand on her shoulder.

"Between him and Jackson, I've had quite enough fretting." Not that it would end anytime soon. She hadn't expected it to, but some days it was harder than others.

"You want me to stop pestering you, don't you?"

"Never." She smiled and leaned her cheek on his hand. "But yes."

"You need anything, let me know. Did you bring it?"

"Yes. I have my gun in my lunch pail. Anything else?"

He chuckled. "Nope. Just making sure you come back in one piece."

"If you send Mr. Hamm to check on me, I'll get mighty riled up."

"Just how I like ya." Cole winked as he pulled open the door.

Jane shook her head. She pulled open her drawer and wasn't able to stop the gasp. The chair clattered to the floor when she flew to her feet. "Damn it."

"What is it?" The door still hung half open as Cole ran back across the room. His brow furrowed when he looked in her drawer. "What is it?"

"I'm not certain, but it wasn't there yesterday when I locked up." Her hand shook, but she pulled the envelope out of the drawer.

Before she could open it, Cole set one hand on hers, and the other on his holster. "I'm gonna make sure there ain't no one else here."

"Of course," she whispered. Once he'd freed her hands, she ripped open the envelope. Cole disappeared from sight, and she sank into her chair again.

The pages were filled with notes, what appeared to be medical notes. Jane swallowed against the burgeoning lump in her throat and pushed up the top of the paper. *Constance Pinot Querney.*

"No one's here. Jane?"

"They're from the asylum. He took some of Constance's—no, Clara's—medical records from her time in the asylum. These are sloppy. Maybe the doctor's notes during session. They would have been copied neater later."

"How do you know that?"

"Daisy does it all the time." Jane bit the tip of her pinky, reading the scrawls as best as she could. "It says here he thought Clara was cleverer than she let on. Clearly terrified, but most likely saner than suspected. He recommended she go to trial."

Cole leaned on the desk beside her. "Anything else?"

"The Pinots pushed for her to remain, saying she wasn't behaving as their Constance would." She flipped the page. "All of these medicines. They tried so many. She fought so hard at first they had to restrain her and use syringes. Then she began to be compliant. They were able to change to powders and tinctures. That must be when his notes changed suspicious."

"Jane." Cole tugged the papers from her hand.

She didn't move, staring where the papers had been. There were so many more words, more notes. Things Clara had said. She had to read them all, memorize them. They had to help, for they were Clara's words. Clara's raving, drug-addled words.

"Jane?"

"Sorry." She set her hand on his offered one. "I don't know what to do with it all. I need to read the whole thing."

"You will. First, come here."

She didn't argue, only rose to step into his arms. With a deep sigh, she let his embrace ease the rising nerves. "We have to do something."

"Damn straight."

"Promise me."

"What?"

"If the worst happens…"

"It ain't gonna." He released his tight hold on her. Like a caged animal, he paced the room until she slammed the door shut and locked it. "It's not gonna happen, so I got nothing to promise. I won't let it happen."

Not to be ignored, she pushed forward. "Don't close yourself off again. I couldn't bear it."

"You'd be dead, so it don't matter none, does it?"

"Please, Cole. I need to know you're going to be all right. Jesse will. He's got David. I need to know you'll be all right. I need you to promise."

"I can't."

"I'm scared." Sanctuary. His arms were around her again. For a moment everything was going to be all right. For a moment.

"You still ain't heard nothing from that Hodgkins guy?"

"Or woman. No. Nothing. I spoke to Norman today. He offered to send the telegram a fourth time, but I don't see the point. It's been weeks since the first, days since the third. Not a word."

"What did you say?"

"I keep it simple." She turned to lean back against him, where she could see the papers he'd dropped on the desk. She laced her fingers with his. "They just said: 'Need to talk. Annabel Lee'."

"What are you gonna do about it now?"

"I don't know. I can't go there. Not with things so uncertain. I'm sure David wouldn't approve of me leaving town again."

"Someone should. Find this Hodgkins person." His fingers ran up her arms, drawing goose bumps. "Maybe he'll have answers."

"Who would go? David and Michael both are tied here. I won't let Mike call one of the Young brothers, even if he does keep hinting at it. They've had enough pain."

"Why not me?"

He couldn't be serious. That would mean he'd leave. She needed him too much. Panic rushed through her. "No."

"I'd be back. Yankton's only a few days by train."

"I need you here."

"There might be answers there."

"I know." It was maddening how logical he was being. This was not the time for logic. It was the perfect time for logic. This was a no-win situation. He was right. The answers could be there.

He turned her around to face him. When she tried to avoid it, he tucked his finger under her chin to pin her under his intense gaze. "You need to find out the truth."

"We all do."

"I gotta do this for you."

"You do know what that means, don't you?"

Tension tightened his arms around her. "What?"

"You need to fix things with Graham. Someone has to watch the saloon."

"You can."

"Not alone. I have a job. Cuddy can't work every day."

"You just want me to change my mind."

She couldn't help it; she giggled. It was ridiculous. After all, she had much more convincing ways to change his mind. She gave a fervent shake of her head. "No, I absolutely hate you leaving, but you're right. I need the truth. Everyone needs the truth."

"Annabel Lee, huh?"

"'And neither the angels in Heaven above, nor the demons down under the sea, can ever dissever my soul from the soul of the beautiful Annabel Lee'."

"Come here, Annabel."

And she did.

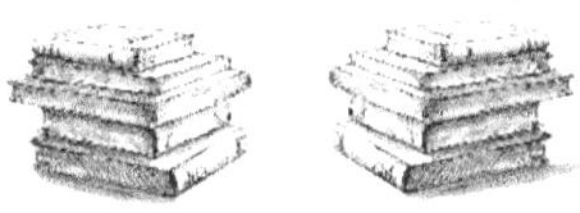

It is easier to forgive an enemy than
to forgive a friend.
-William Blake

"I'm not doing it." Cole slammed the glass he'd just dried on the counter.

Nonplussed by his latest fit of temper, Jane continued cleaning. She bent to pick a stray playing card off the floor. An ace. All their cards were accounted for last she'd checked. "Seems someone has been cheating. We'll need to start checking sleeves. And yes, you are. You have to."

"I'm not."

"Child."

"Nag."

She slipped the card into her belt and tugged a cloth from the other side. To give him a chance to cool off, she wiped the table down with care. Between her asylum records appearing on Wednesday and the appointment with Lloyd and Mr. Greensburg on Thursday, tensions had been high. Nothing was going as planned, and that made them even more nervous about him leaving town.

"No," he snapped before she'd finished wiping the table down. "What about you? I told you days ago to get your things on over here."

"I'm not moving into the saloon for even the two weeks you're going to be gone. I have a perfectly good home."

"It ain't safe."

"Nothing is."

Silence.

"You need to talk with Graham." She set a chair in place firmly. The argument had been raging for days. To the point where she felt they were reading lines of a play. "Like it or not, he is still your business partner."

"Only until I can be rid of him."

She wiped down the next table. "Then you will close the saloon down while you're gone? Just close the doors and walk away? Leave it to rot with no customers, pray the whores remain until you return?"

"Hell, no."

"Then like it or not, you need Graham." Once the floor met with her satisfaction, she moved behind the bar. A few feet away from Cole, she set her hands on the edge of the counter and hopped up onto the bar. "I have a job that actually pays me money to work."

"I'd pay ya."

"I do this for you, not for money. I can't be here all the time, and you can't work Cuddy that hard. You're leaving in a few days, and that isn't enough time to hire another trustworthy bartender. I doubt you want to leave Sly in charge."

Cole's lips curled. "Not putting him in charge of the money."

"Exactly."

"Don't trust Graham neither."

"Nobody would expect you to yet. However, he is repentant. He is determined to make amends, and that is a step in the right direction." She braced her hands on the bar and slid toward him. "For many years he's been your best friend, yet you cannot forgive one error?"

"It was a huge error."

"So was mine. You forgave me."

"That's different." The stubborn set of his brow wavered. Her so-called 'nagging' was having the right effect.

"Not entirely. You need him so you can go to Yankton for me."

"Don't need that bastard." He'd moved between her legs and gripped her thighs. Stubborn lines creased his forehead instead of the lines of laughter she preferred to see around his eyes.

"If you want my help at all while you're gone, you have to talk to him." Jane set her hands on his shoulders. When he met her gaze, she lifted a brow and tried to be stern as possible. "If you don't at least try, I won't lift one finger to help."

"You're trying to threaten me?"

"You bet. Will you at least try?"

"Will you stay here while I'm gone?"

Her lips drew in tight against her teeth. It meant too much to move in, even temporarily. Tempting, though it might be, she couldn't do it.

"It's safer here." At the firm shake of her head, he frowned. "I won't go if you don't."

"Your threat means nothing. You'll go. It was your idea."

"No threats?"

She shrugged. "Don't think you have one that would work. I have enough threats outside of these walls. You are no threat to me."

"I got something else I could do."

"Oh?"

"Bribery." His hands left her thighs to lift her skirts.

"Oh. I like that idea."

He chuckled. "So do I."

Compromise makes a good umbrella, but a poor roof; it is a temporary expedient.
—James Russell Lowell

"I don't believe it. How ever did you manage it?" Kat leaned over the bar to get closer to Jane. She flashed her teeth and gave a sharp tug to Jane's sleeve. "Tell the truth. Was it a trick? Or perhaps a bribe?"

"No." Jane laughed. In truth, she'd been tempted to bribe Cole to talk to Graham about their situation. It took almost a full week to make him agree without the help of such trickery. "All it took was a good solid threat. I reminded him that he already had a partner and until he at least tried to work things out with Graham, I wouldn't lift a finger to help. If I didn't help in any way, he wouldn't be able to go."

"And what about your end of the deal? Has he been trying to bribe you?"

A pleasant heat filled Jane's cheeks to accompany her nod. With a sigh, she leaned against the wall next to Katherine. "Oh, he's been trying. He has failed. But he's tried."

"Why don't you do what he asks?" Kat set her hand on Jane's arm and gave a gentle squeeze. "Cole isn't the only one that wishes it. I believe we would all feel better."

"I don't think it's a good idea. The implications of what it could mean."

"Then keep it temporary." Kat's eyes widened and her smile drew wider than seemed possible. "Oh, my. Unless you don't want to keep it temporary."

"Katherine," Jane cut her eyes to her friend in warning, "you know that isn't the case. Everything is temporary. For me. I can't do something that could mean so much."

"You practically are anyway."

"I need to get back to work."

Katherine giggled. "Of course you do. Then again, the saloon isn't really your job. So is it work?"

"Hush. Be gone." Jane laughed and pushed her friend out of the saloon. "I'll see you at supper."

"If Cole lets you out of his sight. Two days isn't much time."

"Impossible." Jane set her hands on her hips and shook her head. Laughter shivered through her before breaking free when Katherine flipped the tail of her bodice at her. After a final wave she headed inside.

A signal from the corner where Cole and Graham huddled drew her attention. Cole shook his glass at her and pointed to Graham's coffee mug. If she wasn't so determined that the two finish their conversation, she would have balked.

However, it looked like they were making progress, so she complied without complaint. At least not an external one. She got more of both their drinks, carrying them back toward the table.

"I'm trying. I can't promise that I'm not going to." Graham took the coffee cup with a shaky hand. He set it down, squeezing it tight. "Best I can do."

"It ain't enough." Cole frowned.

Jane squeezed his shoulder, frowning at him before setting down his glass. It wouldn't do any good to be stubborn about it. Everyone deserved a second chance if they could have one. She'd told him as much last night.

Cole downed the whiskey fast, smirking when she set a beer next to the empty glass. With a wink at her, he turned back to Graham. "You can't drink while you're here working. Maybe then you won't be so keen on destroying the place."

Jane nodded and headed back to the bar to set down the tray she'd used. She sucked her lips between her teeth to hold back her sigh. That was one thing handled. Having him leave was going to be hard enough without that tension.

"Jane." Michael walked right up and wrapped his arms around her.

"Michael...what are you doing here?" She squeezed him tight before releasing him from the hug. He'd been so intent on being against her return to Cole that she'd not seen much of him at all.

"I was just at the depot." His smile faded as he reached into his pocket. "Norman had a letter for you."

Throat dry, she could barely rasp, "It's the same script."

"I thought so."

"He's been in town how many times, and we've not seen him, but then he leaves again and sends letters? I'm sick of this game."

"Open it." He squeezed her hand. "Might as well see what he has to say."

Jane opened the letter slowly. She kept her back to the corner, scanning the few words. "'No rest for the wicked. All criminals turn to preachers under the gallows. You will soon see'."

"Clara…"

"'Many cliffs and ravines. It's dangerous for little boys'," Jane finished in a weak whisper. She folded the letter quietly and tucked it back into the envelope. "He's waiting for something…but it won't be long."

"He's trying to scare you. Obviously thinks he can intimidate you."

"Well, he can't."

Michael took her hands in his. "Then why are you shaking?"

"I'm not frightened for me." She took a long, shaky breath to steady herself. "I mean, I am a little, but I've known for some time that my future does not look promising. It's Jesse. He's the one I'm worried about. And Cole."

"Don't make me tell you again," Cole's voice rumbled just behind her. "I'm gonna be fine."

She was certain she jumped three feet. Her heart stopped for a moment. "Cole, don't do that."

Cole's brow furrowed before he looked at Michael. "What's going' on? Why's she acting plum crazy?"

"It's nothing."

"She got a letter," Michael spoke over her. "Another one from the maniac."

"What?" Cole's hand tightened on the edge of the bar, his knuckles turning white. "What did he say?"

"More idle threats." Jane laid her hand on Cole's. If she hadn't been so focused on him, she would have bothered to give Michael a scathing look. He would have ignored it, but it might have helped her mood. "You're going to find answers. It will be over soon anyway. It doesn't matter, right?"

"Jane," Cole's eyes flashed, "what did I tell you?"

"Not now." When Michael's hand landed on her shoulder, she tensed. Cole's short nod relaxed her the slightest bit.

"We're going to figure this out, Clara. Lloyd has been working on it." Michael squeezed her shoulder. "He'll figure something out."

"Stop trying to comfort me." She spun around. "Lloyd has nothing. I don't want false platitudes. Unless Cole finds something significant, it's pointless."

Cole pulled her closer. "I leave in two days. With any luck, I'll be back in a couple of weeks."

"God willing." She leaned back into his chest.

"Ain't got much to do with it." Cole chuckled. "Not with me, leastwise."

Michael quirked a brow. "On that note, I'm going to go tell David about the latest letter. He'll want to know."

"Thank you." She refused to pull away from Cole, even to give Mike a hug. After the letter, she wanted to feel safe. She needed it. "Tell David I'll see him tomorrow. If he wants to see the letter, I'll have it with me."

"Of course." Mike leaned in and kissed her on the cheek. He muttered, "In any other situation I'd argue. In this one, I have to say…listen to Cole."

She pursed her lips and looked down until he'd left. "I should get back to work."

"No. It's Graham's test." Cole started leading her toward the door.

She glanced behind them in surprise. Graham was there, working behind the bar. Her protests were silenced until they stepped out into the open air. She planted her feet in place the moment they were outside. "Are you sure? He's shaking like a leaf."

"You're the one that told me to work it out." Cole kept moving until he leaned on the hitching post. "Right now is his test. If he doesn't take a drink much as he wants it, he can stay on."

"I see." She walked up next to him, leaning on the post. "You don't trust him."

"Hell, no. You're gonna have to keep an eye on him."

"He'll love that."

"Don't matter none." Cole's hand closed over hers. His fingers laced with hers and pulled her arm closer. He didn't look at her, his thumb tracing circles in the back of her hand.

He lifted her hand, brushing his lips along the back of it. He switched hands, wrapping the now free one around her waist. Close as can be, he rested his chin on top of her head.

Words failed. For all of their scandal-causing scenes in the public eye, Cole reserved such quiet notes of tenderness for moments behind closed doors. She didn't have a problem with it; in fact she expected it. It was the norm. This was the exception.

Emotions started to bubble up, ones she'd rather not face just then. She cleared her throat and used her fingertips to push him back a little. He took the hint and shifted, but kept their fingers entwined.

"So Graham's gonna leave you alone. No more threats or nothing. Said you came to some understanding."

"We'll see how long it lasts. Doesn't mean he'll enjoy seeing me as his keeper."

"Don't care." He ran his fingers along her forearm. "He wants to stay as partners, that's what he's gotta do."

"All right."

"You need to stay here."

"I won't have this argument again." She tugged, trying to pull her hand free. His grip was like a vise, holding her firm. "Cole, please. I have my own house. I can't live by fear."

"Your house is outside of town. Close to the depot. Bastard's been around here, and there ain't no one that saw him. It's just not smart."

"I have a gun. He won't be able to take me."

"I'd feel better having you in town. Not alone like you'd be out there. Mike agrees with me. It's better—it's safer." His grin grew wider when she gasped. "Yeah, we talked about it."

"I guessed as much when he told me to listen to you. I don't believe the two of you. You can't agree on a damn thing...except this? Let me guess, you started the conversation by telling him you were leaving?"

"Sure did. Cheered him right up."

Every effort to smack him was thwarted, leaving her squirming in his arms. "Cole Mitchell, let me free."

"I want you to stay here. In my room."

"I can't." She stilled, resting her head against his chest. She was losing this argument. It wasn't one that she was sure she wanted to win. Despite the implications, the fact that he'd asked meant everything. Even if it was just for her safety.

"Please."

"No." It was weak. She couldn't even muster a little force to it. "I shouldn't."

"I want you to. Not just because it's safer."

The sag of her defeat tensed up until she was trembling. He hadn't needed to say such a thing. She was going to say yes anyway. He couldn't mean it; it was just a bribe. She had to brush aside the implication, make it playful. "You just want to enjoy every minute before you leave."

He didn't return her smile when she turned up to him. "Jane."

"I'll stay."

"Thank you."

"So." Her voice faded. She needed to move past it for now. "Two days."

"Yup."

"Not much time."

"Nope." His fingers brushed along her cheek. Within moments, his lips closed over hers, searching, tender, pulling her closer, holding tight. He pressed his forehead to hers and took a deep breath.

"I'll be fine. Whatever happens, I'll be all right."

"You damn well better be."

"If something happens, it's not your fault. It's not Michael's."

"Can I blame Graham?"

It was ridiculous. It was silly. It was pointless. It was what they both needed, and her laughter joined his low chuckle. "If you have to blame someone, I guess that's all right. I'd rather you blame Johnny, or whatever his name is."

"Think I can handle that."

"Good." They were wasting time. There wasn't enough time. "A shame…"

"What?"

"Just a couple of days. Doesn't seem like much time. Yet we're standing out here in the sunshine."

"Just standin' here."

"Seems rather pointless."

"Sure does." Cole shrugged. "But what can you do?"

"I guess we could find something to fill our time."

"Like what?"

"I don't know. Books." She bit her lip to try to prevent the smile tugging at the corner of her lips.

"Books?"

"I have a few upstairs." She let loose the wicked grin. There was no doubt he'd understand what she meant. "We could…read…all night…"

"Guess it's a good thing I learned to read."

*Absence from whom we love is worse than
death, and frustrates hope severer
than despair.
-William Cowper*

Cole tugged on the girth strap once more before he pulled down the flap. When he turned around finally and spotted the package in Jane's hands a dark frown creased his brow. "What in blazes is this?"

"Amazing as it may be, Graham and I agreed about something." Jane held the bundle out toward him. "You need a much better coat for such a journey. This one is wool. We don't know how long you'll be gone and the weather is taking a turn. Already it is cold enough to send everyone huddled around the stoves."

"I ain't taking it."

"Yes. You. Are." She shoved the wrapped package hard into his chest. At this point this was a ridiculous argument. Everything seemed ridiculous. All she wanted to do was scream at him to remain in Dominion Falls, but the last thing she needed to do was that. The trip he was taking had to be done. If not for her, then for those Clara had left behind.

He pulled her close, the coat still between them like a barrier she was sure they needed. "You're fussing."

A hum of annoyance was all she could manage before extricating herself from his arms. Determined to not fall apart, she bent to grab the burlap bag filled with food off the floor. She handed it to him after he'd shoved the new coat into his already brimming saddlebags. "I had Cora make you enough food to last you to Yankton. You shouldn't need to buy anything until you arrive."

He tied the bag to the saddle and sighed heavily. After a moment he turned back. The grimace that twisted his handsome features tugged her heart more. "Anything else?"

"That's all." She couldn't stop the shaking of her hands. They moved toward him of their own volition so she yanked them back to clasp them behind her back. The past few hours they'd spent together, saying all that needed said in the privacy of his room.

Saying goodbye.

She was worried Johnny would go after him the moment he left town, and he was worried about the same happening to her. The sense of foreboding did nothing to help her keep things calm and collected. Their goodbyes were concluded. All that remained was for him to leave.

"I'll send a telegraph soon as I get there."

Her nod was too strong for decorum. She didn't dare look at him. His shoes would do. Boots wouldn't make her cry. Boots lifting into his stirrups wouldn't—or maybe they would. All of it meant he would leave. Soon. It was unstoppable now, and a soft whimper slipped free.

Eyes screwed shut, she cleared her throat to erase the lump. He should be in his saddle by now. It would be safe to open her eyes. When she did so, she realized it wasn't safe. He was right there, his face an inch from hers.

His arms went around her waist. With one step, he had her pushed against the stable wall. The inch was gone, their lips locked in a sweet embrace.

His tongue searched the planes of her mouth, and she responded in kind. The salt of her sorrow added to the bittersweet lingering.

She gripped the lapels of his coat. Desperation surged forth and she tugged him closer. One last goodbye. It wasn't long enough; it would never be long enough. He pulled back, and she didn't dare fight him no matter the clench of her heart.

Slow as possible his hands came back around her waist. Just the tips of his fingers were left, the lightest touch of his lips. One gentle push from his fingers to keep her still and the cool night air rushed back between them.

An invisible barrier they couldn't dare to cross. He had to go, and she had to let him. They both would pray it wasn't a wild goose chase. That it wasn't too late.

She forced a smile, dead set on lightening the moment. It wouldn't make it easier, but any minute he'd be leaving and she'd do him no good to be a sobbing mess. "I told you. You're far better with actions than words."

His finger pressed into her lips and he smirked. "Keep that mouth of yours shut much as possible. Much as ya like to think otherwise, you ain't so great yourself."

"Yes, sir." The smile stuck on her face. If it cracked, she would.

With a brief nod, he hopped into the saddle and got his reins situated.

This was it. There would be no more foolish delay. She would be strong. If it killed her, she would. She returned his wink, still smiling like a fool, as he turned to ride out of the barn. There would be no running after him, no desperate calls. She'd been a fool long enough. Grateful as she was to have him returned to her side and for his support, the best way to let him do so now was to let him leave. Find answers.

Steady steps led her to the doors, and she waited there. At the fence gate Cole was still astride his horse, but leaned down to talk to Graham. Their words were muffled and distant, but knowing them didn't matter. In moments he would disappear into the dark and snow. They hoped that by leaving at night and boarding a train elsewhere, Johnny wouldn't realize at first that Cole was gone.

She didn't move from the spot. She couldn't. Her legs had grown weak, wobbly. One step and she'd collapse.

Finally he moved, riding out of the corral into the cold night. It wasn't until she couldn't discern him from the dark that she found the energy to move. She rushed up to the fence next to Graham and stared into the night.

Graham set his hand on her back. "Sorry."

"Whatever for?"

"You know what."

Perhaps the closest he'd come to both an apology and a note of sympathy. A nod was all she could manage in reply. Before she could stop herself, she grabbed his hand. "Thank you. I should get back inside."

"Jane."

"Yes, Graham?"

"Thanks." When she didn't reply, he kept talking. "For helping me when I'm shaking. For convincing Cole to give me a chance. For what you said to Becky."

"For helping you sneak around with Linh so this time no one is the wiser?"

"That too."

"I'm not doing any of this for you, Graham. I'm doing it for Cole." She thought she might be losing her mind for everything she was doing for Graham. Truth was, the happier he was, the less likely he was to upset Cole. "He still considers you his friend, no matter how mad he is at you right now. A good friend, at that. He didn't like what you did, but it was the first time."

"I'm not going to mess up again."

"At least not until I stop helping you." She smirked. "And if you screw up once I do, I'll come back to haunt you after my hanging."

Before he could reply, she turned and rushed toward the building. It was impossible to stop the smile that was forming. Graham sputtered behind her, likely trying to figure out if she'd really said what she had.

"Wait. You don't believe in ghosts do you?" His laughter filled the night as he jogged toward her. "Jane, wait."

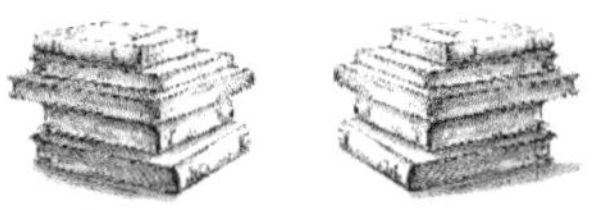

Sorrows gather around great souls as storms do around mountains; but, like them, they break the storm and purify the air of the plain beneath them.
—Jean Paul Richter

Outside the saloon the snow dunes were several feet deep. The morning after Cole had left, Thanksgiving morning, the storm had begun. All through Thanksgiving and the day after the storm had raged and howled.

Jane did all she could to keep busy, but as only a few men made it through the storm to the saloon a good portion of her time was spent in useless cleaning. Or poring over the notes from the asylum, or ever more useless cleaning.

Somehow Michael had made his way down the street with a basket of food from Cora's for them to nibble on during the storm. Of course, Jane was far from hungry. However, at Michael's insistence she'd complied. The storm had finally passed and Jane was left to wonder if Cole had made it over the mountains before the worst had hit.

The worst part was not knowing where he was. She'd made him promise not to send a telegram until he'd made it to Yankton. A decision she was beginning to regret.

Michael whistled and waved his hand in front of her face. A half smile belied the amusement behind his furrowed brow. "Have you heard a word I've said?"

"No," she admitted with a sigh. "Not a one. Sorry."

"I'm sure Cole's fine."

Jane shrugged and wiped down the bar again. At least with the storm passed there were actual customers now, and quite a few of them. Having customers added life and activity that the saloon needed, or rather that *she* needed. So far Graham had been as good as his word and hadn't had a drop to drink when at work. Then again, maybe it was easier when the saloon wasn't full of men tossing one back.

"Jane?"

"Sorry." She offered a weak laugh. "I haven't been sleeping well. I haven't been able to see Jesse since the storm started, only this lot."

Michael glanced around when she waved toward the whores. "You get along with them well enough, or so it seems."

She shrugged a shoulder. Sometimes she wondered on how well she got along with a few of them, but for the most part things still went smooth. "I do, when there's plenty of distraction. Most of the girls don't like to talk about their pasts, and we ran out of conversation pretty quick. Plus, they didn't care for me making them clean every inch of this place, and themselves."

"I see."

She pulled out a tray and lined up several whiskey glasses and two beer mugs. Once the drinks had been poured she carried it out to the larger table to hand them out.

Michael grinned as she resumed her post behind the bar. "You seem to be enjoying this, Jane. Watching over a saloon."

"There are worse things to be doing with my time, I suppose."

"That isn't what I mean, and you know it."

"I'm quite certain I don't." Her lips tightened to cover her smile. Truth was, she did enjoy it. Last thing she'd do is let Michael think he had an upper hand.

"Liar."

"Perhaps." She poured him another cup of coffee. Her smile grew when Graham walked in the door. "Graham? What in heaven's name are you doing?"

Jane thought she detected the hint of a blush on his already ruddy face. He held up the banjo he was carrying. "You mean this?"

"Yes."

"Mabel's got it in her head to have a dance or something for Christmas. She's been pestering me to help out the band with my plucking."

"I didn't know you played." Jane giggled. "Can't imagine those clumsy hands can make good music."

"Jane," Michael snorted, "don't poke the bear."

"You aren't funny, Jane." Graham's laughter said the opposite. He poked her with the end of the banjo before setting it down. "It's been a while since I played, but don't seem to have forgotten."

"I still don't believe you." Jane shrugged. "You've been known to bluster."

"Sounds like a challenge." Michael chuckled at Graham. "Going to take her up on it? Or can you just play with a band to cover your horrible squawking?"

"Come on, Graham. Show 'em." Wills grinned. "But only if Janey'll dance with me while you do."

"I'd be willing. If Graham can play, of course." She set her hands on her hips. Dancing might make her ankle ache, but it still sounded like a good time. "What do you say, Graham?"

"Will it shut you up?" Graham laughed at Michael's loud guffaw. "That's right. Ain't nothin' that shuts you up."

"I promise to be quiet for a full hour if you play well enough." Jane smacked Michael's arm and stuck her tongue out at him. "It may well kill me, but I'll do it."

"Hell, I'd do it if she shut up for an hour." Bert laughed when she threw a pickled egg at him. "What?"

"Watch it, I'm the one that made sure Heather was available for you."

"She's also the one that gave us that show with Cole," Wills muttered at Bert. "Best be nice to her."

"I heard that, Wills." Jane laughed. "You've been running your mouth all over town."

"You ain't embarrassed. What does it matter?" Wills held up his beer. "I'm just showing my appreciation."

"Hey." Michael's nose wrinkled. "I'd rather not hear it. It is my sister you're talking about here. So what say you, Graham? Save me from the talk?"

"For an hour of peace and quiet, I can play a bit." Graham picked the banjo back up. "If it's a promise."

"Promise. Now play." She untied her apron and dropped it on the bar. A few notes stilled the remaining chatter in the saloon. With a grin, she stepped into Wills' arms. "Shall we?"

A lively tune tumbled out of the banjo, the screech of tables being shoved aside joining in. In moments the floor was cleared, and several couples danced in the space. Jane laughed, moving easily with Wills, even though she couldn't remember ever dancing.

Before she knew it, she'd been traded off to Bert. Several times she switched partners until a shadow outside the door caught her eye. Through her laughter, she slipped out of the dance.

The moment she recognized the figure just outside the door, her heart fell. It was David. He hesitated to enter. That could only mean one thing. The door started swung open, and her hand was grabbed.

With a yelp, she was pulled back into the dancing patrons. Laughter and cheers continued around her, but this time she couldn't join in. Soon as she could, she pulled free of Michael's arms.

David stood at the bar, not saying a word. He couldn't even look at her. That wasn't good. Nothing was good.

"I need more time." A squeak in her voice belied her fear. She cleared her throat. "Cole's not back. Just a few more days, David."

"Someone alerted the marshal. He'll be here on this afternoon's train. I'm sorry, Clara." His hand rested on her shoulder as he called her Clara for the first time in months. The old name was a confirmation of what was happening. His hand shook, and his hat was pulled so low she couldn't see his eyes. The break in his voice was enough. "I gotta take you in."

"David, no." Michael's shout stilled all action.

Red heat filled Jane's cheeks. This couldn't be happening. Not now.

"I'm sorry." There was no doubt he really was. Regret filled every syllable until it was heavy and slow. "Nothing I can do now."

"It's all right." How she'd found her voice, she'd never know. It was weak, shaky, but it was there. "I'll be all right. Cole will be back. He has to be."

"We still have time. Could be weeks before we get a judge." Michael squeezed her arms.

"There's no more time." David finally lifted his head. Moisture shimmered at the edges of his eyes. "Judge'll be here on Monday. So will a witness and the Pinots."

"There's gotta be something we can do." Graham set the banjo on the bar. "Something to delay until Cole can get back."

"No. No delays." Jane straightened her back. "I said I would face my punishment when it was time, and I meant it. There will be no delays. No more waiting."

"But, Clara," Michael turned her toward him, "you've got to fight."

"I will fight with what I have. I won't delay the inevitable. It's time." Every word crushed its weight down on her. There could have been a full herd of horses on her heart at this point, and it wouldn't have felt any different.

"I'll wire Cole." Graham's hand on her shoulder about dropped her to the ground. It was too much. "Get him back here real quick."

"No."

"Jane," David frowned, "he should know."

"If he turns back now, it may be too late anyway. If he finds something, it could help you. Help Mike." She cupped David's cheek. "He may have answers that I can't give you. We have to let him finish. Without rushing, without coming back here where there's nothing he can do but watch."

"Still think I should wire him," Graham grumbled, his hand dropped from her arm. "He'll get mad if he don't know."

"I'll take full blame. Please, let him do what he needs to." Jane had to get out of there. Away from the ogling crowd. It was time. She'd said she'd accept her fate, and that was just what she had to do. "Let's go."

"Clarabelle, let me get Ma."

"She'd never make it in time. She already thinks I'm dead—don't open that wound just to pour salt on it." Jane grabbed David's hand. "We need to go. Now."

"I can't ignore this, Clara." Michael grabbed her. "Please. I have to do something."

"Walk away. If it's too much, walk away. Now."

"I can't do that. I'm going to be here." Michael folded her into his arms, but she didn't accept it. Her body remained stiff until he pulled back. "Clara."

"I need to go now. Don't come to the jail. Please." She spun on her heel and left the building. The cold air assaulted her lungs, lifted goose flesh on her arms. She'd forgotten a coat. It didn't matter now.

Kat ran toward her. Another sympathetic person she couldn't face, not yet. She had to figure out how to handle this first. The propelling hand of David at her elbow was both her salvation and her damnation.

Each step toward the jail echoed through every muscle until her brain pounded. Prison. Death. The noose. Only in her nightmares had she faced those realities.

Words were one thing. With words she could stand up to anything, face anything. Once reality crashed down, words were of no use. There was nothing she could do now. Nothing she could say.

A past she couldn't remember was destroying a future she'd never forget.

Like quicksand dragged on her limbs, she struggled to reach the door. David's pace was not any easier. Once the door opened and she saw the yawning dark entrance of the cell, she froze.

"Clara."

That name. It struck her soul deep. He knew it was over too. That's why he used it. Clara was already dead to him. "I'm sorry. I need a minute."

"Take your time. I'm not going nowhere."

"It was just so much easier to face when it was an idea."

"I'm going to be here the whole time. You won't be alone. You're never going to be alone. I promise."

"If I get sentenced to the gallows…" Her heart stopped as her fingers wrapped around the cold metal bars. The cold ran through her to her toes, encompassing the fear and hardening it.

"I told you I'd be there. I'll hate it. I told you; you won't be alone."

"Cole, tell him…"

"We'll deal with that if it happens."

"Thank you, David."

When she straightened, he put a supportive hand on her waist.

She pulled away and stepped into the cell, the world spinning around her in a swirl of pain, fear, and confusion. Turning around, she watched the bars of the door move closer inch by inch. Suffocatingly close.

With a clang, the door closed, and the world went black.

The melancholy days are come, the saddest day of the year.
Of wailing winds and naked woods and meadows brown and sear.
-William Cullen Bryant

"'Leaves that the night-wind bears to earth's cold bosom with a sigh, are types of our mortality'." Arthur frowned. He opened his mouth to speak again, and then shut it. Rather than go on with the poem, he toyed with the edge of the page with his finger.

Jane didn't move. Her forehead pressed against the bars between them. The words he read were dark, but she'd always found hope even in the darkest of poems. With a soft sigh, she closed her eyes. "Go on, Arthur."

"You sure?"

"Yes, please."

"I don't know, Jane. It don't seem happy."

A smile tugged the corners of her mouth. She had to turn this conversation around. The very fact Arthur was there bothered her. She gripped the bars and focused on the next words. "'The tree that shades the plain, wasting and hoar as time decays, spring shall renew with cheerful days, but not my soul again'."

"Sure don't seem happy to me." He closed the book with a snap. "You said there was joy in every poem."

"And I meant it. Didn't you hear it in what I cited?" She pulled her head away from the bars. The boy shook his head, and she allowed a small smile. "The fact that life continues to live itself. Time continues to turn. One person's life or death does not change the whole of the world."

"But, it still seems to end real sad."

"Just go back. It starts sad as well, talking about the 'mourn and cheerless gale'. After that, the words show that even in strife there is beauty. And there is, Arthur." She focused on a point beyond his head. Beyond the tiny jail. Beyond what had become her life.

"Still say it ain't hopeful."

"It isn't one of Longfellow's more cheerful pieces, I'll grant you as much. What else do you expect from a poem about autumn?" Jane laughed, and for the briefest moment felt the joy behind it. "I know, how about this one?"

Arthur's gaze lifted, a grin already forming. "You gonna recite?"

"Of course." She rose to her feet, walking across the small cell to where he'd been sitting. Fingers wrapped tight around the bars, she grinned right back at him. "'Tell me not, in mournful embers, life is but an empty dream'?"

"Longfellow, *A Psalm of Life*," Kat's smile light up the jailhouse. The dreariness faded in the light of her friend's arrival. "So good to hear you quoting such a marvelous poem. But, really, if you're going to do it, do it right. Give the boy the best lines."

Jane laughed, knowing immediately what she meant. "'Trust no future howe'er pleasant. Let the dead past bury its dead. Act—act in the living present. Heart within, and God o'erhead'."

"Exactly. Live in the now." Kat squeezed Arthur's shoulder. "At least, I'm assuming that was her purpose in reciting that to you."

"She's real good at making poems speak things I never thought they did." Arthur nodded. "What else does it say, Jane?"

"Just a moment." Within two steps, she'd crossed the cell to her cot. She picked up the well-worn book from her pillow and clutched it to her chest. In the six short months she'd owned it, the pages had become worn. It was one of her favorites. She ran her thumb over the cover and sighed before carrying back over to the bars.

Kat smiled at her over Arthur's head, despite the tears shimmering in her eyes. "You carry that everywhere, Jane."

"Here." Jane slipped the book through the bars. She smiled at the young man. "I want you to have it, Arthur."

"But Jane."

"Please. I want you to have it." Jane squeezed his hands to quell any further protest. "It has some of my favorite poems in it. Longfellow's words always speak to me. Pick out a few of your favorites and we'll read them on your next visit."

"It don't seem right."

"I think that's up to me to decide. You have a gift with words too, Arthur. That should be encouraged. I want you to have this. Someday perhaps you'll have a big collection of books as well." Jane shrugged. "I could think of no one better to share it with."

"Your ma is looking for you, Arthur." Kat stepped closer to the cell. Her sharp gaze didn't waver from Jane's. "She said something about some chores you forgot."

"Oh. I forgot to sweep the store." Arthur flew to his feet. "Will I get to see you again, Jane? Tomorrow?"

"I hope so. Perhaps tomorrow evening after my day is complete." Jane managed to keep her smile until he darted from the jailhouse. In an instant, her strength crumbled away and she dropped her forehead to the bars. "It isn't right. I wish Cora would tell him to stay away. He shouldn't have to see this."

"You didn't protest when he watched the hanging of the horse thieves last month." Kat wrapped her hands over top of Jane's. "And you will not be hanged."

"What else could happen? I could be exonerated? Kat, even if they fail to prove murder, there are other crimes here. Ones they can prove. Fraud, for instance."

"Let Lloyd try to get a lesser sentence."

"And spend my life in a cell like this? Or worse, an asylum? I would rather swing than rot."

Kat sighed. "We need more time."

"More time for what?" Days had passed since Cole's departure, since her arrest, and there had been no word from Cole. No sign of hope. She was afraid that even if he did find something, it wouldn't help her. The marshal was certain the fraud charge would be enough if he could not get murder. "The only thing that is left would be to find something to help Michael and David understand why Clara did what she did."

"You are *not* Clara."

"I know."

A harsh clang rang through the bars when Kat hit them hard once, twice. "There has to be some way to make them see that."

"Marshal Lewis is convinced that this is yet another deception. I don't blame him. I have no doubt he is not the only soul that believes as such. Johnny certainly believes I am using his lessons to my benefit. Graham and Daisy thought I was being deceptive for quite a long time. I think Graham still has his doubts."

"Cole will be so mad you didn't send a telegram."

"I know. But he had to do this. If anyone told him, he would have turned around immediately. There is nothing he can do to help me here. And C. Hodgkins is our only hope for some truth. Some clue into what might have happened." A shudder ran through her as the grim reality hit her in the gut again. "Now I can only hope he'll return before…before the end."

"Don't say that."

"I accepted my fate long ago. I had only hoped it would end different."

"He'll be back. He'll be here and yelling at you for doing it this way."

"The hope that he has something to make this easier for those Clara abandoned, for Michael and David, perhaps even for Cole…that's what is getting me through."

"Nothing will make this easier. We don't want to lose you, Jane."

"I've lived this past six months with all that I could, Katherine. I do not regret one moment. I can't. It will sustain me when I need to be Clara for this trial, and I must be her, the woman I despise and don't remember. My memories of my life will carry me."

"It's not enough." Kat reached through the bars to clasp her hand. "Fight for who you are, Jane. You're not Clara. You didn't do this."

"I was Clara once. She did." Jane pulled her hand free and returned to her cot. "I am afraid. If I give into the feeling that six months was not enough, I will not be able to take any of this. I am afraid that Cole won't make it back. If he doesn't—"

"He will."

"If he doesn't. Do you still have the letter? You will give it to him for me?"

"He'll never forgive you."

"I'm getting used to the idea of that."

"Clara," David stepped into the jail with Lloyd hot on his heels, "Cole is all right. Supposed to be in Yankton first thing tomorrow."

"He made contact before he got there? He wasn't supposed to do that." Jane buried her face in her hands. By doing such a thing, he might have alerted the wrong people to where he was going. The clank of the key unlocking the door drew her head back up. "David?"

"Marshal Lewis is with the judge and the Pinots. They just got here. Figured you'd want to see Kat for a few minutes. Plus, your lawyer's got the right." David pulled her to her feet and hugged her tight. "I'll be guarding, so don't you try to run."

Jane managed a weak laugh because she knew he expected as much. She hugged him back briefly. The second she released him, she was completely unprepared for the strong hug Kat captured her in. "Easy," she gasped, "you don't want to knock me unconscious."

"Well, you need to be hugged. Deal with it." Kat's weak laugh didn't match the tears in her eyes. She wiped at the tears on Jane's face. "Now what's this about the telegram, David?"

"Here you go, Mrs. Schaffer." Lloyd held it out. "At least Norman said it was meant for you. Who is Annabel?"

"Clara's code." Jane smiled and took the telegram. "And it's Miss Young. David and I are divorced. It's best that I do not go by Clara Schaffer. He will be the one—"

"I'm not talking about it." David cleared his throat. "Just read your telegram."

> *Annabel,*
> *Delayed 2 days. Will get where I'm going tomorrow. Be home when I return.*
> *C.*

Jane let out a shaky breath. "I'm sorry, Cole."

"I want to make sure you're ready for tomorrow." Lloyd sat in a chair right outside the cell. Unlike Kat, he didn't breech the doorway. It spoke little of his faith they would be successful. As though behind those bars was where she belonged. "We have already discussed your plea."

"You mean my lack of one?" Jane folded the telegram with great care. When she resumed her seat on the cot, she clutched the paper to her chest.

"What do you mean, lack of one?" Kat gasped. "You are saying you're not guilty, aren't you?"

"Actually, Miss Young is refusing to plea." Lloyd nodded. He adjusted his glasses and opened the folder he'd carried in with him. "In most cases, I would advise against such a thing. With Jane—I mean Miss Young's case—I, and your mother's lawyer, think it's smart."

"How so?" Kat resumed her pacing. "That doesn't make any sense. Why wouldn't it be better to make a plea and stand by it? Show you believe in yourself."

"You're making me dizzy. Stop." Jane slipped the telegram in her bodice before she leaned back against the bars. "Why would I make a plea? I cannot say I am not guilty. But also cannot say I am guilty to crimes I have no memory of committing. If I had more information perhaps, more than the word of a maniac…"

"Will she be hanged?" Kat's voice cracked. She wrung her hands. "If found guilty?"

"It is more likely for many reasons, including her preference for the sentence." Lloyd frowned and dropped the folder onto his lap. "Although I'd still like to talk to you about your decision to waive your right to a jury."

"Now I know you've lost your mind." Katherine gasped. "The jury is your best chance."

"She's right, Miss Young." Lloyd frowned. "The judge is one man and could easily be swayed by bribery."

"I'm aware of this." Jane remained silent until the two of them staring wove under her skin. "I've made friends in this town. Good friends with good men. I won't ask them to swear to be impartial and decide my fate. I won't let them face being bribed and intimidated into taking sides against me."

"If they're good men, then they won't be." Kat began to pace again.

"They're good men without two nickels to rub together most days, and many with shady pasts. If someone like Jackson goes after them, I wouldn't blame them for caving, and I won't give them the chance." Jane folded her arms across her chest. "Let them continue to be good men and allowed to show their support if they choose."

"Jane, stop this now." Katherine spun toward her. "Please. Stop being so logical, or illogical—I can't figure out which you're being. But stop, and get yourself out of this mess. You aren't Clara. I can't bear the thought of you being hanged."

"Katherine," Jane sighed, "we've talked about this."

"And I'm this close to breaking you out of here and having Cole take you far away. Far away where you can be free of this." Katherine took a shaky breath.

"I'd come right back, and you know it."

"Not if I hit you on the head hard enough." Before either of them could stop it, they both burst into laughter.

The ridiculousness of the notion that a simple hit about the head would clear her memory as nothing else had done for months proved far too amusing. It served to break the mounting tension wonderfully.

Katherine sank onto the cot next to her. "You're really doing this, aren't you?"

"Going to trial? Yes. I have a lawyer and everything."

"Jane."

Jane squeezed her hand. "Go on, Lloyd. Let's finish going over this again. Let Katherine hear it. Maybe it will help."

"Nothing will help." Katherine's head settled back against the bars.

"She's got that right." David wasn't even looking at her. His arms were folded against his chest.

Jane closed her eyes, picturing Cole. "I know."

The charge is prepared;
the lawyers are met, the judges all ranged
(it's a terrible show!).
—John Gay

Much to Jane's disappointment, Lloyd lost the first most important argument. Their hope had been to have the trial in the church, where a clean and sober environment could be observed, especially with Lloyd's appreciation for beer.

The judge had laughed at the idea, and so the trial was being held in the saloon, in Cole's home and business, where she'd been living ever since he left. It felt like a slap in the face and based on Jackson's smug smile, he agreed.

The location hadn't kept her friends from joining but did blessedly keep the children out. Every inch of the saloon sat packed with people, so at least that was good for Cole's income, if not for her.

Beside her, Lloyd kept his thirst quenched with a constantly refilled mug of beer despite her protests. Behind her, the presence of Kat and Michael both assured and worried her. The judge had a whore on each side, and his whiskey cup was bottomless as well.

The whole thing was a circus. Still, she refused to give in and lose hope. Not just yet. When the prosecution's key witness took the stand, she lifted her chin to meet his gaze.

"Mr. Darius." The lawyer for the prosecution had been paid well. Kat told her he came from St. Louis and was popular and very wealthy because of his ability to win. Jane noted Mr. Quinn's drink was nothing more than water. "Would you tell us what you saw on the train platform the nineteenth day of December, the year of our Lord 1870?"

"We were all waiting on the platform. All of us in groups." Mr. Darius nodded in her direction. "I remember she was standing with that man, the one that died. They were talking real quiet-like. Huddled up close. She kept looking around, maybe to see if we was watching."

"Objection," Michael muttered behind her. "Damn it, Lloyd. Object."

Jane waved her hand behind her chair in an attempt to quiet him. Even if what the man said was speculation, she had to hear it. She wanted to know what had happened that day.

"They'd told us near-four times that the next train was passing right through. We were to stay away from the tracks, but they were close." Mr. Darius shrugged. "I looked away when I heard the train. When I turned back, it was happening."

"What was happening, Mr. Darius?" Mr. Quinn moved closer. "What did you see?"

"He was falling, and there she was. Her arm still out from pushing him." Now Mr. Darius avoided her gaze. "Screamed like the devil, she did. We all thought she'd done lost her mind."

Maybe she had. Jane closed her eyes and lowered her head. If only she could remember. Defend herself in some way. Quinn's continuing line of questioning sounded far away, distant.

She tried to comprehend the full extent of what was happening. How she'd let this happen. What a complete and utter fool she'd been. Now it was too late for any good to come. Even for the brothers Mike had sworn could help to do anything to assist.

"It's a mustang court," Michael muttered in her ear when the judge called for an hour's recess so he might enjoy a whore before Lloyd made some attempt at argument. "We need to do something. Now."

"What? What can we do now? I've made a mistake, all right?" Jane grasped his hand and held it close. Fear and confusion welled into a jumbled mass of nerves.

She shook so hard Michael drew her close. "Clarabelle."

"I should not have waved my right to a jury. I was trying to spare these men any pain. I'd hoped the system would not be so swayed before it arrived. I was a fool, though I thought I was being smart and kind and now I'm scared."

"I know." Michael kissed her forehead and held her in a strong hug. "It'll be over before any other lawyer can get here. The judge is in Jack's pocket. The marshal might be too."

"I don't think the marshal is. He simply does not like or trust me. But yes, I have little doubt you're right about the judge." Jane straightened when Kat and Lillian walked up. Somehow, she managed to put forth an attempt at a smile, though she couldn't attest to its strength. "Please don't offer whatever it is you're about to offer, Lillian. I don't think anything can help now."

"Had I known your judge would be Benjamin Wallace I would have called on Mr. Daugherty to get you moved to Denver, where you were more likely to receive a fair and just trial." Lillian's brows turned down. "But I'm afraid you're quite right."

"Don't say that. Please, mother. There must be something we can do." Kat chewed on her lip, wringing her hands. "It can't be as simple as that."

"Benjamin Wallace is the worst judge in the territory. Easily bribed and he loves a good hanging. Also, once he's assigned to a case that's sure to add to his notoriety, it's almost impossible to get him off of it." Lillian sighed. "Not even Mr. Greenburg was able to get the judge's name for me until he stepped off the train. If it eases your mind at all, Jane, a trial with a jury wouldn't have mattered. Wallace gets his way."

"I wish David would hurry over here to take me away. I cannot watch Jackson gloat any longer. I did this." Jane stayed close to Michael.

"Jane." Michael sighed and held her close. "No, you didn't do this. You didn't do anything wrong."

"I certainly didn't help matters with my behavior toward Jackson when I first arrived, or in recent weeks. It's irrelevant now. We all knew this was a very strong likelihood." Jane tilted her head to meet Michael's gaze. "Go now. I do not want you causing trouble when the verdict comes. Go home. Tell them the truth about Clara. Tell them I am sorry."

"No, Clarabelle." Michael squeezed her shoulders. His forehead pressed to hers with desperate intensity. His breath seemed to stop before it re-emerged in heaving gasps. "I can't."

"Say goodbye, Michael. Say goodbye to Clara, to me. Go to your family. I am so sorry I was such a miserable sister to you." She wrapped her arms around his neck and held on tight. "Don't put yourself through this torture any longer."

"Jane," he buried his face in her shoulder and held on tight, "I…"

"I know." She took a deep, bracing breath. "And when you come back to Dominion Falls, ask Daisy to start courting. The lovesick routine is rather pitiful."

He guffawed into her shoulder and pulled away. "You're rotten."

"Always."

"I love you, Clarabelle."

"Clara loved you too. And so do I."

Letters are among the most significant memorial a person can leave behind them.
—Johann Wolfgang von Goethe

Cole's head lolled to the side. He jerked awake with a start. Sleep clung to him like a heavy blanket. He rubbed his eyes to clear the exhaustion away before he looked out the window across the snow. The train was moving fast, already on its way back to Colorado. It wouldn't be fast enough. Something told him nothing would be fast enough to get him home.

Before he'd ever got to Yankton, dread had settled into the pit of his stomach like a boulder. The anxiety had prompted him to send the telegram early. He had to let her know how long the storm had delayed him getting over the mountains.

There'd been no response as expected, though he'd partly expected a scolding. Something. From someone.

Jane had forced them to keep quiet, he was sure. He'd likely get a lecture like he'd never heard once he returned home for sending that telegraph.

He hoped, prayed, he'd get that scolding.

His heart twisted in a knot as he considered the alternative.

No. It couldn't be true. She'd be there. If anything had happened, she'd not have the sway to keep others from contacting him. Certainly Graham wouldn't listen to her, he didn't like her much.

Plus, Cole had made the man swear as part of his repentance to keep an eye on Jane. Protect her. Get her the hell out of town if anything happened.

He'd heard nothing. That meant she had to be safe. It had to mean she was safe.

He tubbed his hands over his face to try to rub away the panic racing through him. The trip had been nothing at all like he'd expected.

Upon reaching Yankton, food and lodging had sounded like the best thing. Well, besides getting home. He'd gotten neither. There was no rest for him. The urge to return home was too strong, and he was beyond thrilled the luck was on his side.

A miscommunication had gotten him answers fast. They had no idea who C. Hodgkins really was. By asking for him in the crowded depot, all that had been heard was the name as he'd yelled it. They'd thought he was Hodgkins.

Cole wasn't dumb enough to correct them. He made quick use of Jane's code to attain the large bag that now sat in his lap. After that he'd bought a private sleeper room on the first train back to Colorado.

He hadn't been in Yankton half an hour.

Now he was going home. All he could think about was getting off the train, getting home to Jane, finding her alive and well. A vast expanse of time stood before him before that point. Time to worry and wonder what was happening back home.

Time to read.

The thought sparked his mind back to life and he straightened. The bag in his lap was heavy, filled up to his chest with letters. It wasn't like he'd needed to keep the thing in his lap—the sleeper was private, after all. Something had made him keep it there, safe.

Maybe it was the faint hint of her jasmine perfume that floated out of the open sack. There were countless letters. It would take days to go through them. Days that he had. His trip would be long.

He reached into the bag and pulled out a letter. Her flowing script was clear, the postmark from almost a year ago. A few more weeks and none of these letters would have been there. A few more weeks and they would have been too late.

The telegraph operator said that he'd been just in time. That as per the original agreement, he'd been prepared to forward the letters on after a year of silence. Where they'd be forwarded, Cole didn't know. It no longer mattered, he'd gotten there in time.

A. Lee nee Poe

St. Louis, Missouri

Missouri. She'd been in Missouri. He turned the letter over in his hands, running his fingers along the seal. C. Hodgkins no longer mattered. These letters were from her. Maybe they'd have the truth.

He ripped open the seal without any further hesitation.

My dearest Michael,

Michael? The letters were meant for Mike? Why the subterfuge? Who was C. Hodgkins anyway? And if these letters were meant for Mike, why wouldn't he know who C. Hodgkins was?

Wickedness is in the midst thereof; deceit and guile depart not from her streets. Psalms 55:11

This will be my final letter. I've taken so many risks, I only hope it gets to you. One year from the date of this letter, you'll finally know the truth. I hope it will help to ease your mind, as writing them has helped keep me sane.

Or, at least as sane as I could be in these miserable circumstances wrought of my own design, my own naivete.

I can no longer hide from you, or the world, the things I have done. Having learned the truth, and knowing this last job for what it is, the truth will be revealed. I only hope that by the time you receive this letter, you'll see that I've accepted my comeuppance and faced my fate with courage.

It is not an end I ever wished for—but I cannot, and will not, try to hide from my punishment. It is just. I hope it causes you far less pain than the past seven years of my silence.

The end is near. My luck has run out, and it is my fervent hope that you receive these letters before he finds them. It took me years to learn enough to end this charade. It is a risk, a great one. I may see my end before I'm able to face justice, but the time has come. I will no longer let him control me. To help me become something other than who I was.

I wonder if I truly remember who I was. Clara seems so far away, so long ago.

I will be strong, dear one. For Jesse. I will see that he is returned to his pa. Where he belongs. Where he should have been from the start. Where he would be today if I had not been so blind. Such a fool.

I will right the wrongs I've made somehow. I will stop HIS web of lies. I will suffer for my own mistakes—but if it ends HIS lies, it will have all been worth it.

Tomorrow we leave for Manitou. That is where I will end this. He has become far more vigilant. He suspects, I am certain. It no longer matters. I will see this end. I will make sure of it. Now that I know the whole truth, I can't possibly continue.
God give me strength.

Cole didn't move a muscle. The letter quivered with each bump of the train.

The letter sounded so much like Jane, like her words before he'd left for Yankton. Reminding him that memory or not, she'd once been Clara. That if the stranger was right, she was a criminal.

It was strange seeing Jane's words so closely mirrored in a woman he didn't know. Never knew. Yet knew so well.

There were still so many unanswered questions. How had she sent these letters? What exactly had she done? Who was the man?

There were too many questions, and far too many letters to go through. He'd started at the end, the letter on top. Postmarked a year ago. He had to go deeper, find the truth. If it took the whole trip back.

His fingers wrapped around the rough burlap, gripped the edges of the seam. In one swift movement, he turned the contents onto the floor. Letters scattered across the worn carpet, slipping down the pile of aged paper and ink.

He sank to his knees, rifling through them. Over the next several hours he put them in order, as best he could. Some were in stacks of letters on the same day, others suffered the distance of months, one break almost a full year.

The first letter after that time difference pulled his attention, what had made her wait so long? Had she been ready to leave sooner? He slipped the envelope through his fingers.

A tingle in his leg reminded him how long he'd been scrunched into the tiny space. With a grunt, he extended one long limb out, rubbing the thigh to erase the tingling of tiredness. He was far from finished. Nothing would move him from this spot. Not even the aches of his immobility.

Since he already held the letter in his hand, he ripped it open to see if it held the answers to his questions. The postmark was in Massachusetts this time.

> *Michael,*
>
> *It's been so long since I've been able to write. HE has been extremely suspicious for quite a long time. At first I continued to write, but had to burn many letters before they could be sent.*
>
> *Then I had to give up. Give him no reason for suspicion for a while.*
>
> *Just in time, he has left me alone again. The thought of escaping I told you about in my last letter has become impossible.*
>
> *I must learn the truth first. Find out what happened years ago. If the child lived or died.*
>
> *Was he David's?*
>
> *This last turnabout was high society, Michael. The kind of society we never saw. Above even Ma's family. I can't believe that*

we managed to fool them, but then again, I completely believe it. Like HE has always said, they are so blinded by their own status that they miss the little details.

I'd be lying if I said that on days like this I didn't find it intoxicating. To be someone so…so very much not Clara.

To wear a mask that none can see through. To pretend I'm not the awful creature I've become.

But at night.

At night the mask falls away. There is no hiding in the dark. The ghosts of my past creep up and claw at me, leaving me bleeding and broken. I want to get away, but I fear that it's too late for me now.

How could I get away from HIM? HE knows me too well. HE formed me into this thing that I am. This fraud. This horrid creature. This thing that I hardly recognize.

There are days that I miss Clara's life so much it aches deeper than I ever knew a person could hurt.

My soul gets wrenched in two. Bursting. Leaving pieces of my shattered heart scattered behind me like a trail. But unlike Hänsel and Gretel, it will not lead me back home.

My home is gone. There is no home to return to. For I am no longer Clara. I haven't been for so long. I hardly remember her.

Would you recognize me today, Michael? Would you still love her today? Would you still love me?

King Solomon said that your own soul is nourished when you are kind; it is destroyed when you are cruel. I was not intentionally cruel, but I wonder just how much of my soul is left. How much of Clara still exists, or is she gone forever?

There are days that I remember it all. The precious children, the ones I taught for four years out in Utah. Their faces are etched into my mind; their laughter lingers in my ears, seared into what is left of my soul.

And David. My love. He could never love me again—not as I am. He loved Clara—strong, independent, fiercely loyal Clara. How did I forget what I was? How did I fall so far from what he could love?

I was so weak.

I gave in so easily. Did you think I could?

HE did. HE knew. Somehow, HE knew.

HE is so good at deception. HIS web of lies is so tangled I wonder if HE even knows what the truth is any longer. I must find a way to escape. I must free myself of this life, even if that means I will die for the crimes I helped him commit. Even if I must commit a few myself to find freedom.

First I must find the truth. About what HE did to me when the child was born. What HE did with the child.

I must learn the truth about the depths of darkness in my own soul. For I must have suck darkness to be here now. Poe is my one companion. His words speak to me as they never have before. Perhaps it is because it is only in the dark that I can see the truth; that I can remember.

And the raven never flitting, still is sitting, still is sitting,

On the pallid bust of Pallas just above my chamber door;

And his eyes have all the seeming of a demon's that is dreaming,

Cole replaced the letter fast, ignoring the shudder that ran down his back. Before she'd ever lost her memory, Jane had separated herself from her past. Not very well though. She still clung to it. She hated it, and clung to it.

How had she managed to do this? She said she'd had to burn many letters to avoid getting caught. But there were still so many.

The first letter that had been sent was aged by seven years in a depot. Time, dust, and grease almost obscured the date on it. The return address. Jane's flowing script was jagged and uneven, rushed.

The letter inside was the same. Short. To the point. Sloppy. So unlike Jane.

Michael,

This is my test. If he finds this before you see it, I am dead. I have to try. So much has happened. So much you need to understand. I need to understand.

What have I done?

HE leaves me alone now. For short spurts. I have money now, and for enough money, you can accomplish most anything. I will try to send you letters, Michael. I will make arrangements for you to receive them if the worst happens.

I pray I can make you understand.

I pray that I can understand.

I am safe. That is all I can tell you now.

I promise answers.

Once I find them.

For now I am safe. I am happy...somewhat. HE treats me well. HE teaches me what I need to know. But HE also wishes me for himself. HE will not share. Some days I almost understand why.

I love you, dear one. I'm so sorry for hurting you. For hurting David.

Forgive me

I do desire we be better strangers.
-William Shakespeare

"Constance? Please tell me it's you." The strange woman's voice was soft. A southern lilt carried the words in a delicate cadence to Jane's ears.

She didn't move. Lying on the cot, her hands lay folded on her un-corseted stomach. The wool of the simple gray dress scratched her wrists. No, she couldn't answer. She couldn't face this person.

Jane's eyes closed against the present. It was too much. She knew who this stranger must be, and it wouldn't do her any good to answer. She'd seen her at the trial. A quiet woman, delicate. Her features lined from years of worry. Of fear. Of disappointment. This would be one more disappointment for her.

Mike had been right. The trial was little more than a mustang court. Already, she'd been found guilty after two very spotty days in the mockery of a courtroom. Judge Wallace was more interested in drinking and whoring than the trial.

After very little cajoling Jane had agreed to let Lillian make whatever attempts she could to stop the trial. Unfortunately, it had been to no avail. Her words had proven true, and with Wallace as the judge, her case wasn't going anywhere. Now she waited on his next round of whoring to end so he could sentence her.

It was the words of the witness that still haunted her. His tale of how she'd killed Mr. Querney and the horror of her behavior after.

Jane was sure the man was telling the truth, but not that he remembered correctly. He'd admitted it looked like she'd stumbled, that he'd seen her outstretched arm as the man fell.

Then she'd screamed. Screamed for so long the doctor had drugged her. That's all he knew. That's all he'd seen.

The murdered man had been in Jane's nightmares. The mangled body. The unseeing eyes.

"Constance, please."

She couldn't bear it. First Clara, now Constance. Why didn't anything make sense? She was tired. Tired of trying to make sense of it. It was time to accept it. Whether or not she'd killed the man no longer mattered.

Clara was a criminal.

"Constance." The woman's voice broke.

Jane drew her eyes open. It would do no good to ignore her, strong as the desire may be. "Mrs. Pinot, I'm not Constance."

"But I saw you. Every week in that asylum." A ring clinked against the bars. "Please. Let me see you."

The shackles were gone, but Jane felt the full weight of them lingering on her wrists. Tugging like a thousand sins until her heart sat in her feet. She pushed against the imagined weight to sit. The woman she'd been had robbed this woman of the truth. The least she could do was face her.

"Come closer. Allow me this." The gray hair that had been so neatly contained in the saloon now looked rough.

Wisps of silver caught the light as they sprung from their confines. Every step Jane took closer showed each worry line of the woman's face in vivid relief.

Jane approached, getting right up close to the bars. "I'm sorry, Mrs. Pinot."

"You look so much like her. It's possible that you are."

"Do I really? Or do you just really wish I did?"

"We searched for so long."

"When did she go missing, Mrs. Pinot?" There was no denying the torture in the woman's eyes. Jane could tell she'd been a beautiful woman before the loss of her child. Now she was tired. Age and worry claimed her.

"Ten years ago. In the middle of the war. We thought we were safe, with the general in the position he was." The woman's head sank to the bars. "I wanted you to be her. I needed you to be."

"I'm sorry to have caused you this grief. It was never my wish to cause anyone such pain. I wish I had answers for you. I remember nothing."

"You were in Manitou."

"I don't know. It seems as though I was."

"You were the one that wired Jacob."

"I don't remember." Jane gripped the bars, willing her legs to hold. "I remember just one moment with him. I think I told him everything. I just don't know what it was I told him. I don't remember his death."

"But it was you."

"Yes. I think it was."

"Why did you do this? Make us think our Constance had come back to us? I held your hand in the asylum. I made sure you were cared for."

"I have no answers for you."

"That is not good enough." Her pitch grew shrill, desperate bony fingers gripped Jane's. "Do you know what happened to her? To her child?"

"No." Jane tried to pry her hand free. "I'm sorry. I'm so sorry. Please."

"You must know. You must. You pretended to be her. You let me believe you were her."

Jane stumbled back when she got her hand free. "I might have known once, but I don't now. I wish I could remember for you. For your husband. For my own selfish reasons. I just can't."

"You are a very cruel woman. To rip the last bit of hope from an old woman like this. How can you bear it?" Her kerchief was pressed to her face, muffling the words, doing nothing to stop the streaks of sorrow.

"I can't." Jane turned away. Her own tears clung tight to her eyes, refusing to fall. It wasn't time for them to fall yet. They were tears of her own making, ones that she didn't deserve to shed. Not this time. "That is why I will accept my punishment without a fight. It is deserved."

"Jane," Katherine's singsong call broke through the cold cruel stillness. The aching pain of Mrs. Pinot stilled with a sniffle. Katherine's gasp broke the silence. "Oh no. What are you doing here? Michael."

"It's all right, Kat." Jane didn't dare turn around. Her façade would crumble. She couldn't now. "Mrs. Pinot just had to see for herself that I am not Constance. I'm certain she will leave now."

"Katherine? What is it? Oh." Michael was far from panicked. He sounded angry. If he'd left when she tried to send him away, he wouldn't have to deal with this. "What are you doing? You weren't granted permission. I'm sorry, Mrs. Pinot, you must leave. My sister is not supposed to speak to you."

"It is she that spoke to me." A slight quiver crept into her voice, and Jane cleared her throat. Weakness was not allowed. A knothole on the wall took the brunt of her concentration, forcing her into calm. "And she is done. No harm done."

The murmur of voices, a quiet shuffling. Jane still didn't turn around. The door to the jailhouse closed, and the thud of a basket on the desk sounded. The smell of pot roast, cornbread, and beans assaulted her nostrils. Cora had cooked a feast. A last supper perhaps?

"Jane?"

The knothole still needed to be studied. Her hands were shaking too much. She would be strong. It was a necessity. "I'm fine."

"Then why won't you look at me? What did she say, Jane?" Katherine's footsteps paced outside the cell. "What did you say to her?"

"What I've said to everyone. That I don't remember. I don't remember. I don't remember." Clouds. Storm clouds so thick the sun was blotted out. That was what it felt like. Her memories were the sun. There was a time when life was the sun. Now that was gone. Her only hope was a gust of wind to blow away the clouds.

"I know you don't, Jane." Katherine's pacing stopped. "Damn it, will you look at me? I need to see that you're all right."

She could be calm now. It was entirely possible to keep it together when she saw Katherine's face. Slow as molasses, she turned, forcing her lips into a tremulous smile. It would hold. It had to—oh, damn. It wasn't holding.

"Oh, Jane."

"Jane. Geez, Clarabelle. I'm so sorry. I didn't mean to be gone that long. Cora roped me in—Clarabelle." With a clank of metal, the door flew open and Michael had wrapped her up close to him.

"Don't. Please don't. Please." Too late, the sob escaped. She gripped his vest and buried her face in the soft suede to cover her tears. The salty rivers would leave stains. She needed to stop.

"I should have stayed." Michael ran his hand along her hair. "I never thought she'd come in here. I only meant to be gone a few—"

"Shut up." Muffled against his chest, she didn't have the strength to put any force behind her words. It didn't matter. He listened for once.

"You need to get some food in you, is all." Katherine's pain cracked her voice, but she made herself do the busy work of preparing a plate. "Then you'll feel much better."

They all knew it was a lie. Feeling better seemed a long way off. It was more of the same lie. The denial of what was coming. They would succumb to it. It was so much easier than the truth.

All along she said she'd be ready to face her punishment if it came, but she was wrong. She no longer wanted to face her punishment. She wanted to live.

But she was going to die.

The judge had yet to make his decision; the trial wasn't over, but she knew it. As sure as she had always known Jesse was hers.

Accepting it was one thing.

Living it was an entirely different matter.

She wasn't strong enough. How could she be strong enough?

Facing death should be far easier than a life of this guilt. This interminable guilt for the suffering Clara had caused.

Yes. Death was easier.

To die for faction is a common evil,
but to be hanged for nonsense is the devil.
–John Dryden

"Are you ready for sentencing, my dear?" Judge Wallace set down his whiskey glass. He leaned his elbows on the table tapping his fingertips together. A sly grin curved his features. The man was enjoying every second of this moment.

A wave of disgust curled down her spine, but Jane did her best to force her features to remain impassive. She gave the judge a simple nod. "Yes, sir."

"I must say, I am glad you helped this all run so smoothly. In my years of experience, juries just muck things up and I like them simple." He slurped his whiskey. After a moment he sat back. "All right, then. Clara Young, you have been found guilty on all counts of capital murder and fraud."

Jane twisted her fingers in her skirts to keep panic at bay. To be sentenced in the place she'd called home and spent so many hours of joy and pleasure seemed an extra cruel twist of the knife to her already painful situation.

The entire crowd in the saloon and the snow-filled streets beyond the door remained silent. It was like the world was holding its breath in anticipation of the ruling.

Judge Wallace must have enjoyed the show, for he remained silent. He curled a lock of Iris' hair around his finger. "Both severe crimes. They deserve just punishment. Even more so as you have avoided your fate so many years with lies and subterfuge."

Jane stared at a point beyond his head. If she looked at anyone, even the judge, she might lose her tight grip on her emotions. Everything hurt from the lock of tension she kept on every quiver of fear, horror, and grief.

"You are sentenced to be hanged." Wallace spoke louder when a collective gasp filled the room. "At ten in the morning on Saturday you will face the gallows."

Jane jumped when he slammed his gavel into the table. Ice ran through her veins and she clenched her skirts tighter to be sure her hands still worked. Somehow she'd held onto the faintest sliver of hope until that moment.

The moment the words were said aloud and her fate was sealed.

It would all be over soon. Way too soon.

Saturday was only two days away. There was no chance Cole could make it home in time. She wasn't sure whether that would be a blessing or a curse. Maybe it would be better if he didn't have to witness it.

Her death.

Oh, heaven help me. Her knees gave out, yet she hadn't even realized she was standing, much less walking.

"Come along, Clara." David's strong and sure hand guided her through the clamoring crowd. Along the way he kept everyone at bay, even Kat.

Considering her state of mind-numbing panic, she was infinitely grateful for his thoughtfulness. She might have thanked him if her mouth would work and form the words she'd always been so fond of. She was quite certain her body only moved because he propelled it down the street.

He guided her into the jail where he shut the door against the crowd and their discussions, their debates, the calls of support, and a handful of sobs. He gripped her arms when she swayed. "Easy. Sit down. That's it. Here. Drink some water."

Jane stared at the cup he pressed her hands around. "I am going to die."

"Yes."

"Soon."

"Yes."

"Where's Michael? Has he gone? Please tell me he left. He shouldn't see this. He shouldn't have to see—"

"He's gone." David pulled a chair into the cell and sat across from her. "Drink."

She might have protested, but he pushed the cup to her lips, and the cool water soothed her parched lips. A shudder coursed up her previously numb legs, into her spine until her teeth chattered. All along she'd known, worried, feared, and been certain it would happen. And yet, "I didn't think it would all happen so fast. I thought I'd have time."

"I know."

"I need more time. Oh, David. What of Jesse?"

"He'll know about you." He set aside her cup and took her hands in his. After a moment he rubbed them. The simple action sent warmth into her near-frozen soul. "I'm going to make sure Jesse knows all about his ma. Both parts of his ma."

"I'm so sorry. I was so stubborn."

"You wouldn't be you if you weren't."

"I hope Cole found something. You deserve answers. Answers I could never give you." She closed her eyes and took a ragged breath. "That's the last shred of hope I'm clinging to. That you, and Michael, and Jesse all get the answers you deserve. You didn't deserve this."

"Neither did you. Neither did Clara. I'm sorry."

"You have nothing to be sorry for."

"I do. I'm sorry I didn't believe you." He cupped her cheek. "I thought you were trying to spare my feelings because you were with Cole. Maybe you remembered, and cared too much to hurt me that way."

"What changed your mind?"

"This, right now. You'd save your life if you could. If you remembered anything, maybe you could."

"I hope you find happiness, David. If Lee makes you happy, don't let her go. She's a good woman, and you deserve the best. You're too good for the likes of me, you always were."

"Cole is just rotten enough."

She laughed and nodded. "I think he's a better man than you give him credit for, but yes. He's just rotten enough."

"I said goodbye to Clara long ago. Not sure how I'm going to say goodbye to Jane."

"Don't. Jane wasn't real." She smiled, but the trembling she'd thought contained to her clenched hands reached her lips. "I wasn't real."

"Yes you were. You are. And we're going to miss you so very much."

Rather than respond, she glanced away. She picked up the water and took another sip. Now that the shock had faded an eerie calm washed over her. "Michael went back to Buffalo, then?"

"That's where he was heading. He said he would tell them everything. I'm to send a telegram ahead of him so he'll know when he arrives."

"I have told Cole what to do with my effects."

"And he listened?"

"It wasn't an easy conversation," she admitted.

Many times over she'd tried until she'd forced her hand in the days before he left. In painstaking detail she'd listed everything. She'd made him listen, though he fought her every step of the way.

She took a deep breath and forced herself to keep talking. The shock remained at bay when she focused elsewhere. "The books will go to the library. I have asked that what money I have go to Jesse. It is far from a fortune, but it should keep him well cared for so you don't have to worry for a few years."

"You didn't have to do that."

"I know, but whatever happened, it's my fault he was lost for so long. I have given him so little, I didn't even give him his ma. It's the least I can do." She set her hand on his arm. "There's one more thing."

"Why do I think I'm not going to like it?"

"My homestead."

"No."

"It is still half in Michael's name, but he has the Silver Saddle and his own land. You and Jesse don't need to stay in Cora's crowded store. It's silly."

"I don't know." He shook his head. "It doesn't seem right."

"Please. It has room for you both and room to grow should you chose it." She bit down hard on her tongue, doing her best to keep her tears at bay. "And please try to give Cole some leeway when he gets back. He's not going to handle this well."

"There's only so much I can do."

"I know." There was still so much that needed to be said, that she needed to do. Yet, she'd done everything to prepare for this.

"What can I do?"

"There's nothing left to do. You can't take away the pain, much as I know you'd like to. All you can do now is your job."

"You won't be alone."

"I know."

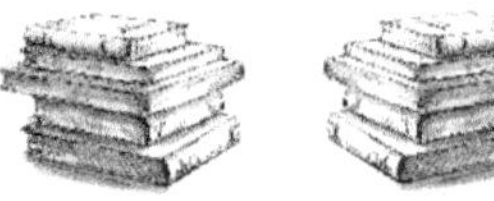

The realization that one is to be hanged in the morning concentrates the mind wonderfully.
-Samuel Johnson

"Yes. I saw it happen when I was in medical school." Daisy's testimony rang through Jane's head. *"The drugs have different effects on different patients. Some it only calms, others…"*

Jane had avoided looking at her. She'd done her best to block out the testimony. The knowledge that her time in that horrid asylum could be the cause of her amnesia was painful. Or perhaps the injuries she'd suffered after her escape might have done so. Or both. All of Daisy's knowledge and they still didn't know any more than they had.

"He was falling, and there she was. Her arm still out from pushing him." Mr. Darius had avoided her gaze after that. *"Screamed like the devil, she did. We all thought she'd done lost her mind."*

Maybe she had.

It wasn't out of the realm of possibility.

"I'm sure this is another of your deceptions." Marshal Lewis had been cold. Unforgiving. Yet, she'd almost say there was softness there. Pity, maybe. Maybe he did believe the amnesia. But he still saw her as a criminal. *"I just can't figure what it is you want out of this town."*

Life. Freedom. Love.

The train whistle blew off in the distance. Long and low.

"Think this'll be the one, Clara." David gripped the bars. "There's still time."

"For what?"

"For Cole to get back."

"It might be better if he doesn't."

"Clara, you don't mean that."

"I do." Jane rose to her feet, shivering. "That way he won't have to see it happen. That way by the time he gets home, it will be over and done. If he's here, he could cause trouble. And…"

His warm hand enveloped hers. "It'll be easier for you."

"So much."

"You didn't give me a chance, Clara." David's rough hand smoothed along her cheek. His thumb brushed the apple. "You've got to do it right this time."

"You mean actually die? Instead of just disappearing?"

"That isn't what I mean, and you know it."

"Kat has all Cole needs. In more ways than one." Jane sighed as she sank onto her cot again. Katherine had agreed to reveal the truth when her daughter arrived. To ease her soul as much as it would ease Cole's. She'd also made Katherine and Michael promise to get Cole out, not let him close up. "I won't be leaving him with nothing."

"I'm not supposed to understand that, am I?"

"Not in the least."

"Clara."

"Yes, David?"

"What about Major Webb?" David sat on the chair just outside the cell door. "What about his offer to try to help? To get your sentence lightened."

"It was very generous. Very tempting. Not right." She stared at her hands. Her books were gone. She'd made them take them away with the sentencing. There was nothing left of Jane. It had to be Clara. Blank, unethical, criminal Clara. If she faced this as Jane, she wouldn't make it to the gallows.

"But maybe…"

"No more maybes. It's over, David. I don't want Al to put his neck on the line for me. I must face this."

"It's death, Clara."

"Considering Clara is already dead, it is nothing."

"You're still here." David's head thumped against the bars. His hat spun in his hands, anxious. "That means you aren't dead."

"Clara is. I'm a construct of a few months. Nothing to miss." She gasped. "Oh God. That's what she said. About your marriage. Not enough time to miss. Easily forgotten. Oh God."

"Clara." The train whistle sounded louder, interrupting his reply. "Look at me."

The bars were all she could see anymore. The blank wood walls. Looking at David was far too painful. He'd been hurt so much by Clara, and her as Jane. Why was he still here? "Why are you still here, David? How can you look at me? Try to comfort me? You didn't deserve any pain, but I've caused you so much."

"I've loved you from the moment I saw you, Clara. Yeah, you hurt me. That's just pain. There's more than that. You gave me my son." His hand wrapped around hers, and his hazel eyes came into focus. "I forgave you long ago. Just having you in my life is good enough for me."

"You have such low standards for life if you believe that."

"You don't give yourself enough credit. Besides, what man wouldn't fall for a woman as welcoming as you were?"

"Does that mean you fall in love with every whore?"

"No whore here, Clara. You didn't take money; you took my heart."

"Oh, you're going to make me sick." Jane's nose wrinkled, and unbelievably, a laugh burst out. "You are such an incurable romantic."

"It got you to laugh, didn't it?"

"I really hope that's why you said that. If you really talked like that, I'd have to have Cole take you out and show you what a real man is like. Or just put you down so I can be out of my misery. I can't take such overt sweetness. It sits poorly on the palate."

"There's the spirit we've all come to enjoy." David smiled. "Hold on to that."

"Why?"

"What in hell is this about?" Cole burst into the jail, throwing off his coat before he grabbed the bars. His face pressed to the bars, desperate. "I thought I told you to still be here when I got back, Jane."

"David," Jane's voice cracked, and she squeezed his hand, "could you?"

"I'll be outside if you need me." David stood and adjusted the chair closer for Cole. "I'm sorry, Cole. She wouldn't let us send a telegram."

"She was in jail. What in blazes was stopping you?" Cole's eyes flashed, and he shoved the chair across the room. "Let me in. I gotta see her."

"Not now." David straightened, his hand on his holster. "Middle of the day, marshal still pops in now and again. Later."

"David."

"Cole," Jane's resolve snapped, "listen to him. The marshal doesn't even trust the hanging to be done because—"

"Hanging?" Cole turned back to her. "It's done already? I been gone for a week."

"Nine days. And, yes, I'm to be hanged in the morning. Fraud. Theft. Murder."

"No."

"Yes." Jane didn't move an inch. Cole's fierce gaze held her tight. "David, please."

"I'll be right outside." David sighed and left the building, closing the door behind him.

"How did this happen? What the hell did you do?"

"I didn't do anything." Jane stayed as far from the bars as the cell allowed her to be. If she got too close, she'd give in to her emotions. She'd worked too hard over the past day to push them aside. To forget Jane. To become Clara. "I think he did it. Someone alerted the marshal, the judge, the Pinots. It wasn't me. I swear it."

"Jane, you can't be hanged. I ain't gonna let it happen."

"Just how do you propose to stop it?" Wool rubbed against her hands as she twisted them in the folds of her skirt. Every muscle started to shake. Why couldn't he have stayed gone? It was so much easier to not feel when he wasn't there. "It's too late. It's over."

"No." The loud clang of metal rang through her head, filling her ears, blinding her with tears. The silence that came after was more deafening. He didn't say anything for a long time. "Did you fight?"

"With what?"

"Your words. You're so damn good with them."

"Words are nothing without knowledge. Knowledge is something I had nothing of. Not regarding Clara."

"You didn't want this. Clara didn't want this. She wanted away from him."

"What?"

"She stayed until she found out about the kid—and then to try to save him. Wanted to put the bastard behind bars. Reveal everything."

"Was she a criminal? Did she do these things?"

"She had no choice." His hands wrung the bars. "Jane. You gotta come here."

"I can't." She clung to the wall, unable to move. It still wasn't possible to get closer. It was all supposed to be blank. Unfeeling. Much easier. "How do you know?"

"Letters."

"Letters?"

"That's what was in Yankton. Letters. Addressed to C. Hodgkins, but you wrote them to Mike. Told all about what you did, what you didn't do. The times he put you in the hospital for disobeying. Stopped a year ago."

"When Mr. Querney died. When I went into the asylum. When Clara died."

Muffled voices sounded from outside, and the door opened. Jane swallowed against the lump of emotions beating their way out. When the mayor, Archie Hill walked toward the door with the key, she shook her head. "Don't. I can't."

"David said to tell you that you have to." Archie turned the key. "David's taking Marshal Lewis to supper. You've got an hour."

"Archie, don't. Please don't open the door." Her knees buckled. No. She couldn't bear it. If he got near, that spark of life would revive. It needed to be squelched. It hurt so much more to feel it. "Don't let him in."

"You already let him in. Not going to stop him now." Archie pulled open the door. "One hour. I'll give you a five-minute warning. It's the best we can do. Make it count."

She curled in a ball, blocking him out. It couldn't happen.

One touch was all it took, and everything spilled over. A wail ripped from deep in her gut, and her arms went around his neck. Wrapped in the sanctuary of his arms, it had always been so safe there. Not even there was safe now.

"Jane. You didn't—"

"No. Don't tell me. I don't want to hear any more about Clara. Nothing more. It's done and over."

"I can't do this. I can't let it happen."

"I need you, Cole." She shifted in his grasp until she pressed close against him as close as possible without actually sitting in his lap. One hour was all she had left with him. To make him understand, to tell him everything, to feel again. Just one more time.

"There's gotta be something I can do."

"There is." She brushed her lips across his. "Promise me."

"I can't."

"Promise."

He picked her up, and then sat on the cot with her in his lap. "I'll try. Best I can do."

"Live, Cole. Don't close off again. You didn't do this. You did what was in your power to stop it. You gave me everything."

"I gave you nothing."

"You gave me everything." Her forehead pressed into his as she took ragged breaths in an attempt to hold back tears. "I had nothing…nothing real. You gave me memories. Good, bad, everything in between. Memories that are mine, not some stranger's. Enough memories for a lifetime."

He pushed her back, setting her beside him. Shoulders hunched, he stared at his boots. "Lot of good they're gonna do you now."

"It does more good than you think." She reached out and inched her fingers along his jawline. Resting her hand on his cheek, she turned his eyes toward hers. "Once you leave after this hour, I don't want you to come back to see me. I don't want you there tomorrow. Stay away from the gallows."

"No."

"This is going to be so difficult. I don't want to remember this. I want to remember the good. I want—"

He grabbed her hand and yanked her close. "You want memories, you get them all. Didn't you say that nothing is worth forgetting?"

"Promise to remember that."

"I promise."

"Don't say goodbye. It's too sad."

"Jane." He pulled her closer, until their foreheads pressed together again. In seconds, she was across his lap, his fingers digging into her thighs. He took a ragged breath. "It ain't fair. It ain't right."

"Please remember our time together. All of it."

"Couldn't ever forget."

"Please remember me."

"Always."

No greater grief than to remember days of gladness when sorrow is at hand.
—Friedrich von Schiller

Simple. No petticoats, no corset. One well-cut layer of fabric.

Plain. Rough black wool. No adornments, not even a visible button.

A dress of death. Her death.

Pale skin shone back at her in the mirror. Shaking hands pulled her tresses into a simple bun. No hat, no coat. The bitter, cold temperatures would mean little to her welfare. Illness couldn't claim you if you were already dead.

A tendril of steam rose from the cup of tea on the table. The scent was strange, exotic. For a brief moment it pulled her from her self-reflection. Not her usual orange tea, David had insisted she drink this.

He'd said it came from Black Moon, and perhaps it was her state of mind that made her not balk. Or maybe it was just his assurance that it would help ease her nerves. The way she'd been feeling all morning, it seemed like a good thing.

Dignity.

That was what she wanted to have when she made that walk. Not to be a blubbering mess of a woman.

Her hands wrapped around the warm cup and pulled it close. The heat soaked through her then, creeping up her arms. With a sigh, she took a sip, letting the warmth run through her to her belly. Ease the tremors of cold.

It could warm her body all it wanted, but it couldn't warm her soul.

Half an hour.

That was all she had left. Half an hour before she would make the walk to the edge of town to face her fate. The one that she'd said she was ready to accept. The one that she wanted to run from now.

She took another sip of the tea and smoothed her hands over her hair again. All that was left was to finish her tea and sit with Reverend Greene. There would be no other visitors.

Cole had ignored her request. He'd stayed more than the hour. He'd stayed the whole night, outside the bars, talking to David when she ignored him. Not once did he mention Clara or the letters again. He was just there.

At dawn David had made him leave to give her time to get ready and collect herself. To meet with the reverend. To re-gather her strength. Cole's presence had been both soothing and painful—reopening the gaping maw of her emotions, pouring salt and salve on them at the same time.

Calm evaded her.

Now it started to return. The tea almost gone, her body's trembling began to cease. A calm she didn't feel in the pit of her stomach coursed through her body.

At least the shaking had stopped.

"Jane."

"Please call me Clara now, Reverend. Clara is the criminal. Clara is the one facing her punishment." Jane turned from the mirror, picking up what was left of her tea. She forced a smile when David opened the cell doors for the reverend. "Thank you, David."

"A last visit with the clergy is part of the law, Clara. No thanks are needed." David wouldn't look at her. The weight of his task pulled his features into lines she hadn't noticed the day before.

Michael was gone, far off on a train bound for Buffalo to tell Clara's family of her ultimate fate. Something Clara hadn't been good enough to do.

Reverend Greene took her free hand and squeezed it before taking a seat. "It has been decided, Clara. There will be a service."

"No. There shouldn't be, not for a criminal. A simple prayer over the grave will be well suited." Tears stung her eyes, but failed to fall. Within moments, they were gone again, the tension in her shoulders leaving. She would have to remember to thank David for the tea, if her mind would function properly.

"Clara will not have a service. Her grave will be presided over just as you have asked." He opened his bible and turned the pages slowly. "Jane, however, is not a criminal. She is a good woman that has done much for this town."

"That isn't necessary."

"It is. Not for you. For your friends. Your family. This is difficult enough for them to bear. You will not deny them this."

"Thank you, Reverend." Jane took a ragged breath and finished the last of her tea before she gave into the tears again.

"Do not hesitate to ask, Jane." His sharp green eyes settled on her. A hint of a smile appeared, the sadness in it not lost on Jane. "You have never held your tongue before. This is not the time to start."

"I do not want to sound as though I don't have faith."

"You couldn't. I know you, Jane. You have faith. It is not surprising that it has been shaken. Just remember to walk by faith, not by sight."

"I was once Clara. I did all these things, though I do not remember." She was tired of repeating it, but it was so painfully true. "I have asked forgiveness—I have prayed until my knees are bruised, my hands cramped, my eyes dry. Will I be forgiven? Or am I damned?"

"You have asked forgiveness for sins you did not commit. Not this spirit. You share the same body as she did, but since you woke up, you've lived well and strong, even if some sins persist. The weaknesses displayed by Clara do not live in you."

"But they do." She gripped the edge of the cot. If she could, she would run now. Hide. Or would she? "The urge to do things she would have done is strong. To run, to hide, to pretend Jane and Clara never existed."

"Having the same weaknesses doesn't make you the same. It's how you deal with them that matters. You've learned from Clara's mistakes." Reverend Greene smiled. "And if it's forgiveness you sought, I'm certain it was granted."

"I'm scared."

"Psalms twenty-five, verse fifteen to the end."

"'Mine eyes are ever turned to the Lord; for he shall pluck my feet out of the net. Turn thee unto me, have mercy upon me; for I am desolate and afflicted'." Her mind slowed, and the racing thoughts stilled.

When his hand closed over hers, she continued the verse. "'The troubles of my heart are enlarged. Oh bring me out of my distresses. Look upon my affliction and my pain and forgive all my sins'." It was getting difficult to remember now, to think clearly.

"'Consider mine enemies, for they are many; and they hate me with a cruel hatred." He picked up when her voice trailed off. "Oh keep my soul and deliver me'."

"'Let me not be ashamed, for I put my trust in thee. Let integrity and uprightness preserve me, for I wait on thee'." Her head drooped to her chest. She gripped his hand tighter.

His free hand closed over hers. "'Be strong and of a good courage; be not afraid, neither be thou dismayed, for the Lord thy God is with thee whithersoever thou goest'."

Fingers now lax, Jane closed her eyes. Strong and of a good courage. She'd been forcing herself to be strong for so long now. Could she make it this last distance? Would there be peace after that?

"It's time." David's soft voice startled her.

"I think she fell asleep," Reverend Greene said quietly.

"Good. She didn't sleep all night. I think the tea helped." David's hand moved under her arm. "Clara, I need you to get up. Walk. I know it's tough. I've had that tea before, so I know what it does. It is difficult to move once it sinks in, but once you get there, you can let go."

"David, why?" Jane let him help her to her feet. Her mind poured sluggishly over what was happening. Still her mind wouldn't function properly. The tea. Something with the tea. "What is it? What did you do?"

"You've been suffering plenty. Didn't see no reason for you to suffer this last hour, or at the end." He squeezed her arm. "It's just some herbs. Helps relax you, puts you unconscious. You can fight it for five more minutes, Clara."

A cold wind whipped her back into consciousness. Her body jerked awake for a moment before relaxing again. "This isn't happening."

"It's all a dream," he concurred. Helping her cope. Sweet, but it didn't make it any more true. The gallows stood in sight. Just six short steps onto the platform. The noose was already in place. It would be a short drop.

Lack of oxygen wouldn't matter much if these herbs knocked her unconscious. If she thought she could form a coherent sentence, she'd thank him. Another cold blast of wind hit her, and she blinked. "Thank you. For trying."

"Hush now, Clara." David's hold on her arm remained tight. Holding her upright. Leading her right to those steps. Just a few more feet.

Frozen, she finally saw the crowd. Unlike they'd been at the hanging of the horse thieves the month before, they were somber. Still. Quiet.

"Clara, up the steps."

Oh, yes, walking. To her death. To the noose. In front of all of these people. Her friends. The lives she'd had touch her own. The only people she knew.

They were still silent. Kat clung to Norman, tears in her eyes. Daisy was close at hand, her expression unreadable. Al, his hat in his hands, appeared unwilling to look at her. Mr. Hamm had tears on his cheeks. So kind. Caring. Everyone was so quiet. Eerie silence.

Except for one group. Off to the side, a struggle disrupted the quiet.

Cole.

Held back by Graham, Archie, Bert, and Carl. Fighting against them all. He shouldn't have come.

"It's time for the mask." David's low voice cut under the increasing volume from Cole's struggle.

She inclined her head in a small nod, her eyes on Cole. When the mask lifted over her head, he stilled. One moment was all she had left to let him know what she'd failed to in the past months. One moment, and she took it.

Her mouth formed the words she'd been too afraid to say aloud. *I love you.* The burlap covered her eyes, but not the sound of Cole's shout or the increasing struggle, cursing of Graham, and then the subsequent silence.

The noose looped over her head. The burlap was rough, like sand on her skin.

How could she know that? Had she seen sand? Felt it between her toes? Questions, so many questions. She'd never know the answers.

Everything grew muddled again. She no longer felt the cold. Her hands were tied, but the rope failed to sting. David's heavy footsteps across the boards to the lever sounded like they were going through mud.

Her senses were failing one by one. Reverend Greene's voice had become unintelligible. Cole's shout now a whisper. This was what David had meant. Already she was slipping away.

Floating.

No, falling.

A flash of light.

Blackness.

Death--the last sleep?
No, it is the final awakening.
-Sir Walter Scott

It hadn't happened.

The whiskey helped convince him of that fact.

Jane wasn't dead. She couldn't be.

Clara Young Hanged

December the 2nd, 1871 at 10 a.m., Clara Young was hanged at the edge of town for crimes committed.

Marshal Lewis and Dr. Pearson confirmed death at 10:15 a.m.

It was a short notice. Unworthy of her.

Jane Doe, Deceased

Survived by many friends, those she considered family.

Jane's numerous contributions to Dominion Falls will not be forgotten. Not by the families she helped in the outer settlements. Not by those who enjoy our now-overflowing library. Not by the men she sobered up, or the women she brought them home to. Not by the merchants whose wares she bought when their patronage was low.

Not by him.

She was in every inch of his room. He hadn't dared step foot in it yet. Not that it did him much good. Sitting in the storeroom, he could still feel her there. See her face the first time he'd touched her. Feel the soft silk of her skin.

The newspaper caught fire fast in the flames of his match. He couldn't read her death notices anymore. It hadn't happened. It wasn't real.

Cole stumbled to his feet, kicking the bottles of whiskey aside. He'd go to his room because she'd be there. Waiting for him.

Not one soul dared approach him on his way to the stairs. Every pair of eyes watched him, driving the pain of remorse into him like sharp needles. "Get back to your booze."

The shuffling, low murmur of regret. The silence of her absence. The hollowness she left behind. She'd been helping him for mere weeks, and the saloon already felt empty without her. Emptier than it had without Graham.

His door stood as the last barrier to reality. He couldn't cross the threshold. If she wasn't in there, he didn't know what he'd do. She had to be in there.

Oranges and jasmine. This scent was hers. It overwhelmed him. She'd been the last one in his room. Their room.

The door clicked, locking him in with her ghost. She was everywhere. She'd been staying there just two weeks, and she was everywhere. Her clothes hung from nails, peeked out of a trunk. Toes of shoes poked out from under his bed.

The silver-handled brush on the dresser. The delicate carved comb.

The books.

Everywhere.

Under his bed, spilling out next to the shoes. One on the pillow. A stack of three on his desk. On the shelves between the items from his past she'd put on display. On a chair she'd put by the window in his absence.

Whitman on the table next to the bed, where it had always been. Still open to her favorite passage.

> *...The furious storm through me careering—I passionately trembling;*
>
> *The oath of inseparableness of two together—of the woman that loves me, and whom I love more than my life—that oath swearing...*

His hands shook. The book flew across the room, thumping to the ground and bouncing back open. "No. *It ain't right.*"

She was here. Everywhere. Suffocating him with her presence. How could he be so stupid? How could he have let her in? Knowing it could only end in pain.

He'd had no choice. She'd been inside him from the minute he'd picked her up. Weaving into his life silently, then not so silently. Damn her for leaving. Damn her.

She had to go. He couldn't keep her here. It was too much. It would be easier to manage without her.

Fabric shredded when he yanked it from the nail, flew up in his face when he crammed it in the trunk. The perfume bottle clinked, threatening to break.

It didn't matter.

Nothing mattered. Not anymore. Not without her.

He shoved everything deeper into the mass of clothes. The brush, the soaps, all of it.

He sat on the trunk to shove down the top as fabric dripped from the edges, out of the opening. Even when it was forced closed, fabric still spilled out. He stood and shoved it out the door before turning around.

Her books. He hadn't touched them. They were everywhere, and he moved fast. Papers fluttered, spines *thunked* together, until he had a pile to his chin.

He froze. No. Not the books. He couldn't let go of them. Of her.

Without any care, he shoved them onto his desk and stacked them in a messy pile.

No. That wasn't good enough. She deserved better.

One by one, he lined up books on the shelves. Between his things, on empty shelves. Neatly, carefully.

Whitman was the last book. The first book. Its place was by the bed. Where she'd always kept it. It went right back where he'd found it.

The books were her. She would never stop haunting him. He would not deny her.

He'd promised.

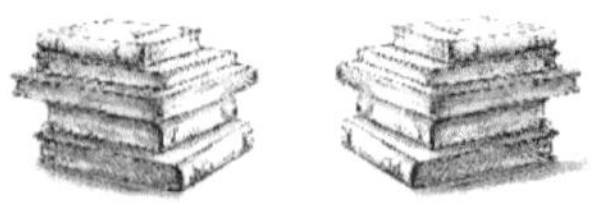

Black.

Cold.

Pain.

Pain so intense it radiated through every limb; ripped through her soul, into her heart, her head.

Was this Hell?

Her mouth opened, but no sound escaped. She couldn't scream, couldn't cry. Her arms folded across her chest.

Darkness pressed down around her.

Suffocating.

Claustrophobic.

She gasped for air, her hands flying out.

Wood. Right above her head. Around her sides. Everywhere.

A coffin.

No.

No. She wasn't dead.

Pain was pushed aside, and she shoved, kicking. Screaming silently.

No.

Gasping for air, her lungs closed.

No.

There had to be someone there. Someone to hear her. Someone to end the horror.

No.

Praying. She couldn't die like this.

God help me.

The coffin wiggled under her panicked pounding. She froze.

Air was so short, and her throat on fire. It was so black.

Pounding. Kicking.

Silent screams.

"What the hell?" Graham's muffled voice.

Someone had heard. She pounded harder, screaming in pained silence.

Wood creaked, cracked, and splinters rained down on her arms. Her hands pounded against air, then thick arms were around her. She still couldn't see. Couldn't speak.

Screaming silence.

"Jane? How in hell are you alive?"

Other Books in
The Dominion Falls Series

Independent Brake
Derailed
Dark Territory
Green Eye
Runaway Train
Home Signal
Red Zone

Upcoming Books in
The Dominion Falls Series

Dust Raiser
Blizzard Lights
Dead Man's Swish
Birdcage
A Highball Arrangement
Ball of Fire

Books by Sarah Cass

The Tribe Series
The Tribe
The Wolf
The Chief
The Raven
The Lake Point Series
Santa, Maybe
Deep-Fried Sweethearts
Stalled Independence
Witch Way
A Thorough Thanksgiving
Eve's New Year
Heartstrings & Hockey Pucks
Luck of the Cowgirl
Stars, Stripes & Motorbikes
Free Falling
Love for Hire
Haunted Hearts
Stand Alone Novels
Masked Hearts
Leap

About the Author

Sarah Cass, author of over twenty novels in 4 series, is devoted to giving her readers well-crafted, emotional stories, with depth to even her secondary characters—to give readers a full world to explore. Stories that explore not only the labyrinths of the heart, but the nightmares of the soul. A RONE finalist, she is also owner and creator of Redefining Perfect. By day, she's a nurse, a mother, wife and cat-mom to 4 mischievous beasts. By night she crafts stories that take her across centuries. From the old west of Dominion Falls, to the small town of Lake Point for the holidays, and even into the paranormal land of Shifters and Magic in The Tribe. She loves hearing from her readers. Visit her at www.authorsarahcass.com

Divine Roses Ink
DivineRosesInk.com